Storm Constantine's Wraeththu Mythos

I0653774

Para Imminence
Stories of the Future of wraeththu

Storm Constantine's Wraeththu Mythos

para Imminence
stories of the future of wraeththu

Edited by Storm Constantine
and Wendy Darling

Stafford, England

This is a work of fiction. All the characters and events portrayed in this book are fictitious, and any resemblance to real people, or events, is purely coincidental.

Storm Constantine's Wraeththu Mythos:
Para Imminence: Stories of the Future of Wraeththu

Cover art, story frontispiece and Wraeththu Mythos logo: Ruby
Interior Illustrations: Page 92 Andy Bigwood, Page 119 map Maria Leel & Gordon Leel; Pages 36, 132, 321 Jason Fullwood
Editors: Storm Constantine and Wendy Darling
Interior Layout: Storm Constantine

Set in Garamond
IP0035

First edition by Immanion Press, 2012
An Immanion Press Edition
http://www.immanion-press.com
info@immanion-press.com

ISBN 978-1-907737-45-9

contents

Preface – Storm Constantine   6

Introduction – Brad Carpenter   10

A Tour of the House – Storm Constantine   13

The Etherline – Wendy Darling   43

The Lakes of Lunil – Andy Bigwood   75

Ascension – Maria J. Leel   97

The Lady – Daniela Ritter   121

The Bridge – Martina Bellovičová   135

The Dehara of Navilasalem – E S Wynn   161

The Colour of Words – Victoria Copus   171

Antiques – Wendy Darling   201

Give Us This Day – Fiona Lane   215

Destiny of Choice and Chance – Suzanne Gabriel   247

Ai-Cara 1515 – Martina Luise Pachali   285

The Skies of Miyacala – Andy Bigwood   311

Beyond a Veil of Stars – Storm Constantine   326

History Lesson – Maria J. Leel   350

Afterword: We Might Be Doomed, but That Aside -
Wendy Darling   358

About the Contributors   364

Preface

The Persistence of Hara

Storm Constantine

Wraeththu have been with me for the greater part of my life. My first rather ham-fisted (and half-finished) stories about them began in my mid-teens. It wasn't until I was twenty-six that I began work properly on the full-length novel that became *The Enchantments of Flesh and Spirit*, first volume of the original Wraeththu trilogy, which was published in 1987. This was followed by *The Bewitchments of Love and Hate* and *The Fulfilments of Fate and Desire*.

For the benefit of anyone who might pick up this book and has never read a Wraeththu novel or story before, Wraeththu are an androgynous race that rise from the ruins of humanity, who have virtually wrecked the planet. The original Wraeththu (or hara) were 'incepted' from human beings; it wasn't until later they realised they could actually reproduce among themselves. Procreation for hara is not quite as simple as it had been for humans. The underlying tension and *ache* behind the original trilogy was the thwarted relationship of two of the main characters, Pellaz and Cal. While hara fumbled with their new condition and sought to find balance and then evolution, and Pellaz rose to be a leader among hara, the unfulfilled yearning of Pell and Cal stole like mist through the stories, strangely becoming an entity in itself. If anything, the energetic soul of that yearning informed Wraeththu as a whole; I certainly see it as having an effect upon the future of the race.

After the first trilogy, I waited nearly fifteen years to return to the world of Wraeththu. The new trilogy (*Wraiths of Will and Pleasure, Shades of Time and Memory* and *Ghosts of Blood and Innocence*) were more mature novels, but then the writer herself was more mature! It was interesting to return to that world, older and wiser, even though it had never left me. I'd been forced to write about other worlds by the industry, and it was only with the advent of new publishing technology, plus the support of my American publishers TOR, that I was able to bring new Wraeththu books to life – through TOR in the States and through Immanion Press, set up for the purpose, in the UK and Europe.

If I were to say I'm surprised Wraeththu are still with me so vibrantly it would be a lie. It never entered my head, as an aspiring writer, that hara would ever be anything but *persistent*. While I suffered more than I should have done with monumental screw-ups concerning distribution and management of my early Wraeththu novels, (which contributed wholly to me being unable to sell more Wraeththu material for years), I've managed to survive as a writer, and for that I'm grateful. I've seen many other writers, who I knew in the early days, fall by the wayside, disillusioned, burned out or just tired of fighting the industry. It is not an easy path to follow if you want to earn a decent living, unless some huge stroke of luck sears like lightning from the sky. But for some of us, despite what life might throw at us now and again that gags our muse, writing is in our blood. We'd do it whether we were published or not. For us the lightning strikes are within, and unceasing.

One thing I would not have guessed when Wraeththu first began is that it would be persistent not only for me but for others, and other *writers* at that. I'd read so much good 'fan fiction' over the years that I wanted to give something back to these people who loved Wraeththu as much as I did. The idea for regular short story anthologies of the best of Wraeththu fiction sprang from this. Three of the writers in this collection (Wendy Darling, Victoria Copus and Maria J. Leel) also have Wraeththu Mythos novels published through Immanion Press (*Breeding Discontent, Terzah's Sons* and *Song of the Sulh* respectively).

Following the success of our first shared anthology, *Paragenesis*, Wendy and I wondered what the theme should be for the next one. *Paragenesis* explored the origins of Wraeththu and it seemed interesting to us to visit the extreme opposite of the harish timeline: how hara might develop hundreds, if not thousands, of years in the future of the original novels. We threw this idea out to the writers and got some wonderful tales in return. Some of the authors had also contributed to *Paragenesis*, but we're pleased to welcome a few new faces too.

As for my own contributions to this collection *A Tour of the House* was inspired by a visit to Shugborough Hall, a National Trust property near where I live, which was once the home of Patrick Lichfield, the Fifth Earl of Lichfield, a cousin of the queen and a respected photographer. Shugborough has appeared – if only briefly – in several of my stories and novels throughout the years; it continues to be an inspiration. It is, of course, home to the famous and mysterious Shepherd's Monument, which has featured in many books and TV documentaries and is rumoured to be linked to the story of the Holy Grail. Shugborough and its gardens, its monuments and follies, ooze atmosphere that I never fail to find intriguing.

I visited the place in 2011 after not having been there for a while and found that Patrick Lichfield's personal apartment had been opened to the public following his death in 2005. It's no secret that the earl led a colourful life; he counted many party-animal celebrities among his close friends in the 60s and 70s, and there's no doubt that they got up to a fair amount of shenanigans at Lichfield's stately pile during that time. You only have to look at the photographs adorning the walls of his apartment to see that – The Rolling Stones, The Kinks, and various super models, and wild child actors and actresses of the day arranged in sultry poses amid the grounds. What I found absolutely fascinating as I walked through the rooms, looking at the photos and Lichfield's personal belongings, is that the coach-loads of conformist, mostly elderly tourists would have been horrified by the activities that might once have taken place at this outwardly-dignified stately home. Now Lichfield's rooms – and who knows what dramas might have been enacted there? – are just a museum. I felt sad about it, wistful, sorry for all those Bright Young Things who were now only wisps and memories but who had once filled the apartment with life and, I'm quite sure, a storm of wicked laughter.

When I left Shugborough that day, the feeling would not leave me, and I sat down and wrote *A Tour of the House* virtually in one sitting. I had not written so freely for years.

The second story, *Beyond a Veil of Stars*, began life before *The Enchantments of Flesh and Spirit* was even published. It was one of my very early Wraeththu stories that just didn't get finished. Its original title was *The Claws of Wraeththu*, and sometime in the late 90s, when I first became introduced to the thriving Wraeththu fandom on the Internet, and used to visit their chat room once a month or so, I suggested this story should be finished like a game of Consequences. One of the fan fic writers would write a few paragraphs to continue the tale, then pass it to another writer, who would do their bit and pass it on, and so on. Inevitably, it all got a bit silly but was a fun thing to do at the time. I always meant to finish the story properly myself, and because I was pushed for time to do a second piece for this book, browsed all my half finished Wraeththu tales and decided to work on *Claws* again, although it *did* need a new title very badly. I always knew how I *sort* of wanted it to end, but struggled with how to do it years ago. Now, going back to it, I could polish it up and finish the tale as I originally wanted it to be. The denouement seemed obvious to me now, whereas in the past I'd run into rather a dense cloud with it. The idea behind the piece, which I shan't mention here because of the spoiler factor, *has* been done before, but when I first began work on it I wasn't aware of these other stories; some of them were written far later than my original idea anyway. I could have changed it all, to avoid these similarities, but then felt the story deserved to be completed as it was begun.

There are some great stories in this collection, marvellous visions of what the future might hold for harakind. In some, Wraeththu explore far beyond the confines of the earthly realm, in others hara are reacquainted with the ancient past of their race or of humanity. It was a delight to read and edit these stories, and I hope that more anthologies will follow.

For now, read and enjoy, and a big thank you to everyone involved, who contributed to bringing this new collection to life.

Storm Constantine
October 2012

Introduction

Brad Carpenter

Just thinking about this collection has me excited and a little nervous with anticipation. I know that these stories will reflect the future of Wraeththu. The initial battles of survival will have long been fought and won. Humanity will have all but disappeared. Now there's a bigger question to ponder. If Wraeththu is the future of Humanity, then what is the future of Wraeththu?

I had delayed myself from reading these stories for way too long, holding off for just the right moment to take the plunge. But now, finally, the time has come. I open up the document from Storm containing the collection of short stories, and I start reading. It doesn't take long before I find myself transported back into a world that I find so pleasingly familiar, and yet so deliciously different. It's as though I'm a Wraeththu Rip Van Winkle who has woken up to find that centuries have passed, and that the universe has expanded to new and exciting proportions.

The rich world created by Storm Constantine in the "The Wraeththu Chronicles" and "The Wraeththu Histories" has long inspired legions of fans to craft their own stories. In this latest call for submissions, authors were offered a wide scope for this collection, and the result is stunning. "Para Imminence" is a provocative collection of short stories set in the future at various points in the Wraeththu timeline, taking place on Earth, in space, and in other realms.

As one might expect, the wide scope encouraged for this collection has resulted in a broad range of intriguing and relatable themes. For example, if these exotic androgynous creatures represent Humanity's best potential having come to fruition, would life then seem too perfect? Would there still be enough obstacles to challenge them? What would Wraeththu technology look like? Now that the species has been around long enough to experience a natural lifespan, what would that look like? And how would they deal with their own mortality? What relationship might Wraeththu develop with their gods, the Dehara? And what would Wraeththu think of Humanity so many centuries later? Would any humans still exist? And if so, would this highly evolved species discover that they still had something to learn from Humanity?

The insightful answers explored in this collection are quite stimulating. In Wraeththu times yet to come, space exploration will have taken on entirely new dimensions, and yet, future generations will still be learning how to overcome and respect each other's differences. And as is often the case with our own culture, the future Wraeththu history books will have been shaped a bit by "the victors." I found it fascinating to see how these future Harish citizens viewed the events of the past that we know so intimately from Storm's original books.

One my favourite aspects of the Wraeththu Mythos is that I can always find aspects of myself within the characters. Adding vast amounts of time and space to the equation has only made that all the more true. When you step back and observe the beautiful mosaic created by these stories, it seems to reflect back an even greater sense of our overall potential. It's comforting to see how, even in the context of alternate times and dimensions; Wraeththu provides the most optimistic mirror Humanity could ever hope for.

A Tour of the House

Storm Constantine

A Tour of the House

The house had not been lived in for over a decade, yet somehow, even as a museum or a place of learning, it still retained an ambience of homeliness. We Dwell in Forever. But the hara who had so named the house were long gone.

Gred stood in the doorway, shaking the rain from his umbrella, water dripping from the tendrils of his long dark hair that hung over, or were stuck to, his face. A har standing beside the reception desk indicated his umbrella should be placed in a stand with several others. Water pooled on the cream marble floor. Outside the sky was blue-grey with summer storm, while the foliage of the soaring ancient trees was acid green against it. Within the house, the double-doors of highly-polished oak stood open to the day, but the hallway was dark, smelling of rain and trodden grass.

Other visitors were clustered around the desk, looking at informational guideleafs. A soft-voiced guide, dressed in a uniform of moss green tunic and loose trousers, was gathering a group of hara together, ready for the next tour of the house. Gred decided grudgingly to join them. He had travelled far on this pilgrimage. He had wanted to visit for so long. Part of him resented having to share the experience with so many others. But he was just a tourist, like them. There would be no special privileges.

The tour would begin in five minutes. Gred closed his eyes briefly, a ghost at the edge of the crowd. He thought about the feet that had walked these marble tiles, that had descended the sweeping stairs ahead. He thought of the tragedies and romances of history, wrapped up in legend.

"We shall start with the lower west wing," the guide said.

The group turned as one towards a corridor that led off to the left and followed the guide, who moved slowly, allowing everyhar to absorb the surroundings, examine the fittings, the pictures on the walls, the atmosphere itself.

"The house was built in the style of the type of country mansion found in ancient Alba Sulh," said the guide. "During the human era, this estate was undoubtedly occupied by a moneyed family attempting to emulate the lives of Sulhian gentry."

A soft ripple of laughter spread through the group.

The guide smiled indulgently at the follies of the past. He paused before a painting. "The hara who came to inhabit this house during the Upheaval were susceptible to the same impulses. Here, for example, is a portrait of our tribe founder, Terzian, with his horse and dogs. In style, it resembles the antique paintings of high-ranking humans that would have been found in all the large houses of ancient times, especially in Alba Sulh. There are many pictures within the house in this style. Useful for us because they tell us much about the hara who lived here."

The artist had captured a day very similar to today, Gred thought. Early summer, searing green foliage, a purple sky gravid with storms. And Terzian, young and proud, his yellow hair a shock of corn against the bark of an old oak. His horse; whites of its eyes showing, yet standing calm. At Terzian's feet lay the hounds, looking up at him, tongues lolling. This was a har who had built a tribe, slaughtered thousands, human and hara alike. Long dead, but living in a picture. Gred wondered if the portrait had hung in the house following Terzian's death or whether it had been very recently brought out from storage, unwrapped from dusty cloth, simply for the benefit of tourists.

"Do any of the family still occupy any of the rooms?" somehar asked.

The guide shook his head. "No. Although the family have only recently donated this property to the Megalithican Heritage Trust, no Parasilians have occupied it for at least eighty years. Until about ten years ago, it was used as a centre for the Galhean Arts Brotherhood, who lacked the funds or resources – or indeed inclination – for proper upkeep. The family did little to maintain their ancestral home. We still have much restoration work to do."

"Why did they leave?" Gred asked.

"Marlet har Parasiel had a new house built for the family following his chesna-bond to Ambel har Unneah. Some say he was plagued by ghosts..."

Again, a ripple of laughter.

The guide made a languid gesture with one hand. "In fact he

15

thought it time for the family to move away from the past and the looming shadows of those who had come before. Megalithica had changed, as had Galhea. History, especially of the volatile kind associated with the early Parasilians, should remain in a museum. This is what the house has become."

Madness, Gred thought. *How could anyhar leave this place, its ghosts, its histories? Somehar having no imagination or no heart.*

The guide was gazing at Gred speculatively. "It is rather like reading a novel," he said. "The stories are romances, probably less than half true. Nohar wants to live in a story. The new house is very beautiful. Parts of it are open to viewing twice a year." His smile had become somewhat tighter. "Now, shall we continue? To our left is the family sitting room."

Most of it was roped off to protect the elderly carpets and furniture. A small area was provided for everyhar to crowd into. There was a smell of ancient dust, perhaps caught in the heavy drapes at the windows, which were tall and with wide sills, where hara might once have sat to gaze out at the gardens, the long driveway, lined by poplars, which wound towards the town. There was also a green smell; a whiff of pine. In the fireplace, long unused, was a vase, filled with a glorious display of evergreens: several species of ivy twined around sprays of fir branches and sprigs of holly. The guide indicated this. "The foliage display you see was a tradition upheld by the family in remembrance of tiahaar Cobweb, who was Terzian's consort in the early days of the house and subsequently lived here for nearly three centuries. We have reinstated this tradition."

"Why is it in the fireplace?" somehar asked. "Did they burn it as a tradition too?"

Yet more laughter.

The guide was grinning now. "No, it originally stood upon a side table between two of the windows. When we took over the place, there was still a fragmenting old display there that had perhaps remained from the days of family occupation."

"Did you keep it?" Gred asked.

"The display is replaced regularly," the guide replied. He sniffed dismissively. "Members of the family who were in residence would meet here in the evenings. It was sometimes used to entertain guests known well to the Parasilians. An informal room."

Two large unyielding sofas, several stiff padded chairs; all looked uncomfortable and far from informal to Gred. "Are these the original furnishings?" he asked.

The guide shook his head. "Unfortunately, the original furnishings that remained were beyond repair. The items you see here are our attempt to recreate the room as it once was. They came from another house we care for." He rubbed his hands together. "Come, we have the dining-room and the main reception salon further along this corridor."

As the group moved on, Gred lingered a moment, gazing back into the room. Here, Cobweb had sat upon the floor before the fire, perhaps sketching in one of his notebooks. Many of those remained. One was on display in the museum in Immanion, held open at a page, under glass. You couldn't touch it. Gred held out his hand to the air of the room. It was all still here, just a little.

"Tiahaar?" The guide was calling him.

"Excuse me," Gred said. He caught up with the rest.

In fact, there was very little left of the original appointments. Megalithican Heritage had filled the rooms with furniture that belonged elsewhere, to other lives. What was the point of trying to emulate the past when the pieces were merely mismatched impositions? Empty rooms would have been better or even the rotting remains of what the Trust had found when the house had opened its doors to them and let them in. Cobweb might have approved of the Galhean Arts Brotherhood. No doubt they had made a mess, not cared at all about maintaining an image of the past. They had just lived here.

The original mahogany dining table remained, although the guide complained it had to be covered with a cloth, since the GAB had used it as a cutting table for various projects and had ruined the surface irreparably. The guide talked about what a magnificent piece it had once been. Gred wondered why the Trust hadn't replaced it. He nearly said so, but held his tongue. Places were set for diners as the Trust assumed they would have been. Multiple sets of cutlery, several different glasses for several different wines. Delicate, gilt-edged crockery.

Gred could only think of gloves left on the table, and books, some pencils, a few feathers and stones from the garden that harlings had brought in to show the family. Crumbs on the table cloth, knives smeared with butter laid across plain white plates.

Cold cups of coffee, half drunk. This was what he'd always imagined when he'd heard stories of the past; he had always felt he'd 'seen' beyond the dry facts into these colourful lost lives. He was quite sure the Parasilians would never have eaten off the polished table, except when distinguished visitors were present. Most of the time, it would have been swathed in rough white linen. Gred thought of shoes kicked off beneath the chairs. Mud traipsed in from the stable yard. He thought of laughter. Sullen silences. An argument. A reunion. Simmering lust. A sharp-tined fork plunged into a hand. He knew that story, how Tigron Calanthe, long before he became Tigron, when he was still mad, had stabbed Terzian with a fork in this room. The Varrs had sheltered Cal when he'd needed sanctuary. In their way, they had helped save him. News had come to this room also, as the family had sat to eat breakfast or dinner. Gred could visualise the door flying open, somehar rushing in with something to say. Sometimes something bad.

In the reception room, with its views of the terrace where urns still stood, resplendent with ferns, the guide talked about how the Parasilians had entertained there. "Terzian initiated the custom for all the seasonal festivals to be celebrated here at the house. Hara from Galhea were invited, and festivities were held outdoors so that everyhar from the local community could be accommodated. Within the house, high-ranking hara, their friends and family, plus members of Terzian's militia, would gather in this room. The family maintained this tradition until they moved to their new residence. The Galhean Arts Brotherhood, of course, did not continue it."

"Do the family still hold these festivities in their new home?" somehar asked.

"The house is open twice a year for viewing," the guide replied. "Those times coincide with a couple of festivals and there is some entertainment provided in the grounds during the evening. I believe there is a guideleaf about it in the entrance hall."

"I suppose all the famous hara of the early days of Wraeththu came here at some point," somehar else said. "Would Tigron Pellaz have been in this room?"

The guide nodded. "Undoubtedly. He visited the family before he became Tigron, and thereafter remained a constant friend, especially to tiahaar Cobweb, who was often an advisor to him."

Gred smiled to himself. So few words to describe such a huge history. *"Visited the family before he was Tigron..."* This idiot had no idea. Gred gazed about the room from beyond the tasselled ropes that kept everyhar away from where events had actually happened. He closed his eyes and inhaled. This room would always be redolent of Natalia, the winter festival. The flames would have been ferocious in the imposing fireplace. The sideboard to the left of the room would have been heaped with traditional, seasonal fare. The air would have been heavy with the scents of mulled wine and sheh. And among the guests, a thousand embers of feeling.

It was true that the Aralisians, the ruling dynasty of Immanion, had often spent Natalia here, especially so in the later years of Pellaz's reign. Galhea had become the capital of Megalithica eventually, the small agricultural town expanding into the metropolis it was today. In those days, the house had been on the edge of the town. Now its hill was surrounded by roads and parks and suburbs. The Parasilians and the Aralisians, separated by an ocean, remained close allies if not close friends. Yet the magic had somehow seeped away from that famous alliance. The characters who played the stage today were not the towering, vibrant creatures of history, who had shaped early Wraeththu, who had bled for it.

The guide broke into Gred's thoughts. "You are a student of history?" he asked, somewhat archly. He must have noticed Gred's absorption in the house.

"In an amateur fashion," Gred replied.

"You are from Almagabra?" Was that a slight note of accusation? Gred's accent coupled with his olive skin must have given him away.

Gred smiled, inclined his head. "Yes, I am. As you can imagine, Galhea holds great interest for my harakin. It is a large part of our heritage, or shall I say our *combined* heritage, since for Parsics, this area is also of great significance." That sounded too pompous.

The guide had narrowed his eyes. "You are Gelaming, then."

Gred was tempted to lie. "That is my tribe, yes."

"Then naturally this area holds racial memories for you," the guide said dryly. "The Gelaming concentrated their efforts in

19

Galhea, especially after the death of Terzian."

"I thought that Imbrilim was their centre, to the south," Gred said. "The Varrs, then later the Parasilians, always maintained control of Galhea." So far, the term Varr had not been mentioned in the tour speech.

"Superficially, yes," the guide replied. He perhaps became aware how the tour group was starting to feel uncomfortable and smiled brightly, raised his voice. "The history of this area is colourful, but again much of the detail has been embellished over time. Shall we move on?"

The group visited Terzian's private office, a small room now empty but for a desk and chair. The guide did not speak about how some of the greatest decisions of Megalithican history had been made in this room, nor that it had been Terzian's son Swift's office for a great deal longer than it had been his father's. The guide did mention that the desk and chair were original, though.

From there, the group moved on to the domestic quarters, the kitchens and laundry. These had been reconstructed and filled with copper pans and other antique-looking artefacts. Wax vegetables and fruit were placed neatly on the table.

While the guide spoke about the day to day running of the house and what tasks the staff had engaged in, Gred stared at the table. It too was original. He tried to think of festival times, when the kitchens had been busy and fragrant with cooking, but all he could see in his mind's eye was a time of panic and fear. The attack on Galhea by the Teraghast tribe was fairly well-documented, and Gred had read all he could find on the subject. Now, he could only visualise the body of Ithiel har Varr laid out this table, his throat cut. He'd been killed in the town when the Teraghasts had attacked it, all those centuries ago. Hara had brought him here, the house's defender. It had been a time when grim decisions had been made. Swift had been absent then, dealing with the aggressors further afield. Gred visualised Cobweb, Swift's hostling, alone and frightened, having to rally his hara round him in the face of limitless threat. This house had died for a while after those times, when the Teraghasts had sacked it, and the family had been forced to flee into temporary exile.

Some of the Parasilians had remained Varrs at heart, Gred had no doubt. He could not think of a figure like Ithiel, such a prime if quiet mover in the early days, Terzian's right-hand har, becoming Parasilian in anything but name. They could call their tribe something else to hide the past, but it had never left them, not really. Perhaps that was another reason why Marlet had built his new domain, on the other side of the town, far beyond the river, surrounded by trees. This hill could not be seen from there.

There were no roped-off areas in the kitchens and the tour group was free to walk through the rooms and touch things. Two hara brought refreshments on a tray – the traditional local sheh liqueur and hot tea for those who preferred it. Gred took a glass of sheh. He smelled it but didn't drink it. He wandered from room to room. Part of him wanted to weep, another part simply wanted to sneak off like a harling and explore the rest of the house on his own. The guide, no doubt, would notice.

Once the refreshments had been consumed, the tour continued. Now the group was taken upstairs to view the bedrooms. To Gred this seemed slightly voyeuristic. However, the reality of what he saw banished that feeling. The rooms looked twee, too tidy, and again furnished with items from other houses. Cobweb's chamber held no feeling of him, and neither did Terzian's. The group was shown the bedroom used by Swift before he came of age, and the quarters of Tyson and Azriel, other sons of the house. Strange how so many hara had lived in these rooms since those times, yet they were still referred to as belonging to their original occupants. Gred thought of later Parasilian harlings lying awake at night, besieged by history. It must have lived on here. It must have haunted the place. In many ways.

"The attics were only opened up and refurbished following the siege of Galhea," the guide said, as he led the group towards the narrow staircase that led to the upper story. "When the family returned to Galhea, they found the house had been badly damaged. Tiahaar Cobweb had parts of the attic converted into a studio, as he was something of an artist. He also commissioned a new apartment for himself up here."

Is it going to be mentioned he made a chesna-bond with an Aralisian, Snake har Aralis, Pellaz's own brother in fact?

"Tiahaar Swift, who was by then Master of Galhea, took over the east wing on the first floor with his immediate family."

No, didn't think so...

Gred felt cheated of the experience he'd wanted to have, but for that he'd have had to be alone. Two great Wraeththu dynasties had combined in this house. Battles of many kinds had been fought and won, or fought and lost. But the years had not nurtured the alliance of the two houses. Now they were only the most distant of relatives and there was an undeniable distaste of the Gelaming branch on this side of the ocean. It was reflected within the entire tribe, hence the guide's frostiness upon discovering Gred's origins. No mention was made of the Aralisians who had once called Forever home: most importantly Cal, then Snake and his son Moon, who had formed a chesna-bond with Tyson har Parasiel. To Gred, it felt like these hara had been erased from the house's history, undoubtedly because of being Aralisian. In part, perhaps the Gelaming's reputation as relentless conquerors was deserved. But that had been only the start. If it hadn't been for that great alliance, perhaps the world would be a different place now, and not a better one. The guide had alluded many times to history being rewritten with a romantic slant, but it seemed clear that in Galhea it had been rewritten in more than one way.

The guide led the group back downstairs; the tour was over. He told everyhar about the restaurant in the converted stables, and where maps could be found for those who wished to explore the gardens.

But there was one final sight to be shown before the group left the house. This was a reception room off the entrance hall, somewhat unprepossessing and allegedly used rarely by the family at any time in its history. The guide said that Terzian and Swift might have met lesser dignitaries in this room or received messengers. But it was famous now for only one reason and that was because a portrait of Cobweb hung over the fireplace. Why it had been placed here, in this unloved corner, Gred couldn't guess. Perhaps once it had lived in another room.

The tour group expressed an audible gasp when they saw it, perhaps even those who'd seen it before.

"Yes, it is magnificent, and strangely bewitching," said the guide. "It was commissioned by Tiahaar Swift when his hostling was one hundred years old."

The portrait was of a willowy har with pale luminous skin and abundant black hair, dressed in flowing garments of pale green. He was depicted sitting upon a stone wall in a dark and secluded corner of the gardens. He seemed to shine from the picture, his deep brown gaze at once melancholy and whimsical.

"Is it... embellished, do you think?" somehar asked. "I mean, was he really that... arresting?"

"There are other pictures," the guide replied. "I think we can safely say that tiahaar Cobweb was indeed as beautiful as the legends say."

Gred went to the restaurant and ate a late lunch of very good cold roast chicken and salad. He drank one large glass of the local sparkling wine, made from 'flowers of the field' as the menu said. He sat alone, his mind strangely empty. Outside the sky had cleared a little and the wet stones of the courtyard beyond the window of the restaurant gleamed and sparkled in sunlight. Gred had picked up a map of the gardens. He was savouring the moment before he began the last part of his tour, this time thankfully without company.

First he visited the lake with its blanket of water lily pads and cuffs of yellow orris. A mass of huge orange and silver fish haunted the banks, expectant of food from the tourists. To Gred they looked like entrails, squirming and tangled as they were. He had nothing to throw to them. The sun was hot now, although dark clouds still roamed the distant sky. A shimmer of steam rose from the lawn as Gred walked barefoot across it, his sandals dangling from one hand. The umbrella was a nuisance, awkward and damp beneath an arm. He walked around the lake towards a folly of tumbled stones. Here, evergreens scented the air. Gred put his sandals back on. The stones were rough beneath his feet, sometimes sharp. He was surrounded by 'presence'; he could put no word to it other than that. If he concentrated hard enough, could he summon the past to him like moving pictures? He wanted to know everything about the hara who had lived here in the distant past, but most of the details were lost. He felt Wraeththu had a tendency to tidy away their history, embarrassed by their early heritage, tainted as it had been by the humanity that had lingered in the harish psyche.

He saw the summerhouse as shards of whiteness through the trees. No other tourists had come to this spot as yet, perhaps most still engrossed in leisurely meals at the restaurant. The summerhouse was round, its wood painted ivory. Within was a central pool with a fountain. Water spattered onto the stone bench that surrounded it. Gred sat down and closed his eyes, listening to the music of the water. His heart felt swollen with love. *I was born into the wrong time*, he thought. He yearned for the passions of the past. At thirty-five years old, very young by harish standards, he felt momentarily ancient, displaced in time. He sighed, opened his eyes, and found that somehar was sitting next to him. He physically jumped and uttered a smothered cry.

"Excuse me, I startled you," said the har beside him. This har was dressed in clothes of dark green, perhaps an employee of the Trust, since his garb resembled their uniform. He had very long black hair, covering him like a shawl. He did not turn to face Gred, which seemed a little odd.

"It's fine," Gred said. "I was lost in my thoughts, didn't hear anyhar come in here."

"It has always been a place for meditation – of one kind or another." The har laughed softly.

"I've been on the tour," Gred said. "I was hoping for more history."

Now the har turned to face him and Gred's chest contracted. For a moment, he could not draw breath. That face. Those eyes. "You are... you are Parasilian?"

The har nodded. "Yes. I expect the family resemblance is obvious. As is yours, of course."

"Er... mine?"

"Aralisian, yes?" Again the har laughed. He reached out and touched Gred's arm briefly. "Don't worry. I won't tell a living soul."

Gred risked a smile although he was feeling light-headed now, disorientated. "That is probably for the best. Do you work here?"

"No, I just watch them."

The har must be quite old, Gred decided. He had a translucent quality to him, which was often seen in older hara: the slow fading to spirit. But the resemblance to hara like Cobweb and Swift was shocking. Gred hadn't expected that. His mind was a maelstrom. He should use this moment to ask for information and stories, but his tongue was a stone in his mouth. He felt shaken in a peculiar way.

"I'm glad you came back," said the har.

"I... this is the first time I've been here."

"That's not what I meant. You should visit the family. I can tell you haven't."

"They moved from here," Gred said. He felt that was reason enough to explain why he hadn't visited them.

"Forever is a leaky old place," said the har. "Don't think too badly of Marlet. I try not to. Anyway, the Meglets probably look after the place far better than we ever did."

"Meglets!" Gred laughed. His unease was fading. "It's such a pity they've rammed the rooms full of things that don't belong here, though. I would have preferred emptiness to that."

"Well, they have to earn enough funds to maintain the place. Most visitors want a theme park, not reality. Marlet and Ambel took most of the furniture with them to Murmur Heights. You'll see more to your taste there, I'm sure. And they *will* talk to you, if that's what you want." The har touched Gred's arm briefly again. "Perhaps it's time for old alliances to be rekindled."

"I wonder why they ever faded. I sometimes think it might be because hara are embarrassed about the past, don't want to be reminded of it."

"It's not just that," said the har. "Things happened over the years. Petty arguments. Differences of opinion. The Parasilians didn't want Immanion to have its fingers in the Megalithican pie. And by that time, all the original players were gone. Emotional attachments were gone. But I do think Marlet would be open to patching things up a little. Times change."

"Yes. Thank you." Gred paused. "Perhaps I could go to the Heights with *you*?" He wondered if that was too presumptuous.

The har studied him for a second. "I stay here mostly," he said. "You don't need me to guide you. Just say I sent you."

"Who... sent me?" Gred asked.

"They'll know." The har stood up. "It will rain soon. You'd better set off." These words were clearly a dismissal.

Gred also got to his feet. "I will. Thank you. It was... very interesting to meet you."

The har inclined his head. "Pleasure to meet you too." He walked to the door and out into the green light.

Gred couldn't follow. He was rooted to the spot. Then the rain came and he was released. Outside, he opened his umbrella and fled back to the house.

Gred took a float car to Murmur Heights. He wasn't sure if this was really the right thing to do or what kind of welcome he might expect. But the strange har in the summer house had affected him deeply. He kept trying to dismiss the thought he'd met a ghost, but it nagged at him seductively.

There were guards at the gates to the Heights, to whom Gred presented his identification. The guards appraised him warily. Aralisians on Galhean soil again? They did not obstruct him unnecessarily, however. It seemed there was little fear in this land of hara who might wish the family ill.

The front door to the Heights was opened by a har in a green uniform of flowing garments, much like the uniform of the Trust employees and the har he'd met in the summerhouse. Rather stiffly, Gred told this har who he was and that he hoped that the family would not mind that he'd come to visit.

"Come in," said the har. "This is a surprise. I'll tell tiahaar Ambel at once. Tiahaar Marlet is not at home." He gestured for Gred to come into the hall. It was indeed a beautiful house, full of light. "Allow me to take your coat and umbrella."

Gred shrugged off his coat and handed the items over.

"Thank you. Please sit here. I won't keep you waiting long."

Gred sat down on the chair indicated to him. He felt slightly breathless.

Presently, a tall mature har, with a plait of chestnut hair hanging heavily over one shoulder, and an open, good-natured face, came into the hall. He was dressed in loose tunic and trousers of a colour to match his hair. "Hello. I'm Ambel har Parasiel. I believe you are a relative, if somewhat distant!"

Gred stood up, bowed his head. "Yes, tiahaar. Thank you for receiving me. I am Gred har Aralis."

The har waved an arm at Gred. "Hush. No need for formalities. What brings you to our home?"

He gestured for Gred to follow him, and Gred noticed how similar this house was in layout to Forever. They would turn left and presently come to the family sitting room, and they did.

"I've always been interested in the history of our two families," Gred explained. "And then I had the time for a protracted holiday and thought I'd come over here. I went to Forever today."

"Fascinating place, isn't it?" Ambel said. He indicated Gred should sit down on one of the sagging old sofas, which embraced him like loving arms. "I've ordered tea for us. It won't be long."

"Forever is a wonderful house," Gred said. "But then, so is this one."

Ambel looked around him. "Yes... In some ways we were sad to leave Forever, but it is a... *heavy* place. We both thought it was better for the younger generations to have a new home, somewhere lighter and not so damn haunted." He laughed.

"Really haunted?"

"But of course. What can you expect? It was never *our* house, Gred. Not really. It belonged, and still belongs, to the hara who created our tribe and who shaped early Wraeththu. It's right that the house is now for everyhar. It's their history."

"I felt there wasn't enough of it there."

"Well, there's so *much* of it, and the Trust don't like to dwell on the melodrama, as they see it. We have plenty of old pieces here that we brought from the house, if you want to see them. Marlet will be back soon. He can show you his collections. But I warn you; it can be boring after a couple of hours!"

"Thanks. I'd like that, and I *won't* be bored."

"You must stay here, of course. Have you booked into a hotel in town?"

"Not yet, no. That's kind of you."

"Kind?" Again Ambel laughed. "Don't be ridiculous! We'll want the gossip from Immanion too. There is a lot to talk about." He paused. "Marlet was only recently thinking of contacting Sahaan, you know. We wondered if overtures would be welcome."

Gred grimaced. "If you contact anyhar, make it Tulsel. Sahaan is not the most affable of hara. Tulsel is. He's my high-father."

"Well now we've contacted you, so we're halfway there," Ambel said. "What a fortunate coincidence!"

"Somehar... somehar told me to come here. He told me to say he'd sent me. One of your relatives. I met him at Forever."

Ambel frowned slightly. "Oh, who was that? I can't think of anyhar who'd be over there today."

"He didn't give me his name, but he was an older har. He looked very Parasilian, if you know what I mean. It sounds mad, but I did wonder if he was a ghost, to be honest."

Ambel drew in his breath, rolled his eyes. "I see. Why am I not surprised?" He shook his head. "He's a stubborn old beast. He won't leave, you know. His rooms here are barely touched."

"You mean it's somehar who still lives at Forever? The tour guide said all the family had left."

Ambel paused a moment. "Technically, we did. The har you met is not a ghost, but he might as well be. It was Cobweb."

Gred couldn't speak for a moment, and yet he had known all along really. "That's impossible. Surely?"

"He won't leave this world, Gred. He should, but he won't. Don't ask me why. Everyhar else has gone to wherever they go. He's not like us. He's not wholly *here*. He doesn't really have to 'live' anywhere."

"But nohar lives that long. Do they?"

Ambel shrugged. "Like I said, he's not quite *with* us. It's not something we talk about with outsiders. As far as everyhar else is concerned, Cobweb faded nearly a century ago. He keeps himself to himself most of the time. But he would have seen Pellaz in you, no doubt, so decided to communicate."

"Does the Trust know he's still... *haunting* the place?"

"Not officially, no. Marlet has told him he shouldn't hang around there during the tourist season, but I suspect that the Trust secretly likes the idea of ghosts. The visitors would no doubt relish it. I expect Cobweb does manifest from time to time when the mischief takes him."

"Does he ever come here?"

"Sometimes, usually just to make me jump. I'll be in the house or the gardens then suddenly he's there beside me, criticising whatever I'm doing, or complaining about the Trust, or demanding I make him a meal. He doesn't have to eat much, but occasionally enjoys the experience of good food. I sometimes think he's still around because he's just too stubborn and awkward to move on. He's not sad, though, and that's the important thing. If he's happy, he can do as he likes, in my opinion."

"This is hard to take in," Gred said.

"Understandable," Ambel said airily. "We're just used to him. I realise it must be rather a shock. Which is no doubt what Cobweb intended. I'd be grateful if you didn't talk about this too much. We don't want to attract attention to Cobweb. He's persistent but in some ways fragile."

"Of course. I'll be discreet." Gred smiled. "I'd give anything to be able to talk to him properly, though."

"Who knows? He might comply. He might not. I can't predict. Ah, here is Zaya with our tea. You've met our housekeeper, of course."

The har who'd let Gred into the house had appeared with a tray.

"Do join us, Zaya," Ambel said. "Gred has had a Cobweb experience over at Forever."

Zaya pulled a humorous face. "Oh dear. Nothing too alarming, I hope."

"Not at all," Gred replied. "I want to say... without sounding too sentimental... that I'm really glad I've been welcomed here. I wasn't sure what to expect."

"I suspect this wariness has maintained the distance between our kin long after any stupid arguments in the past were long forgotten," Ambel said. "I'm also glad you came, or that Cobweb interfered enough to send you to us."

When Marlet came home, he was not alone, and suddenly the Heights was filled with noise. Hara and dogs spilled into the room where Gred still sat with Ambel. Introductions were made; a list of names and a sea of faces Gred could not remember. Hounds jumped up at him, eager to lick his face. He felt slightly overwhelmed, but he'd never been good with crowds. Marlet was something of a throwback to the Terzian strain, as he lacked the fey dark appearance of Cobweb's type, being fair of hair, tanned of skin; a har of the outdoors. While he was ostensibly ruler of Galhea, the post was mainly ceremonial; day to day government of the Megalithican tribes was the domain of the Hundred Fires, the name for the ruling council of the country. Marlet was a land custodian, more at home in the fields than in any chamber of government. That was clear.

Marlet was more restrained than Ambel had been in his greeting of Gred. He wasn't hostile, or even impolite, but the reticence was plain to see. Gred didn't feel he should make too much effort to break that down. This might appear artificial. Marlet must take him as he was.

"Is it your duty as envoy of Immanion to meet with us?" Marlet asked.

"No," Gred replied. "Nohar knows I'm here. I didn't want to

be burdened with any diplomatic tasks. I just wanted to be here in Galhea, see for myself."

"You are discontent," Marlet decided. "You seek solace in the past."

Gred uttered a wordless protest, but Marlet held up a hand.

"No matter. You're welcome here. I hope you find what you're looking for."

Dinner was a raucous affair, with multiple family members and their harlings and pets stuffed into the dining-room. The food was excellent but the din soon made Gred's head ache. Everyhar had to shout to make himself heard, cats jumped on the table, and were only occasionally brushed off it when they became too unashamed about stealing food, harlings squabbled and eventually ended up running around the room, yelling at one another. To Gred, it was like a madhouse. His own family were restrained and courteous. Harlings sat quietly at the occasional big family gathering. Animals would not be allowed in the room. Now, Gred faced a barrage of questions from the Parasilians, some of them quite presumptuous, who apparently found the Aralisians pompous and easy to mock. His own questions, the ones he ached to ask, lodged in his throat. He couldn't bring himself to ask them.

Eventually, Gred pleaded exhaustion and asked permission to retire. It occurred to him that the Parasilians were in actual fact very like how he'd imagined their ancestors to be; informal and numerous. He recalled the fantasies he'd had earlier in the dining-room at Forever. Reality was something different.

Ambel escorted Gred to the room that had been made ready for him. "I can see the family have tired you out," he said. "They mean well, but they are rather draining, I know."

Gred smiled. "A little, although I envy you as well. I have nothing like that. I live alone mostly, keep away from the family. They are not as intimate with one another as yours are."

Ambel eyed him speculatively. "Don't feel you have to join in with all family gatherings while you're here. You're free to come and go as you please. Zaya will see to your meals if you prefer to be alone. Just let him know."

"Then I would be a poor guest. Forgive me, I'm simply not used to this kind of life."

Ambel put a hand on his arm. "Sleep well and sleep long. I usually take my breakfast late, in the orchid house. You are welcome to join me there. Around 10. Just ask a member of staff where to find me."

Gred inclined his head. "Thank you." He opened to door to his room, was about to step inside.

"This room..." Ambel said, rather suddenly.

Gred paused. "Yes?"

"As you'll no doubt have noticed the Heights was constructed to the same design as Forever. You will be sleeping in Cobweb's room, the one he originally had. Well... its copy."

Gred nodded. "Thanks... Perhaps I can dream more here than if I stayed in that travesty of a room back at Forever."

"Indeed you might," Ambel said. "Goodnight, harakin."

Alone inside the room, Gred sighed and leaned back against the door. A lamp glowed dimly on a table beside the low bed, which was spread with a beautiful embroidered coverlet of dark green and cream that depicted a tangle of birds and trees. An oil burner on a chest beneath the window released a gentle scent of jasmine. Fresh fruit had been left for him in a green glass bowl, along with cordials and a pitcher of water. Gred mixed himself a drink from an essence of 'flowers of the field', most likely the same that were used to make the wine he'd drunk earlier. He gazed out of the window at the gardens. A wind had come up, making the trees dance. Everything was utterly dark close to; in the distance were the dim lights of the town like snakes of fire.

His drink consumed, Gred took off his sandals and went to lie on the bed fully-clothed. He knew Ambel had put him in this room for a specific reason.

How do you tell when a ghost enters your space? Does the air go cold, condense, and an unreasonable feeling of terror shingle the skin? Or is it more subtle than that, a simple awareness you are not alone, and that the presence with you is 'other'?

After maybe twenty minutes of staring at the wall, thinking of not much at all – perhaps in readiness his mind was clear – Gred saw a shadow by the door, which resolved itself into a shape that walked towards him. He sat upright on the bed, hands braced against the coverlet. Was he afraid now? He didn't know.

"They will have told you, of course," Cobweb said. "May I sit down?" He didn't wait for a reply but seated himself graciously at the end of the bed. He seemed to waver like a mist, more like a ghost now that Gred was sure he was not.

Cobweb folded his arms and regarded the speechless Gred. "Such a sad soul," he said. "What are you searching for here?"

"Meaning," Gred replied awkwardly.

"Ah, I can't give you that. Life is such a strange, cruel thing isn't it? I look back on mine and it's as if it happened to another har, or it was a book I read. I don't know when it changed and I found myself in the other half of life. I can't remember it happening. When I was in the first one, I thought nothing would ever change, and then I would die, but it's not like that. The life of youth is another world to the one I live in now. It dies but you are not dead, you're just this older har and the past has gone, many of the hara you loved with it, even though they might still live. You wake up one day and realise most things you took for granted have disappeared or been done with. You are somehar else. But you can remember so well..." He sighed, then smiled with great warmth. "I should not be here to heap you with melancholia. In truth, I feel no grief, only an astounded wistfulness. But that is not how you feel, is it?"

I have been given a chance, Gred thought, *so rare and brief; I must make the most of it. Every second will count.* "No... I feel... lost." He shook his head. Couldn't he put it better than that? Words eluded him.

Cobweb waited patiently. Gred felt the har trusted the words would come. And so they did. "When I look at the world, in Immanion, it all seems so... *bleached.* It doesn't feel real to me. I don't think any other har feels the way I do. We live in a prosperous country, we have peace, we have art, we have exploration, we have learning. If there is darkness in the world, it is far from our door."

"That is what we worked for all those generations ago," Cobweb said softly. "It didn't come easily, I assure you. There were dark ages."

"I know and that is why I yearn for those days, those hara," Gred said. "In peace have we become somehow less? Is it only conflict that drives a har to passion and greatness?"

"Perhaps so," Cobweb said, "but perhaps also you are an anachronism. All those hara in Immanion – and indeed around us here now – are content in the world that was made for them. They do the things they were supposed to do – the pioneering frontier is within. Or they explore the Otherlanes and beyond, seeking the mysteries of the multiverse. That's not so bad a life, free from war."

"No, most hara would say it is the perfect life."

Cobweb reached out and squeezed one of Gred's feet. "But not for you, poor harling. I would be a liar if I said those early days weren't cauldrons of great passion, daring and courage, even though we lived in blood and terror many times. Love was an anvil on which our hearts were forged. All that was human within us was a bonfire, raging always. And that is perhaps what is lost to me now." He frowned. "What a quandary. I wonder why I'm still here, but there is no call for me to the ancient graveyard and beyond. Even though my loved ones wait for me there, and will wait for me forever, this world is still my home. I would not say I am here by choice, but then I have no great yearning to leave it either. And it is your home also, Gred har Aralis. So what is to be done with you?"

Gred laughed weakly. "I would not presume for you to sort *that* quandary out!"

Cobweb pursed his lips, thought for a moment. "The hara who are not already in bed will still be sitting round the dining table. It won't be hard for us to sneak out unseen. Well... for *you* to do so. I go where I please, seen or not. I'll clear a space for us. Come." He stood up.

"Where?"

"Where do you think? Silly harling. We'll go to the house."

Cobweb took Gred to the stable yard, again a copy of Forever's. True to his word he had 'cleared a space' for they ran into no family or members of staff. "This is so typical of us now," Cobweb said, as he led the way. "These float car things stabled alongside our horses. We still use horses, although some hara with the gift can fold through an Otherlane in the blink of an eye. I regard these inconsistencies with affection."

"Car or horse?" Gred asked. "Or will you fold us there?"

"I was never a great lanes traveller," Cobweb replied, "despite being the grateful recipient of many other gifts. I *think* myself to where I want to go most of the time, but could never take anyhar

33

with me. And I do appreciate speed and comfort. We'll take a car tonight."

It seemed incongruous to Gred, if not utterly bizarre, for Cobweb, this being of myth, to take the driving seat and competently pilot one of the Parasilians' sleek grey float cars out into the night. He steered it above the trees, where the stars were watchful sparks. He left the lamps unlit and the roof open, so they wafted through the darkness as if on a magical carpet.

"This seems absurd to me," Gred said. "I would never have imagined you driving a float car."

"Whyever not? The energy that vitalises them is the pure source, made from hara themselves. That to me is magic. Also, a car is less likely to have a funny turn and throw you into a ditch. Ah, here we are."

Cobweb landed the car softly on one of the lawns at the back of Forever. There appeared to be no security at the house. There were no lights to be seen.

"They just lock up at night and leave this place unguarded?" Gred asked.

Cobweb chuckled. "Galhea, for all its pretensions to grandeur, is still a country village at heart. Everything is safe here." He sighed, gazed up at the house, which glowed pale in the starlight. "I am still deeply in love with the old place. Perhaps it is the house more than anything that tethers me to this world."

Gred ducked a formal bow. "Then, tiahaar, it would please me greatly if you would conduct a tour of the house – this time a proper one."

Cobweb inclined his head. "Of course." He offered his elbow for Gred to link with. "Come."

They entered the house through a window-door that led into the old family sitting-room. It was ostensibly locked but the mechanism was so old a gentle shove made it give way. Now Gred was on the other side of the ropes that earlier had fenced the room from him. It made him feel spectral, somehow.

Cobweb lit a candle, and Shadetide shadows danced across the walls.

"I don't know how you can bear it," Gred blurted, "coming here now, it not being your home."

"I had to get used to many things or go entirely mad,"

Cobweb replied. "The time for tears is done. At least I have the choice over which memories to revisit, and I choose to remember all that is good. Forever deserves no less."

"Are there ghosts here other than you?"

Cobweb laughed. "Me, a ghost? Ha!" He patted Gred's shoulder. "Well, there are quite a few. They are simply memories, the house dreaming, or thinking aloud, as it were. There are no chained souls here, Gred, only thoughts."

"You must miss everyhar, though. It seems cruel you are left alone."

Cobweb said nothing. He was prowling round the room, examining the appointments and ornaments, few of which could have once belonged to him.

"I mean," Gred continued awkwardly, "I know you have family – lots of it – but it can't be the same, surely? I don't wish to pry but..."

"These are the things that eat at you, I know," Cobweb said. "You want more than ghosts, don't you? You want to be able to slip through a chink of time and find yourself back here, hundreds of years ago."

"Yes. If I am honest, yes." Gred paused. "If you are honest, isn't that what you would want too?"

Cobweb considered. "My hara call to me," he said. "Quite often. Snake, Swift, Tyson, all of them. But it is as if I say back to them, 'wait a minute, I'm not quite done'. I don't feel any urgency to join them because they are always there, and at the same time, always with me. Time means nothing in the realm they call home now. Perhaps they are sitting waiting for me to join them for dinner, and then, when I do join them they'll have waited only five minutes, even though centuries have passed in this world. I'm not alone, Gred. I don't feel that way. All I lack is physical closeness, and after all this time that is not something I crave or need in order to survive. Not in this world at least." He smiled wistfully, perhaps thinking of his chesnari who waited for him somewhere 'other'. "But would I go back?" He was silent for a moment. "No. Because now I can relive all that is good, and there was much that was bad. There are certain things I would never want to live through again, nor would I want those I love to relive them."

Gred frowned, nodded. "Yes, I can understand that."

Storm Constantine

36

"You would not enjoy them either," Cobweb said. "Early Wraeththu were savage, Gred. You would be shocked, terrified even. When Cal, your ancestor, lived here, he was ravaged, ruined – in his mind. He came back to us, some time after his first visit with Pell, believing that Pell was dead. He had killed the har he thought partly responsible on the way to us, in the most gruesome way imaginable. He murdered one of the greatest hienamas our kind has ever known, the har who was one of the first of all incepted Wraeththu."

Cobweb stared at Gred, who felt his shock must show plainly on his face.

Then Cobweb nodded, as if satisfied by what he saw. "Cal was a husk for a long time and suffered greatly to overcome all that he was. Many early hara were tormented like that. They had seen, and lived through, so much that was terrible, unspeakable. And the ruin wasn't always confined to the mind or spirit. When I first met Snake he was horribly disfigured, one half of his body crippled."

Now Cobweb paused, perhaps reflecting on that time, and Gred found he was able to speak, somewhat inadequately, he felt. "I'm sorry... I didn't know. It was wrong of me to assume..."

Cobweb shook his head. "Some things you will not have been told or read. To you, I expect Pellaz's famous consort Calanthe is remembered only as a wise and mighty ruler."

Gred grimaced. "Not entirely, although obviously there is a lot I don't know."

"Much," Cobweb agreed. "This room..." He turned in a slow circle, hands on hips. "Here I loved. Here I saw harlings grow. Here I spent priceless moments with friends and those I loved. It is a good room. Here I remember Snake, whole again, cured by what we found in the deepest mysteries of aruna together. That is a beautiful memory. But if we were to go Terzian's office, you would feel death sentences hanging over you. If I showed it to you as it really was, you would smell blood... carrion... You might even see it, some of it."

"Did you... did you love Terzian?" Gred asked.

Cobweb appeared to pull himself in, become somewhat more reserved. "Of course. He was a great and powerful har. Whether I would have loved him if he'd been only a farmer or something is another matter. I am not blind to realities. I was drawn to powerful hara, as many are."

"But you were one of them too."

"Not initially. Those around me contributed greatly to who I became, not least your ancestor, Pellaz. We were alike in some ways. He too came from humble beginnings, but it was right he became all he was. Anything else would have been a waste."

"I never met him," Gred said, somewhat bitterly.

"Yes, well, he was impatient to get away," Cobweb said. "This world and the hara in it often annoyed him, and it got worse over time. This world *does* age you, Gred. It makes your physical being grow thin; it's just part of what this realm is, even if you're a har who can live for centuries, perhaps even millennia. But what's inside us never fades or grows feeble. Some choose to fade away over time until they are blown like gauze into another life. Pellaz wouldn't wait for that. He wanted somewhere else, so off into the Otherlanes he went. Others close to him chose to join him at the time. They were done here, so they sought a new world. Perhaps that was his way of 'going back', only it was starting anew."

"I was never told that," Gred said. "They never tell us that. They say that Pellaz and his kin faded. They went to a mountain and were taken to what is beyond."

Cobweb snorted derisively. "How biblical! I suppose they don't really know what happened or it's what they want to believe. Perhaps Pellaz did go to a mountain to open a gate. I can't remember. All I'll say is this: if he was standing here now, he'd call you insane for the things you desire. He'd say, 'get out of this realm, young har. If it bores you, there are limitless exciting places to discover'."

"Is that it? I'm just bored of my life?"

Cobweb shrugged. "Only you can answer that. I'm not sure if you're capable of withstanding true danger and excitement, but if you are, the Otherlanes and its realms is where they lie. But if you go there, and I mean truly go deep and explore, you might not be able to return. And then you might regret your decision, lost in an alien environment where you would never feel at home. Pellaz had outgrown his home; it was different for him. You are young, full of fancies and desires and yearnings. You have a lot of living yet to do in this world."

"Perhaps... perhaps I should look for Pellaz," Gred suggested.

"Not yet," Cobweb answered shortly. "If a harling leaves the nursery before it's ready, reality will rapidly cause its demise."

"I don't feel that young," Gred said. "In fact, quite the opposite. I suppose every har is young in comparison to you, though. I understand your impatience with us."

"It's not impatience," Cobweb said. "Anyway, did we come here to have this conversation or to explore?"

"Both, I think."

"Then let's explore now."

Cobweb led Gred through every room in the house. The stories he told were not of conflict, courageous deeds, terror or destruction. He spoke of small amusing things, such as silly words Swift had spoken as a harling, various awkward romantic affairs that had taken place, arguments that had ended in humiliation or farce. They had come to one of the bathrooms on the second floor. "Tyson was terrible as a young har," Cobweb said. "He would push the harish system to its limit. I remember once a distinguished Gelaming visitor found him unconscious on this bathroom floor with his trousers round his ankles. It took some time for the har to push open the door since Tyson was lying behind it. Tyson's excuse was that he'd been meditating and had gone on some strange travel vision. In reality, he was just blind drunk and had fallen off the toilet."

Gred laughed. "You're not doing a very good job of persuading me the past is not a good place to visit. I wish I'd known all those hara."

"They're just stories," Cobweb said. "Make your own."

"In Immanion?" Gred asked incredulously.

"Even in Immanion there must be hara you'd want to know. It's just finding them."

"With my face, that's difficult. I carry the baggage of the Aralisian dynasty. Few hara beyond Phaonica's Mount are at ease with me."

"Then go somewhere else. Be somehar else. The world isn't exactly small." Cobweb sighed. "You've only looked at a very small part of it, haven't you?" He shook his head. "By all the dehara, this takes me back! I might as well be lecturing Pellaz again when he was having one of his *episodes*."

"Perhaps that was why I was drawn here."

"I'm beginning to think that was likely," Cobweb said dryly.

They had come to the threshold of Terzian's bedroom. Cobweb had left it until last. Even all the rooms on higher stories of the house had been explored first. "So much drama lingers in here," Cobweb said. "Really, most of it is embarrassing now. We were so self-obsessed."

"Tell me a drama."

Cobweb rubbed a hand over his face. "Oh, I'd rather not. Not one of my personal ones, at least. But Terzian died here, in that bed. It's the original."

Gred approached it.

"Lie on it," Cobweb said. "Pearls were delivered there, a har died, many loved."

Gred laughed shakily. "Now history frightens me a little."

"You see? You know your skin will crawl if you lie on that bed. My skin crawls in this room too. It's one of the bad places. Swift tried to live in it for a while. He soon saw sense."

There was a silence. Then Gred said, "Thank you for all this, Cobweb. I really appreciate it."

"My pleasure. I sometimes like to indulge myself and tell the old stories. The family have heard them a hundred times, so are a poor audience nowadays. There are a couple of the harlings I quite like. They seek me out all the time, and now and again I'll let them find me. It doesn't pay to lose my mystery and be too available. They love it, anyway."

"I wish I was one of those harlings."

Cobweb stepped forward and embraced Gred. "But my dear thing, you are!"

The tour was over. Cobweb and Gred went back to the sitting-room, where Cobweb extinguished the candle, now burned to a stub (a ghostly story for tomorrow's visitors?), and they went outside. Cobweb pressed the window door shut and the tired old mechanism clicked back into place.

"I will never forget this night," Gred said.

Cobweb took hold of Gred's arm again. "But it's not over," he said. "How about we return to the Heights and assault Marlet's collection of rare sheh vintages? I have many more stories to tell and now, quite frankly, they are bursting to be let out."

"I'd like nothing better," Gred said.

They talked until morning, when the staff began to appear in the kitchen to prepare breakfast. Cobweb and Gred were still seated at the kitchen table, with two empty bottles of sheh before them. Gred felt happily, woozily drunk. But not tired. The staff did not seem surprised to see Cobweb there but had perhaps been trained by Ambel not to register surprise in such circumstances. This was still Cobweb's home, if only his 'other' home. A har discreetly made coffee and placed it before them.

"You should sleep," Cobweb said.

"But then you'll be gone, and it will be over," Gred replied.

"Never that," Cobweb said. "Have your adventures, Gred. Find hara you like. Fall in love. Take aruna with a har who makes you feel as if the act was created solely for you and him. Go into wildernesses. Find mysteries. Then come here to tell me of them."

"You'll let me find you?"

"You'll have to wait and see, won't you?"

Gred slept for three hours and then sought out Ambel in the orchid house. Beyond the arched windows, the day was clear.

"I heard you had a sleepless night," Ambel said, indicating Gred should take a seat beside him at the wrought iron table. "It isn't often the staff come across Cobweb in the house."

"You knew he would come to me," Gred said.

Ambel shrugged. "Strongly suspected. He *is* difficult to predict. But I can see that in some ways he has inspired you. You feel a lot lighter to me today."

Gred nodded, grinned. "It was an unforgettable experience."

"And did he help you choose a path?"

"I think it was more like he told me to make my own map. I'll have to think about it."

"Cobweb once told me that he and Pellaz would argue fiercely sometimes. Pellaz didn't always like the advice Cobweb gave him. But invariably, he took it." Ambel handed Gred a glass of tea. "Well, enough of the past. I hope you will stay here for a while with us, and then when you return to Immanion we can initiate greater contact between our families. That, I personally believe, is one of the paths to go on your map."

Gred paused. "I think..." he said eventually, "that the hara in my country have changed far more than those I've found here. I don't mean it to sound rude, but in some ways being here *is* like stepping back in time. You might be disappointed by my harakin. They seem to me to be dour and dull in comparison."

Ambel laughed delightedly. "Perhaps they need some shaking up! Pellaz and his kin were never dour or dull, I *do* know that." He reached out to take one of Gred's hands. "And also, young har, bear in mind that the hara of Phaonica's Mount are not the entire population of Almagabra. I think you've been locked in your rooms for too long! Never mind braving the daylight enough to come here. Perhaps there are places for you to explore closer to home."

Gred pressed Ambel's fingers, held onto his hand; an intimate gesture he could not remember doing even with his own hostling. "Cobweb said the same."

"You see?" Ambel released Gred's hand. "Now, breakfast. Then you can delve into Marlet's collections. I'm afraid it's been mentioned we should have a dinner gathering while you are here, so hara from Galhea can meet you. Is that acceptable?"

"Yes, it's the first step, I suppose."

"Good. You never know what might come of it."

As Ambel set about preparing a plate of food for Gred from the various dishes available, Gred stared out of the window at the sky. Overnight, his life had changed completely. It was like shedding a skin or perhaps even emerging from a pearl. He felt, for perhaps the first time in his life, a sense of excitement, as if events and experiences – and hara – were gathering unseen amid clouds around him. They were not dark clouds, merely a shifting mist that concealed what was to come. He would walk into that gladly.

The Etherline

Wendy Darling

The Etherline

The young har's body was sprawled comfortably in a cosy armchair, legs hanging over the upholstered arms, eyes closed, but his mind was far, far away.

Marila in Alba Sulh was talking about a dream he'd had, involving an ouana-lim that migrated all over his body. As they were pondering the possible meaning of this, Fendron, down in Almagabra, connected and said he had to talk about a new har he'd met, but Luka, engrossed in dream talk, told him to wait a few minutes and try back later.

It was only mid-morning but Luka had already been in conversation with a dozen different hara. Some chats were only quick exchanges, check-ins before work, while others, like Salvador in Megalithica revealing that he was with pearl, had been long and involved. There might be another half a dozen conversations to go, depending on how long he could keep on connecting to his friends on the etherline.

"Tell me how you felt about this in the dream. Were you upset? Were you—?"

Luka paused. The distinct awareness he had of his physical body had alerted him that he was no longer alone, in a physical sense.

"Sorry, have to go, Marila. Hostling here," Luka apologised. Then he opened his eyes.

Helan was standing in the bedroom doorway, slowly shaking his head. "You never listen, do you?"

Luka flung his legs back towards the carpet and crossed his arms over his chest. "I *do* listen. I just don't always follow instructions."

Helan sighed. "Too true. Which is why I'm here. First off, the dogs need feeding, which I seem to have to tell you every day. And second off, your father needs his lunch brought to him."

It was the same as always. *Should have known things were going too well online today*, Luka thought. He wanted to argue, as he sometimes did, plead for more time, but the mention of his father gave him pause. Helan would not stand for Torbek to wait on his lunch, which he ate before noon since he often went out at dawn.

"All right, Hel," Luka conceded. Carefully grasping the enhancer on his lap, he stood up and placed it on its stand by the bed. "I was having a lovely time, but I suppose dogs and fathers need feeding."

Helan, who had entered the room, now put a hand on his son's shoulder. "You should spend more time having a 'lovely time' *here*. At home. In the village. Not—" he made a sweeping gesture in all directions, "out there with people you don't really even know."

Luka studied his hostling's hand, and silently counted to ten. How many times could they have this same conversation? "I'm a grown har, Hel."

"Barely," Helan said sharply, "and your father and I are getting tired of indulging you and your obsession. You've got to start being *here* and doing *useful* things." He took his hand away. "And yes, I know I've said this a hundred times to you, but just yesterday Tor was saying he'll be needing help with plantings. You can't just spend your days surfing the etherline."

Luka strode over to the closet and yanked out a pair of boots and a light jacket. "Alright, alright, guilt trip received, hostling of mine. You don't see the point of the etherline. I get it. But I'm *not* conceding, I'm just going out and doing those chores because *then* I can come back here later and continue what I was doing, hopefully uninterrupted."

Helan straightened up Luka's coat collar and embraced him lightly. "I suppose that's the most I'll get from you for now." He stepped back. "The food is—"

But Luka was already out the door. "I *know!*" he called from the hall. "Dogs' food in the bin, Tor's lunch on the counter, don't forget the water bottle. I *know!*" And then there was the sound of footsteps on the stairs and he was gone.

In the sky over the vineyard, the sun was just beginning to thin out the thick gray of spring clouds. The air was chill and damp, a fact Luka wished he had remembered when selecting his coat. Thrusting his hands deeper into his pockets, he began the climb up the rutted steps of the terraces to where his father would be working to ready the vines.

The dogs, kept in a run beside the house, had been fed and exercised. In the distance, Luka could still hear them barking happily, no doubt still horsing around with one another. Luka himself had spent enough time as a harling among the pack, horsing around as one of them, that he could interpret the dogs' language almost as well as any other foreign language.

Those days in the dog run seemed long gone, however. Although it had only been a year since his feybraiha, to Luka the young har, the time between his life as a harling and the present day seemed a vast chasm. One day he had spent his time blissfully wandering amongst the vines or reading books in a chair in his hostling's office, or running into the village for market day... and then the next day he was deep in conversation via the etherline, hands grasped around the enhancer, equally oblivious to home, vineyard and village.

Up until his feybraiha, the etherline had been something forbidden to him. No matter how Luka pleaded with his parents, his friends' parents, the local hienama or anyhar else, he had always received the same answer: "Not until you're older. At least past feybraiha." And thus his heart's desire hung tantalisingly over the border of adulthood. While most harlings looked to feybraiha as the time of bodily changes and their first experience of aruna – something both longed for and feared – for Luka this milestone chiefly meant access to what to him seemed an outlandish and magical land: the etherline.

His parents had asked him many times, before and after his feybraiha, why the etherline so fascinated him. Yes, they agreed, the ability to join a network of harish minds from around the world was a marvellous thing, useful, and a further sign of Wraeththu's superiority over man, who had needed wires and electric waves to communicate similarly. But no, it was not the be-all and end-all. Learning a trade, making friends in the world, raising a family – these were all more important and more fulfilling in the long run. Helan in particular had no interest in the etherline: "There are enough marvellous hara right in the village, enough mountain scenery and waterfalls and sunsets, to keep me satisfied the rest of my life. Why should I close my eyes and seek better elsewhere?"

Yet, making his way up the slope of the vineyard, Luka couldn't help his mind from straying to the world of the etherline.

He thought of Marila's dream, of Salvador's pearl, and wondered about the new har Fendron had met. A pity he couldn't link up that very moment, but even with all his experience, Luka still found that connecting on the go just wasn't possible. Sitting in a chair, lying in a field, sprawled in bed, yes, it was easy, but climbing a small mountain while carrying a backpack and hearing crows caw overhead? No, it wasn't possible.

Looking up the slope, Luka spotted a shock of bright copper hair peeking out from behind a high row of tangled, bare vines. His father. With hair like that – like Luka's own – Torbek was as usual easy to spot in the field of blacks, browns and greys. Luka quickened his pace and made his way up the path.

"Ah, lunch at last!" Torbek announced cheerfully, as soon as Luka had appeared at end of the row. He set down the bundle of twine and heavy shears he had been working with and wiped his forehead with the back of his coat sleeve.

Luka handed over the bag lunch and the water bottle he'd just fished out of his backpack. "Helan is busy and sent me up with this."

Torbek accepted his son's offerings. "'Course he did. Lucky he could manage it. Dragging you away from your invisible 'friends,' that is." Torbek held his lunch bag in one hand and with the other, raised the bottle and twisted the top off with his teeth. After spitting the top down to the ground, he took a long swig.

Luka didn't take the bait. Not that it would do him any good, he knew. When his father decided to lecture him on this subject, it wasn't necessary for him to actually make any replies. The best he could hope for was to keep things short so he could return to the house as quickly as possible.

When Torbek had satisfied his thirst, he nodded in the direction of a nearby boulder. It had long been a favourite spot for lunches and afternoon snacks. Luka followed his father over and together they settled on a flat, mossy seat the boulder thoughtfully provided near its bottom edge.

After a suitable amount of time, and making a suitable dent in his sandwich and the muffin Helan had sent up, Torbek began the expected lecture. "Luka, your hostling and I are concerned about you."

Luka kept his eyes rooted to a spot across the valley, determined to hold steady against yet another well-intentioned assault.

Torbek continued. "I know I've said that before, and so has Helan, but all this time you spend on the etherline isn't in your best interest. There's nothing wrong with doing it, of course, but it's the amount of *time* you devote to it – at the expense of other things."

Against his better judgment, Luka couldn't help but respond to this. "Other things? Like what… Like grapes?"

Torbek chuckled. "Well, the work is good, fulfilling, and the land is lovely, but I was thinking more of other hara. A young har like you shouldn't be cooped up in his room. The village has a half dozen hara just your age and others you might like as well. Some of them quite attractive, too. I've seen them myself. I don't spend all my time up here with the vines, you know."

Luka suppressed a groan. "I *do* spend time with other hara, *especially* hara my age!" he protested. "Just because they're not here in the village, they don't count?"

When his father didn't reply, he went on. "Besides, the village hara are so provincial. Most of them only know the very basics of the etherline and I don't think any of them has their own enhancer. They borrow their parents' or go to the library."

"Luka, you're spoiled, you know." Torbek took a healthy bite of sandwich and chewed it while shaking his head slightly. "We gave you money towards the enhancer because you wanted it so badly, but we didn't know you'd use it as a way to hide from the world."

"Hide?" Luka stood up and rubbed his hands together. It was cooler at the top of the vineyard. "But I'm *not* hiding, I'm out there every day with other hara!"

Torbek patted the mossy seat. "Sit down. You know what I mean." He looked up expectantly until Luka resumed his seat. "I mean that for all you obviously consider the local hara, especially those your age, 'provincial' and 'underprivileged' when it comes to your virtual world, they do have something you don't have. Can you guess what it is?"

Luka raised an eyebrow. "Um… Not sure. More chores?"

"No, that's not what I was thinking of. I was thinking of something you might actually *like* to have more of." Torbek winked. "Aruna."

Luka put his hands over his face and sighed. "Tor! I can't

believe you said that!'"

"And I can't believe you're *not* interested." Torbek pulled at Luka's hands and once they were away from his face, held them steadily. "You're young, Luka, and aruna is important for everyhar, but especially the young. You need to explore, find out what you like. It makes you stronger, too, as I'm sure Johnna taught you."

Luka nodded. "Yes, but—"

"But nothing. Your etherline world might provide a lot of things, but aruna isn't one of them. Unless I am even more clueless as a parent than Helan sometimes thinks I am. You might talk about it 'online' or even describe it, but you can't actually *do* it."

Luka had to concede this was true, but still he rolled his eyes. "And your point is?"

Torbek squeezed his son's hands. "Aruna, my darling pearl. Down there. In the village. Go!"

Luka stared at his father, open-mouthed. "You... What, is this a chore?"

"It shouldn't be, Luka." Torbek stood up. "Now, thanks for the lunch and all, but please do me a favour and stay out of the house all day. Go to the village. Come back later. Tomorrow, even. If your hostling wonders where you are—"

"OK, OK!" Luka agreed, standing up and brushing off the back of his pants, dirty with bits of moss and dead leaves. "Fine. As orders go, this one shouldn't be too hard. And it keeps me from having to beat the rugs tonight, which I think I agreed to do."

"I'll take care of it. Now: Go!" Torbek shoved Luka playfully towards the downward-leading path. "Have some fun in the real world," he added softly.

Down in the real world of the village, Luka found his "chore" was harder to take care of than he'd expected. By that hour most hara were working. It was too early in the year for hara to be lazing about in the park, although he did spy some older harlings conspiring around the fountain. Just a year ago, he would probably have been one of them.

After walking about for about fifteen minutes, Luka decided he had to think strategically. Where would be a good place to spot hara and be spotted? As it happened, he was standing next to the village library, which was directly across the square from his favourite pub. Luka smiled to himself over the idea of procuring some reading materials to take with him for a "reading" session at the pub.

Inside the small library, the atmosphere was predictably quiet. The har seated at the front desk, Tomas, smiled warmly and beckoned Luka over.

"Ah, little Luka, it's been too long," Thomas began, then checked himself. "Sorry, not so little anymore now, are you?"

Luka suppressed his impatience. He wasn't sure he had visited the library even once since his feybraiha. And no matter how much time he had once spent there, today he was not in the mood for chitchat.

"Sorry, I'm just popping in. Wanted to grab something and take it off to read at Bekker's."

Tomas' eyes lit up. "Ah!" He rose from his chair and went to a nearby bookcase. "That reminds me," he said over his shoulder. "Just recently, a copy of *Vedallion* came in. I remembered how you had been pestering me about it, so I set a copy of it aside." Tomas returned to the desk and handed Luka a plump novel. "I had a feeling, and a hope, that you might return here again and I could give it to you."

Luka didn't know what to say. The book was one he had passionately wanted to read. He had indeed asked the librarian about it over and over again. It was a second novel by a har whose first novel had set his imagination on fire. The first novel was as old as Luka.

"Thanks," he said, brushing his hand over the cover. "I had almost—" he began, but then stopped. He had been about to say he'd forgotten about the book, but that wasn't true at all. He had remembered it numerous times over the past year, even brought it up in conversation on the etherline. A few times he had even thought to check at the library to see if it had come in, but he always seemed to remember in the middle of the night when the doors were locked. And then in the daytime his mind would disappear into the ethers far beyond the village.

"Yes, well, thanks," Luka concluded lamely.

"You're very welcome," said Tomas, who after noting the book loan in a ledger, looked up at the younger har and smiled.

"Truly, I'm so glad you're back. I've been worried."

Luka did not give the other har time to elaborate. He didn't particularly want to listen to another lecture, which he suspected is what the conversation would turn in to if he mentioned where and how he'd been spending his time.

"Thanks again." He raised the book in one hand and waved it in farewell as he backed toward the door. "Perfect for the pub."

Given the early hour, Luka was able to secure what for his purposes was the ideal seat at the pub. Nestled in a corner, he had a full view of most of Bekker's, including the bar and entrance, and there was even a mirror that showed hara behind him. Not that there was anyhar worth looking at when he sat down, but Luka was thinking ahead a couple of hours, when hara would come in during their lunch break and, under the pretext of reading his book, he could scope everyhar out.

Luka put his feet up on the bench and leaned against the wall as he took a drag off a clove cigarette, which they'd been selling up at the bar. He'd also arranged for a plate of bread and butter and a large mug of tea, heavily mixed with cream and sugar, with a hint of cardamom. Fragrant smoke drifting around his shoulders, Luka was projecting himself into the physical world, with hopes that would trigger physical attraction.

But first there was the book, *Vedallion*. Luka ran his fingers over the cover and a frisson of electricity seemed to run right up his arm. Books were always best, Luka thought to himself, before you started reading them. In the moments before, you could imagine anything you wanted, indulging in high hopes and fantasies. The last book had been so good, this one had to be equally marvellous or, possibly, even more marvellous. What wonders would it contain? How and where would it transport him? Would it make him ache? Would it fill his head with dreams? Until he began reading, anything was possible.

The cover was deep purple with a sketch of a mountain embossed into it like a carving on a pub table. *Vedallion: Reaching the Summit* was the full title, written in script across the top. Across the bottom, the fabled author's name, Diek har Sulh. In Luka's mind's eye flashed an image of the author he'd concocted as a harling: a slender, black-haired har like the hero of the first book. There'd been no actual author picture to contradict him and flipping the book over and then cracking it open, Luka found this was true of the new book as well. He had a name for the author and the knowledge he was from Alba Sulh, but that was all.

Dragging on his cigarette, then sipping tea and munching on bread and butter, Luka began to read. He was almost hesitant at first, wanting to dive in, yet at the same time, wanting to savour the moment. He didn't want to read too quickly. It was a thick book, true, but at the outset, there was a feeling akin to standing on the edge of a deep chasm. He could fall and fall, if he wasn't careful. It had happened with the previous book. It could happen again.

A couple of hours later, Luka was indeed in a faraway place. Three mostly empty cups of lukewarm tea sat at his elbow, while the remains of a sandwich rested on his plate, but how or when they had been consumed, Luka had only the vaguest idea. His eyes, ears and everything else had been all for the book. If he nodded his head at the waiter or made his lips form words to order sustenance, it had been out of habit, not conscious thought.

Diek har Sulh had once again swallowed Luka up and engulfed him in a strange and yet completely compelling world. *Vedallion*, like its predecessor, *Ipstillion*, was set in a world apart, of the past that may or may not have ever been. The characters lived on Earth, or something like Earth, and seemed in many ways like hara, except that rather curiously, they were human, men and women, just like in Luka's history lessons.

"She," "her," "him" and "his" were words that at first, as a harling, had thrown him, but soon he had grown acclimated to them and after a while, he almost didn't think of the peculiarity – the fact he had never met a human and probably never would. Luka had of course plunged into the stores of the library to learn more about hara's predecessors on earth – anatomy, drawings, their decline, all that – but still, in a way, humans were more of a fantasy than a reality to him.

And so that day in the pub Luka had dived so deeply into the world of *Vedallion* that it wasn't until he felt a hand on shoulder that he realised somehar was standing next to him speaking. He dropped the book to the table in surprise.

"Oh, sorry!" gasped a slim young har, taking a step backward. "I didn't mean to startle you."

Luka did not recognise the har. "No harm done," he said quickly, marking his place in the book with a corner of his napkin. "I wasn't paying attention."

The other har's eyes caught the gesture. "It's a good book." This was not a question.

"Yes," Luka agreed. "You haven't actually read it, have you?" The har nodded enthusiastically. "You *have*? Really?"

"That's why I came over here. I glanced down and saw the front cover when you were tilting it up a few minutes ago. Then I saw you attached to it!"

The har took a seat on the other side of the table and drummed his fingers on the worn oak. "I'm Matti, by the way."

"Luka. Are you new around here?"

Matti laid his palms flat on the table. "My family moved here a couple of months ago. But you're not new?"

"Quite the opposite," Luka replied, chuckling. "I was hatched here, lived here all my life. My parents own Moel Vineyard."

Matti looked impressed. "I've heard of it. My parents drink your wine often. I'm not allowed to, at least not now anyway."

"Not now?"

Matti's fair face flushed. "Since I'm about to start my feybraiha. They say alcohol is certainly soothing but also might just confuse me more."

At these words Luka stretched back in his seat a bit and studied the young har more closely, using not only his eyes but his harish senses. Not through feybraiha yet! He should have noticed. The harling wasn't shy and was easy to talk to, but for the purposes of this afternoon, he wouldn't be suitable at all.

Luka steered the conversation back to where it had begun. "So, you're a Diek har Sulh fan like me? And you've read this?" He patted the thick volume.

"They're my favourite!" the blond near-adult gushed. "I read the first only last year and then just before we moved, *Vedallion* came out. My parents got it for me as a present – a way to make it up to me for moving so soon before my feybraiha was due."

"I just started it this morning, after I found out the library had it," Luka explained.

Matti eyed the book. "Oh, so you've only just started. I thought maybe you were rereading it." He considered. "Well, I won't spoil it for you!"

Luka gaped in mock shock. "I should hope not!"

"No, no, I wouldn't... I promise!" Matti burst out. "But could we talk about the first book?"

Although it was a tempting prospect – he had never discussed the book with anyhar beyond Tomas and his own parents – Luka once again thought back to his alleged purpose for being in the village in the first place.

"I'd love to chat over this book and the other one..." Luka began, "but I tell you, Matti, I can't do it right now."

Matti cocked his head. "Oh, you've got to be back at work or something?"

"Not exactly." Luka looked the younger har steadily in the eyes. "The reason I don't want to talk books now is that I'm here in the village to look for a har. A har for – and I'm sorry, you're in feybraiha, it's awkward – aruna."

Matti gulped. "Oh."

Luka winked playfully. "And though you are charming, you really won't suit me. Again, sorry if this is awkward. My parents actually sent me down here to get out of the house and meet hara – and so far I haven't done much but read!"

If young Matti had been embarrassed by this, he certainly didn't show it. Instead, he leaned across the table and whispered. "Well, I can help you there, tiahaar. I have an older brother and he's right here in this pub!"

Upon awakening, Luka's first thoughts were of dreams and not the events of hours past. Images and feelings and urgencies swirled in his mind, some from the world of Diek har Sulh, others from the world of the etherline. Connections, messages, indescribable certainties.

Gradually, however, the dream thoughts drew back and his surroundings came to him. This was not his bed. The window, through which the moon shone half full, was not his bedroom window. And the har next to him? His name was Helm, but beyond that he knew more of his body than any details.

Matti had proved an adept matchmaker. After a short introduction, during which Luka found himself a bit embarrassed, he and Helm had come to a mutual understanding. The har would certainly "do." Following a silent exchange with his older brother, Matti patted Luka on the arm, told him "see you tomorrow," and headed out the door.

Technically, tomorrow had arrived. Luka had awoken some hours before dawn, feeling warm and sated. Aruna had been a most pleasing affair. Helm was five years older and evidently far more experienced. Not even on the etherline, where as his hostling had speculated, hara did indeed discuss intimate matters, had Luka heard of some of the pleasures Helm had shown him. After one particularly satisfying bout, Luka had had to stifle a laugh at the thought that his father had been right in his lecture: He had indeed been in need of a good roon.

Eyes now adjusted to the darkness of the room, lit only by moonlight, Luka made out the shape of the wine glasses left on the bedside table, along with a platter of half-eaten cheeses, bread and olives. Luka raised himself up on his elbows and reached for a few of the leftovers. After following Helm down a narrow lane to his family's house and sneaking in the back door and into the bedroom, they'd found the small meal already set out. The mystery was quickly solved; Matti was very thoughtful, Helm had explained.

Luka chewed on an olive and thought back to his dreams, still drifting about as trails of steam, and then he thought further back, to the pub, to the book, to Matti. Remarkable to have run into not only the book — finally — but a fellow fan, on the same day, in a little mountain town. All at once he had several things to look forward to, none of which he had been expecting when he'd woken that morning at the vineyard house: another dive into the fantasy world, somehar to discuss that world with (even if he was a harling) and a flesh and blood har with some remarkable talents.

Scooting back down, he carefully turned on his side and, beneath the warm cocoon of the blankets, draped an arm over Helm's bared shoulder, then ran his fingers down his companion's spine. With his other hand he moved lower. Helm murmured wordlessly, then with a sigh, fluttered his eyes open. "Still here?" he whispered.

"Still here," Luka replied, putting the covers over their heads.

In the morning — the real morning, with sunlight streaming through the bedroom window — Matti came knocking, bringing an invitation to breakfast.

"You can meet our parents," he informed Luka. "And no, I

didn't tell them you were here, they just know it." Matti, who had picked up the tray of food, blushed. "Even I felt what you were up to overnight!"

"It's alright," Luka assured the harling. "We'll be there in a couple of minutes."

Once Matti had gone out the door, the two hara began to get cleaned up and dressed. Helm took the opportunity to fill Luka in on his family. "Matti's always been precocious. His favourite thing by far is reading. Brings home all sorts of ideas from the library or from talking to hara he meets around. He's not shy."

Pulling on a shoe, Luka nodded. "I got that right away. And what about your parents?"

Helm stood at the mirror combing out his long blond hair. "Their names are Berga and Torst. Berga is a teacher and Torst studies history."

Luka, through with his shoes, looked up. "Really? Harish history or human history?"

"Both, actually. But more often than not, human." Helm was now standing at the door. "It was Torst who introduced Matti to those books you two are into. Myself, I tried to read them but it wasn't my thing. I'm more interested in art. Anyway..." He grasped the doorknob. "Breakfast?"

At first breakfast was a cosy affair. The kitchen table, normally set for four, was crowded with settings for five and extra food for the visitor. Berga was gregarious, asking Luka questions and refilling his coffee cup with every sip. When Torst discovered Luka's parents owned the vineyard, he dove into a conversation about wine. This would have gone on longer but Berga had to be off to work at the school and Torst was meeting somehar early at the library. "Take care," he said, kissing Matti on the top of his head and winking teasingly at Helm.

Luka leaned back in the seat, glad for more breathing space. "By Ag, you're all such talkers!"

Helm chuckled. "We are that. Mind you, they're probably going to gossip about us all through their walk." He dug into a last remaining hunk of eggs. "By noon they'll be planning a bonding ceremony."

"You're joking!" Luka exclaimed. He fidgeted. "You are, right?"

"Yes, I'm joking." Helm began to stack up the dirty plates. "Not that they won't gossip, but no pressure. It's not like I haven't brought somehar home before!"

Matti began to gather the coffee cups. "So what about your parents?" he asked, on the way to the sink. "Do they pester your visitors? Or you do bring them by entirely in secret?"

"Trysts in the vineyard?" Helm jested. "Could be romantic."

Luka found himself acutely embarrassed. "Well, actually... I, um... don't have any visitors. No trysts in the vineyard either."

Matti gaped. Helm set down the stack of plates. "What? Well, where *do* you have them, then? In the village?"

The situation was not improving, in Luka's opinion. "I... just don't have any. No visitors, no trysts."

"But you're so fine!" exclaimed Matti. "I mean—"

Luka waved away any apology. "No, it's OK. I just prefer to spend a lot of time by myself — or well, actually not by myself, but with hara who aren't here in the village."

Helm looked quizzed. "Wait, how are you alone and yet with other hara?"

"The etherline, of course," Matti answered, taking the words out of Luka's mouth. "Not that I know much about it, but we went over it in school and I read a lot about it."

Luka nodded. "That's exactly right. I've got a whole host of friends, from all over, and spend time chatting with them all."

Helm's expression continued to be one of puzzlement. "I don't quite understand. I was shown the etherline, how to use it, and I find it useful for connecting with hara, especially since we've moved, or for getting answers to questions..." Helm paused a few moments. "But for just talking and talking? Hara you — you haven't met?"

"Oh, I've met them," Luka corrected. "Met them online. Some I discovered on my own, others are friends of friends... others I don't even remember meeting but talk to every day. I'm on the etherline for hours, all the time. I have an enhancer, that helps."

Helm got up and brought the plates to the sink. He stood looking out the window, which gave a view of the mountains. "Talking all day to hara who aren't here but are there — over the mountain, across the sea even. Never would occur to me..."

Luka felt himself growing nervous. Given the lovely time he'd had so far, he really didn't want to get another lecture. Also causing unease was the fact that in talking about his online friends, he realized he had been away from the etherline almost a full day. The urge wasn't strong yet, but he suddenly felt an itch to get back to it.

Helm was back at the table. "But each har to his taste. And I should be grateful you have that habit."

Luka raised an eyebrow. "Grateful why?"

"Because if you spent more time rooning you wouldn't have jumped into my bed last night!"

They all laughed.

It was chilly and bright as Luka and Matti climbed the hill up towards the vineyard later that morning. A flock of ducks flew overhead, returning from their winter home in the south. Trees and flowers were coming alive and awake.

Perhaps this influenced Matti's choice of topic: Feybraiha.

"I didn't want to say it in front of my brother," he began, "but I really meant it when I said I *felt* what you and he got up to last night." His fair cheeks coloured. "Not just the sounds but... the feelings."

"I'm sorry," said Luka, still walking.

"Don't be," Matti soothed. "I'm just saying, I'm near my time. For feybraiha."

"Ah." They paused at the end of a road to let a cart and horse pass. "You probably are. Does it... hurt?"

Matti nodded. "Not until last night. My guts are churning. Feel like a bowl of soup put on the stove for slow boil."

They resumed their climb. "It's like that. Was for me." Luka reflected. Had it only been a year ago? "But don't worry, it's only temporary and usually doesn't last long. I know I was so grateful when it was over!"

"Your first aruna, you mean?" Matti said laughingly, probably trying to sound knowing.

Luka stopped in his tracks. "Well, I meant happy feybraiha was over, mainly because I wanted so bad to finally get to use the etherline."

Just as that morning in the kitchen, Matti gaped. "You wanted the etherline more than you wanted aruna?"

Luka felt sheepish but nodded. "My parents couldn't understand it either." They had finally caught sight of the house.

Luka thought back to discussions that had taken place there. "But since I went through the ceremony and took aruna and went to Johnna for basic training — and I'm an only harling — they got me an enhancer, once I had been trained in etherline and knew how much I needed one."

"The enhancer allows you to have conversations over long distances, doesn't it?" Matti asked.

"Yup. And I wanted to talk to hara far away. The idea — it just excites me so much. It's like you can be in one place but at the same time be a dozen other places at once."

They had reached the short path up to the house. "But now we're here, so why don't I introduce you to my hostling and then get into the book!"

When they came inside, Helan stepped out from the kitchen. "Ah, you're back," he remarked, wiping his hands on his pants.

It was time for introductions. "Yes, I'm back. Hel, this is Matti. We met at the pub yesterday." The harling nodded and smiled appropriately. "Matti, this is my hostling Helan. He and my father run the vineyard."

Matti looked suitably impressed. "My father loves your wine." He glanced around the large, homey family room and then up the hall. "Er, do you have a bathroom I could use?"

After giving the harling some quick directions, Helan eyed Luka appraisingly. "He's a harling, Luka," he said quietly. "You didn't—"

"No!" Luka whispered. "Not him! I met him at the pub. We got to talking about books. Later he introduced me to his older brother." He couldn't help smirking. "His *very* handsome and *experienced* older brother!"

Helan smiled. "I'm glad for you. But what are you up to now?"

From his bag Luka pulled out the book. "Went to the library yesterday and the new Diek har Sulh book was there waiting for me. Matti is also a fan."

Just then the harling appeared down the hall. Helan turned to him. "So you've dragged my Luka away from the etherline?"

For moment Matti looked confused but he quickly recovered. "Oh, you mean talking about the books? I guess so. I'm not allowed to use the etherline until after my feybraiha."

Helan nodded slowly. "Which will be soon. Speaking of which, have you or your parents chosen anyone? To be your first?"

Matti, predictably, coloured. "No, not yet. But they will soon. They'll have to."

Luka suddenly felt Helan's voice in his head. *You really should do him a favour.*

What? He considered for a moment. *Maybe. I'm not saying yes but... How do you come up with these plans so quickly?*

Some things are just obvious.

By this point Matti had clearly caught on that some form of silent communication was ongoing. He waited patiently, curious but polite.

"Well, glad you had fun in the village," Helan said brightly. "Now go off wherever you were going to. I'm making a stew, which will be read in an hour or so. Sound good?"

It did. Luka guided Matti to the stairs up to his bedroom.

Although he had only been gone from it a day, to Luka his bedroom seemed to have the look of a room abandoned for a good length of time. A light layer of dust had gathered on his desk and bookshelves, while clothes were piled in an untidy heap near the wardrobe, the bed unmade. On its stand the etherline enhancer stood slightly askew, evidence of the haste with which Luka had left the room.

"Sorry for the mess," Luka apologised to Matti, who stood examining the books. "I don't have a lot of visitors." He gestured to the bed. "Here, sit. Unless it's too grubby."

Matti turned and grinned. "Don't worry. You didn't see my bedroom. Total sty, as my hostling says." He hopped up on the bed. "Comes from caring more about reading than tidiness."

Feeling the room could use some fresh air, Luka was opening a window. "Your brother's room was tidy."

"He's an artist, but an orderly one," said Matti.

Luka set his bag on the desk and pulled out *Vedallion*. That he would continue to read — and discuss later with the harling. But *Ipstillion*, which he pulled off the book shelf, was fair game. Settling down on the bed cross-legged, he set it down on a pillow. "Where shall we begin?"

After only a few minutes, it was clear to Luka that Matti hadn't been feigning interest in Diek har Sulh and books. After a half an hour, Luka was thinking the harling reminded him an awful lot of himself — before his feybraiha. After an hour, Luka was thinking how he should thank his parents for making him go down to the village. Elsewise he'd never be having such a wonderful discussion.

Matti matched Luka not only in enthusiasm but in the amount of background reading he had done — aided by his father's studies in human history, as well as library research similar to Luka's. Another commonality, more unexpected, came to light just as Luka had speculated on what happened next in the story — and realized that he'd most likely be finding out soon when he continued reading *Vedallion*.

"I used to wonder about that all the time..." he told Matti. "I'd stay up at night acting out scenes I imagined might happen."

Matti nodded. "I did that too. I'd write the scenes down sometimes, like a play. And then I started doing stories."

Luka cocked his head and sat up straight. "Stories?" He got up off the bed and moved toward the desk. "I did that, too." He rummaged in a drawer. "What were yours about?"

Matti described a number of different scenarios involving characters from the novel, as well as original characters he'd created himself. "Of course some of them — my speculations — turned out to be totally wrong, according to what happens in *Vedallion*, but it was still fun to speculate. And some of my guesses were right!"

Luka returned to the bed holding a sheaf of papers. "Here're mine. Some of them are probably going to be embarrassing..."

Together they browsed through the stories. Some were, as Luka had indicated, clearly based on the immature notions of a harling, but others were more insightful.

"I really like this one," Matti remarked, holding out a particularly thick bundle, held together with a clip. "Or at least the start of it. I'd like to read more later."

Luka felt flattered. "Oh, really? Thanks. Well, I guess you can borrow it to read. You can borrow all of them, if you like."

"Really?" Matti was grinning as he arranged the stories in a neater pile. "That would be great."

Luka got up and replaced *Ipstillion* on the bookshelf. "Sure. I can finish *Vedallion* and you can read my juvenile stories. I'm sure you'll be done faster but meanwhile, maybe we can meet up in a few days."

"I'd like that." Matti came over to the door holding the stack of stories. "And I've really liked talking to you."

"Likewise. Now let's see if my hostling's stew is ready and you can have lunch with my parents."

Once Matti had left — a bottle of vineyard wine in his possession — Luka returned to his bedroom and began to read. His eyes did flicker over to the enhancer, his mind to the etherline, but after being away for a day, another few hours couldn't hurt, he quickly reasoned. And besides, there was the book and promises of finding out if any of his speculations about future plot had been true.

Luka made a nest for himself in the bed, propping himself up on a mound of comforters and pillows. This wasn't entirely unlike the pose he sometimes adopted for etherline adventures, but his mindset was different. With a book, the adventure was in his own head and to some extent, the mind of the author. The trip was at his own pace, no interruptions from far-flung friends or even his parents, who were far less likely to interrupt reading than etherline sessions.

And so Luka tramped around in the world of Diek har Sulh and his cast of humans. He relished certain scenes especially — those with his favourite character, Daniel, along with certain scenes where humans dabbled in magic, even if in those days before Wraeththu, magic had not been as widely understood. At times the humans struck Luka as terribly fragile, succumbing to diseases and uncertainties that would hardly bother hara. Were these really the beings that had pushed the planet to the edge, whom Wraeththu had slaughtered and incepted until their present-day near extinction? Had it been necessary?

After a couple of hours, Luka was half-way through the book and had supplemented his nest with an additional pillow and his bedside table with two cups of tea. The sun was beginning its descent as he finally put the book down and stretched. His head was still abuzz with questions, even if the buzzing was a bit muffled by sleepiness. What was going to happen to Daniel? Were any of the characters going to die by the end? He hoped not but was sure someone would. The suspense was great and yet he was drowsy. His thoughts continued to drift and soon he was asleep, book at his side, afternoon sunlight warming up the blankets.

Daniel was in danger. He had thought he was safe, had convinced himself that nobody — at least nobody who mattered — would ever find out about him. If someone did find out, they couldn't really, care. Could they? It was all bluster, right? People really *cared* about these things?

People cared. And people hated. They hated Daniel for what he believed and for what he was. The differences seemed insufficient to cause hate. Wasn't there enough room in the world for all?

Daniel had been locked up. There were no chains but neither was there freedom. He was going to be "corrected." The authorities, his parents and all the rest of them would see to it. No more blasphemy, heathen magic, explorations — either of ideas or the unscrupulous people with whom Daniel so often associated. And certainly no more explorations with Richard, with whom he had been caught.

Richard. Where was he? In the same building? Daniel couldn't remember. He started to reach out for Richard in his mind but then he remembered why he had been locked up. Richard! How was he to—?

Luka woke with a start. He'd been having a nightmare about Daniel — a nightmare *as* Daniel. He'd been captured. Luka felt a sense of panic, of urgency, as if Daniel were a flesh and blood friend of his. He had to get him out!

But Daniel had not been captured, Luka realized as he gradually woke from the dream fog. Daniel had been in danger but none of the rest of it had happened — not in the book. A presentiment? Or a story idea? Luka turned the idea around in his mind and decided to finish the book before writing anything.

Luka looked around the room. From the angle of the sun — and the fact Helan hadn't woken him for dinner — he judged he had only slept for an hour or two. Enough to recoup a bit of the prior night's lost sleep and for his spirit to cook up dreams.

Luka sat up, patted the book at his side, stretched and yawned. His eyes fell on the enhancer. Now would be a good time to go online.

Pulling one of the comforters from the bed and snagging the

enhancer with his free hand, Luka settled into place in his armchair. He nestled the enhancer on his stomach as usual and rested his hand gently upon it.

Closing his eyes, he flipped the switch inside himself that would prepare him: quietness, openness, perceptiveness.

Then: *Up, up, up. Outward. Seeking.* Finding the thread, the trickle, the hints of the torrent that was the etherline — always flowing, if a har knew were to look for it.

Within a few minutes of diving in, Luka found himself in an eddy with several of his friends: Fendron, Marila, and Zak, along with a har he didn't know.

"Luka!" the first three greeted him, all at once. Then, ahead of the others, Zak: "Where have you been?"

Luka sensed through the ethers that his friends indeed had missed him. "I was just away for the day. There were things doing."

"Well, we wondered," said Fendron.

"This is Lin, by the way," added Marila, indicating the new har. "He's from Morla."

This was a familiar ritual: Hellos, questions about how long one or another har had been offline, then introductions. Luka could manage these things in his sleep. The exchanges continued, with Luka contributing at the proper intervals.

"Anything interesting on your end?" Zak asked Luka, Of all the hara present, Zak was the one who got on with him best.

"Yes, actually," Luka replied, thinking of all that had transpired in the past day. "Went to town, got into a new book, met a couple new hara, rooned last night and then this afternoon I had a crazy dream."

Marila laughed into the ether. "You were busy!"

"What was the dream?" prompted Zak.

Luka thought back. "Well, I don't suppose it would make sense unless you've read the book I'm reading, since it was about one of the characters. I had a dream all about how he was in danger, sort of in prison, and going to be punished."

"Punished for what?" questioned Fendron.

"Among other things, for being a human man and rooning other human men," Luka explained. "It makes sense if you know the book."

"If you say so," said Fendron. "Human men couldn't roon

human men? How does that make any sense?"

"Men were only supposed to roon women," Luka told him. "The humans were divided up in that way, only this human and some others didn't agree with the division."

Luka felt Zak inspecting him closely. "Are you sure you're all right, Luka?"

"Yes. Why?"

"Just that I've never heard you talk about books before. What happened to you while you were away?"

Luka was nonplussed. He didn't consider talking about a book an unusual thing and wouldn't have even if he hadn't been talking books just an hour before — which he had.

"I told you, I started reading a new book," he explained. "Nothing weird about that. Problem?"

"No problem," said Zak. "Just wondering."

The conversation swirled off in another direction after that. Fendron had a new roon partner. Marila was going on a trip to Freyhella. And Lin was starting a new job at a library.

"Maybe you can recommend some books to me," he joked to Luka. "I might be starting work surrounded by books, but I'm not a huge reader myself. My job there is actually teaching technology, things like etherline use. But I have to get familiar."

"I'd be happy to help," Luka offered.

Not too long after that, he decided to make his exit. He sensed dinner would be ready soon and besides, there wasn't anything to hold his interest — at least not as much as the half-read book he had waiting for him, plus a story idea.

"Meet you later," he said in farewell. When that would be Luka wasn't exactly sure.

Over the next few days, Luka continued on with *Vedallion*, nibbling into it like a piece of fine but rare cheese, aiming to make the enjoyment last as long as possible. However, by the fourth day, sitting on the seat-boulder at the top of the vineyard during a break from helping his father, Luka knew it was time to finish up. What was the point of stopping with only thirty pages left? Even if he did, he'd spent the whole afternoon distracted by the thought of it.

He'd managed to make the book last through careful discipline, as well as a decision to see if he could re-engage in a few of the things he used to do more often. If just one day away from the etherline could bring a book, Matti and his brother into his life, what could several days do?

And so Luka had, besides reading, helped out his father in the vineyard and his hostling in the office. He'd gone for long walks in the fields. On a couple of occasions he'd curled up late at night with a notepad jotting down story ideas. And the night before, he'd arranged a roon with Helm, a "tryst" in one of the vineyard's store rooms. As before, Helm had demonstrated considerable talents.

Luka had also kept up with the etherline, of course. He caught up with Fendron about his new roonfriend, checked to see how Mila was recovering from his pearl, and earlier that morning, had described to Zak in detail a few of Helm's talents. The sessions were enjoyable, but they didn't last nearly as long as they used to. Quality, not quantity, Luka told himself.

This change in behaviour had not gone unnoticed by Luka's parents. While Torbek was discreet in his approval, telling him that he'd known a good roon would do him good, Helan seemed to glow every time he spotted Luka away from the etherline. Reading a book or heading out to work with Torbek, Luka would sense eyes upon him and see Helan's gaze trained in his direction. Just that morning at breakfast, Helan had confessed, "I'm glad to have my son back at the table."

Now Luka's mind was floating amongst the clouds with Diek har Sulh's prose, as it soared toward the story's climax. Lightning could have struck and Luka would have read on — carefully, desperately, soaking up every last world. Daniel's fate, Richard's fate, and the fate of the whole world hung in the balance, until almost the last page.

And then it was over.

Luka closed the book and held it. It seemed to thrum in his hands like a living thing, but that was probably the sensation of blood pounding through his fingers. Luka's heart was beating fast. The rush of the book had led him on a race inside his mind. And now he was gasping and catching his breath.

Vedallion, he decided, was even better than the first book.

The next morning, Luka headed down to the village. After four days in the vineyard hills, walking down cobblestone streets and past local shops was a refreshing change. His destination was not the shops, however, nor was it Bekker's, his pub of choice. Instead, he headed into the library. Tomas was at the front desk, just as Luka had hoped.

"So, how was it?" the librarian inquired cheerfully, putting down the book he'd been reading. "Worth waiting for?"

Luka nodded emphatically. "And then some! Thank you so, so much for setting it aside for me!"

"Not a problem." Tomas looked him up and down. "You're almost glowing!"

"Am I?" Luka glanced around the tables and chairs of the library's first floor. "Well, I might be. It was fantastic!" He lowered his voice. "And I thank you, but I must tell you, I was hoping to find someone here. Matti?"

Tomas chuckled. "That one! Another Luka, head always in a book. He's upstairs."

"Great." Luka turned to go, but then Tomas spoke up.

"So, not ready to return the book?"

Luka glanced back. "Oh, I'm sorry, no, not quite. Still digesting it. Also, I'm discussing it with Matti. Bit of a two-har book club, you could say."

"Unsurprising. Two of a kind, I'd say," Tomas remarked.

Luka found Matti curled up in a comfortable chair at the far back corner of the fiction section. One glance and Luka knew something wasn't quite right. He approached carefully.

"Hi there." At this, Matti looked up. Luka noted the book in his hands. "*Ipstillion*, huh?"

Matti stared up, wide-eyed. "Yes. But how did you find me?"

"Well, finding you in the library doesn't seem like such a long shot, does it? Besides, I asked Tomas at the desk."

"Oh." Matti glanced down at the book, looking ill at ease.

Luka took a seat in the chair opposite and studied his young friend. He was blushing. "So, what's up? And what's wrong? If I may ask."

Matti looked even more uncomfortable. "Oh, I'm fine, just lonely and…" he shrugged, "I've started my feybraiha."

That explained the discomfort as well as the blushing, Luka thought. "Well, congratulations and empathy are in order, then. Congratulations for reaching what is an important milestone –

and blah, blah, blah – and empathy for the stinkiness of the whole thing. It's not a fun time really. Only when you're done is it fun!"

Matti didn't smile but he did look less upset. "Well, I hope so. I feel disgusting."

"Sorry about that. Nothing to do but wait." Luka paused before changing the topic. "But in good news, I finished the book!" That generated a smile. "And I loved it! Even better than that one!" He pointed at *Ipstillion*.

"Cool. I thought so, too." Matti was quiet for a few moments. "But..." The harling wrung his hands. "Not to side step that, but there's something I wanted to ask you and since you're here..."

Luka waited expectantly. He had a good idea what the question would be.

"Would you... Would you be my first?"

This was just the question Luka had expected. "Of course. I'd be honoured." He stood to go. "Just make sure I get an invitation to your party. And tell your parents I'll be sure to bring a few bottles of wine."

Looking immensely relieved, Matti also stood up. "Thank you. It's all I've been thinking about, but I only met you once, so—"

"No worries. Now take care of yourself and I'll see you soon. The sooner the better, right?"

Over the next two weeks, Luka spent a good amount of time preparing for his role in his friend's feybraiha – enough time that both his parents took notice. Helan was delighted when Luka mentioned he was going into town for a meeting with the local hienama, to the point of hugging him and patting him on the head, which Luka thought was overkill. Meanwhile Torbek cackled when Luka presented his request for the wine. "Only too happy to contribute, my son!"

By the day of the party, Luka had everything prepared: a new outfit, a small cart of wine, and a special gift he had worked on every day – a package of stories. The main story was the longer one he'd come up with while reading. That was intended to be the only one, but he finished it so quickly he realised he had time to add a couple more. Then he'd created several illustrations and finally created a cover. Binding it up with vineyard twine, he set it atop the wine in the cart and headed into town.

The party, begun in mid-afternoon, was lovely. Helm had put

on his artist hat and handled the decorations, both inside and outside. Springtime flowers were everywhere, including Matti's long black hair, which was braided with tiny white snowflake flowers. The young hair looked lovely, if nervous.

Finally, after a good amount of the wine had been drunk, the ceremony was complete and the sun was falling behind the mountains, it was time for Luka and Matti to retreat back into the house.

The young har's bedroom had been decorated with the same white flowers as his hair. It seemed a small room relative to his brother's, mostly because its walls were jammed with full bookshelves.

"It's not usually this neat," Matti explained, "but for this special occasion, and with nothing to do but be uncomfortable the past two weeks, I managed to pick it up."

Luka drew Matti toward him by the waist and kissed him softly on the cheek. "I wouldn't care it were messy as a pig sty. Right now I only care about—" And he tipped Luka onto the bed.

Several hours later, once both hara had pulled themselves down from the ceiling where they'd been seemingly floating on their aruna high, Luka revealed his present.

Matti was ecstatic. "You did this for me?" He stared at the cover, then flipped through the pages. "This is—Wow. I don't know what to say!"

"Well, at least tell me what you think when you've finished. Hopefully it's not too horrible," Luka kidded.

"Based on the stories you gave me when we first talked, I don't see how it could be," Luka countered. "You told me they were silly, harling stuff, but I don't know... Most of those stories were very good."

"They were? Are you still high on aruna?"

Matti hugged Luka around the shoulders. "Definitely, but I really did like those stories. I am so happy to have more. Which reminds me..." Stretching half out of the bed, he pulled open a drawer in his desk. "I wrote a story, too!"

When Matti thrust the pages into his hand, Luka chuckled. "Two of a kind," he murmured.

"What?"

"Something Tomas said to me at the library. He says you remind him of me, back when I was younger."

"You're only a couple of years older than I am, Luka."

Luka nodded. "Well, seems like longer, and anyway Tomas meant the me before my feybraiha and the etherline."

After this conversation they became distracted with the physical again, but in the morning they picked up the thread.

"I was wondering," Matti said, after a few minutes into the conversation, "if you've ever used the etherline to talk about this stuff. The books or these stories of yours."

Luka thought about it. "Not really. I guess I've always thought of them as separate things. Even recently, when I've gone online to talk with my friends, I haven't really discussed what I've been doing."

"Why not?"

"Well, I guess I didn't think they'd be interested." Luka considered. "We talk about all sorts of things but like I said, I just put those topics in two separate buckets really."

Matti was leaning against the headboard, picking stray snowflake flowers out of his hair. "Well, I think it would be worth a try. When you teach me how to use the etherline, can we give it a shot?"

"I'm teaching you?" Luka reached around to pull out a flower Matti had missed, then kissed him on the temple. "Well, that's news to me, but I'd be happy to."

They ended up sharing breath and putting off breakfast for some time, distracted again, but by the time Luka left later that day they'd agreed on lessons and a plan to go do some exploring online.

"I think I've found someone!" Matti exclaimed. He wasn't speaking out loud, but in the virtual world of the etherline. With a month's practice and eager determination, he had joined Luka in trying to find fans of Diek har Sulh.

Luka excused himself from the conversation he'd been having with Lin in Morla and shifted his attention over to his friend. "Who is it?"

They settled into what the two of them thought of at their chat space. They were in fact physically sitting in the same room – Luka's bedroom – but carried out their conversation online when they were in a session.

"It's a har named Marila," Matti replied. "In Alba Sulh."

"Marila? I know him!" Luka wondered at the coincidence. "He was one of the first people I met on the etherline from far away. What does he say?"

"He says he has a friend who knows Diek har Sulh!"

"Really?" Luka was genuinely surprised. "And does this friend use the etherline? I mean, can we get in touch?"

"I think so. Well, if you help me." While he had progressed fairly quickly, Matti was still learning the ropes.

The last few weeks had been an enjoyable time for both hara. Between etherline lessons, talking about the world of the books and writing stories – together and separately – Luka and Matti had kept both busy and happy. They had also managed to connect the two worlds – Diek har Sulh and the online world. With Matti's encouragement, Luka had taken the initiative to question his many etherline contacts about the books. To his surprise, a handful of them had read them as well. And these friends had friends. Gathering the threads together, it seemed there were at least a dozen Diek har Sulh fans online. But finding someone who actually knew the author? This was a first.

"Come with me," Matti projected. "Marila said he was going to try and summon his friend."

Luka followed Matti out of their created chat space and into the one Matti had been in with Marila, who was now joined by another har.

"Luka!" Marila exclaimed. "I never knew you liked Diek. You should have mentioned it!"

"It just never occurred to me. So who is this with you?"

"Gab. He's also in Alba Sulh," Marila explained, "though quite a distance from me. And he knows Diek!"

Luka focused his attention on the new har, who felt friendly. "Wow. How do you know him? For how long? You are so lucky!"

Gab hesitated, then replied, "Well, it's funny, because I didn't meet him because of his books. I met him because I'm interested in history and he was in a chat group about the history of Alba Sulh."

"A chat group?" Matti asked. "A chat group on the etherline?"

"Of course!" said Gab. "Diek is an absolute etherline fiend."

"What?" Luka broke in. "Say that again."

"Diek is an etherline fiend," Gab repeated, as if stating the obvious. "It's amazing he manages to write these giant books

71

given the time he spends online."

Luka was stunned. He never thought for a moment his favourite author would be online, let alone an "etherline fiend," as Gab had put it. The possibilities…

"So," Luka began slowly, "do you think you could introduce us? I mean, we – Matti and I – are big, big fans, and we are interested in history, too."

Gab considered. "Sure. Now, I happen to know that he's not on today, he's in Kyme doing a big book reading, but he'll be back in a few days. Check in with me in three days and he should be back."

"We'll certainly try."

Neither Matti nor Luka could believe the turn of events. Immediately after the etherline session, they sat in Luka's bedroom talking so long and so intently that Helan had to open the door and wave at them to tell them dinner was ready. He'd been calling for ten minutes.

"I thought you were on the etherline together," Helan commented. "But you're not. That's good."

"Actually we were on it earlier, dear hostling," Luka put in, following Helan down the hall. "But it's not all we do. And anyway, you know I've been teaching Matti."

"Corrupting him," Helan teased. He stopped and patted Luka's arm. "Just kidding. I know you two have been doing other things – writing, helping Torbek and, well, engaging in that most sublime of harish pastimes. A good thing!"

The two young hara exchanged knowing looks. Indeed they had continued to share aruna, although Luka had not been exclusive, as Helm's talents simply couldn't be dismissed. Neither brother seemed to mind sharing Luka, although they certainly didn't want to share him at the same time.

Three days later, as promised, they sought out Marila, who, when they found him, wasn't alone.

"I've been waiting for you," Marila announced. "And so has Diek."

Matti and Luka were equally stunned. "It's… It's an honour," Matti managed.

Diek projected an image of himself. Luka found he had been

right in picturing the author as black-haired.

"I so seldom find myself talking to fans online," Diek began. "As much time as I spend here, my fans tend not to be interested in this technology. Although it isn't so much 'technology' as another world or an extension of the world."

Luka readily understood this. "Exactly. I will say that until recently I didn't use the etherline to talk about your books or meet fans before. But now that I've been doing it a while, it seems so obvious."

"Does it?" Diek questioned. "Let's talk more."

And so they did, Luka telling his story and Matti his, then Diek sharing a story longer than either of theirs. Diek was one of the original users of the etherline. "People are surprised, thinking I spend my time constantly writing or hiding out in library history sections, but I loved the possibilities of meeting like minds in other places. I would have loved to have done this as a teenager."

"A... what?" Luka questioned, before he could stop himself. "Wait, were you human?"

"Incepted, yes. A long time ago. I won't give my age – we've just met – but I suspect I'm old enough to be your high-high-high-father or something like that."

This news stunned Luka. "I've never met a har who was incepted. Well... No, I don't think I have."

"And I've never had such a long conversation with fans online. We should do it again. Right now, my chesnari is probably waiting on me. I'm supposed to make dinner."

Somehow the idea of Diek har Sulh needing to go make dinner struck Luka as hilarious. But then again, authors do of course have regular lives, he reasoned.

"We'll meet again," he promised. "On the etherline, where anything is possible."

Back in the bedroom, Luka sat on the bed next to Matti.

"Did that just happen?" he asked.

Matti elbowed him playfully. "'Course it did." He stretched out his legs and stood up. "I was right."

"Right about what?" Luka questioned.

"About using the etherline to find fans and stuff. And, as it turns out, Diek!" Matt stood studying the bookshelves.

"Though it wounds my pride to admit it, yes, you were right. I hadn't thought of it. But you did!" Luka patted the bed. "But now let's celebrate."

Matti turned. "How?"

"Let's stay offline a while."

The Lakes of Lunil

Andy Bigwood

The Lakes of Lunil

Tia. Nix har Kenned, Guardian of the Stepping Stone Islands, Keeper of the Eternal Gardens of Carnavrillion, and most puissant Nahir Nuri of the Ermine Robe. Invites Tia. Carse har Tuaththua, a student at Kyme, to a celebration of Lunalunil in full at the Midnight Garden of Carnavrillion:

...said the card, its edges dipped in gold and its surface imbued with emotions of respectful sincerity and invitation. It was accompanied by a prepaid intercontinental gate pass.

Naturally I told all my friends and suborned them into the selection of my clothes, a new hair style and suitable magaric charms.

Being careless with those I loved most, I left a scribbled note to be given to my parents and headed off to the other side of the world.

Most of the caste-titles on the invitation had been meaningless to me, their arcane significance known only to those of the highest caste. The important title was the last one. This Nix har Kenned was a Nahir Nuri, a master of the agmaric arts, what a human would have called a magician. Only one in a hundred thousand ascend to his level of awareness and ability. Quite why so potent a har should have an interest in a mere library student from half way around the world was a mystery to me.

One of the good things about the modern world was that a properly-conducted ritual could find exactly the right har for almost anything, be it finding a good emergency plumber or a top deharic intervention consultant. Some of the high caste even used the seeking ritual to pre-select witty and engaging guests for important functions. How better to impress the Tigron than to be surrounded by pleasant and alluring company? If this was one of the latter, then I'd really have something to tell my parents!

Disaster!

The celebration was in full swing when I arrived. The grand entrance I had planned in my mind had long since turned to dust. A realm gate translation inbound from the otherworldly realm of Three Lunamoons had been waiting on the correct resonance. With an arrival from a deep reality pending, all of the local intercontinental traffic had been left to chat amongst themselves. Fortunately the partying was more wild than formal and it seemed likely that I'd not caused offence.

I watched shyly from the back of the crowd as the Nahir Nuri with the flame red hair drew his symbols, invisible to normal sight but glowing brightly on the etheric plane of reality.

At this stage, it was impossible to say what the delicate pattern would represent; it could be as simple as a gathering of good fortune for the watching audience, or something incredibly complex and precise, an application of agmaric energies that changed reality in a tightly-prescribed and intense manner. It was almost a dance, his hands tracing the agmaric energy in the air, the ghostly forms intricately-sculpted and as fine as spun glass. I could feel the tightly-constrained power. Even though the pattern wasn't complete, it was clearly a thing of great potency.

I knew for certain that if I were attempting this ritual, it would look like a finger painting by comparison.

"What will it do?" I asked the har next to me, taking a sip of honeyed wine.

"Shhhh! Watch!"

The pattern continued to expand. The Nahir Nuri whirled about, hands moving faster, one hand adding new elements, the other reinforcing older parts of the pattern before they dissipated into nothingness.

To the left, a veiled and hooded figure emerged from the crowd, clothed entirely in black silk with the exception of his right arm, which was exposed to the shoulder. Reverently the newcomer raised a musician's triangle in his ungloved hand and struck it twice.

Ting! Ting!

The sound echoed, ricocheting around the planes of reality, becoming louder and causing the pattern to wobble. For a second the Nahir Nuri almost looked scared - and then his fingers were moving, a blur of speed adding further detail.

Without warning, the majhahnic pattern blew outward, a filament of golden-white energy passing through my chest, filling me with a fizzing warmth. For a second I feared that the Nahir Nuri had lost control… and then the sky exploded in a swirling panoply of otherworldly glory. Fireworks of the mind.

The crowd howled in wolf-like exultation "Wraeeethhhhoooo! Wraeththooooo!"

The vast and delicate weave of energy lingered above the heads of the revellers, gradually drifting upward. I felt awkward and out of place. Everyhar was getting seriously drunk, but I felt I had to stay sober. A good impression might be vital.

At first I assumed that the majhahn was the end of it, but an hour later the Nahir Nuri's assistants re-emerged respectfully ushering the ribbon clad dancers away from the centre of the garden.

With great care, a device was erected and aimed at the celestial body our first ancestors had named Lunalunil. When our race emerged from the shattering of humanity it had been the fashion to rename every settlement, river, mountain and sea. Historians in Kyme were rumoured to get into fist fights about which set of ruins had been which human city. In the case of Lunalunil the primitive race had simply called it 'the moon'; missing the significant etheric and deharic aspects entirely.

Reaching out with my mind I attempted to understand the aura of the device they were setting up. The very least I could do was be familiar with the Dehara who had been invoked in its making.

To my surprise there was nothing, the device was completely inert.

"It's a human artefact," said a voice at my shoulder.

I glanced around, my eyes widening as I recognised the Nahir Nuri, who was using a towel to dab away the sweat from his earlier exertions.

"Really?" I blurted, forgetting my manners.

"Yes, really, Carse har Tuaththua," replied Nix har Kenned with a lopsided grin. "It's a telescope. They used it for seeing over long distances. You have no idea the lengths I had to go to to get it. You will note that the conservator of the Colurastes doesn't even allow me to touch it; adjustments may only be done by his personal staff."

"Why not just perform a remote viewing? Unless... You're worried that a viewing will disrupt the pattern of the majhahn you performed."

"Precisely. The observer effect. Here, come and look. It's important that you understand." Nix waved me toward the device and indicated a tube sticking out at right angles from the body of the telescope. "Look in there."

I bent over and put an eye near to the end. At this close range, the deadness of the manufacture was almost distracting. Any Wraeththu-manufactured device would have been alive with its maker's marks.

A scratched and dirty piece of glass sat between me and Lunalunil's image, distorting and pulling it closer. There was movement, wisps of etheric energy at the very edge of perception. Gradually the pattern of tiahaar Nix's dance came into view, an annular disc filled with a lacework of invocations that contracted until it seemed to match the Lunalunil's circle exactly.

"And... Now!" said the Nahir Nuri

I felt the surge as the etheric pressure suddenly dropped. Intuitively I kept my eye to the lens. A second, two seconds, and suddenly the eyepiece was filled with a blinding light as stored energy pulsed into it.

I glanced up, noting that tiahaar Nix seemed to be grinning from ear to ear.

"The surge took at least a couple of seconds to reach the pattern...' I began, "that means... the distance... That majhahn was in orbit?"

"They said you were good and so you are, Carse. Yes, the stage two nayati deployed was at a range of approximately 235,000 miles. But not in orbit, beyond orbit."

A bunch of revellers staggered past, interrupting the moment and giving me a moment to think it all through.

To project one's will over such a distance was a breath-taking achievement. If it were made public, Nix har Kenned would become the most famous har of modern times. His experiment today would herald a new era. With a nayati in geostationary orbit above Eartharuhani, a sending might be bounced from Forever City to Immanion Central almost instantly.

I paused, stopping my train of thought. tiahaar Nix wasn't doing that. If he were, then he wouldn't have disguised the majhahn as a party trick. Which also meant this wasn't finished, there was something more.

"Lunalunil. You've sent that majhahn to Lunalunil."

"Exactly. The real obstacle was the navigation. The first few dozen evocations went wildly off trajectory. Ironically, the answer to the problem was almost as old as that telescope."

"How so?"

"If you want to hit a target as far away as Lunalunil, you have to be absolutely precise about everything involved, the angle of launch, the Eartharuhani's speed, Lunalunil's, their relative movements, the mass of the projectile. You can't just go with what feels right."

I nodded "And all of our majhahnic training is aimed at seeking out what feels right and feeding energy into it."

"Which is why it was so valuable to find that humans had already done all the hard work, said Nix. "They'd calculated how to get something weighing a couple of tons to land in a place they called The Sea of Tranquillity. Quite why they did that is a complete mystery. Anyway, once I had that, all I needed to do was make sure my majhahn simulated the mass of their object."

My head began to hurt just thinking about it. A majhahn is ethereal; it doesn't exist in normal reality at all and definitely doesn't have mass.

"With respect tiahaar Nix... Why? Why go to Lunalunil at all? Just getting a majhahn into space is going to change how our world works. You're going to be the most famous har in all the world realms when word gets out."

"Because that's easy. I do things because they're hard. If I absolutely have to suffer being famous, it's going to be for something that will merit it."

His eyes flashed with a diamond-like determination that left me wondering what he considered to be hard enough. A moment later the steel left his eyes and he grinned, bathing me in the warmth of his personality.

"Of course the hard part is all going to be about you, Carse. I need a pair of volunteers, you see. If I must be famous, I want there to be somehara even more famous out there to deflect the worst of it." He patted my shoulder "Fortunately, my precognitive abilities are finely tuned and I was able – with the aid of Miyacala of the Airs, peace be with him – to locate a pair of appropriate young candidates, you being one of them."

It's not easy when someone knows your weakness and plays to it so cynically. Vanity and hunger for attention are without doubt my worst traits. My friends have often teased me by comparing me to legends like one of the Cobwebs or Caeru the First. Unfortunately, I was fairly certain that I lacked the dress sense and the singing skills of either.

"You want me to pretend to invent your majhahn technique? It would never work."

"No. Of course not. That would be absurd. No. What I would very much like is for you to agree to be the first har from the world of Eartharuhani to set foot on Lunalunil."

I felt the odd sensation of the world suddenly shrinking around me and the impression that everyhar was looking at me... which they weren't. It was the sort of sensation that they described in caste school as a 'destiny call', a feeling that everyhar was trained to look out for. The moment when a dehar reveals to you one of life's crossroads and points the way.

I shivered and nodded decisively. "I feel the path under my feet. I don't know that I'm the right har for it, tiahaar Nix, but I can sense that I'm going to be tangled up in this."

"Good. We'll start with standard realm transitions and work you up from there. For now, come over to the bar; you look like you need a drink. I've got some of the new Veralic wine. It self-carbonates when the seal is broken..."

The gates that led to the other-worldly realms stood in a circle, each one as tall as ten hara and wide enough for a small cargo lifter. Vehicles would enter the approach pattern, become sympathetic with the reality they intended to enter and then move through the gate, looking less and less real as they departed.

Gates were delicate and the agmara energy that powered them was produced in the 'traditional' way by pairs of Gatekeepers. It was a job that required a pair of hara who loved each other deeply, had a high libido and iron discipline. Plenty of couples reckoned they had the first two, few had the third.

I was to visit one of the furthest realms, a place on the very edge of perceivable reality. Usually expeditions of Astronomists headed to YYgdrasilium Aerie and stayed for a month before attempting to return. I was instructed to transit six times a day for a week.

I was still screaming as I hit the ground. Nix har Kenned hadn't prepared me; probably that was deliberate. When you use a gate to hop between continents, you stop existing for less than a blink of an eye. When you are being sent to a place like the Aerie, you don't exist for a measurable amount of time. It's weird, you don't exist, and therefore you shouldn't be able to think or feel time passing or anything.

Unfortunately, my subconscious noticed a gap and promptly filled it with a random assortment of emotions, physical sensations and memories.

A hand reached down and pulled me to my feet.

"Ssstings doesn't it" said my helper, offering me a glass of mango juice.

The hand holding the glass was delicate, with fingernails painted to resemble serpent-heads. My gaze continued on up the arm until I realised I was looking at possibly the most interesting har I'd ever seen. It didn't show in his face or body as he was as lithe as any and beautiful in a Colurastean sort of way; the thing that attracted my eye was subtle, his etheric aura, which shifted and flowed like the northern lights.

"Yes. Stings like a kick in the ouana." I agreed "Thanks. I'm tiahaar Carse har Tuaththua." I gave the har a formal hug of greeting.

"I'm tiahaar Ss'Ss§s'û 'Sharktooth' har Ponclast-Colurasste. Welcome to the realm at the sscentre of a galaxy."

"Har... Ponclast?"

"An affectation from my harlinghood. I thought it made me sound dangerou§ss to know."

"You really are filling me with confidence."

He grinned. The complete wildness of his expression was scary and intoxicating. I could well imagine him as a first generation Wraeththu, running wild, incepting humans right and left.

"And I use Sharktooth or Sharky because honesstly unles§s you have a Coluraste's forked tongue in that cute mouth of yours, you're gonna mangle the name Ss'Ss§s'û."

Whilst he'd chattered on, I took a couple of calming breaths and thought through a quick mind-calming meditation exercise to dampen the effects of the gate transition. When I finally had time to take in my surroundings, I found I was standing on a platform sculpted from a living tree. It had been given agmaric encouragement and stood three times as tall as its natural brethren some twenty feet below.

I ignored the alien plant life. On any other realm-world it would have been fascinating, but on YYgdrasilium Aerie it was a distraction. Overhead was this realm's true wonder; a galactic core that filled the night sky from horizon to horizon. Billions of pinpoint stars so closely packed that the lunamoons were in silhouette. All I could do was stand open mouthed gaping at the wonder of it.

"Worth the pain? YeSs?"

"Yes. Image crystals don't do this place justice... Ss'Ss§s'û... Did I pronounce that correctly?"

"A little more ssibilance on the '§'. But not badly done for a son of Tuath." He looked me up and down appraisingly. "Sseriously, my new friend, call me Sharky. I'm the har that Old Nix has picked to go with you to Lunalunil. Whatever else, that guarantees we're going to be close."

I gazed back, my mind a bit clearer, and his personal aura now had a sort of fractal quality that just seemed to suck me in.

I bit my lip trying not to stare vacantly at him.

He nodded to himself as if deciding something "Come, walk with me. We have to replenish our agmara levels and rebalance before each return trip, so we might as well get to know each other a little."

"Of course." I smiled archly. "I am eager to learn from an experienced arunic rebalancer."

"I promise we won't step through the gate until I have you so thoroughly arunic that your ears glow."

"Well, that's something I'd like to see."

The week passed quickly in a series of highs and lows. The agony of the repeated gate transitions balanced with the frequent sessions of aruna we needed to recover our agmaric energy levels.

On the final day of my gate training, as a Rosatide gift for Sharky, I purchased a sculpture of a rose spun from silver and inlaid with the fragrances of flowers.

He smiled, hugging me close. "Thank'sss it's wonderful! Oh and all of that extra 'arunic rebalancing' we've been doing hasn't gone to waste. I might not have gotten your ears to glow but it did allow me to make real progress in my own pet project."

"Really?"

"Yes. I've been trying to find out which galaxy it is out there. The other Astronomists have been split on whether it's our own, or what humans called Andromeda, or one of the Majhahnalic clouds. Today the higher plane entity who is associated with that galaxy's etheric influences spoke to me. His dehar-name is Andrii and he's not any of them."

"Is that as big a deal as I think it is?"

"Only to a few, but yesss, yes it is. This place is a lot further away than anyhar realised. Which confirms that realm travel isn't constrained by anything so mundane as physssical distance. It also means that anyone creating majhahns here has a very powerful local dehar to evoke."

I tried to look as if I understood the significance. Sharky ruffled my hair as if I were a freshly hatched harling "Don't worry, Carse. Just share breath and you'll see what it means to me."

Obediently I did as I was told, tasting his exultation and the grandeur of it. I also got a very good taste of his feelings toward me... apparently the Rosatide gift had generated exactly the response I'd hoped for.

"What did you learn?" asked Nix har Kenned.

"Being non-corporeal is severely disorientating for the unprepared, tiahaar Nix," I replied, sipping the fine wine that had been provided by the Nahir Nuri's silently aloof staff. "The key is to know what to expect and have your mind in the right place. It took a while, but I can cope with that now."

"Good, good. But don't expect your trip to Lunalunil to be identical to going through a realm gate, Carse. The majhahn I've created is very different. You will be hit by a completely new set of sensations to overcome. That's why you two didn't get the standard six months of gate training and were sent to the most difficult destination on your first hop."

"I see the logic. I've been thinking, though. Lunalunil is airless, right? If we just step through the equivalent of a gate we're going to suffocate within a minute or two."

The Nahir Nuri smiled. "Except that you'll freeze instantly or boil away first, depending on if you are in shadow or direct sunlight."

"Really? I didn't know that," Sharky said.

"On the plus side, gravity is low. So you won't need to worry about being crushed to death."

Sharky stuck his tongue out at him.

"Seriously though," Nix continued, "I'm into doing things that are hard, not impossible. I've had the best tailors – top hara in their field – working on custom built Lunil-suits cut to your measurements."

I sat straighter; this sounded a bit more like it!

The Nahir Nuri slid a pair of gate passes across the table. "You and Sharktooth are scheduled for a final fitting tomorrow. Learn how to use the suits; they will save your lives.

"I present the mark one Lunil-naut suit," said the har posing before us. He gestured at the clothes hung upright, dangling from the ceiling like puppets.

The suit seemed to consist of mummy-wrap leggings that ended in silver bands at the ankles, skin-tight embroidered trousers with a fringe along the seam, a flouncy silk and leather shirt with baggy ruffed cuffs and more fringes. It was a look that wouldn't have been out of place on a Cirabin pirate.

Next to me, Sharky had already stripped naked and was pulling on the second Lunil-suit.

"It looks good on you, Sharky," I said. "But is it airtight as well as fashionable? "

Instead of answering, Sharky picked up the mug of coffee on the workbench and poured the contents on his embroidered sleeve. A pattern woven into the fabric glowed etherically, repelling the beverage as if it were liquid mercury.

"Now that's impressive!"

"One of the first spin-offs from tiahaar Nix's research," explained the tailor with a sniff, clearly unimpressed by Sharky's normal level of exuberance. "If tiahaar Nix were a business-har, he and I would have Tigron-level fortunes, just for the waterproofing majhahns. Unfortunately he says it's—"

"Not hard enough!" Sharky and I completed the sentence together and grinned at the shared joke.

On an impulse, I quickly snatched a sharing of breath with Sharky, communicating the pleasant level of mutual attraction that we'd established during the gate training. I made a note to follow up on how we were feeling later.

The tailor cleared his throat theatrically. I blushed and focused my attention on the Lunil-suit.

"So if airtight was one of those easy things, what's hard about this suit?"

"Ah that would be..." he said gesturing dramatically to the work bench "...The Collar of Lunil and Astelle."

On the bench stood two wooden torsos cut off at the neck. Resting on the shoulders of each was a pair of silver shoulder guards etched with majhahnic patterns and linked together by a necklace-like ring that circled the head at about chin level.

"Are those... rubies?"

"Also diamonds, emeralds, amethysts, jet and opal. All necessary to evoke the correct combination of dehara," the tailor said proudly. "Slip the one near the window over your head and do a standard calling of the quarters to activate it."

I quickly did as I was instructed, discovering that the shoulder guards included padding to the underside and buckles for attaching to the Lunil-naut suit.

In my mind, I summoned the four dehara of the quarters greeting them and asking for their aid, a task that I did almost subconsciously. Energies flowed and the collar came to life forming a bubble of force around my head. My hair was moved by a breath of wind from somewhere behind me and in front of me a series of remote viewings sprang to life.

One of the images that hung before my eyes was recognisably Nix har Kenned's study. I focused on it and it expanded to fill my perceptions.

The Nahir Nuri glanced up. *I see that you have the collar on,

*Carse.**

Yes, I sent in reply. **I'm picking up good detail of your study and your thoughts are coming through clearly.**

As they should, given where it's designed to send from, he replied, closing the sending at his end.

"You were communing with tiahaar Nix?" asked the tailor.

I nodded.

"OK, good. And do you see a row of sigils for the major dehara just above your eye line?"

"No."

He took a small tool – a Macaw feather bound in leather with a silver tip – and inserted it into one of the collar's supports, twisting slightly.

"And now?"

"A Miyacala Sigil."

"...and now?"

"I have four now, just the Aghama sigil missing."

He gave the feather one final turn. The row of sigils rotated upon themselves forming the floor symbol for a grand nayati in etheric space.

"That got it," I said. "Is that what I think it is?"

"If you are seeing a micro-nayati consecrated to the primary dehara, then yes."

"Then we have a problem. My caste level is nowhere near high enough. I might be able to interact with two prime dehara at a stretch, but evoking all five is going to fry my soul."

"It won't be like that. The Nahir Nuri does the actual interaction, you two just have to be present in order to be a focus of intentions."

Nix har Kenned insisted that both Sharky and I visit home before we launched. I showed my friends some crystals of me and Sharky, the first few depicting us trying on the Lunil-suits – I'd not told them what they were for. I also showed them a crystal of the two of us on Carnarvrillion's beach, catching fish with a traditional Cirabin spear. After that, a few crystals of us dancing, one of us bartering with a Cirabin raft merchant, and a few more of Sharky posing next to some recently-excavated human ruins, where two weird statues had been found. One statue had a duck's head; the other was big eared and was supposed to be a mouse but looked nothing like one.

My old roommate gave his current lover a knowing look and drew the symbol for the blessing of a joining in the air. I blushed a deep vermillion, much to their amusement.

Fortunately I was rescued from a merciless interrogation about my *'new friend'* by the thudding of running feet and the arrival of another student from our class, pushing the curtain door aside and shouting "The Roselanes! Hara of the Roselane tribe have created a majhahn in orbit!"

We went outside, and there it was, a pinpoint of agmaric energy flying overhead sending back a simple **Here!* *Here!* *Here!** that faded away as it dropped toward the horizon.

Further down the street, I could see the senior scholars of Kyme gathering and heading toward the Great Library. Many of the students followed. This was big! There would be implications.

"I need to get back to Carnavrillion," I said, heading in the opposite direction.

"Back so soon?" asked Nix har Kenned, setting aside the egg-sized emerald he'd been etching.

"But... the Roselane. They've reached orbit!"

"Yes. They so desperately wanted to be first. It seemed a shame to disappoint them."

"So... You knew what they were planning?"

"Relax, Carse. Even if they created a majhahn identical to ours, it would still need time to reach Lunalunil. That race was won weeks ago. All that remains is the mundane chore of getting you harlings to your destiny on time." He looked at me with a steady eye. "Besides, if we launched you early you'd pop out the other end too high. I have no interest in being the first to create a pair of hara-shaped craters."

I felt the tingling run up my spine as he said it. Half anticipation, half fear. The self-doubt was there waiting like a familiar. Fortunately it was only one of those false emotions that every schoolhar learns to face down in his earliest lessons.

The final days of preparation seemed to pass with both infinite slowness and lightning speed. Nix har Kenned wanted me to think up a first message to send back to the hara here on Eartharuhani. A task that was harder than it seemed at the outset and left me frantic for inspiration, until the hourglass had run out on me. With no time left to think up anything, I made the decision that I'd just say whatever popped into my head.

The mission plan was simple enough. Step through the majhahn; construct a tent-like pavilion so that we could sanctify a permanent nayati. Pay our respects and give devotions to the deity Lunil, Dehar of Dreams, pick up some Lunil-rocks, (if Lunil agreed to part with them), and then by taking aruna generate sufficient agmaric potential for a majhahn home. Easy.

It was sunset; time for us to go to Lunalunil. Sharky and I stood in the clearing by the beach. I would step through first and Sharky would follow. The four quarters of a majhahn burned brightly with the agmaric energy of a prime dehar. I had my eyes closed; I didn't want to lose my sanity by looking at the higher plane divinities directly.

Nix har Kenned danced, weaving the difficult patterns around me. He'd been right. It was almost exactly *not* like passing through a realm gate.

Where the gate had been a void, this was the opposite; I was surrounded by an overload. White light blinded me, a roaring noise escalated until it was no longer a sound at all. The smell of dark earth and blossom tickled at the nostrils, demanding a sneeze. Release. Suddenly all of it was gone, converted into a sensation of unstoppable movement. The world was gone.

I imagined that I held Sharky close, using him as a mental anchor.

Intense, I sent

Yeah, just a bit. Keep focused. He's still weaving it.

For a short eternity everything seemed calm, the only sensation that of time passing.

Without warning my mind was filled with a sending getting louder and screaming *Here! HERE! HERE!*

The Roselane! I screamed.

In an instant of clarity I understood the disaster that was unfolding. The distortion of reality that the Roselane had put into Eartharuhani orbit happened to be on exactly the wrong flight path when the Nahir Nuri launched me toward Lunalunil. The two manipulations of reality had entangled on the etheric plane and were now in the process of merging into something new and unplanned.

I wondered if anything like that had ever happened before but couldn't think of an example.

I could feel the raw power of the Roselane's majhahn interacting with Nix har Kenned's creation, boosting some parts and overlaying others, changing the emphasis of Nix's intention. Where the human trajectory numbers had been a spider silk-thin strand of the original majhahn, they now formed the main conduit for the Roselane energies. Going exactly and precisely where the trajectory led was now the primary goal of the mutated enchantment.

I could sense the Nahir Nuri dancing, desperately trying to adapt and reconfigure the delicate web of his majhahn. But the emphasis was wrong. I could sense things getting away from him.

At the same instant, (or much later), I stopped thinking and just existed, swept away on the distorting reality.

I coughed, spitting out the cold lifeless grey dust that my face was resting in. I pushed myself up only to find that I'd shoved harder than I'd needed and was flying. A few heartbeats later I stopped flying and fell back at a leisurely pace. The ground still hurt me when I landed.

Sharky? I sent

No reply.

Tiahaar Nix?

No reply.

I sat for a moment, calming myself. A quick invocation pulled up the collar's display. A variety of icons danced before my eyes, all of them generating feelings of comfort and correctness. Whatever was blocking my sending wasn't a problem with the majhahnics at my end.

The thought that I might be entirely alone wasn't a good one. Without Sharky as a partner with whom to generate agmara, I wasn't going home.

Death wouldn't be quick or easy. The microscopic realm-gates woven into my collar would keep me supplied with fresh air from Eartharuhani. I could sip water from a tube that led indirectly from a mountain stream near Immanion Port. Unfortunately we'd not expected to need food.

Slowly I undid one of the pockets of my lunil-suit and set the crystal in it on the ground in front of me. I could still do the experiments even if they had to send somehar else to pick them up.

Without warning, the ground began to vibrate. The tiny dust grains danced and my memory crystal fell over. Instinctively I ducked, sensing something coming toward me from behind at shoulder height. A ferocious blizzard of particles flashed into nothingness as they hit the majhanic field that surrounded my head. For a moment I feared that the cumulative reality of the luna-dust might overload my helmet.

The dust settled slowly revealing some sort of machine, its white side emblazoned with a human tribal marker.

^chsk^ Tranquillity Base here. The Eagle has landed. ^chsk^

I scrambled backward behind the rim of the crater. Aside from the breeding program on the Isle of Men, humans were as extinct as the elephant. The implications were terrifying. The collision of the two majhahns must have thrown me into a different reality... or an earlier one.

A figure in a white lunil-suit emerged from the vehicle, descending clumsily, his boots kicking up a cloud of dust.

^Chsk^ One small step for a man, one giant leap for mankind. ^Chsk^

I hopped backward, trying not to leave many tracks. There was no telling what they'd make of unshod footprints, or what impact it might have on the flow of history. Fortunately, the creature was too busy erecting one of its red, white and blue totems to pay attention to me.

Three craters later I discovered a hiding place between pair of large boulders. Shadows as dark as Ponclast himself beckoned me in.

I sat for about three hours throwing pebbles, watching them create tiny craters in the dust. In the distance, the two humans moved slowly about their ugly spaceboat. Every plan I could think of had some vast stumbling block. I could maybe ask for a lift home. But that would probably banjazzle the entire time continuum. Or I could perhaps attempt to create my own realm gate. Of course I didn't have anything like the agmaric energy needed or the skills of Nix har Kenned. I could create a nayati and commune directly with the prime dehar Lunil, although it was likely I'd fry my mind in the attempt.

Putting a hand in my pocket I felt the pitted surfaces of the memory crystal still warm with its agmaric charge. What if...

I pulled the crystal from my pocket and examined it; the swirling patterns etched into its surface were only visible to the etheric senses. If I remembered my biology classes correctly, humans could only see light. So if you ignored the memes slowly rotating around its core it looked exactly like an ordinary luna-rock.

I vigorously rubbed the crystal in the grey dust. There. Now it was a definitive Lunalunil rock.

Concentrating, I 'gave breath' to the crystal, pouring my feelings and memories into it. The humans would never detect the message and hara had only learned how to record breaths in the last decade. Sure, my ancestors would sense the rock was special, but not know why. With luck, my message in a bottle would eventually get to some har who could untangle me from time.

The human was digging, slowly, deliberately shovelling luna-rocks into the container beside him. He'd been at it for fifteen minutes and had consistently faced toward his spaceboat and the

Eartharuhani beyond.

I supposed that, at some level, even his brain could feel the powerful deharic song radiating from home with its simple message: *I Live!*.

Aiming carefully, I pulled back my arm and threw the crystal toward the open container... and watched it slowly drift to the ground several feet beyond in the low gravity.

Caeru's wrath! Is nothing going to go right today!

^Chsk^ "You say something, Neil? Over." ^Chsk^

^Chsk^ "Negative. Over." ^Chsk^

Oh great! I thought to myself. They'd picked from their best and one of them was very slightly psychic.

I stayed still for a minute, expecting shoveller to turn to look toward the newly-arrived crystal and then remembered that there had been no sound to attract his attention. Unfortunately, that didn't alter the fact that the crystal wasn't in the bin.

There wasn't any alternative. I sprinted as best as I could, grabbed the crystal and slammed it down into the rock samples. Out of the corner of my eye I could see the human begin to turn, his mirrored helmet facing almost directly toward me as I made the safety of the rocks.

^Chsk^ Neil. Check my suit readouts. Over. ^Chsk^

^Chsk^ Problem? Over. ^Chsk^

^Chsk^ I just saw a goddam Sioux brave complete with a feather in his hair run past and steal a moonrock from the sample container. Hell of a thing. I figure I must have a build-up of CO_2 or something. Over. ^Chsk^

^Chsk^ Better come back in. You were only down for five more minutes on the moonwalk. And let's keep talk about a War Chief off the record. They're going to have a hard enough time believing we actually made it here without getting all Jules Verne on us. Over. ^Chsk^

^Chsk^ A-firmative on that. Over. ^Chsk^

I let out a long sigh, making a note to thank every dehara who might have influenced reality in my favour.

The white-suited figure hopped clumsily back toward the spaceboat and then stopped, bending awkwardly to look down at its feet. Slowly he bent down onto one knee bracing himself with one hand... peering at my footprints.

Struggling back to his feet, his expressionless, mirror-smooth visor looked directly toward me for what seemed like an eternity. Slowly, he reached into his sample container, removed my message crystal and threw it so that it landed between my feet. In what seemed to be a deliberate move, he turned his back on me and walked directly away, only turning toward his spaceboat when he was close to it.

I just stood there, trying to comprehend the magnitude of my failure. I was still there ten minutes later when the human's spaceboat exploded.

The craft fractured at its mid-point, the white skull-shaped head shooting upward, leaving the golden bottom half standing like a decapitated Sedu. No, not exploded... Launched... The humans were going home with their stolen rocks.

As they receded, their craft becoming a small star overhead I sensed something, the beginnings of a whisper in my mind getting louder.

Here? Here? Here?

Here, I thought, filling it with bitter irony. The other half of the entangled majhahn had obviously survived somehow and was still sending its message.

He's Here! Here! Here!

My eyes flew wide; it wasn't an echo of the Roselane's majhahn. Somehar was searching for me! Sharky? Activating my collar's transmitter I sent *HERE!* imbuing the word with as much agmaric energy as I could feed into it. Completely drained, I slumped to my knees.

Dust began to stir, tiny grains dancing and slipping aside to form patterns, swirling geometries that centred on the human craft but spread outward to cover the crater's floor in fractal perfection.

It was the dehar Lunil's mark repeated as a fractal at every scale. Tiredly, I focused my mind up a level so that I could see into the first levels of the etheric plane. As expected, the pattern's true majesty was reserved for the higher plane of reality. Sheets of blue-white light projected upward from the dust, filling the sky. The nearest sheet of it sliced straight through my wrist, completely unaffected by my arm's claim to be real.

The light became more intense. Blinding. I tried to stop myself from seeing, but it was futile.

Like everyhar, I had trained from an early age. I'd learned the correct protections and forms of address to use when interacting with the god-like beings from the higher planes of reality. None of it applied. Instead of being the one in control, interacting with a small portion of a dehar's vast awareness, I was the one being summoned.

The light filled me, until thought itself wasn't possible.

The Lunil-light faded abruptly to darkness. I could hear lapping water, and when I moved my foot, water sloshed aside. Everything was blurry and out of focus, but it appeared that the Lunalunilscape had been transformed. The craters were still there; but now they had the seeming of ornamental lakes fringed with black-barked trees, lit as if by the light of Lunalunil.

The garden was also achingly familiar. Whenever I or anyhar else called upon the Dehar of Dreams as part of a majhahnic ritual, this was where he would be... his demesne... The Lakes of Lunil.

The remnant of the human spaceboat was also present, but had become a throne, the spindly metal legs having transformed into small trees that now held the sumptuously-cushioned pedestal. Lunil, the Dehar of Dreams, sat there with his feet crossed at the ankle, his chin resting on delicate fingers. Like the human before him, he gazed directly at me, his eyes obscured behind a glistening blindfold of golden silk that was one of his symbols.

The humans... I think I've changed history, I started to send.

That dream has already been dreamt. Memory fades as the rippling waters become still again, whispered the dehar in a voice that was at once distant and aloof. *The celestial dance is not changed by so small a thing.*

But what about me? I asked selfishly

I have told Aruhani that your dream continues little one, said the Dehar of Dreams referring to his equal, the prime Dehar of Life and Death.

Lunil gestured silently and the runes burned brightly again, engulfing my mind in cold still whiteness.

Carsse?

Carsse? Come on, har, don't do thiſs to me!

I hurt. I hurt all over. Actually it felt worst around my head.

Opening my eyes, all I could see was the gold foil side of the human's boat pressing up against the magharic field of my helmet.

Sharktooth? I sent.

I felt him hug me close. *Carsse! Thank all the dehara! You had usss worried there for a sʃecond.*

I gave the spaceboat a thump and pulled myself shakily to my feet.

When we landed, we had exsstra momentum from sʃomewhere. You sslammed sʃtraight into the ʃide of that that thing. Whatever it iss, sent Sharky in a rapid-fire burst of thought, tinted with deep concern.

Human spaceboat, I corrected

sʃeriously?

Oh, yes. They went home in the other half.

Other half? he asked, sounding sceptical.

I wanted to explain it all, but my head was still throbbing and the details were beginning to feel a bit woolly around the edges.

Either that or it's the Throne of Lunil. Take your pick, I replied noticing that the human tribal markers weren't where I remembered them on the spaceboat. In their place was an almost invisible symbol of Lunil.

Looking around, I couldn't see the red white and blue pole-totem and the footprints had all been blown away by whatever the humans had used to hurl themselves back into space.

Now that you're back with us you need to focus on the mission, sent Nix har Kenned. *We'll ditch the communing meditations and the evocation rituals this time. Just send some words for the Wraeththu back home. Once that's done, I'll switch off the monitoring so that you two can set up the pavilion and generate sufficient agmara for your majhahn home.*

The words that I'd spent several days writing felt like soft mush in my head. For reasons that I couldn't quite pin down I sent something that I'd heard somewhere... or maybe I dreamed it.

This is one small step for a har... one giant leap for Wraeththu-kind...Wraeththoooooo! I sent to the world and then switched to a private sending. *And as for you Sharky Ponclast, two words... Ears and Glow.*

Ascension

Maria J. Leel

Ascension

My hostling despairs of me. "Shu'nay," he asks, "what are you going to do with your life? It's high time you decided."

And I just shrug my shoulders helplessly and say, "I don't know."

As always my hostling then tries to recruit my father. "Speak to him, chesnari. Make him see sense. He's a dozen years past feybraiha now – it's time he settled into some kind of career."

And my father holds up his hands, shakes his head and says, "There's plenty of time."

I was born into one of the rich families of the western coast of Megalithica and there's tribal blood running through my veins, very diluted these days, of course, but it's there. You can tell by the bronze tint of my skin, my near-black eyes and the dark silken nature of my hair, which I wear unfashionably short. I remember an ageing relative, (one of my hostling's family, naturally), cooing over me when I was a harling. "Oooh ... you can see the Chumash in him ... and you know, don't you, Shu'nay, that you're named after the plant the ancients used to weave their baskets ... you *do* know that, don't you?"

I recall the consternation I caused when I said that Shu'nay wasn't my name.

My hostling was apoplectic. "What is your name then, if Shu'nay isn't good enough for you?"

I couldn't answer him and chose, even at that tender age, in future to keep my thoughts to myself.

I have bad dreams sometimes too; of blood and bone and tearing flesh. I'm not sure if they're mine or belong to somehar else. There are things I do enjoy, though. I like to walk, especially in the rain, and I love to swim. I adore the feeling of water on my skin. We're lucky where we live; down on the coast there are a plethora of beaches and inlets and just inland any number of rivers. I also like to surf the knowledge. You can plug yourself in to all the latest ideas. The knowledge has been around for centuries. They used to surf in the old days. I researched it once for a school project. They used chunky plastic boxes with lots of wires – very cumbersome and limited too; just visual and auditory. We've used sensor-discs for decades now. You just lie back and place the disc over your third eye chakra and then you can smell and feel and taste, see and hear whatever it is you want. And then when you're done you just slip the disc back into its little case, put it in your pocket and go about your business. If it gets low on power you simply leave it in the sun to recharge – or even better go surfing in the sunshine and you can work on your tan at the same time.

I play a lot of war games when I'm surfing; alternate realities. I have done since I was a harling. Maybe that's where all the dreams of blood come from?

My hostling, of course, disapproves. "Shu'nay, you'll never be a success or win the respect of your peers if you waste your time on such trivia."

A couple of years ago I got quite interested in the Atlantis Project. Well, it was difficult to miss – the entire planet was in thrall, glued to the vis-casts or engaged in mass surfing parties. There were bodies lying about everywhere with little discs stuck to their foreheads. It's not every day that a continent that has been resting peacefully at the bottom of the ocean is brought back to the surface. I found it quite fascinating how quickly the landmass re-vegetated, forests springing up in a matter of months and the ancient cities erupting from the earth as if they'd just been waiting for the opportunity.

I didn't hide my interest well enough though, because my hostling pounced upon it and decided this was where my future lay. He persuaded my father to use his business contacts to get me a post at the university working on the Lemuria Ascension Project. "Something basic to start with and then Shu'nay can work his way up." So that's where I've been for the last eighteen months.

The project leader is one Professor Mojigato, Moji to his friends; I have to call him Professor Mojigato. On the day I arrived in his office, he looked me up and down, sized up my potential in five minutes flat and gave me duties commensurate with my abilities. I hand out name badges to visiting dignitaries, serve wine at faculty socials and just generally potter about keeping the office and the lab tidy. My hostling is happy that I am gainfully employed and I am happy as my working hours are short, so that I can spend the afternoons swimming in the waterfall-fed lake in front of the university.

The university, itself, stands half-way up a mountainside with views over the bay and the Mantle of Tagaloa beyond. A steel and coloured-glass structure, but of that glass they use that's made from plants? That cellulose stuff? So that it's a bit bendy and can withstand earthquakes? We get rather a lot of those. I mean, this area's always been prone to that kind of thing but apparently it's got a lot worse during the last couple of centuries.

This is part of the reason for the Lemuria Ascension Project – to tame the Ring of Fire. I could be cynical for a moment and say the citizens of the countries surrounding the Mantle of Tagaloa want a piece of the limelight that those countries encircling the Girdle of Tiamaat, where Atlantis now stands, have so recently been glorying in... But there are some genuine good reasons. Not least, as I say, to placate that extensive zone of volcanic and seismic activity that traces the outer limits of the Mantle of Tagaloa or the Ocean of Fire as some would call it. Our mystics have long believed the increased incidence of tsunamis and earthquakes to be an indication from the depths that Lemuria was ready to ascend once more.

More prosaic, perhaps, but no less necessary, is our need, as a species, for more landmass. Despite our best endeavours our numbers continue to rise; our ever-increasing life-span; our resistance to disease; the short duration of childhood in our young. It is not uncommon to have seven generations of a family dwelling under one roof. And whilst our needs for sustenance are met by the myriad of food forests, which mimic the structure of their natural counterparts, production on multiple layers; so much kinder to the earth and higher in yield than the abhorrent agricultural practices of humanity, still we need more land.

When Atlantis returned to us, she brought with her a revolution in science and technology – gargantuan leaps forward that would have taken decades, maybe centuries, otherwise. We're hoping for something similar from Lemuria. On Earth we have otherlane technology pretty much sussed. For instance, I choose to walk to work every day because I enjoy the exercise. I could, however, step outside the family front door, open a portal and emerge, seconds later, on the steps of the university; I could, if I chose, take a day-trip sight-seeing in Immanion. Transportation has, therefore, pretty much become redundant except, perhaps, in the pursuit of leisure. But we're never satisfied are we? We always want more. Lemuria, it is hoped, will be the jump point for mass travel to other worlds, other realms. Mythology has it that the ancient Lemurians were higher in frequency and did not fully manifest to the physical. It's hoped that Lemuria will have a similar effect on the harish form. So, quite interesting stuff I suppose and it's all useful in placating my hostling which is my major objective.

Well, everything was going along quite swimmingly. I was doing my little job, getting under no-har's feet and keeping safely out of the way and then the Big Day arrived. As the date for the planned ascension got nearer an edict came out from Paz Marca, Chief Scholar from the Library at Kyme and overall project co-ordinator. Rumour has it that he can trace his family history back to Batalha, the great scribe, and Batalha is known to have had Lemurian ancestry.

Anyway, this edict listed all those hara who were to be present at the actual ascension event. The Mantle of Tagaloa is littered with islands, each one believed to be a mountain top from the great continent beneath. The plan is to station hara on each of these islands and then they will work together to raise the land from the bottom of the ocean. So this decree bore all the names of those who'd been selected and my immediate superior, Professor Mojigato, wasn't on the list ... *but I was*. Moji was livid.

Inevitably, I was summoned to the Professor's office. He sat there, quietly steaming, behind his desk. He indicated a chair and then, in highly controlled tones, asked, "I just want you to explain exactly how you've pulled it off."

Hastily I assured him I hadn't pulled anything off.

"Don't get smart with me you little..." And he broke off abruptly, angry beyond words but not yet ready to sacrifice his dignity. He had his academic reputation to consider after all. He took a measured breath and then tried again. "I've dedicated years to the Lemuria Ascension Project. I've been working towards this all my adult life. So how is it that you swan in here for all of five minutes, contribute nothing of any real value, and then get selected to the ascension team and I don't?"

I shrugged helplessly. I had no answers to give. It did seem very unfair on him.

The Professor was now in full flow. "So easy for you I suppose? So easy for one of the sons of a wealthy west-coast family? Just a word in the right place and their lazy good-for-nothing son bags a prized place on the most prestigious project of the century?"

"I'm sorry Professor Mojigato, I don't know how it happened."

He clicked his tongue impatiently. "I expect your father, egged on by your simpering hostling, greased the palms of a few of his business associates... Is that how it works?"

I glared back at him, nettled at last. He could insult me as much as he liked, that was all just water off a duck's back, but he was being utterly unfair about my parents. Okay, they drive me crazy but in this they were innocent of all charges. Yet still I tried to mollify my employer. "Look Professor, I don't know how this happened, really I don't. Can I contact Paz Marca at Kyme for you? Tell him there's been a mistake and that you should take my place on the team?" I smiled in what I hoped was an engaging way.

If anything Mojigato's pale glare got several degrees colder and he pointed a long and angry finger at the door. "I don't need your charity, you gormless little no-har. This opportunity is utterly wasted on you. Now, get out of my sight. I don't want to see you at this university again and don't expect your job to be waiting for you when you return."

I beat a hasty retreat.

The run-in with the Professor upset me far more than I would have expected and I slept badly that night. As usual I was visited by my standard unpleasant dream; blood, bone and tearing flesh. I had a week to kill before the selected party of the Lemuria Ascension Project were due to depart. Obviously I couldn't go to the university; Professor Mojigato would have had me bodily ejected and that would have just been plain undignified.

My hostling was thrilled that I'd been selected, believing it to be my reward for hard work and dedication – I hadn't the heart to tell him that I'd been all but sacked from my job. So each day I performed an elaborate charade. I'd leave the family home at the usual time, walk in the direction of the university, once on the edge of the campus I'd open a portal and transport myself to the coast. There I'd spend my day among the dusty booths and side shows on the beach, lie in the sun breathing in the salty tang of the ocean or chat to the street vendors whilst the seabirds screamed overhead. Curiously I didn't feel much like surfing the knowledge, which would have been my usual distraction. Mostly I just sat on the sand, staring out to sea and wondering what my future held. Then at about the right time I'd transport myself back to the outskirts of the university campus and walk home. And that's how I spent my time until the day of departure arrived.

Startlingly fast, I found myself on board ship, sailing west towards a chain of islands. Our specific destination was one particular island called the Island of Flowers, once believed to have been the highest peak of one of mountain ranges on the great continent of Lemuria. Odd isn't it? That this outmoded form of transport was selected? I mean, it would have been far more efficient to just open up a portal and step through. But it was thought best that the project members had time to clear their minds of all distraction before the actual ascension began, and a journey at sea would be just the thing. They were right, too.

I hadn't realised just how much the argument with the Professor had distressed me or how disquieting I'd found having to lie to my parents like that. It's curious, but since being on board I'd felt far more like myself; that the thoughts I was thinking were *my* thoughts. Maybe it was just being away from home, or more specifically away from my hostling. I was still getting the bad dreams though, every night; blood, bone and tearing flesh. But now if anything they were more vivid, more personal and I could hear screaming too.

However the days made up for it. I had no idea that sea travel could be so pleasurable; standing on the deck of a ship as it pitches and rolls across the ocean; the rhythmic motion; a hint of brine in the air; the sound of the surf. I'd travelled by ship before, of course, when surfing the knowledge, but even with all the artificial sensory stimulation it's *nothing* like the real thing. Most days we had a family of dolphins racing alongside our bows. For two pins I'd have jumped in with them, they looked so joyous. The hara on board were all delightful too. They brushed aside the concerns I had that my selection to the project team was a mistake. "Relax, Shu'nay, you're here for a reason. Believe it." So I tried.

Rumour was rife around the ship that Paz Marca, the project co-ordinator from Kyme, was on board. That he was, reputedly, the descendant of one of my childhood heroes, Batalha the Scribe, interested me intensely. As well as being a field researcher and great luminary of Kyme, he'd also penned many books for children. I'd read all of them, of course, whilst surfing the knowledge, but my family also possessed two leather-bound volumes of Batalha's adventures and I loved them, the feel of them, the smell of them. So... a link to one of the champions of my youth there with us on board... We'd not seen him. Apparently, he was in deep meditation in his cabin. I considered him an idiot. Missing it all? Or maybe sea travel was just old news to him. But I loved it. Sitting with my back to the forward cabins, warm timbers beneath my feet, salt spray in my hair and laughter on my lips... The next day we were due to arrive at the island... and I realised – I was scared.

I awoke as the dawn light crept in through the porthole near my bunk. My dry mouth and knotted intestines were testament to the anxiety that had made its presence felt the previous evening. I sat up and looked out of the tiny window. We must have arrived at our destination during the night, and we were now moored up close to a beach. The island lay invitingly beyond a stretch of sparkling ocean; white sands leading to rain-forested valleys, backed by a seemingly sheer curtain of glassy rock that probably reached to the gods themselves. My guts gave another twist and I winced. Today was the day I was going to be found out. A mere underling, a gormless little no-har, fit only for passing around glasses of wine and handing out name badges; and this one of the highest profile exploits in harish history. How had I got myself into this mess? I sat on my bunk gnawing at fingernail after fingernail and staring out of my little window.

The island really was most alluring; all fluted cliffs and emerald green pinnacles; cascading waterfalls plummeting down into deep, narrow valleys; scalloped beaches and sea caves and a large craggy sea arch with a white sand spit running right through it. And that ocean, crystal blue and calm – you could lose yourself in waters like that. No boat has landed on that beach for millennia, a tradition from before recorded time, a tribute to the gods of creation. And to honour that tradition we were going to swim in and nothing, not even my imminent discovery and inevitable being sent home in disgrace, was going to stop me making that swim. Maybe they'd take pity on me and let me explore for a few hours before sending me away. And anyway, I'd even get to see the famous Paz Marca. That was bound to impress my hostling.

So I sat gazing out of the porthole until the call came to go up on deck and ready ourselves for the swim ashore. Not everyone was as enthusiastic about this prospect as I. They'd taken me at my word when I said I was a strong swimmer. Each of us was fitted with a transparent, waterproof rucksack; cellulose again. Air bladders were inflated along the sides. Those of us who had identified ourselves as stronger swimmers also had our backpacks loaded up with food and other provisions, bedding and the canopies under which we would sleep. The weaker swimmers carried no provisions and it was they who looked unenthusiastic.

The ship's captain gave us final instructions before we entered the water. "Take it steadily. Strong swimmers ensure you swim alongside the weaker swimmers to assist them if there are any difficulties. Paz Marca will greet you on the beach; he swam over just after day break."

I frowned. I had been watching from my porthole since dawn and I had seen no-one.

I was partnered with Lemel, a shy and diffident research student from the University of Oseney in Alba Sulh. He splashed along, a look of grim determination on his face. I took his hand and encouraged him to relax and take longer strokes. After a while, he did and stopped gritting his teeth, allowing his face to soften into a smile. To me, the experience was an unalloyed delight, and I longed, at the earliest opportunity, to be back in the water unencumbered by backpack and weak swimmers. I was born for this.

Too soon, we reached the shore, but not soon enough in Lemel's opinion. I helped him through the shallows to the firm sand beyond.

He turned to me, his pale hair plastered to his head. "Thank you."

I brushed aside his thanks and unclipped my backpack.

He did likewise and began to wring out his robe. "I wish I could enjoy the water as you do. I never learned to swim properly." He pulled a rueful face. "Too many hours in the classroom I think."

I shrugged. "I spend all my spare time in the water, have done since I was a harling," and then, equally ruefully, "and not enough hours in the classroom."

He laughed then. "But you love it so."

I was surprised to hear a voice say, "I'll teach you if you like." I was even more surprised that the voice was mine.

Lemel turned his eyes to mine and held them for a long moment. Then he smiled. "I'd like that."

I smiled too, I'd found a friend.

Lemel's gaze shifted to something beyond my left shoulder. "Oh! Here's Paz Marca."

I turned and beheld the strangest looking har I'd ever set eyes on.

He was about average height, but his skin had a curiously mottled appearance, as if the pigment was irregularly dispersed. Patches of his skin were as dark as black coffee, but there were paler areas of pure peach, interspersed with streaks of translucent pearl. He looked for all the world as if he had been painted. If he was a pony we would have described him as piebald. The irregular pigmentation continued into his hair, which was the texture of wool and worn in heavy two-tone locks down his back.

Paz Marca stood before us and held his arms wide. "Welcome," he intoned. "Welcome to the island and to the culmination of our lives' work. Let us begin by sharing a meal together. Bring the provisions further up the beach. The sun will soon dry you but we'll kindle a fire – this will be the focus for the storytelling to come."

We did as we were bidden. The backpacks were carried to the point where the sands gave way to rounded pebbles, firewood was gathered and a meal prepared. Lemel and I were sent with an empty backpack into the rainforest to gather fruit. The trees were laden; guava and grapefruit; mountain apples and melon; papaya and passion fruit. We picked enough for a meal and carried the brimming rucksack between us back to the beach. When we reached the sands I stopped and gaped. "The ship is gone," I wailed.

Lemel looked across at me and laughed. "But of course. Think about it Shu'nay, if we are successful and raise Lemuria, any ships in the vicinity would get stranded on a mountain top or washed away in a tidal wave. We will try to contain this as best we can but all shipping must retreat to a safe distance."

I nodded; it made sense, but it meant that once my perfidy was discovered I would not be sent back to the ship. Perhaps they would just open a portal and send me home?

Lemel laid a hand on my arm. "Just consider, Shu'nay, all over the Mantle of Tagaloa groups like ours are gathering on islands that were once the mountain peaks of Lemuria. Have you heard of the island of Ostara? It's where the ancients carved great stone heads, fine of feature and enigmatic of gaze. Imagine, once Lemuria is risen again, no more will they stand with their backs to the ocean, instead they'll form a protective ring around a sacred mountain top."

I swallowed, hard. Lemel was so knowledgeable, I felt foolish in comparison.

"Hi, you two," a voice called from the other side of the fire. "Hurry up, we're getting hungry here."

Hastily we took the loaded rucksack across to the fire where the contents were quickly sliced up and laid upon wooden platters. There were also, I noticed, spreads of delicious looking breads, fragrant cheeses and spiced meats and several carafes of freshly-squeezed pineapple juice and coconut milk. I spotted a stack of polished coconut shell halves and handed them around, I knew my place. We sat around the fire, about twenty of us in all, and helped ourselves to whatever we fancied. Paz Marca, I noticed, ate only the fruit that had been collected. He did not touch any of the other delicacies that were on offer. Strangely, I found I was minded to do the same.

When we had all eaten and drunk our fill, a bowl of spring water was passed around so that we could clean our hands.

Paz Marca shook the excess water from his hands and clapped them together. "And now, it is time for the storytelling. First we will find out everyhar's name and where they come from. There will be no name badges here, it is beholden on each of you to learn and remember one another's names."

I squirmed with embarrassment; I've always hated this sort of thing.

And so they began, the introductions, working their way around the circle, getting ever closer to me; scholars from the colleges of Almagabra; researchers from the Malitan healing houses; theorists from the universities of Alba Sulh and Freyhella, Alke-bulan and Megalithica; scribes from Kyme ... and then it was my turn. Hastily I told them I was Shu'nay from the west-coast University of Sancruzien and I assisted Professor Mojigato. I hoped they would pass swiftly on – no such luck!

"How is old Moji?" one of them asked. "I haven't seen him in months."

"Why isn't he here?" another chipped in. "He's dedicated his life to this project..."

There was an embarrassing silence.

Paz Marca spoke, "Professor Mojigato did not fit the selection criteria."

A murmur of dissent passed around the circle. I just wanted the ground to open up beneath me. Lemel placed a reassuring hand on my thigh and squeezed gently.

Paz Marca held up a hand for silence. "Thank you..." he paused and glanced in my direction but I noticed he did not look at me, "...Shu'nay. And now, if we may continue?"

Lemel gave me another reassuring squeeze and told his story.

When we were all done Paz Marca thanked us again and said, "Since the subject of the selection criteria has come up, we'll deal with that first. It relates to the final days of Lemuria so I will begin by reminding you of that story."

Now that Paz Marca was speaking I had the opportunity to study him more closely. Before I'd been hard pressed not to stare but now, like everyone else, I had reason to fix my gaze upon him. Hara are famed for their physical loveliness. I suppose I've grown used to the regularity of feature and varying degrees of beauty. Paz Marca is not like that, although he is physically arresting. Now that I was closer I could see that the irregular pigmentation was not confined only to his skin and hair but extended also to his eyes; one a crystalline blue and the other a vibrant hazel. And his features were not regular either, almost as if his face could not decide who to be. I also noticed that, though his eyes travelled around the circle as he spoke, he never once made eye contact with me.

"Remember," Paz Marca said, "that for centuries Lemuria was peaceful, productive and harmonious. Then the citizens became ruthless, greedy for expansion, for material wealth and sensory pleasures. The land became dispirited, and during this time unprecedented storms ravaged the fields and ruined the crops. Tremendous earthquakes rocked the continent and huge tidal waves inundated coastal areas. Then one day a giant volcano in the Hata Valley erupted, spewing molten lava over the city of Hatamakula, and a violent earthquake shook the land and blocked the flow of the mighty river causing it to back up into the valleys. For days all was silence, the survivors clung to a pitiful existence on the mountain tops. Then the great river burst through a fault and poured into the recently erupted volcano. A terrific explosion followed that lifted the mountain bodily from its foundation and flung it some three hundred miles. Further explosions and fractures allowed the ocean to flood in. Lemuria convulsed and disintegrated and was lost to the ocean floor. It's a wonder anyone survived, but survive they did. They were washed out to sea and the lucky ones found themselves torn up trees, mats of vegetation and even canoes to carry them.

"The reason," Paz Marca continued, "that each of you is here is that you all have a genetic link to those survivors. Every one of you has an ancestor who once walked upon Lemuria. Those survivors were born on the currents to far off lands and became the Maori, the Bramha, the Aborigines, the Maya, the Hopi and the Chumash..."

Chumash? I zoned out for a moment. I had Chumash ancestry. Maybe my hostling had something to be proud of after all? I began to relax a little. This explained why I was chosen for this project and Mojigato wasn't. I still didn't feel I deserved to be here though, I'd hardly *earned* it. When I turned my attention back to Paz Marca I discovered he was telling a different story.

"At its height, I'm sure you recall, Lemuria enjoyed a golden age. There was no theft, no unemployment, no poverty. Every man and woman had work according to their ability, and opportunity was limited only by one's ambition. The single crime that occurred in this golden time was the crime of passion, and for this the laws of Lemuria were really quite drastic. There was no capital punishment as such. If a citizen committed murder, they were banished to an unpopulated land with provisions and the essentials to sustain life for just one year. To keep the citizenship of Lemuria pure, the family and relatives of the offender would also be banished from the motherland but, in their case, to a more civilised dependency."

I shivered. It was barbaric.

Paz Marca continued, "Recently, I have undertaken several dream quests and have unearthed details of a genuine case."

I felt Lemel stiffen beside me, his eyes alert. "This is new."

Paz Marca closed his eyes and took a deep breath; he exhaled slowly. "During this golden era, a couple lived in the capital city Hamakulia. They were much in love and popular with all who knew them. Vitima was a sculptor and his wife, Culpado, wrote beautiful poetry. They had been married for several years but had not, yet, been blessed with children." He opened his eyes again. "One day, a poisonous friend of Culpado's, who was envious of her happy life, told Culpado that Vitima had been seen in the company of another woman. Culpado instantly dismissed this as nonsense but a seed of anxiety had been planted within her and it began to grow. She contrived to follow her husband as he went about his business, and she discovered that he did, indeed, spend time with another woman; taking her notes and bringing her flowers. The seed of anxiety began to blossom in shades of jealousy and wrath. One night, as Vitima lay sleeping in their bed, Culpado caught up a jewelled knife that lay in the fruit bowl. She took it to the bedroom and used it to cut out her husband's heart. He died with her name on his lips and she was discovered sitting upon the floor, rocking back and forth, with Vitima's heart clutched to her own. The seed of anxiety had borne its bitter fruit – regret. Vitima was buried with all honours and his sculptures placed in prominent positions around the city. Culpado's work was destroyed; every sonnet, every volume of poetry was reduced to ash and the unhappy woman herself was banished to an empty land with just the bare means of survival. One of the tools they sent with her was the jewelled knife she'd used to mutilate her husband."

There was silence for a moment. One har swallowed thickly and asked, "And what of her family? Were they all banished too?"

Paz Marca sighed. "She had no family. Her parents had died long before and she was an only child. Her lack of family is the one fortunate aspect of the whole sorry tale."

Lemel spoke up. "And was Vitima guilty? Was he courting another woman?"

Paz Marca shook his head sadly. "His love was reserved for Culpado alone. He bore love tokens to the other woman for the sake of a friend, who was too shy to do so himself. Culpado had nothing to fear."

Silence fell again as each of us considered the implications of Paz Marca's narrative. The storytelling continued, migrating to happier topics; tales from the seven rivers; legends from the Thibi valley and the mysteries of the sea coast marshes. But I was unable to get the tragedy of Culpado and Vitima out of my head. How had she coped alone? How had she lived with her guilt? Had she killed herself quickly with the jewelled knife that had been left to her or had she died with agonising slowness when her provisions had finally run out?

Around noon, the storytelling circle broke up and each of us was left to our own devices. We would assemble again for the evening meal.

"Wander the forests," Paz Marca suggested. "There are temples and waterfalls and pools. Get yourselves attuned to the energies of this place."

As we had been sitting, an onshore breeze had formed, turning the seas choppy and giving the once crystalline waters a sandy murkiness. Few of us chose to remain on the beach. We wandered inland, past the pebbles and boulders to the fairyland fernery that lay before the rain-forested valleys. Lemel and I had given the area scant regard as we pressed on into the forests in our quest for fruit. But now we looked around us at the lush and feathered leaves, the scarlet hibiscus and the blue jade vines. Here we set up the canopies under which we would later sleep, and then groups and pairs and individuals melted into the forests seeking their own communion with the island that had once formed part of their ancestral home.

Lemel and I chose a path and followed it steeply upward until it brought us to a flat area where a temple of twisted stone stood beside a deep, ripple-free pool. Carved steps led down to the water. Inevitably Lemel went to sit within the temple, closing his eyes in meditation, and I cast off my clothes and sank into the water. It was clear and warm and not in the least brackish, fed, I mused, by some underground freshwater stream. I lay on my back in the water trying to disturb the surface as little as possible. I became conscious of Lemel's eyes upon me.

His mouth curved into a smile. "That looks so good I might just have to join you."

I sank beneath the surface then reappeared with water streaming from my hair. "Do," I encouraged him.

He shrugged off his clothes, leaving them in a tidier pile beside mine. He slipped in beside me and instantly the expression of mild terror was back on his face.

I had to stop myself laughing. "Take a small breath," I suggested, "and go and sit on the bottom for a few moments."

He managed about five seconds before resurfacing, choking and arms thrashing.

I caught hold of his shoulders. "Are you dead?" I asked. He shook his head as he got his breath back. "Before you learn to swim," I told him, "you must first learn to float. Will you trust me?" He nodded again and I placed one hand behind his neck, the other at his waist and laid him back in the water. At first he held himself rigidly stiff but gradually he relaxed and I was able to remove first one hand and then the other as he learned to make the small movements and adjustments that were necessary to keep him afloat. Once I was happy he had mastered it, I lay back and floated right alongside him. We relaxed like that until our skin began to wrinkle, then we got out and reclined, naked, on the sun-baked rocks overlooking the ocean. The sea breeze could not reach us here.

"Do you think this is what Paz Marca had in mind when he suggested we got ourselves attuned to the local energies?" Lemel murmured sleepily.

"I think this is exactly what he had in mind," I affirmed

decisively. "I was born to lie on these rocks and swim in these pools."

I must have dozed for several hours and my dreams were a complicated mix of anxiety over the tragic fate of Culpado and the usual dream of blood, bone and tearing flesh. This time though, the screaming was that of a woman. I shivered as I awoke and my stomach gave out a loud growl.

Lemel looked over at me. "Should we get back and help prepare the evening meal?"

I nodded and we threw on our clothes, hastily descending the forest path. On our return to the fernery, we found hara milling about filling platters with sliced fruit, cuts of meat and hunks of bread. I assisted in preparing a herbal infusion and noticed, as we sat down to eat once again, that more of the party chose to follow Paz Marca's example and eat and drink only that which originated from the island itself.

As the platters were cleared away Paz Marca snapped his fingers at me. "Hi, you. Sorry, I can't remember your name. Come here a minute."

"Shu'nay," I said through gritted teeth as I unwillingly followed the beckoning finger. Perhaps name badges would have been a good idea after all? I threw a glance at Lemel who shrugged in return, then I turned and followed Paz Marca to the beach.

This was it, I thought, as I trudged along behind him. This was where I got told that, despite everything, I didn't belong here and would be sent home.

Back on the beach, the onshore breeze had turned offshore once more and the sea was calm again. The warm wind gently caressed my bare arms and carried with it the floral scents of the fernery. The fire we had used earlier as a focal point for our storytelling had burned to embers, but a telltale glow hinted that it was not yet dead. Paz Marca waved a hand and a collection of driftwood rose from where it lay scattered across the beach, flew steadily through the air, and came to rest upon the embers. A solitary finger of flame reached up from the ash beneath, and the fire flickered to life once more.

I blinked my surprise. The skill is not uncommon; caste training would allow most hara to acquire the gift of telekinesis. The truth is, the majority of us simply don't bother. We've grown indolent now that our lives are so much easier. Paz Marca clearly wasn't one of the majority, but then that was no surprise at all.

Paz Marca indicated a spot by the fire. "Won't you sit down?"

I sank down to the sand and he sat beside me. "I detect a certain discomfort in you," he began, "a sense that you feel you truly do not belong here...?"

"I know you're going to send me away," I interrupted, "but please, before you do, please tell me what became of Culpado? I need to know."

Paz Marca sat open-mouthed at my rudeness. He blinked several times. "Very well," he said, shaking his head, as if to clear his disbelief. "Culpado was, as you know, sent into exile. She had with her only the bare means of survival and also the jewelled knife. Many times she looked upon that knife with despairing eyes and thought to take her own life... But she did not. She opted to survive, never to forget and to find some way to atone for what she had done. She was careful, used her rations sparingly, taught herself to hunt and learned the fruits that could and could not be eaten. She lasted far longer than the year the Grand Council had intended. But the winters were harsh and there came a day when she had food left for only one more meagre meal."

I swallowed hard. So she had died a slow lingering death. I pitied her. Despite the warm breeze and the fire before me I shivered.

Paz Marca looked at me, for the first time making eye contact, and he read my expression. His mouth curved into a half smile. "Just one more meal," he repeated. "And then the miracle occurred. Fate was not yet done with Culpado. A traveller came upon her; a man from the great island civilisation of the east. Even in her wretched state, he saw the beauty in her and, as they began to converse, he recognised her wit. He carried her from that place to his ship and then on to his home on the islands amongst the wine-dark sea. He quickly fell in love with her and she, though she did not love him in return, married him in gratitude and was loyal to him; she gave him sons and daughters. She took a new name and under the name of Marazi she began to write poetry again."

"So she survived? I'm glad."

"Oh yes, she lived to a very great age."

"And you saw all this in a dream quest?"

"I see it in my dreams, yes..."

I seemed to have lured Paz Marca into storytelling mode. I intended to keep him there. "And what of Batalha of Kyme," I pressed. "Is it true he was your ancestor? I read all his books as a harling. My family have two of his volumes bound in leather. They were my greatest treasure when I was young."

Paz Marca leaned back holding up his hands, half gratified, half embarrassed. I cast about for another topic, I had to keep him talking but Paz Marca shook his head firmly. "Enough," he said. "I have answered two of your questions, now it is time you answered one of mine."

I sat before him dumbstruck. Nervously I licked my lips.

"Tell me, Shu'nay..." He spoke my name as if it stuck in his throat. "Tell me, why is it that you believe so fervently that you do not belong here?"

I felt the tide of blood rise in my face. My skin burned. I looked down in shame. "Everyone here has devoted years to study, worked so hard, so diligently..." I gestured helplessly. "I have contributed nothing." I raised my eyes again and saw that Paz Marca was looking at me with slight distaste.

"In your words I hear the voice of Professor Mojigato." He shook his head again and leaned forward earnestly. "Listen Shu'nay," and this time he said my name with greater ease. "I can show you a breath vision of Lemuria that will wipe out the need for years of study. You'll know it. Of that I am certain and then you'll be assured that you have every right to be here." *Share breath? Me? With Paz Marca?* The gods must have taken leave of their senses. "Yes, alright." I heard myself say.

Gently, he reached forward; gently, he took my face in his hands and, equally gently, our lips connected; his breath honey-sweet, edged with citrus. Slowly, steadily he sent a stream of images to me.

Now, he said, from somewhere within the depths of my brain. *Now tell me what you can see.*

We appeared to be suspended above a great continent, land stretching away towards the sea far beyond. *We're somewhere above the Rhu Hut plains,* I said, *looking south to the city of Hamukulia and beyond.* How did I know this?

Go on, Paz Marca prompted.

Hamukulia is the hub of the wheel from which project the seven river *valleys and the seven mountain ranges of Lemuria. From here I can see the Clarion Mountains at the southern end of the Rhu Hut plains, the thickly-forested tribal valleys of Judi, Opu and Beni, the Chi, Thibi and Upa rivers and the sea coast marshes shrouded in mist.**

Paz Marca broke the connection with me but still he held my face in his hands. "Now tell me," he said, looking deep into my eyes. "Tell me that you do not belong here."

"How do I know all this?" I spluttered.

"It is deep within you," he replied. "It is deep within your soul, your very being – you were Lemurian once." He took his hands away from my face. "Believe it Shu'nay. It is the truth."

My mouth was completely dry. I did not know what to say. I believed him. The images were too strong, too powerful and the knowledge too certain to be ignored.

Paz Marca pressed a hand to his brow and shook his head slightly. "I find it strange that you asked about Culpado. Even though she survived, her punishment continued. The penance she inflicted upon herself was to remember her crime through each and every incarnation she experienced." He paused. "That, and condemning herself never to love again, until she could properly atone to Vitima, the beloved husband she had robbed of life." Paz Marca sat up suddenly. "A great wrong was done and reparation must be made."

I watched as he drew from his sleeve a knife; ancient-looking, keen-edged and with a jewelled handle... *a jewelled handle?* "There must be a sacrifice, an offering of blood, here on the sand."

I pulled back in horror, the hair standing up on the back of my neck. Was this the reason I'd been brought here? The disposable little no-har fit only for menial duties? I might not know what I wanted from life but one thing I did know was that I didn't want to be dead.

Paz Marca raised his eyes to mine and caught the expression. Unexpectedly, he laughed. "Oh no my dear, not you." And he sliced down viciously into his own left arm. Blood fountained onto the sand. He gasped and dropped the knife. After a moment, he ran his index finger the length of the wound which immediately sealed leaving a scar. "That should be sufficient," he hissed.

I looked at the sealed flesh. When our species first ascended from humanity, each and every new har had borne a similar scar upon one of their arms.

Paz Marca's eyes sought mine again and I could see the pain reflected there. "You are still uncertain I see... Shu'nay." He spoke my name with infinite gentleness. "It is time for you to wake up."

Confused, I shook my head again. I didn't understand any of it.

"Will you share breath with me again? I want to help."

But the question held more than just benign concern and an earnest desire to be of assistance. I could hear the unspoken plea there too. *"Save me..."* Without thinking I leaned forward and pressed my lips to his. Startled, he pulled back at first but then plunged in and I saw the story of his lives: the joy of a Lemurian childhood; the delight of first true love; the despair of imagined betrayal; the horror wrought with the jewelled knife; exile and rescue; a new life; many new lives; each of them without love or connection; remembering always the blood, the bone and the tearing flesh; his final human incarnation, the crazed and distressed boy, who could bear the burden no longer and sought to destroy himself; the bliss of inception and the deliverance of a new form better able to carry the memories; Batalha, his first harish incarnation; his wisdom; his travelling; all the hara he'd later become; on and on, life after life; searching always for his first love, Vitima and now, his current incarnation. I saw and felt all this in Paz Marca's breath and then Shu'nay fell away and Vitima sat in his place, arms around the lover who had destroyed him, drinking him in, understanding.

I pulled away. Paz Marca, or Culpado as I thought of him now, sat mute and anxious before me. "I should have explained," I told him, meaning the attentions I had paid, so long ago, to the other woman.

"I should have asked," he half sobbed.

I drew him into my arms. He lay there quietly for a while and then said, "I searched for you for so, so long." His voice was so plaintive it brought a painful lump to my throat. "You were well hidden from me. And then, on the journey here, I could sense you on board ship. It took all my strength and control not to beat the door down to reach you... but the time would not have been right... all those lifetimes I searched for you. Why could I not find you before?"

And suddenly I knew. "I've never manifested before now."

He looked at me, his mismatched eyes wide with wonder. "Never?"

I shook my head. "All my life, this life, I've drifted, having no idea who I am or what direction to take." Realisation hit and it hurt. "I've lived a half life," I gasped.

Culpado squeezed my hand. "And now?"

"Now I know who I am and I see a life before me... but you? You've waited so long..."

Culpado shrugged but I could see the pain in his eyes. "I have, but it was necessary," he said, sighing.

Abruptly I got to my feet. "But that is all over," I said with determination. "Life begins anew."

He looked up at me in confusion.

I bent forward and with finger and thumb picked up the jewelled knife; his blood still bright upon the blade. I held the knife before me with some distaste; my other hand I held out to Culpado. "This has served its purpose I think," I stated, meaning the knife. I hauled my companion to his feet and led him to the water's edge. Foam lapped at our feet. I drew my arm back and flung the knife far out into the ocean. "Let the sea take it," I said. "Let the brine eat away the metal; the currents carry it far from here, dash it against rocks and reduce it to its elements. Let others find the jewels upon other shores and use them for a better purpose."

He sighed again and laid his head upon my shoulder. "And what shall *you* do now Vitima? Now that you know who you are?"

The waves continued to lap around our feet, the air sweet, salty and strong and above our heads the seabirds wheeled and cried. "Soon," I said, "very soon, you and I shall work with the others to bring Lemuria back to the world. We shall have our home again."

"And what of *us*?" he whispered.

I placed my fingers beneath his chin and turned his head so that we looked at one another. "We have the rest of this lifetime to find out and other lifetimes to follow."

Relief flooded his face and he smiled at last.

"And I have a promise to keep," I said. "I must finish teaching Lemel to swim."

He drew in a slow breath and blinked at me. "You were always kind."

"Was I? I haven't known myself to be in this life."

"And what of Shu'nay?" he enquired.

Vitima stood upon the sand, his arm around Culpado, but Shu'nay was not far away. From deep within a voice arose. "So just what is my hostling going to make of all this?" And my laughter rippled across the sea, echoed from the cliffs behind and carried through the air alongside the wheeling birds.

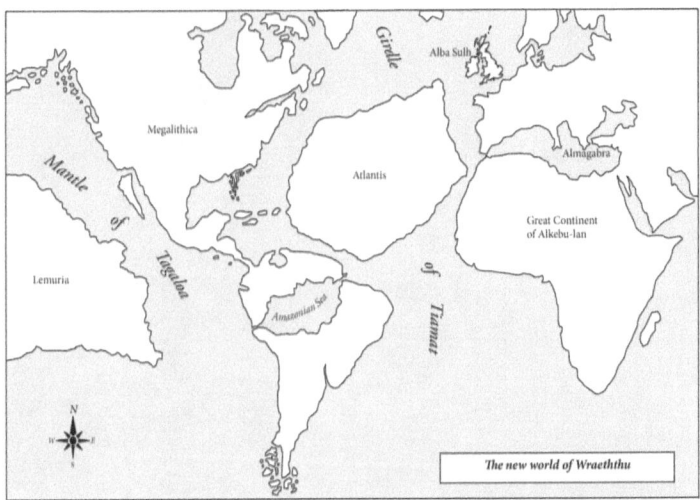

Author's note: Narrative concerning the demise, justice system and geography of Lemuria is inspired by and based on the work of the late Dr Robert Stelle, founder of the Lemurian Fellowship.

The Lady

Daniela Ritter

The Lady

"Why are we doing this again?" Moewe pouted, leaning against the rail of the small merchant vessel.

His eyes were as blue as the waters of the Great Divide, which their ship was sailing, and glinted with barely suppressed anger.

Gull sighed deeply. They had been having this conversation over and over since they left their home on the eastern coast of Alba Sulh. His son was driving him mad. "Because I think the anthropologist we'll be visiting can teach you a thing or two about humans."

Annoyed, Moewe rolled his eyes. "Aw, father, I learned all about humans at school. Who cares about them anyway? They're nothing but ancient relics on the brink of extinction. Pathetic, imperfect beings."

The young har's feybraiha celebration had been a week ago. Gull knew his son could imagine thousands of things that were far more exciting than a history lesson. After all, his son had been invited to join an expedition into a dimension some Otherlanes travellers had only recently discovered.

But how could Moewe ever become a good scientist if he was so blind in his presumptuous arrogance? Plus, the way Moewe expressed himself was no good way of talking about humanity.

Only when his son flinched did Gull realize how angry he must have looked as he thought these things.

"I don't remember raising a racist!" Gull growled quietly.

"Why didn't we at least use the Otherlanes like civilised hara?" Moewe mumbled uncomfortably, changing the subject.

"So that you learn what travelling is like for humans," Gull explained, noticeably less patient than before. "And now quit complaining!"

Harmony City welcomed the travellers with rich sights and scents. Hundreds of neat little white and grey stone buildings crowded the shore. The smell of sea salt, wet wood and fresh fish filled the air.

"You know, the war between hara and humans was not the first time this city was almost completely destroyed."

"Huh?" Moewe had not really been paying attention to his father's words. He was much more interested in some of the younger local fishmongers who offered the day's catch at their stands all over the harbour. The blond one had smiled at him, he was sure.

Moewe had to admit to himself that his thoughts were mostly about aruna these days – how could they not be? Having been an adult for only such a short time, he had not yet had the chance to study all the sugar-sweet details of that new aspect of his life. Back in Alba Suhl, there was a handsome young biologist who was about to go on a certain expedition that Moewe would have loved to join. And now he was caught in an extensive, boring history lesson.

"This sucks," he growled.

Gull laughed. "You tell the people who had to witness the destruction! It all started long before Wraeththu..."

Luckily his father had not picked up he hadn't been talking about the city's past.

They had to walk way past the harbour towards the southern border of the city. Here the houses stood further apart, and in the distance Moewe could make out large fields, where the food for the city's residents was grown.

"It's right over there!" Gull pointed to a lovely little white-washed house, surrounded by beds of different pink flowers, all in full bloom.

Moewe sighed. "OK. Let's get it over with."

Determinedly he marched forward. The sooner he started talking with the anthropologist, the sooner it would be over and he could go home. He knocked loudly on the wooden front door.

A moment later the door opened and Moewe jumped back, startled. His heart was racing. The creature in front of him barely resembled a har. It was smaller than him and... broader. What was it called? *Fat.* Its hair was of a dirty ashen grey. The skin of its face and hands was shrivelled and carved with hundreds of deep wrinkles. On its upper body, which was covered with a terrible green pullover, there were two grotesque bulges. But the worst thing was the stench. It smelt of death. Moewe could smell the cells of the creature rotting. He was revolted and a bit terrified.

"Oh, there's no need to be afraid, son."

Moewe couldn't help but sense the sweetly-dripping sarcasm in his father's voice.

"This is Maria. She's just an old woman. A human, you know?"

"Woman?" Moewe gasped.

The old lady didn't seem to mind his rudeness and smiled at him with curious kindness. "Hello, Gull. And you must be my friend's son."

The lady reached out her hand. Moewe couldn't do anything but stare at the leathery, wrinkled skin and the yellowish fingernails.

Maria shrugged and pulled back her hand in an inviting gesture. "Would you like to come in? I've just made chocolate cookies. Everyhar says they're the best in town."

Gull nodded and pushed his son forward. "You two have fun, then. I have some other business to attend."

"What?" Moewe gasped and turned around. Surely his father wouldn't leave him alone with this creature!

But when he met Gull's strict gaze he knew that the older har was very serious about that. "As a young scientist, my son, you should know that no information is more reliable than that you get directly from the source. That's an important lesson for you."

Moewe swallowed his anger and nodded. He had brought this on himself and he knew it.

Gull said his goodbyes and Moewe was left alone on the doorstep. Maria had already gone and was waiting for him at the door to one of the rooms inside. Moewe felt like he was standing in front of a scary unexplored cave, which was inhabited by a huge, ugly toad. But the more he hesitated, the more disappointed the woman seemed to look.

Moewe sighed and entered the house. He was not a harling anymore, and there surely was no reason to be afraid of some old human.

Maria's face brightened up visibly as she guided the young har through the narrow hall into the kitchen. Moewe noticed that the strange smell that surrounded the old woman faintly clung to the whole interior. He politely held his breath as inconspicuously as possible.

The kitchen furniture was mostly made from white painted wood. Each of the chairs, which surrounded a rather small table, had a fluffy, pink cushion on it.

Maria waved her hand toward the table. "Please, Moewe, have a seat. Would you like tea or hot chocolate?"

"Tea, please," Moewe answered absently. He was eying all the little details and items that made the room seem even smaller than it was: white curtains at the windows, painted pictures of cute little kittens on the wall, dried flowers in a vase on a board beside the kittens, and the plate on the table which carried an overload of steaming chocolate cookies. He had to admit that *they* really did smell good.

Then Moewe's eyes fell upon the decoration above the door and he gaped. A wooden man nailed to a cross by his hands and feet, a crown of thorns on his head. The style was a rather realistic one, and red paint glittered as blood around his wounds. He didn't look happy, but then, who would in this situation?

"It's sometimes hard to believe that this is meant to be a comforting image, right?" Maria smiled understandingly and placed a cup on the table in front of her guest.

Moewe remembered then. Human religion. He nodded his agreement and carefully turned back his gaze back to Maria as she took a seat opposite to him. He still thought she was terribly ugly, but at least she seemed nice.

"So..." he tried to start a conversation. "Your inception didn't work, then?"

It was common knowledge that girls who were incepted sometimes just didn't change, just like there was still a small chance an incepted boy would die.

Maria shook her head. "I didn't want to become parage."

"Why not?" Moewe exclaimed. "How can you prefer—?" He stopped himself before he could say the rude words that lay on the tip of his tongue.

"I had my reasons," she answered, more seriously than the young har had expected.

Right after that she shook her head and smiled again. "Help yourself to the cookies, will you? And now here's your chance. Is there anything about humans you always wanted to know but nohar could tell you?"

Moewe took a cookie and thoughtfully chewed on his first bite. She was right. They were delicious.

"Well..." he ventured. "Don't you feel... I don't know... kind of... lost and alone?"

Maria blinked questioningly, her mouth full of chocolate cookie.

Moewe sighed. "I mean... hara are connected. We use the Otherlanes for travelling, we have mind touch... Humans can do neither."

The woman smiled. "We humans just have to believe we're not alone. And although we don't hear our beloved ones inside our heads like you do, we feel them deep in our hearts. Human mothers know when something happens to their children."

"They do?" Moewe asked with surprise.

Maria snickered. "We are not as primitive as you might believe us to be."

Moewe's cheeks coloured, although he was not really sure why his usual thoughts suddenly caused him embarrassment. He decided to keep the conversation going to distract himself from the nagging guilt, which had just appeared for the first time. "Well, you might have some kind of connection to the ethers, then, but you're still just half of what you should be."

Maria pointed at him with another cookie. "How do you know that what I am is not what I'm supposed to be?"

Moewe wanted to reply that it should be obvious. But then, was it? While he was still fishing for words, Maria chuckled. She was damn good at unsettling him, and that started to get on his nerves.

"Aw, come on!" he started, trying to resume his old feeling of superiority. "You're weak, you become sick, you decay..."

"*Age*," Maria interjected. "Not *decay*. That comes when we're dead. And in that hara are no different."

Moewe grunted and continued his rant. "You age, you're stuck in half a gender. Men become disgustingly hairy and women lie around bleeding and complaining once a month! Try telling me that's a life worth living!"

Maria had folded her hands on the table and become silent. There was a deep sadness in her eyes. "Is that what your teachers told you? That being human is a worthless life?"

Moewe folded his arms defensively. He knew that he had hurt

her, but then, she had asked for it! Yet he had a feeling that he might have chosen the wrong words. "Well that's... not exactly what they said." He cleared his throat, which suddenly appeared to be a lot tighter than usual. "But... you know... humans *are* ugly. You have to agree, right?"

Without a word Maria rose from the table and left the room. Moewe felt extremely uncomfortable. This time he was all too sure that he had been very rude. He probably should tell the woman that he was sorry, but his own embarrassment chained him to his chair. What should he have told her, after all? That humans were beautiful and noble creatures? That would be a lie. He knew the history books. Still, his father would rip his head off when he learned of what had just happened.

While he was still wondering what to do, Maria entered the room again. She looked a lot more solemn now and carried a big book under her arm. When she took a seat beside Moewe, the young har had to resist the urge to move his own chair away. He desperately tried to read her facial expression, to find out if she was now secretly mad at him – or why she was *not* mad any more.

Maria had put the book on the table and now looked into Moewe's eyes with a friendly smile. "Look here, young har."

Moewe followed her outstretched finger. The book was old and a little dusty. When Maria opened it, the pages were yellowish and had stains from ageing. But it also showed other things, interesting things, which he had not seen before. The pages were without text, instead completely filled with photos — photos of a half-naked woman.

This was not cheap pornography. Moewe could see how the pictures had been taken with an artist's eye. The woman did not offer herself, but seemed to flirt with the person taking the photos. Her shoulder-length hair was of a deep brown and her eyes were glittering emeralds. Her noble, high cheek bones, tender face and sensuously curving rose-coloured lips nearly gave Moewe the illusion that it was a har he was looking at. But her firm, round breasts gave her away.

Moewe cast a quick look over to Maria's chest. So that was another thing ageing did to women. No wonder they had been so obsessed with keeping themselves young.

He turned his attention back to the book and carefully turned the pages. A slight tickle in his fingertips told him that magic had been worked on the paper, probably to preserve what was left of it. The pictures now showed the woman in different rooms – standing in the shower, sitting on a sofa, playfully outstretched on a bed – and outside in various natural environments.

"Who is she?" Moewe asked with a trace of awe in his voice.

"One of my ancestors," Maria said proudly. "This book has been in the possession of my family for several generations. My mother told me that this woman had been a fashion model and a soldier's wife. Her husband was called to arms when the first war against Wraeththu started, and he took the book with him and defended it as if it was his wife herself. A rather private memory of home to carry around, I admit." She winked at him. "When things went bad for humanity, my family held on to that book as a memory of times when humans had enough time and safety for the arts. And out of pride for having such a lovely woman in their family tree."

Curiously Moewe compared the woman in the book to Maria. "Did you look like her when you were young?"

The woman smiled. "Some men said I did."

Intrigued, the young har turned another page. The next photo made him gasp and widen his eyes.

The woman stood at a beach, arms outstretched, her face turned to the sky and lit by a summer sun. She was completely nude. Of course, Moewe had seen the diagrams at school and knew what human genitals looked like. Theoretically. The naked truth of what he saw made him shiver, because despite of all of what he knew about humans, he couldn't help seeing her as mutilated. Something was just missing. The thought of it sent an imaginary pain through his groin, which made him want to check if he was still whole himself.

And there was another thing that amazed him. "So... human women shaved, too?"

Maria chuckled. "Well, it's a matter of personal preference."

Moewe nodded absently. He had to admit that the woman in the pictures was indeed beautiful. Now, not *roonably* beautiful, but in a certain exotic kind of way. Like a satyr or a mermaid. A whole different species, totally unsuitable for aruna, but still kind of attractive.

While Moewe was just trying to find a category to sort in the woman's kind of beauty, he turned the page again — and then quickly closed the book.

"Oh, sweet Aruhani," he whispered.

Maria couldn't help giggling.

On the last page the woman had been lying in the sand of the beach. The camera had caught her from between her knees, which she had spread invitingly. Her look had been full of longing. A pink amaryllis flower had rested in her lap, just above her secret cave. For a moment, she had looked disturbingly harish.

"I'm really sorry," Maria said, suppressing another burst of laughter. "I thought you were grown-up enough for that now."

Moewe stared at her blankly. "I am grown up. But this was... most unsettling."

"Cookie?" Maria offered him another chocolate-covered disc as if it was an excuse.

Hesitantly Moewe accepted. He slowly chewed the cookie, until he had regained his calmness. "At least all my questions about human female anatomy have been answered." He showed Maria a crooked grin, which quickly changed into a more thoughtful expression. "But I have a question: If you looked that marvellous when you were young, why didn't you try to conserve your beauty?"

Maria shrugged. "I tried. It just didn't work out."

Moewe frowned. "A few minutes ago you said you didn't try inception."

"And that's true." Maria confirmed. "I didn't try to become parage, but I tried to become a mother and pass on my looks to the next generation. But it seems I'm unable to conceive."

Her mouth still smiled, but her eyes had developed a sad gleam. "I tried for a long time, and with a whole lot of different men. When I finally had to give up, because I had become too old, I had missed my chance for inception. Well, I wouldn't have chosen it anyway."

Moewe now felt a deep sympathy for her. He did not want to make her any more sad, but he had to ask one question. "Why is humanity so important to you that you sacrificed yourself?"

Maria now folded her hands on the table and smiled. "Because I am loyal to my race. I am proud to be human. Over the millennia of its existence, humanity had to face many challenges. Still, we developed many different cultures with different arts and sciences. You might not like the thought of it, but everything

Wraeththu has now is based on the work of humans. Wraeththu took over what already existed. They improved everything, but humanity brought the basics.

Of course, not all of us were scholars and scientists. There have always been destructive individuals, tyrants and emperors, who tried to enslave and suppress people. We had to struggle hard for our freedom — obviously in times of war and secretly in societies that wouldn't agree to certain lifestyles. In some centuries people were hunted and even tortured for nothing more than praying to a different god, or having a different skin colour or loving people of their own gender."

Moewe shook his head disapprovingly. "Now that's just plain stupid! Those are no reasons to hate anybody. Luckily, hara are enlightened enough to not ever have thought of such a thing."

Maria drove the arrogant smile from his face with just one word. "Fulminir."

Moewe blushed furiously. "That's... It was just..." He took a deep breath and sighed. "Damn. You're right."

Maria could not help smiling triumphantly. "You see, both of our races have their flaws. But then, Wraeththu are a lot tougher and use magic easily. Well, there also were great human magicians."

"There were?" Moewe asked, surprised.

Maria shook her head. "You didn't really pay attention to that in school, did you? Humanity delivered a lot of the theoretical magical knowledge upon which Wraeththu based their studies. It just doesn't come to us as naturally as it does to you. We have to work on our connection to the ethers. And even when we do so, we will never be as powerful as hara."

Moewe frowned. "Never as mighty or strong or healthy as hara... I still don't understand why this life is still so attractive to you."

Maria regarded him softly. "Because I admire our greatest trait: Willpower. Just as you say, we will never be as good as hara, but we still have the unbroken will to keep on trying. We have survived all the challenges in our existence as a race, and even as we had to face Wraeththu, we kept struggling. Don't you think a race like us does at least deserve a little chance to keep existing?"

Moewe blinked. "I never thought of it this way. But I think I understand now." He smiled carefully. "I think you... made a very brave decision. And I'm sorry to hear you never had children. It must be very hard to see your dream die."

Maria smiled back. "It is. But I am proud I tried to make it come true."

When Gull knocked on Maria's door again, thoughts rushed through his head. He had spent the last hours drinking tea at a café, silently praying to Miyacala that the dehar might help by granting his son the necessary understanding for humans. He hoped that Maria had taught him the respect that he had failed to teach his son. If there was anyone left who could reach Moewe, it was her.

The door opened and Maria smiled at him. "There you are!"

Gull clutched her hands excitedly. "Did it work out?"

Before the woman could answer him, his son showed up by her side, broadly grinning. He wore a blue, long skirt with a violet flower pattern, which Gull recognised as Maria's, and a white blouse which he had knotted over his chest in a harish manner. The sleeves were cut open up to the elbows and fluttered loosely around his arms when he dashed forward to hug his father.

Gull laughed and hugged him closely. "Seems like you two have been having fun."

"A lot of that!" Moewe agreed, winking at Maria.

His father gently pushed him aside. "Well, I'm sorry to interrupt then, but I have some more business with your new friend, now."

Moewe looked disappointed, so Gull added quickly: "There's a young fishmonger at the market who asked for you. I think you caught his eye when we arrived."

Moewe grinned. "Ah well, guess I have business of my own then. What a pity."

He turned around to face Maria. "Can I visit you some time soon?"

The woman smiled. "Of course you can. Ah, but I can't let you leave just yet."

She disappeared into the house. When she came back she carried a little cloth bag and the picture book.

Moewe eyed her curiously and pointed at the bag. "What's that?"

"More chocolate cookies."

The woman smiled and handed the bag over to the young har. "And this is yours now, too."

Moewe stared at the picture book with big round eyes. "Oh no, I can't keep that. You said it has always belonged to your family."

Maria shrugged. "And I am the last of the family. Someone has to keep watch over the old thing. Admit it, you like the thought of embarrassing your own harlings with the pictures in a few years."

Moewe smiled, took the book and hugged it to his chest. "Thank you very much. For everything."

"It was a pleasure getting to know you, Moewe." Maria replied warmly. "And now go. Don't keep your friend waiting." The young har laughed and waved goodbye.

Maria and Gull watched as Moewe walked and jumped down the road leading to the harbour. It had been a while since Gull had seen his son in such a good mood.

Maria now took him in his arms. "He's wonderful. And he has your eyes."

Gull smiled sadly. "You really aren't mad at me?"

Maria raised her eyebrows. "Because you chose inception? Don't be silly, grandfather. I'm happy for you that you had a chance to have more children after you became har. I was mad when you left grandmother, that's true. But I was only a little girl then. Now that I see what it was that you chose, I dare you to regret it."

The har chuckled and turned his gaze back to the point where Moewe had just disappeared.

"You really never told him where that scar came from, did you?" Maria mused while watching Gull absently stroking his left lower arm. A thin white line on his skin marked the vein below.

"Carpentry accident" the har mumbled shyly. Then he let out a deep sigh. "It's ridiculous being afraid to tell the truth because that would mean someone dear wouldn't like you anymore, isn't it?"

Maria smiled. "It's only human."

The Bridge

Martina Bellovičová

The Bridge

The Remembrance Hall, located in the oldest part of Phaonica palace, is dark and silent, a place rarely visited by anyhar but me and the househara who tend it. The picturesque layout of the long hall is dominated by twenty-five full-length portraits of the Aralisian rulers, their chesnaris and sons. I like to study details in the canvases and try to guess what kind of hara they used to be. Soon, I will have to return to my reality and attend a meeting that I've been afraid of for the past few weeks. For now, however, I can linger.

It's mainly the consorts who interest me. Were they gentle and submissive or did they manipulate the Tigrons? Were they well respected? Did they love their life in Immanion, or did they feel trapped sometimes? Isolia, the red-head, seems to have been somewhat flirtatious. I can see it in his posture, the gleam in his eyes, the way he tilts his head to the side. Morion, the last Tigrina but one, has a streak of harshness in his features. There's something wary about him, as if he were waiting to counter a blow that could come at any time. At the other end of the hall the first Tigrina, Caeru, shines with his pale beauty and loving eyes, even though his smile seems a little bitter.

My portrait will never adorn these walls, nor will one of my son. It's a pity; my Colurastes heritage would add a much-needed bit of exotic charm, but Camael already had two consorts when we bonded. The law provides that only the first can become a Tigrina. The act that allowed the Tigron of Immanion to be bonded with more than one chesnari had been adopted quite early in harish history, during the reign of the third Tigron. It caused an uproar in its time, but in the end the majority of the Hegemony supported it. After all, taking multiple wives from dependant or associated nations was a system that had once worked well for human emperors, and as many had pointed out, the first Tigron had two consorts himself.

I can still recall the first time I laid eyes on Camael. He was a vision in gold brocade, with long dark hair and eyes that, should they but choose, could invite and burn all in the same instant. As the delegation descended from the sky and galloped towards us, he and his *sedu* were a single body and soul, well capable of guiding hara safely through the Otherlanes. Their regal group came to an abrupt halt so close that I had to suppress the urge to step back. Instead, I forced myself to stare directly at him, bold and motionless. For an instant he looked back at me. It was just a moment in time, but a decisive moment, one that set me apart from the rest of our welcome delegation forever. They believed the Tigron came with the purpose of creating new bonds between our tribes and consolidating them, while I was deeply convinced he'd arrived in our corner of the world solely to tempt me with sweetness and seduction, let me taste his breath upon my lips and make me shed my soul for him.

In my relatively short life, I have been called many things, but naive isn't one of them. From the beginning, I knew it wasn't eternal love that had brought us together, and I was aware of my future position in the hierarchy. It was about time, he said, that all harish tribes, even remote ones like the Colurastes, entered the Alliance and pursued a common goal of peace and well-being. I was a part of that deal.

It was a challenge I had accepted, hoping to change the odds in my favour through trickery and seduction. It worked more often than not, or so I thought, until my son disappeared and I learned how little he meant to everyhar but me.

The sky was bright and the purest possible shade of blue, announcing a deceitfully optimistic day: Aspot, the day of the yellow sun. Perched on a massive tree branch, one leg dangling down on each side, Zulkah turned his face upwards and pouted. He hated days like this. There was no place to hide from the heat, no matter how deep into the trees he ventured, no matter how little he wore. The yellow sun was scorching, unlike the black one, the red one, or the sapphire one. On Aspots, Zulkah rarely left shelter, because his nearly see-through skin was sensitive and would form painful blisters.

He stretched, trying to make his branch more comfortable. Extending all his senses at the same time, he sniffed, tasted the air, and listened to the ethereal waves. New souls were being harvested not far away! Privately, he called it "rain", the term being slightly ironic. Back home in Kah'Lil, it generally only rained water, although there had been rumours about a day when red frogs had poured down from the sky. In this world, real rain was rare. However, the place acted as a magnet for lost souls like himself, misplaced in time and space. Every now and then, the sky would crack open and rain them down.

The incomers varied in age, gender, colour, and species. Sometimes, though, more of the same kind would appear during a certain time period, which could be considered a sign of trouble in the world from which they came. Zulkah was the only one of his kind there. Being a solitary specimen was risky; many of the other inhabitants of the world were stronger and could be considered various degrees of dangerous. Thankfully, most of the lost souls faced confusion, and were dealing with the loss of everything they had known in the past. They needed to find a way to survive in a strange environment, or perish. Such a predicament didn't leave anyone much energy to look for trouble. And then there was the Nameless... Zulkah rarely ever approached others. Being quite frail, his strength lay mostly in remaining unseen. He was an observer, a silent presence in the trees. Even here, where nature was an unknown and possibly hostile entity, he seemed to blend with it. But he was also lonely. Fortunately, time was on his side. One day, someone special would land on the planet and be grateful for being taken under Zulkah's wing.

Zulkah leaned against the tree and pulled one leg up on the branch, cautiously observing the sky. Perhaps it would happen sooner rather than later.

Two months ago, when I started attending Hegemony meetings, many high ranking-hara would raise a brow upon seeing me climb the stairs to my seat in the Hegalion that I had been ignoring for years. At present, they all know my predicament and have gotten used to my disruptive presence. When I walk through the main entrance, a number of heads turn to judge the stylishness of the clothes I am wearing, and the honesty of my smile, while the Tigrina pointedly looks away.

"Good afternoon, tiahaara."

A few answer me with greetings or nods. I notice deceptive calmness in everyhar's behaviour. Maybe what I deem to be of utmost importance is just another item on their list of duties for today: funds for a new academy in Megalithica – check; preparations for visitors from Alba Sulh – check; state budget for the next term – check; lost prince – check. It will be difficult to stand my ground.

Finally, the guards close the Hegalion's massive door from the outside and Chancellor Israfel rises to his feet, clears his throat, and opens the meeting. Regular problems are brought up first, mainly pertaining to complaints and requests from various tribes. Now that the Alliance has expanded into the entire world, there are always some. After two excruciating hours, Israfel turns a page in the heavy book he always carries to meetings and addresses the assembled Hegemony.

"And now, tiahaara, I would like to bring up an issue that has been troubling us for the better part of three months; the disappearance of Prince Thaniel. We have spent unaccountable amounts of time, skill, and funds in attempt to resolve it. We have employed our best seers, researchers and scientists, as well as practitioners of the highest caste and asked them to devote their undivided attention to the task at hand. We have performed multiple Grissecons. We have heard the testimony of the witnesses numerous times in the hope that their personal experience could give us some clue as to where to direct our actions. Yet all of this seems to have been in vain, and I'm sure I speak for all when I say that the time has come for a conclusion."

There is a vigorous murmur of what I believe to be mostly assent.

Israfel waits until the noise calms down before giving the others permission to speak.

"It appears you have already made your own decision, tiahaar Israfel?" one of the Hegemons asks carefully.

Israfel looks slightly nervous, but quickly collects himself. "It was not easy. After all, this is a member of the royal family whose life is in question, but... yes. Personally, I believe that we should accept that there is little hope we could still be successful in our search and pull back some, if not all, of our resources."

At this point, Ashtar speaks up. "Excuse me, tiahaar, but I find your words hard to believe." He is my biggest hope today. As the Commander of the EaB division, a specially-trained unit for exploring the realms of the Ethers and Beyond, he is facing the danger that the blame for the failed expedition could fall on his head. It is in his interest to prove his worth and show that EaB is able to correct its own mistakes. "We are fearless enough to travel into space," he says, "we do not shy away from any challenges we may face there and, in the past thirty years, we have made considerable progress in mapping the universe. Naturally, when embarking on such a journey, one always accounts for possible casualties, but in my opinion tiahaar Thaniel is not necessarily one of them. He was alive and well when we last saw him. It seems unreasonable and premature to give up the search."

"I think we should wait to hear the Tigron's opinion on this matter," somehar chimes in.

All the eyes turn to Camael.

I want him to look at me, but he ignores my subtle mind touch and overlooks the entire Hegalion with a serene expression, before nodding in Israfel's general direction. Anger squeezes my throat, and I mentally thank myself for having imprisoned my hair in a tight bun, or else it would intimidate everyhar in my immediate proximity. I know what Camael is going to say, even before he opens his mouth, yet for a moment I allow myself the luxury of doubt.

"Tiahaar Israfel and I have discussed the issue extensively," Camael says in a gentle yet dismissive tone, dissolving my hope instantly, "and have considered all of its aspects. What everyhar should realise is that the real question is not whether we want to give up. It is whether there is anything we can do that we have not yet tried. And if the answer is no, can we really afford to keep up our current activities?"

I don't expect anyhar will come up with an idea. They have been debating this back and forth for the past three months. Everything has been said and done. One can almost hear the wheels in their brains turning. Into the hovering silence, I clear my throat and speak: "We could ask the dehara for help."

The silence changes from ponderous to shocked. The Tigrina laughs shortly, fanning himself with a dainty hand, as if to show that he is trying to hold back a much more spectacular reaction. A few hara start whispering with their neighbours and Camael is glaring at me. Now I clearly have his attention. "The dehara?" he repeats as if he hadn't heard correctly.

"They can see the universe in its complexity, or so I believe.

Perhaps with their help, one could find a lost soul in the realms our minds cannot reach on their own."

The Tigrina frowns. "You speak nonsense!" He aims to discredit me. "Have you ever seen a dehar in your life?"

I shake my head, dejectedly.

"Has anyhar you know ever seen one?"

I can see where this is going. "Not here in Immanion, but among my tribe, hara still worship our dehar, Ophidien, and perform rituals to honour him. We do not consider ourselves so almighty as to believe we can challenge any force in the Universe completely unaided."

Unexpectedly, it is the Chancellor who tries to make peace. "Based upon old records, what tiahaar Lorca is saying is not entirely preposterous. Some of you may remember the tale of the great war, in which Tigron Pellaz and his family fought against Ponclast the Varr. Ultimately, it was connection with the dehara that helped them win the war."

The Tigron smiles, giving us an apologetic smile. "It is an old tale, though, so old that it might as well be a myth. The first ruler of any nation is always material for legends. It's likely, the so-called dehara were just a projection of Pellaz's own magical abilities rather than help from the outside."

"But maybe we could..."

Camael stops me in mid-sentence. "Lorca, this discussion is getting widely unproductive." He gives me a 'we-will-have-a-talk-later' glare, then directs his attention to everyhar else in the chamber. "Any other suggestions, tiahaara...?"

Thaniel had been suspecting that it wasn't a mechanical disturbance that caused their ethereal ship to stop, but as the leader of the expedition, he took it upon himself to leave the presumptive safety of the ship and inspect the parts only accessible from the outside. Time was relative here, but it took him about half an hour to check the entire surface inch by inch. By the time he was about to finish, he had fallen into a misleading state of tranquillity. No danger appeared to be looming, and the whole universe was at his disposal. Right in front of his eyes, there was the entirety of space and time, all forms of matter, energy and momentum, and the physical laws and constants that govern them.

Face to face with such a sight, he couldn't help but wonder, whether he could somehow untie the knots of multiple universes and wrap himself into their threads, absorb their essence and gain the ability to direct the entire haradom towards the most plausible fate. If he could stop everything from moving, and capture the sparkling turmoil under the glass jar of his mind for a single moment, he felt he would reach absolute understanding. Yet at the same time, he knew it was impossible. The universe was expanding, evolving, becoming. It was organic. It was alive. The experience was exhilarating, explosive and liberating.

He was about to open the last external tank, the content of which – a product of Grissecon – was glimmering so powerfully that it was visible through the surface, when suddenly a gush of energy slammed him against the ship's body. In the next moment, he was being jerked in the opposite direction. The ship's door opened and somehar moved to pull him inside, but they weren't quick enough. He felt like he was being swept away by a supernatural hurricane, taken apart into the smallest particles and put together again someplace else.

Only with great difficulty was he able to regain his senses, to find some vague sort of balance and spatial orientation in a place that lacked the usual definitions of right, left, under and above. His eyes turned downwards automatically and he perceived nothing but the universe in its vastness, coiling and uncoiling. It only lasted for a moment, before everything faded and he found himself rushing through a void.

The darkness in the tunnel was full of whispers, malicious, and breathing with danger. At times, it was as if he were listening to sounds made by tiny wings, countless insect surrounding him, but once he started to pay attention, he realised there were indeed voices. And there were shadows, creeping along what he could have called walls, if this were the world he knew... Shadows darker than darkness, so black that they shone with anti-light. He started screaming, but supernatural wind carried all sounds away from his lips.

When he opened his eyes again, the world stood still and the ground was hard and uncomfortable beneath his back. Above him, a blinding, odd-coloured sun was scorching the land and draining his energy. He must have lost consciousness during his fall and regained it after being stranded . . . where? Thaniel attempted to lift himself up onto his elbows, but only managed to do so on the third attempt. His entire body felt like it had been run over by a herd of sedim. *Despair was drawing near and what he saw only worsened his mental state. A bright red desert stretched around him in all directions, except for a little group of trees he could see far away to his right. It occurred to him to look over his shoulder. That was when he saw it, an elven being, barefoot and almost nude, observing him from behind a large stone.*

At sunset, Camael finds me on the large balcony overlooking the sea, where we sometimes hold banquets for his closest friends. I can sense his presence even before he enters through the sliding door, and I feel him walk in my direction. He stops right behind me, his breath warming my hair, and stays there for the longest moment, motionless and silent. The sky is clear and dotted with a myriad glowing stars.

The air behind my right ear tingles ever so slightly, enough for me to discern that his hand had risen to touch my shoulder, but never finished its movement before falling away. Not so many years ago, this sensation would have been erotic, but today it only makes me anxious. I catch myself wondering if he simply doesn't know what to say to me, or if there is another reason for his hesitation. Could he possibly be thinking about pushing me over the railing? No, of course not, he is the Tigron, for Ag's sake! Finally, I turn around to face him.

"Lorca..." His sounds both frustrated and saddened, as if I am making him upset and he is already losing his patience with me, even though I haven't said anything yet. His eyes seem a little wild. "You have to be reasonable. It breaks my heart too, it really does, but one day we will have to accept that Thaniel is lost to us and try to move on with our lives. We might as well start now; there is no point in deluding ourselves."

I hate the tone he uses, like I'm a harling who needs to be placated and has no right to an opinion. "One day, maybe!" I snap. "But that day is in the distant future for me. And... thinking about it, maybe not even then. In the same way you don't stop being a hostling once your pearl has grown up, you can't lose hope in bringing your son back unless you have seen his dead body. I don't understand how it's possible that you feel it differently. Maybe my way of thinking is the one of the hostling, but more likely you just don't give a damn."

"I *do*... care, Lorca." Camael avoids repeating the swear word after me.

I snort at that. Come to think of it, I have never heard him speak in a way that couldn't be considered regal, except in bed.

"I understand this is impossible for you to imagine," he says, "but unlike you, I have to take more than my family and friends into consideration. My view is necessarily broader because the entire fate of Wraeththu lies on my shoulders. I cannot impair the haradom for the sake of one har lost in space, no matter who that har is."

"That, or you are perfectly happy with the sons you'd already had when we met."

Camael bares his teeth slightly; I have offended him. "Now you are just being crude", he says, and then puts a hand on my shoulder.

My hair twists and coils, belligerently attacking his wrist. He retreats, anger flashing in his eyes.

"Alright, enough is enough! First, you embarrass me in the Hegalion, now this. If hara saw…"

"If hara saw? Is that all you care about, public appearance?"

Before I can prevent it from happening, my palm connects with his face. He is quick to grab my wrist, so the strike loses much of its force, but still produces a slapping sound. We stare at each other, eyes wide open, dumbfounded by what has just happened, because it never has before. For a moment, I sense in him an immense power that could crush me like a beetle. Ironically, this fleeting moment also makes me glimpse the har I had fallen for. It only lasts a short time, yet I lean over him and kiss his throat anyway. It is better than ripping it apart.

"You little viper," he hisses, grabbing a fistful of my hair, simultaneously letting go of my wrist.

I allow myself a triumphant smile.

The journey to my rooms is rushed and silent. Not everything can be resolved in bed, but it doesn't hurt to try.

Camael moves into the room, his grace a liquid thing as he lights a flame in a branched candelabra. He always likes to see my skin in candle light; it is like copper or gold, he says, and such am I too; a precious and beautiful thing, though tough and resilient. We sink into the silken sheets and he closes his eyes, baring his neck, waiting for the bite. I drop my robes and cover his pearly body with liquid gold and flowing darkness. He whimpers only a little as I sink my teeth into his skin. This is what he always comes for. Some pure born Colurastes have poison in their bite; mine is a powerful aphrodisiac. The Tigron craves the drug.

His ouana-lim presses against the boundaries of my soume-lam, stretching and slipping inside, slowly, as I lie waiting with daggers and kisses, unsure which ones to use. *Well then, once beloved, what shall I do with you? Shall I plant soft kisses on your neck? Offer you a safe haven of warm thighs? Let your own passion flow... Don't wrench my soul, as I know you will. When lust is sated, give me the reward you know I deserve, because rather than hate, I offer you willingly the sweetest of things tonight.*

Camael's flesh is warm and taut beneath my lips. He tastes of jasmine, power and lust, spiced by anger. His flesh inside me is warm and pulses with blood, boiling with my poison. Like the experienced practitioner in the art of aruna that I am, I bring both of us to ecstasy, but for some reason, even when he explodes within me, I don't feel complete. Pleasure, I realise, is not what I was after.

Side by side, we rest in silence, Camael's breath slowly returning to normal. He could be just moments away from falling asleep, but I am wide awake and expectant.

"So...?" I kiss the place on his neck where I had bitten him earlier... once, twice, three times, until he opens his eyes.

"So what?"

"Have you... changed your opinion?"

The relaxed, satisfied expression immediately leaves his face, replaced by displeasure. "I am sorry, dear. You cannot buy me with something that is rightfully mine." With that, he throws off the blanket and collects his clothing. Before opening the door, he at least has the decency to wish me good night.

I feel somehow dirty, like a kanene – we didn't even share breath. Actually, it is worse, I feel like a kanene, whose customer has run away without paying.

Sleep is elusive; various memories of Thaniel keep swarming in my head and attacking my nerves. They sting with red hot pain, each of them an open wound that can never heal. It's not that I am a clingy hostling, who cannot exist independently without knowing what his adult harling is doing all day. It's not even the fact that I am unable to overcome loss. No, it is not his death that I fear; it is the idea that he may be alive somewhere, lost and wandering in an unknown and possibly hostile world. Perhaps he is falling into an agony of madness, brought on by the fear of having to spend the rest of his life, which may be hundreds of years, in complete solitude. Maybe he is holding on to life with the last of his powers, devoid of nourishment, and days will decide whether he will live or die.

Suddenly, the door creaks.

"Want some more?" I bark into the darkness, certain that it is Camael, even though quite some time has passed since he left. "Is this why you brought me to Immanion?"

There is no answer and no other sound My late night guest walks like a cat. This can't be Camael. At the same time, I am certain my guards would never let an unknown person enter my rooms. The fragrance of gardenias, rich, lush and velvet, complimented with dewy jasmine and spiced incense, pervades the room. It is most pleasant and mysterious.

"It's me," says a voice, so soft it could belong to a harling. The har steps out of the darkness and into the small silvery pool of moonlight that the gap between the curtains lets through. He looks like an apparition in his old-fashioned night gown, subtle face framed by a veil of thick honey-coloured hair that falls almost to his knees. His pale skin is almost translucent, which makes him seem even more fragile than he really is, a trait he developed because he rarely ever leaves his rooms.

"Shaya...?"

He offers me a gentle smile. "May I sit down for a while?"

"Oh... yes, yes, of course."

Shay is another of Camael's consorts. He swiftly crosses the distance between us and makes himself comfortable on the bed next to me, where I have just recently taken aruna with our chesnari.

"Unfortunately, I cannot offer you any refreshments at this time of day..." I smile back at him, trying to pretend it is completely normal for us to have a chat in the middle of the night, while simultaneously attempting to wrap my mind around it.

"Don't worry about it. I will send my househara to the kitchen before I go back to sleep."

We have never spoken alone, just the two of us, though I would have liked to. Unlike the Tigrina, Shaya doesn't hate me, despite having been Camael's chesnari before my arrival at court, and the Tigrina doesn't hate Shaya, because he doesn't consider him a danger. Shaya sleeps most of the time. Camael had found him while visiting the ever so elusive tribe of Dreamers, who reside high in the mountains, hidden from the world, and spend their lives dreaming the past, present, and future of haradom. The young har hadn't given up on the habit when he became the Tigron's chesnari. It seems almost surreal to see him sitting next to me and to hear him address a question that wasn't originally meant for him to answer.

"Do you want to know why you were brought to Immanion?" He understands my silence as confirmation. "Because I dreamed about you."

I can't suppress a gasp. "You dreamed about *me*...?"

Shaya nods, putting a small hand on mine to ease my discomfort. "It was a dream I believed to be very important for our future. In it, I saw a Colurastean – you – ride into Immanion with a harling in your arms. I assume it was Thaniel, because his eyes were blue like his father's. Hara were expecting you and celebrated your arrival, and then the Tigron himself thanked you for teaching us such an important lesson."

I sighed. "See? It was just an ordinary dream. Camael would never do that."

We both laughed, but Shaya was evidently very serious about what he'd come to tell me. "I don't simply *have* dreams like a normal har," he explains, "my mind analyses them at the same time and decodes the hidden, some call it prophetic, meaning. Thanks to the dream that involved you, I learned about the significance of your tribe, the Colurastes, grossly misunderstood and always feared in some way or another, even by themselves. The sacred serpent of regeneration lies in their hearts, whilst ineptitude surrounds them in a haze of evasion that has sprung directly from their own insecurities. Do you even know your entire potential?"

"I don't suppose so," I admit, weighing his words. Despite my initial scepticism towards Dreaming, he is awakening something deep inside of me. I can feel it.

"You can make a change," he says, as if reading my mind.

"I wish I knew how."

"You *will* know in time," he assures me and it sounds as if those simple words are fuelled by an inherent source of knowledge to which only he has access.

A wave of emotions rises inside me, along with uncertain sorrow for this gentle being. "Aren't you sad that you dream your life away sometimes?" I ask him gently, sweeping the mass of hair away from his face.

He thinks about it for a while, then shakes his head. "Not really, no. It is painless, and some of us have to live our lives this way so that others can live theirs."

With that, he lightly kisses me on the cheek and disappears silently the way he came.

In the long, solemn hours that separate midnight from dawn, I lie curled on the bed, the quilt tucked beneath me so that it feels like I am nestled in a burrow, waiting for the sun to warm my ice cold flesh. I lie sleepless, contemplating not defeat, but action. Now more than ever, I realise that I was not meant for this golden cage. Though bonded by blood and long gone love, or the illusion of love, which is essentially one and the same thing, inside I have not been moulded.

They might have made me adapt, yet they have not tamed me. You can pick up a fistful of earth, hold it in your hands. You can shape it, burn it and break it into pieces. Water flows, but it will hold shape in a container. But fire… only one of two things can happen to fire enclosed in a box. It will die out, smothered for lack of nourishment, or it will burn down the sides of the box, flickering merrily at your futile attempts to catch it.

Zulkah approached the new being cautiously, circling it several times before offering him a desert star. It was a kind of fruit or vegetable that grew under earth, drawing nutrition from underground water. It held a lot of fluid that the stranger obviously needed, and could substitute for lack of containers to carry water in. When the new one didn't seem to be accepting it, Zulkah placed it at a distance he could easily reach and took a few steps backwards.

Thaniel regarded Zulkah with wonderment — a weird feyling with tangled hair and translucent skin that didn't burn in the sun, out in the wilderness for so long that his movements resembled those of an animal; he was willowy and tough. Thaniel's heart was beating fast; however, it was the novelty of the situation and a sense of the mysterious, rather than fear, that quickened his pulse. He was struck by a disorienting sense of otherness that was familiar from dreams, but that had never before overcome him while awake. Slowly, he reached for the fruit and tentatively smelled it before biting down. Both its odour and taste was rather putrid, but he had no choice other than to swallow the juices, as his thirst was excruciating.

The elven being smiled appreciatively and put his hand on his chest where the heart was. "Zulkah," he said with distinct articulation. Then, he gestured towards the har.

"Thaniel," he said, then tried to repeat Zulkah's name.

Zulkah nodded, obviously pleased with the successful communication, and started to say something in an unintelligible language dominated by nasals and vocals. Thaniel put a finger on his lips to silence Zulkah and attract his attention. There was only one way the two of them could communicate, provided the being was of a high enough spiritual level. That needed to be tried out. He opened his mind like a book, attempting to touch Zulkah's consciousness, not really breach it, but feel its edges and slowly pry. Surprisingly, maintaining the link was relatively easy, much like it would be with a harling, who has the necessary ability but lacks practice.

"Zulkah?"

The other jerked a little at the sudden voice inside of his head.

"Don't be afraid, please. I don't speak your language, so this is a way we can communicate. You have some experience with it, am I right?"

Zulkah nodded. "It has been some time since I could use it. Not here, back at home."

Thaniel breathed out in relief. "This is not your world then, either? Where are we? How do we get out? Tell me, please!"

"There is a theory that this world acts like a magnet for wanderers of the universe. Many beings lost in the Ethers turn up here, few of them from the same place or of the same species. For those coming in, the atmosphere is like a sponge; it sucks them in and safely brings them to the ground. But for those who wish to leave, it is more like a mirror. The alleyways between the worlds are full of discarnate souls who never quite made it to the other side."

On the surface, life in Immanion hasn't changed for me. Nature still graces us with nothing but excellent weather – courtesy of our hienamas, who have mastered the skill of controlling the weather. Air coaches still roam the sky and ships frequent the port. Big and small problems are being discussed in the Hegalion, now without my presence once more, and the Tigrina is still a grudging nuisance. My exotic appearance still makes me a fine addition to every party and Camael still visits me every now and then for a roon or two, pretending nothing ever happened. Nonetheless, everything is different.

I feel like a caged tiger, powerful in his quietness and undeniably dangerous if given the chance. More than ever before, I spend my private time in meditation or working on raising my caste. When the time comes, I want to be ready. At first, it doesn't occur to me that everything is the other way around - time is waiting for me. It depends exclusively on my own readiness. This new piece of knowledge gives me a sense of restlessness I cannot get rid of.

When the semi-annual Solstice Ball approaches, I feel as if I am about to explode. It doesn't help that the palace is full of hara from various tribes, each of whom is overflowing with a unique sort of energy, the total of which is completely overwhelming to my senses. The beast at the bottom of my soul, the untamed core, is impatient and ready to strike. I feel the urge to dance until my limbs ache and my head spins, to drink myself into oblivion, to be admired, touched, kissed and taken, taken hard. Only then would I feel that I am still me – one of the Tigron's chesnaris, the serpent, the seducer.

I make my hair even more lustrous and bead it with black pearls, slip into my favourite robe, line my eyes with kohl, and oil my skin. Rather than run, I force myself to walk to the ballroom, where I place myself strategically onto an elevated platform, close to the fruit bowl, which means I can both be seen in my festive glory and get drunk at the same time. Unfortunately, before I manage to pick my victim for the first dance, I see that Camael is making his way towards me with an unknown har in tow.

"Ah, Lorca, here you are! Aislinn, meet Lorca, my chesnari who I've been telling you about… Lorca, tiahaar Aislinn is going to be our new Hegemon to oversee the relationships between tribes.

"I am very pleased to meet such a fabled beauty," the har

smiles, and I decide immediately I don't like him, partially because Camael told him something about me, which is always suspicious.

"The pleasure is all mine," I say automatically and let him kiss my hand.

"Well, I have other guests to attend to, so I thought that you could maybe keep Aislinn company," my chesnari suggests with a smile, but it is clearly an order. "He has been looking forward to meeting you."

"Of course, that will be no problem at all," I seethe between my teeth. My evening has just been destroyed.

Even though Aislinn tries to pay me compliments and amuse me with stories from his home town in Megalithica, I remain politely noncommittal, until he finally announces that he feels tired. Happy that I will finally rid myself of the unwelcome company, I agree to show him to his rooms.

As soon as I open the door for him to enter and wish him good night, his tongue is in my mouth. It only takes half a second for me to realise that this doesn't feel pleasant at all and I instinctively bite down. My mouth fills with blood and Aislinn starts to panic.

"Calm down!" I hiss. "I'll call a healer, it will be alright!" While spitting around myself, I try to hold him down; Camael would be less then pleased, if Aislinn reappeared in the ballroom like this, claiming I injured him. Thanks to my hair, I quickly gain an advantage in our wrestling. Perhaps I squeeze a bit too much in my attempt to silence him, I don't know, but all at once his fear makes him think unguarded, loud thoughts, and I clearly hear them. He doesn't understand why all of this happened. He had been told that I would keep him company.

Disgusted, I drop Aislinn on the floor and, without waiting for him to make any more noise, I quickly exit the room, aiming for the back entrance of the palace, the one that the kitchen and stable hara have to use, so that they don't mingle with higher castes. I have had more than enough today; the choice is to leave or to take my anger out on the first har I meet. I storm past the confused guards and out into the night, into the streets of the city below.

Immanion is alive with music, quite different from the violins and harps in the ballroom. The commoners are enjoying their own

Solstice celebration, and it calls to me with the sounds of drums and whistles and laughter and singing voices, some of them off-tune. Yet I don't make an attempt to join in. Instead, I head to the sea, where I can still hear them clearly, yet at the same time release all the emotions and pent up energy that have accumulated within me. It is time, I feel it. I am ready.

The rhythm of the drums is easy to follow, so I slip out of my shoes and begin to dance. My body remembers these movements from before Immanion, all the mad spinning around the fire that often held me until I fainted in ecstasy. The sand is still warm and feels pleasant beneath my feet. My hair welcomes the summer breeze and starts to dance on its own. The songs follow one after another, without a break in the maddening tempo, and it seems that as my excitement escalates, so does the music, as if governed by my innermost feelings.

Throughout the inhabited world, in all times and under every circumstance, myths have flourished – and the very imagination of 'beyond' is the secret opening through which the inexhaustible energies of the cosmos pour into mortal minds and bodies. Channelling my life-force towards a dehar I believe is out there but cannot truly identify, I realise I shouldn't do so empty-handed.

What offering do you make to an unknown dehar? I don't have any idea, but all I can give is my own blood. In mid motion, I bite my own arm enough to draw blood and finish full circle, letting the scarlet droplets decorate the sand. The music stops and, for a moment, reality is only me on the beach, with my quickened breath and the stars above laughing at my foolishness. Then, everything goes dark. This is the original darkness that must have been everywhere at the very beginning of all life. Then, a sudden shift in the air, a mysterious change, not exactly a sound or a physical movement, nothing that could be described, yet it is undeniably there.

"Hello..? Is anyhar here?"

"Lorca... I am here." The voice sounds like sheh poured into an expensive crystal glass. Along with it, I sense an unspoken yet heartfelt invitation deep in my soul. I bow my head and offer my sincere greetings to Ophidien, the dehar of the Colurastes. Around me, the stars begin to shine once more, brighter than ever. The air seems to be made of light itself and through it, I can see multiple galaxies, swirling in slow-motion, worlds dying and being born. It is like being pulled into the heart of fire, which doesn't burn, but fills you with energy and warmth.

"Welcome in my Nayati."

I dare to look up and behold a being who appears to be the most perfect har, covered with shimmering scales. Living hair frames his face, dominated by snake-slit eyes. When he smiles, fangs flash in his mouth, while around us, stars begin to fall.

I know this place from a dream I never dared to dream, the most serene place, where those who are worthy learn the magic of knowledge and creativity to make their own map of reality, the patterns of as above, so below.

"Thank you for letting me come to you." I bow to him again and he invites me to step closer with a simple gesture.

"I am not at all surprised you approached me."

I smile, because these words seem to be a form of praise.

"In some ways, the Colurastes embrace the very essence of Wraeththu, as the serpent has long been the ultimate symbol for androgyny, life renewal and magic. Your tribe is more important than you imagine – and you are, of course, the finest example of your people. Gelaming pomposity didn't change your core, which still innately remembers the time when dehara were respected."

"They said you were just a projection of something we created in our heads," I recall, and then completely discard that opinion. However Ophidien came to exist, I know I'm not simply making him up. Maybe our expectations indeed give shape to a dehar's physical appearance, maybe our effort calls him into being, but the concept itself, the potent energy of which the deities are created, is truly ancient – older than us, older than humans, whom none of the contemporary hara have ever seen, older than time itself.

"But you felt different." He leans closer and cups my cheek in his hand. It makes me gasp with both surprise and intense feeling. A river of soft, velvet pleasure licks at my skin, spreading further, making me think about the fine line between the proximity of two bodies and magic, and how the two could become one on this plane, with this supernatural entity.

"The feeling of an untold destiny has been encoded into the genes of every Colurastes who ever lives, or has lived, to remind them that they are the core of their race. At the same time, the duality of the serpent makes them elusive – they use their gifts in seclusion, while the much simpler Gelaming rule. As such, you are feared weapons rather than respected leaders. You, Lorca, could be the bridge between the two poles; I know that in you."

His words make me shiver because they reach to the bottom of my soul, making me feel naked. I don't want to think about my own future and my purpose, not right now, but I am ready to promise anything. "Can you tell me where my son is and how I can bring him back? If this is what I need to do to gain help from you, I will do it."

The dehar turns to me, his hair twisting violently like hungry serpents, gazing into the bottom of my soul, or maybe stripping it bare, I am not sure, with the gaze of a snake, focused, never blinking.

"This is not a *favour* I am asking, Lorca. It is the potential you either have to embrace or reject. No, I cannot tell you, because some things cannot be simply told. They have to be experienced." He reaches out to me, light pooling in his palm and overflowing on both sides like a waterfall. "Accept all I am offering and prepare to make changes, or return to your life as you knew it."

Suddenly, I realise that I want more than just to find Thaniel. I am drawn to the source of light and knowledge; I want to bathe in it, swallow it, and let it thoroughly transform me. I take Ophidien's hand and the light penetrates my flesh, making me instantly aroused. It is a simple trick, but it works on me.

"I accept."

The ground beneath my feet shifts and as I lose balance; it surprises me that the fall is not painful at all. The floor has transformed into an insubstantial covering, softer than a quilt. Ophidien, moving like a snake, is lowers himself down to kneel between my thighs and lets cold blue fire consume his robes. His scaly skin is soft and sleek as he slides up between my legs to embrace me.

"Good decision," he says. "It would have been such a waste."

The sharing of breath shakes my world. A shimmering of white, freezing energy licks at my mind, while my body is being scorched by the fire of his touch. It is as if a portal has opened right before me and, through it, I can see the universe exploding in bold colours. For an instant, I understand everything about our existence, its origin and its purpose. The knowledge leaves me as soon as our lips part, but a calming shade of it remains.

Ophidien watches in amusement as I shiver with desire, my soume-lam trickling with moisture. It came naturally that I would be soume for him, though I have heard terrifying stories about hara who were damaged by taking aruna with higher beings. I am not even certain if what I am currently experiencing is purely metaphysical or not. It is exciting, standing on the edge of a precipice, with wings outstretched, flying too near to the sun and falling into the abyss, screaming in consternation and gasping in pleasure.

Each touch erases some of the remaining fears and when our hair intertwines, I lose all inhibitions, unable to suppress the natural reactions of my body. Needy, I lock our bodies together with one leg thrown around the dehar's back, which presses me against the hardness of his ouana-lim. It slides into me without the usual ruthlessness of hara, who are interested only in reaching their own pleasure quickly. It is like a thumping heart of fire slowly sinking into an ocean, sending a new wave of heat into the cold waters with every beat. We share breath again and he pulls out almost to the limit, leaving me begging, and as he moves forwards again, I feel all the levels in me opening at once.

This is the art of aruna at its finest, as I have rarely experienced it, the sacred combination of passion and magical energy that can destroy or build entire cities upon release. But instead, something else happens, something I only realise at the stab of red hot pain that disturbs my pleasure. My cauldron of creation has been forced open. Ophidien silences my forming scream by placing his lips on mine. The ultimate release is unavoidable, and as the world around me dissolves into darkness, he plants his seed into me.

"Dance for me again the next full moon", Ophidian says, before I fall into unconsciousness. "Then you will have all your answers."

Thaniel and Zulkah had been hiding in the underground cave for what seemed an eternity, but might have been less than an hour, backs pressed on the wall, holding hands for added security. Everything was resonating through

a deafening howling sound coming from the surface; little stones rolled and jumped across the ground. Thankfully, there were no stalactites or stalagmites or any other bigger structures that could fall and harm them.

The har squeezed Zulkah's hand. "What is it? What's happening outside?"

"We call it The Nameless." Their communication had become completely natural, Zulkah's mind touch gentle as a whisper. "It always comes on the last day of the sapphire sun. All the beings on this planet know by now and are wise enough to hide. Otherwise, you can't survive. The first time I experienced it, there was a group of Hunters not far away. I was hiding from them, which saved my life. They froze on the spot, and so did I. I felt watched, intimately scrutinized, my fullest measure taken in ways unknowable and profound. And there was a sound, just like rain, but not completely. Something beyond it. My chest tightened in fear as I felt something coming down. Like in a dream where you run and you run, but you can't get away. A crushing weight somewhere up there. A growing pressure. When we could finally breathe, the hurricane came. They were taken, all of them, or burnt alive by a fire that resulted from the storm."

"Is it always like this? No one has tried to do anything to prevent it besides hiding or even understand it?"

"Oh, you can't fight it! It would be like trying to change the weather or make a river change its direction!"

Thaniel wanted to say that the hienamas back on Earth had already mastered both of those things, but decided there was no reason why he should. Depression was threatening to take him over. How can you exist in a world, where your life is as fragile as the life of a kitchen mouse?

The next full moon finds me burning sage, standing under the night sky in a circle of candles. It wasn't easy to place them one by one; I have not been feeling well ever since the supernatural conception. The pearl isn't restricting me in terms of movement just yet, but I can feel its hard, round shape in my belly when I bend down. The Moon and the constellations are the same as a month ago, the beach, however, is different.

Camael did not take it well when the healers confirmed that my sudden bouts of illness were caused by the fact I am with pearl. He knew too well he wasn't the father. I could have told him the truth, but he wouldn't have believed it, and in fact I didn't really mind being sent away to live in one of his smaller properties an hour away from the city. It was peace I needed most now, to concentrate on my task.

Every day, I spend a considerable amount of time meditating or visualising the dance I will perform. In the evenings, I sit on the beach and talk to my pearl, like I used to talk to Thaniel when I was carrying him. I have a lot to think about – such as what it will be like to deliver a pearl created with a dehar. But there will be time for that later. Tonight, I shall dance.

The sounds of conflict echoed in the darkness of the underground cave. Zulkah clearly thought he had Thaniel pinned down, but the har was in fact trying to free himself only half-heartedly, because he knew he could easily overpower his new friend and deliver an hard blow.

"Let me go", he finally gasped, and flipped them around with one fluid movement, so that he was pinning Zulkah down. "This is my decision and you have to respect it."

"But you will die, don't you understand?" Zulkah screamed, tears glistening in his eyes.

Thaniel felt incredible pity for his companion. He would be staying in this place alone, under conditions that Thaniel wasn't able to stand even with another, much less on his own. "Zulkah... listen to me," he whispered, the urgent tone of his words adding importance to the message he was telepathically sending. "My hostling has been talking to me ever since the last Nameless. I hear him almost every day. Among other things, he is telling me about a ritual he is performing – to bring me home, and it is NOW. I have to go out. If I am to ever go home, I have to."

"Haven't you ever considered the fact that you were hallucinating?"

"Do I look like a madman to you?"

"No," Zulkah admitted and reluctantly removed his hands from Thaniel's, curling up on the cold ground. "I will miss you..."

Thaniel is aware that Zulkah is convinced that his only friend will die; no one has ever survived the Nameless, but perhaps a quick death is better than a life of despair.

Outside, the sky darkens from blue to ink-blue to black, and the raging cosmic storm paints incredible colours on that canvas. Thaniel has little time to admire them. He manages to take only a few steps before the wind picks up his body and throws it at a nearby rock, shattering it. The last thing he sees are the folds of an enormous snake's body trailing on the sky all the way to the horizon.

Exhausted, I fall into the sand. All the energy I had for the ritual has left me and I can hardly even drag myself up into a sitting position, yet Ophidien is nowhere to be seen. Something is wrong. I must have failed because of my condition; I must not have given it my all like the last time. Will there be another chance next full moon? Would I even be able to try, two months with pearl?

As I fall into despair, suddenly the sky explodes in a myriad of colours and a portal opens, through which the cosmic serpent himself rushes into my reality. Yes, the serpent, which is a symbol of the all-in-all, the totality of existence, infinity and the cyclic nature of the cosmos. It is flying directly towards me, threatening to knock me down. I am too weak to get out of the way, so I only close my eyes before the impact. However, there isn't any: he simply flies right through me. As it happens, I sense Thaniel's presence. Not in the physical sense... It feels more like being intensely loved. Being hugged from the inside.

Thaniel is picking the biggest grapes from the bowl I earlier placed in front of him on the oakwood table, perched on the edge of his chair. His legs are dangling in the air; he has a lot of growing to do until he can comfortably use all the furniture. I don't mind that; in fact I am thoroughly enjoying the extra time we have been given. The months when a harling is dependent on you in every respect are the most treasured ones for every hostling.

"Quit playing with food," I reprimand him when I notice he has stopped eating. Instead, he has lined the grapes up on the table, moving them in circles every now and then.

He looks up with all seriousness, as if offended, and points to a group of grapes. "I'm making the universe. This is the Sun, the Moon, the Earth, and Venus..."

"And that one?" I ask, meaning a lonely green sphere, as far away as his small arms could reach. At first, I wasn't sure if I shouldn't be worried about the strange memories that keep surfacing in him more and more frequently, but eventually I realised he never seems to be troubled by them.

"Different world. Far away." He pauses, uncertain for a moment. "I have a friend there."

"Would you like to visit him?" I ask out of curiosity.

Thaniel quickly shakes his head no and makes a face.

I kiss him on the top of his head, laughing. This time around, he will definitely stay away from the EaB.

"But I'd like to visit father."

That's a new one that I didn't see coming, even though it was logical that if he remembered his stay on a remote planet, he would recall Camael as well. Personally, I could live without returning to the palace for an infinite period of time, but I know too well that it is something I will have to face sooner or later, if only because I have promised it to Ophidien.

"Father?" I am trying to buy time. "What do you know of him, anyway?"

"He looks a lot like me and lives in a huge house on a hill. Hara bow to him, but he gets annoyed by that. He is always tired and stressed, because he works all the time."

The idea of Camael as a busy, troubled har, who gets annoyed if his titles are being used in conversation, is foreign to me. What I remember is the har who sent me away when I disgraced him by carrying somehar else's pearl. I wonder what he would say if he saw Thaniel now and understood the truth. Perhaps the time has come to find out.

"You will see him soon," I promise vaguely.

It is winter when we arrive in Immanion. In mid-afternoon, pregnant light still pours into the streets, reflecting from windows and playing on the walls of the marble buildings. Silent flower petals, driven by gentle breeze, are welcoming in the oncoming change of season. The weather is always pleasantly warm here. It only ever rains in the souls of hara, who once became too enamoured of their own powers and success to acknowledge the deities that transcend them and make them who they are. Reportedly, something similar had been humanity's downfall.

Martina Bellovičová

I let my hair dance with the petals, and as I ride my horse along the central road that leads all the way from the port to Phaonica, hara point and begin to gather, some of them shocked to see the harling sitting in front of me. I can be sure I have been talked about in the time of my absence, because there is quite the crowd soon. Surprisingly, most of the assembled hara greet me with respect.

When I arrive at the gate, Camael already knows I am here and walks out of the palace, escorted by the Chancellor. Naturally, he does not bow to me, and does not say any words of thanks. However, he smiles when Thaniel calls his name. Maybe this can be the beginning. Perhaps I can be a bridge. Meanwhile, the celestial serpent is slowly eating away the minutes and seconds of our lives. And in the palace, confined in his bedroom, Shaya is dreaming another dream.

The Dehara of Navisalam

E. S. Wynn

The Dehara of Navisalam

For hundreds of years, we've carried our dehara with us to the stars. We've carried our rituals, built new nayatis on alien soil, dedicated them to Miyacala, Agave, Aruhani. For centuries, we've started over, much as we did once, long ago, on Earth, but each time, we've brought our dehara with us. We've brought our past with us. We've planted it and nurtured it in open, fertile soil, and not thought once about what gods or dehara may have already lived there, may have been born with their roots in that same soil.

Alien gods.

I am one of only a handful of scholars who believe in and pursue such notions. Most hara are not necessarily opposed to the idea of wholly uninhabited worlds having their own dehara, their own gods, but few carry the passion to seek them out that I and my brethren do. For us, nothing is more important than the knowledge handed down to Wraeththu from dehara, the discoveries they have helped our species make, but there is always more to know. That is why we seek alien dehara. That is why we seek the gods born of other worlds.

For forty-eight years, I have walked this path. I have travelled to hundreds of systems, set foot on thousands of new, untouched worlds. Only on a few have I found traces of prior civilizations. Only on a few have I knelt down and touched the ruins of life, sifted the ashes of another species' apocalypse through my fingers, felt sadness, loss, emptiness. Never, not even once, have I felt the presence of other gods.

I have to admit that when I arrived at the *agha-sedim* station on Sivilamia, my hopes for some grand discovery were already low. I was tired, cold from travelling through the fabric of reality, riding lanes tucked between layers of time, space and the energy membranes of other realities pressing against ours. *Agha-sedim*, that's the label chosen for the beasts we use to journey from star system to star system, but in truth, they share little in common with the spirits we long ago plied the Otherlanes with. *Agha-sedim* are built, forged by hara and dehara, gathered together and tempered more of the stuff between dimensions, the substructure of the universe, than of spirit or raw matter. They are machines, conveyances, though even those crude terms fall wide of the mark of what the *agha-sedim* really are. They are beacons, things that ply space and time and guide us like golden roads, lead us to the realms we picture in our minds. It is we who do the flying. It is our minds, our spirits that make possible the journey.

Sivilamia was a clean, virgin world, a rugged and green paradise on the long, cosmic rim of the wide collection of settlements we'd laid out across the stars. A small group of hara had set up a village there, built a robust agricultural centre where crops were literally sung into blooming, but beyond Wraeththu's presence on the planet, there was no evidence the soil or the skies had ever seen the hands of any species more sentient than insect life in all its history. It was a primal world, unpromising as a source of new gods.

As I had done countless times before in the past, I met with the hienama unofficially in charge of the settlement, who greeted me with the usual quiet kindness. Hara like myself are rarely greeted with any real enthusiasm, and never any hostility, but rather only a smiling ambivalence. We are seen as a breath of dust upon the wind, something old, unimportant, a trace of the forgotten just blowing through. Like a wayward harling, I was offered simple accommodations for the two nights I was scheduled to spend on Sivilamia, then left to my own devices, my own meanderings. Among the settlers, it was my nature to become like a ghost, a passing phantom, barely seen while I moved among them, maybe smiled at once, twice, never lingering long enough to be remembered.

Ryniae changed all that.

Ryniae was young, strong. He'd grown up on Sivilamia, taken his first breath in the virgin air and joined his parents among the farmer-singers shortly after feybraiha. Being born of the stuff of an alien world, he seemed to move differently, sported hair that grew in dark with natural shades of dusky rose and visceral silver. He sang differently than the others, sang songs that seemed to come from somewhere else, some further, deeper inspiration than the songs of his sire and hostling. Perhaps it was that which intrigued me most about Ryniae. Perhaps it was his songs that first gave me hope that Sivilamia might be different somehow, unique.

"I've seen things out in the fields," Ryniae told me that first night. Chance had crossed our paths at the edge of the settlement, when we both wandered to the same overlook, both drawn by the silver-purple of the high, full pantheon of moons hanging brilliant and misty in the sky. Beneath us, the world tumbled down to low, sprawling fields of ferns and elegant, delicate flowers, the first primal petals of an alien world's floral evolution, washed by a rain of moonlight.

"When I was a harling, I used to wander out there," Ryniae gestured out into the distances, passed me a flask of some local flower wine his sire had bottled. "I used to pretend I was a Varr or a Uigenna or one of the other Megalithica tribes you hear about in the history-streams, fighting humans, the Gelaming, fighting to be free."

I said nothing, only sipped the strong floral wine, stared out at the fields while he spoke.

"There are shadows out there in those fields," he said. "Not in the evil sense. They don't feel malicious. They feel playful, they feel like reflections of the emotions and feelings you put into the air, like mirrors," he shrugged, "shadows."

"Some form of life?" I asked, passing the wine back.

"No, this world hasn't evolved anything more profound than scarlet crickets." Ryniae shook his head, laughed. "These things, they're like spirits, fledgling spirits, like harlings, innocent, observant, playful."

"Dehara?" My eyes dropped as the word fell tired from my lips, absent of enthusiasm.

"Maybe." Ryniae took a swig of the wine, brushed his lips with the back of his hand.

Fate and the nature of the greater, subtle workings of the universe have a way of pulling disparate elements together in ways we least expect. I ran into Ryniae twice the second day, first as I was walking through the settlement in search of breakfast, and later as I was gathering a few of my things for a hike out into the fern fields we had talked about the night before. Grinning, laughing at the way things come together, I invited him along with me, asked him to show me some of the places where he'd seen the shadows among the blooms of Sivilamia's primal flowers.

Generally, I'm one who prefers to travel alone, to keep to himself. Loneliness lends itself to a sense of serenity, a meditative quiet that allows for an easy communing with agmara, but there was something about Ryniae that still intrigued me, something beyond the hair, the magenta highlights that flared in the depths of his eyes when the light of Sivilamia's twin suns caught them. It was something more than the strange grace about him, something more than the strange words of the songs he sang as we walked.

"What language is that?" I remember asking.

The edge of a grin pulled at Ryniae's features, tugged at his lips. "Just something I heard once in a dream." His tone was innocent, almost dismissive. Quietly, he turned away again, ran his fingers through the outstretched fronds of tall ferns. "The words bring up simple things, urge all that is green to blossom and grow." He glanced back. "The plants like it."

"You heard it in a dream?" Compared to the elegant way in which he drifted through the fields, I moved like an elephant, weighed down by my heavy scholar's robe and my pack of ritual tools, tripping over every veiny root that traced its way underfoot. "From one of the dehara?"

"You'll be able to move much easier if you leave your pack behind," he said, changing the subject, turned fully to face me. "And your robe."

"I can't," I remember saying, hesitating, watching him as he watched me, seemed to study me with a sort of innocent curiosity. "I'll need my tools at hand to construct a proper majhahn when the time comes to try and contact any dehara that might call this place home."

"You come here searching for alien dehara," he grinned, "and you think that you're going to find any using ways you've carried with you from Earth?" He laughed.

"Agmara and the rituals our species have carried to the stars work only in very specific ways, Ryniae." I shook my head, smiled a little at his innocence. "Your hienama should have taught you this."

"So rigid, pre-formulated, earthly rituals are the only ways to contact dehara, then?" He raised a playful eyebrow at me.

"I don't—"

"Take off your clothes." He grinned, stretched long and beautiful in the brilliant light of Sivilamia's suns. I remember hesitating in that moment, just watching him, simultaneously attracted and confused. Like a cat, he languished in the stretch, his grin wide, lusty.

"How do you expect to get in touch with alien dehara if you don't let yourself become one with the planet first?"

"I don't see how...."

"Relax." He grinned again, slipped out of his ragged tank top and tossed it onto the ground. "Nothing will happen to our clothes. There are no thieves or curious animals here."

Struck by his elegance, the smooth suppleness of his chest, his arms, his sinuous muscles, I lingered there for a moment, soaked in the light of his smile, the brilliance of his skin as he stripped off the last of his clothing.

"Now you." He smiled, and hesitating only a moment longer, I breathed, silently gave myself to him, let his hands caress the pack and the clothes from my body. Beneath it all, my skin was far more pale than his, iridescent almost, but his hands lingered in my curves, traced fingers along the lines of my body in quiet appreciation.

As one, we sprinted into the fields then, ran hand in hand with a grace and freedom I'd never felt in my own body before. In that moment, I felt pure, as innocent as the soil beneath my feet, as clean and free as the sky above us. I felt as if I had shuffled off the weight of my skin, of the body that had been mine, as if I were a wisp of light, of agmara drifting quick on eager winds to some distant red-purple heaven. Beside me, Ryniae was shown as beautiful and brilliant as a slice of moonlight caught shifting through the day, impossibly elegant, a creature of unearthly perfection.

How long we ran, I don't know. Time passed in a fleeting instant as quick as an eternity, as long as a breath. Even as he grabbed me and pressed me down among the ferns of the fields, I found myself smiling, breathless, yet alive with a primal, unbreakable stamina.

"Share breath with me," he whispered into my ear, his tones threading themselves through my being like liquid silk. My hands tightened across his back, smoothed themselves across velvet skin as I looked up, met his eyes, found myself snared by the fire there.

"I am yours, Ryniae," I breathed. "Do with me as you will."

Like the sinuous movements of some great cat, he pressed himself against me then, lips seeking mine, trapping them, taking them even as I rose to meet his. In the sharing of breath came a mist of images, a scent like lilac, honeydew, the blossoms of dusty roses. Ferns rose up all around us, rattled upward in the tones of a distant song until they closed in over us, became a canopy of dark, verdant warmth.

See. . .

In the darkness — where had the daylight gone? — I felt Ryniae's voice more than heard it, let it draw me, lead me through silvered mist and into a moonlit night. Far above us, the pantheon of moons reigned in the endless, star-dusted sky like the faces of grand tigrons, cast their light down upon us, watched us with a quiet and lordly benevolence.

What is this place? Thoughts came as words, echoed as though I had spoken. Drifting, I floated over stones moving in a current of mist, floated toward a hazy light that slowly became the moonlit shape of Ryniae.

Navisalam. He dipped his head in a gentle, smiling nod, the words reaching my mind as thoughts, unspoken but said nonetheless. *It is the name of this world.*

Then... Sivilamia?

An earthly name. He smiled softly. *Given to this world by those who see things only in earthly terms.*

And me? I asked.

You are different. He made a gentle gesture. *You try to see the truth of this place, of other places like this. You try, but you are still so very innocent.*

You are a dehar? I tried. *A god of this world?*

I am of this world. He smiled again. *I am this world. I am all things in this world. I am subtle and strong. I am the essence of self, of life.*

A god, I nodded, *but there are no traces of a civilisation here.* I shook my head. *Gods are creatures of belief and energy. They cannot manifest without a mind to believe in them.*

You still think in such earthly terms. Ryniae floated to me, caressed my face with gentle hands. *There is more to the whole of reality than you realise. In truth, it is open. Your rituals, terms and beliefs give depth and definition to the nature of things as you see them, but they limit you in ways you cannot yet see.*

Teach me, Ryniae. I whispered. *Show me the world as you see it. Teach me to see as you see.*

Open yourself, Ryniae breathed. *Allow me into your being. Let me rise into your core, let me breathe the seed of Navisalam into you.*

I am yours, I said again, and as he embraced me there, in that other-world, I felt him merging with my distant physical body as well, flesh rising against flesh in a ritual I understood, a ritual that came alive with all the strangeness and intensity of something wholly new, something wholly alien.

As one, we soared into brilliance, caught fire, shone like suns. As one, we rose in the movements of a magic both taught and learned. As one, we summoned the future, became like clouds, gently dancing along the surface of a luminous astral ocean.

These are the songs of Navisalam, I heard him say. *These are the ways of the magics of the navi-dehara.* Sounds whispered on visual winds, ripples forming shapes in vibrant mercury mist. *These are the image-words with which you are now trusted.*

I am yours. The words came from me in a torrent, tore themselves from me. All around me, the heat of passion blossomed, bloomed, and then I saw Ryniae's smile flare in the darkness, bringing with it a depth of knowledge that sunk in so suddenly, so completely that I cried out.

When I awoke, I was in my robe again, my body cold, empty. Exhaustion quivered in my thighs as I stood, brushed the dirt from my legs. Where the settlement had been, only fields, flowers, ferns — little fronds dancing in the whispers of a cool summer wind — and a waiting *agha-sedim* now remained. A few feet away, my pack lay discarded, still cinched closed, undisturbed. In the whole of Sivilamia, in the whole of Navisalam, there was no sign of anything harish, no trace that the families, the hienama, the buildings, the gardens, even Ryniae had been anything but illusion.

I remember looking down at my hands then, studying them as if seeing them for the first time, when a lock of my hair drifted into my vision, startled me with the shades of dusky rose and visceral silver I saw streaking their way through it. Blinking, I took the lock into my hands, held it, stroked it, marvelled at the colours there, the way they caught the light just as Ryniae's had, just as his eyes and the moons had.

It was then that the words of Ryniae's songs came to me, the words of the navi-dehara rising up, coursing suddenly through my body in lines and rushes so powerful I had to let them out, had to set them free to dance among the winds. Alien sounds pierced the air as I sang, rolled like magic over ferns and flowers, flowed from me in a gushing river of faith-frequency I didn't want to stop, couldn't stop even if I had desired it. All around me, plants came alive, ferns and flowers blossoming, sprouting, growing, rising so tall and verdant that in a moment the field had become like a forest, thick and heavy with succulent, hanging fruit. I smiled, and as I smiled, the song came to a rolling crescendo, then finished quietly, leaving a powerful silence in its wake.

My grin spread in the wide lines of a happiness deeper than any that I had ever felt before. I felt gratitude, strength, confidence, a sense of achievement so powerful it made me want to howl for joy. For the first time in my whole, long life of searching, I had found my dehara. I had found my alien gods.

"Thank you, Ryniae," I whispered then, spreading my arms to the wide world of Navisalam, to the twin suns and the endless fields of ferns and primal flowers stretching on to every horizon. Tears welled at the edges of my eyes as I took a long, deep breath of that pure, virgin air and whispered again: "Thank you, navi-dehara. Today, I rise from your pearl a new har."

Today, I am at last truly alive.

The colour of words

Victoria Copus

The colour of words

Water whispers as it moves. I lie on my belly in the grass to listen. Water whispers Be. It is easy to Be with Water. Water doesn't turn away. Water doesn't mock. I reach into River and Water strokes my hands the way my hostling strokes my hair. Water is cold and I smell the mountains. Water starts to sing.

"Bear!" a har shouts. "Why aren't you in school?"

Water stops singing. I look up and see Obal, who lives in the house next door.

Obal frowns and says, "Come here right now." The yellow light that projects from his chest and head crackles with annoyance.

I climb the river bank to the road. Obal takes me by the hand and walks quickly toward my house. I run to keep up. Yellow-brown words fall from his mouth. I wave them away to stop them from sticking to me.

When I saw Obal through the open kitchen windows approaching my house with my harling in tow, I sighed and put down the pestle I was using to grind flax seeds. I knew Bear had left school again because I had seen him walk by earlier. My harling had no concept of stealth. It didn't bother me that he left school early since it was new for him. It bothered me that he didn't find anything interesting to keep him at school.

Obal opened the front door and declared, "Dura, I found Bear at the river again."

I wiped my hands on a towel and tossed it on a chair as I left the kitchen. "Thank you for bringing him home," I said to Obal. "This is the second time this week. I don't think he's ready for school."

"Nonsense," Obal said. He seemed to believe it was his duty

to fill in for Bear's absent father, although I frequently told him I was not looking for a replacement. "Three years old is old enough for school. He needs to be around other harlings. You let him live too much in his head."

I smiled as I gritted my teeth. Obal's hand was still around Bear's wrist, and before I said un-neighborly things, I removed Bear from his hold. "You're right, I'm sure."

After Obal left, I leaned back against the door and rolled my eyes. "Next time you sneak out of school, don't let that busybody Obal catch you," I told Bear.

It seemed like Bear heard me but he was staring at something above my head. I picked him up and he wrapped his arms and legs around me. His cold fingers touched the back of my neck. "You're ice cold. It must've rained in the mountains."

I set him down on the kitchen table, took his hands between mine, and blew on them. His smile lit up his green eyes as his gaze met my eyes. I felt a familiar ache in my chest. I missed Bear's voice, his little harling chatter, his laugh. When he had stopped speaking over a year earlier, I took him to all the other healers I knew and they all said that there was nothing physically wrong and that Bear would speak again when he was ready.

I noticed Bear's feet and wondered, not for the first time, if it was possible for Bear to have inherited a trait for hating shoes from my hostling, Terzah. "Bear, where are your shoes? They were your last pair." I put him down on the ground. "Show me where you left them."

I run to Water and show my hostling how when I put my hands in the river, Water sings. I want Dura to Be.

Dura shakes his head. "Bear, I'm not playing. Where are your shoes?"

I run to Rock and place my hands on its warm pitted surface. I feel Rock hum.

Dura looks through the grass around Rock. "I don't see them here," he says.

I run to Tree and point up to the branches.

Dura crosses his arms over his chest. "It's a pretty tree, but where are your shoes?"

I grasp Tree's lowest branch and put my feet on its rough skin. Tree doesn't tell me its secrets unless I climb high. I climb up to the branch where I left my shoes and drop them to the ground. Dura shakes his head but I see bright light shine in his chest and know that he is laughing. He holds his arms up to me and I jump into them.

On the walk home Dura puts me on his back and sings. I snuggle into Dura's bright green light. It pulses with gray in places. I like my hostling's light more than any other har's, but I don't like the gray parts. I run my fingers through the short hair at the back of my hostling's neck. His dark hair is longer in the front and hangs over one side of his face.

Dura stops walking when we see horses in front of our house. Dura is a healer and hara often come to him.

"We have visitors," he says and swings me off his back. "Hello!" he calls toward the horses.

I see two hara step around the horses. One is tall with long black hair. He radiates an indigo and bright blue light that reaches out past his limbs. The other har has yellow hair and his light shimmers, orange and yellow like the sun, around his head and chest. Their lights join together in a way that I have not seen before.

Dura mutters harsh prickly words under his breath. He takes hold of my hand and cold creeps up my arm. He pulls me past the two hara.

"David," the yellow-haired har says. "Don't be like this."

"I'm *Dura* now," my hostling says. "I changed my name after I left New Hope. I told all of you that I wanted to be left alone."

"And we've respected your wishes long enough," the same har says with a smile. "Come on. Invite us in. I know you don't want a scene with your neighbors watching."

My hostling looks over his shoulder. Obal must be watching. Obal is always watching. "Fine. Come in."

"What about the horses?" the taller har asks.

"Leave them where they are," Dura says. "You won't be staying long."

Inside the house, my hostling releases my hand. I move behind the chair next to the fireplace where I can watch the strangers. One of them drops a heavy leather bag next to the door. They wear leather and fur and smell like the mountains. They make me think of wolves and wild things. They stomp on the door rug with heavy boots and leave dirt marks on the wood floor. I wait for Dura to yell.

Dura notices the dirt but doesn't yell. He makes a sharp sound and motions toward the couch that I'm not supposed to jump on. "Please sit. Would you like something to drink?"

"Coffee if you have it," the yellow-haired har says with another smile. I wonder if he always smiles.

Dura walks into the kitchen as they sit. The two hara watch me, and I watch them. The smiling har lays his arm across the back of the couch and touches the other's long hair. The contact makes both their lights stronger. My hostling returns and gives them mugs of coffee.

"You have a harling?" the dark-haired har asks.

I wanted to scream. My brothers were sitting on my couch, drinking my coffee in my house. Seeing them reminded me of the turmoil that happened after our father Zen passed. They had avoided most of it by disappearing into the mountains to leave the rest of us to sort everything out. I sat in the chair that Bear was behind and took a deep cleansing breath before I said, "Bear, come here and met your huras."

Bear moved tentatively to the front of my chair. I suspected that Bear's caution was due to my tension.

"This is Bear," I said. "Bear, these are my brothers, Aris and Zia."

Zia drank from his cup without a word. He watched Bear, but I knew Zia well enough to know that he was looking at more than the external.

Aris scratched his blonde hair and set his coffee mug on the floor by his right foot. I grimaced. He had already tracked dirt into my house. Coffee spilled on the floor would likely be next.

"You look don't look much like a bear, little one," Aris told Bear.

"He doesn't talk," I said as I pulled Bear onto my lap. I hated this part, the part where I have to explain Bear to hara for the first time.

"Doesn't talk?" Aris said. "He can't or won't?"

I shrugged. "He started to talk like any other harling but then he stopped."

"Did you take him to healers?" Aris asked.

I clenched my teeth. "I *am* a healer, Aris. I know what to do when something is wrong with a harling. He's fine. He's made a decision not to speak. Until he changes his mind, nothing can be done."

"What does his father say about this?" Aris asked.

My arms tightened around Bear and he squirmed. I tried to relax. "Don't mistake my hospitality for the desire to reconnect with you. Aris, just say what you came here for so you can go."

Aris and Zia glanced at each other. Aris took his arm off the back of the couch and leaned forward. "Didn't you get Illan's invitation?" he asked.

I rolled my eyes. "I thought it was a joke. I can't imagine Illan committing to a blood bond."

"We're on our way there," Aris said. "We were hoping you would come with us."

I shook my head. "I don't want back in on the family drama. I like my life the way it is. It's quiet. Hara respect me for what I do. I'm not Terzah or Zen's son here. I'm just Dura."

Aris laughed. "For Ag's sake, it's a family gathering. You don't have to give up your entire life. The last time we were together was at Zen's passing twenty years ago. Terzah and Zen wouldn't have wanted us to be strangers. Bear should meet the family at least once."

He had a point about Bear meeting the family. I wanted Bear to know he was part of something bigger. Since it was only a visit, we could leave any time. Even though Aris annoyed me, I didn't hate him or Zia. It would be good to see Michael and Jewel again, but I wasn't sure about Illan. "I don't know," I said. "I'll consider it."

Aris smiled. "I can sense you want to come with us, but we can do this your way. Now, tell us where we can stable our horses for the night. Zia and I will make dinner, and in the morning, after you pretend to think it over, you can tell us that you're coming with us."

I watch from the countertop as my huras make dinner. I snap beans from our garden in half into a bowl. Aris makes loud happy sounds as he cooks. He spills water on the floor and laughs. Zia hisses and cleans up after him. A piece of green bean flies into Zia's hair as I snap. I freeze and watch as it works deeper into his hair. He does not notice.

I sense a heaviness creeping into the air like a draft from a window open at night. I set aside the bowl and jump down. I run to the other room and see Dura staring out the window. The heaviness is coming from him. I hug his legs.

He puts his hand on the top of my head. "Are Aris and Zia destroying my kitchen?" His voice sounds clear but the colour of his words is muddy.

I tug on his sleeve and he picks me up. I move his hair back from his eyes. A tear rolls down his cheek. I catch it on my fingers and kiss it to make him smile, but he doesn't.

"I'm okay," he says. "Seeing Aris and Zia again reminds me of a long time ago."

He carries me into the kitchen and sets me on a chair at the table. He opens a cabinet, takes out four plates and places them on the table, one in front of each chair.

"Please tell me Michael finally split up with Nahala," my hostling asks my huras.

Aris laughs. "Michael and Nahala will be together forever no matter how much they deny it," Aris says.

"I imagine they have an obscene amount of harlings and high harlings by now. I'm surprised that the two of you never had a harling. Or did you?"

Both Zia and Aris stop making supper and look at Dura. "David, is that an attempt to reconnect with us?" Aris asks.

"It's *Dura*, and it was only a question," my hostling says.

"A personal question," Zia says.

Dura puts his hands on his hips. "I take it back, then. Have you met Illan's chesnari?"

Aris brings a pan over to the table and spoons what looks like mud on the plate in front of me. "He came with Illan when

Terzah died."

Dura sits in the chair beside me. The heaviness that comes from him grows stronger and makes the air hard to breathe. I pat his arm and he puts his hand over mine to keep it still.

"I don't even know what happened," Dura says. "It was sudden. One minute everything was normal and in the next it was like emptiness opened in my head and I knew Terzah was gone."

"Hunting accident," Aris says as he puts mud on another plate. "He was chasing buffalo. One came up behind him. Solace said death was immediate. He didn't feel any pain."

My hostling covers his mouth with one hand and nods. I try to climb into his lap but he puts me back into my chair.

"Why didn't you come?" Aris asks. "The clan had a gathering for him and there was another in town. Everyhar was there except you."

My hostling closes his eyes for a moment. "I couldn't... I couldn't face it. After everything that happened when Zen passed, I couldn't do it again. I didn't exactly leave on good terms."

"Nohar was angry at you," Zia says as he sits across the table from me.

"That's not how I remember it," Dura says.

"Illan was angry," Aris says. "Michael was hurt. Jewel was confused, so were Zia and I. I think it was disrespectful that you didn't come to Terzah's gathering. He made you one of his own and you treated him like he was a stranger."

"Maybe if you and Zia hadn't left me alone to deal with Illan and Terzah, I wouldn't have left in the first place. You don't know what it was like listening to the two of them day after day. Michael and Jewel were with the clan. I was the only one there."

I twist in my chair and try to push the heaviness away, but it doesn't move. Zia watches me. I know he Sees. I slide under the table where it is cool and I can breathe.

"Please, can we talk about this later?" I hear my hostling say. "This isn't an appropriate conversation for Bear." He ducks his head down below the edge of the table and gives me the Look. "Come out of there."

I climb back onto my chair. Aris tells stories during dinner and makes my hostling laugh. The air lightens enough that I feel comfortable again but I see the heaviness in a storm cloud above our heads at the ceiling.

After dinner, Dura sends me outside to play. He doesn't make me wear shoes, which makes me glad because Earth likes to speak to me through my feet. When it gets dark, I go home. My hostling helps me get ready for bed, even though I don't need help.

"There are things that I haven't told you that I should," he tells me as he tucks me under my favourite blanket. "It's hard to know where to start."

He fingers the edge of the blanket and sits beside me. "Your high hostling, Terzah, made this. I wish you could have known him, and Zen, too. They would have adored you."

He sighs and touches my hair. "Terzah and Zen took me and my brother in after our birth parents died. We were still humans. They took in Aris and Zia, too, as human boys, and they had two sons – harlings – of their own, Illan and Jewel. Even though we weren't related by blood, Terzah and Zen cared for us like we were theirs.

"Terzah was as intense and fierce as a wildfire. When he thought he was right about something, only Zen could change his mind. After Zen passed on, Illan and Terzah had an argument. Nohar could make them see reason. The argument spiralled out of control. Illan wanted the rest of us to take sides. I wouldn't. A lot of painful words were said. After a year or so, I didn't want to watch the family falling apart anymore, so I left. I cut off contact with all of them. I swore I would never go back, but I still miss the way we used to be when it was good."

I don't like to see my hostling look sad. I place my hands on the sides of his face and move his mouth into a smile. He kisses my forehead. "Good night, little pearl," he says.

I wake later when the only light in my room is from Moon. I think at first Moon woke me, but then I hear my hostling and Aris arguing. The air is thick red and angry. I want to hide, but I don't know where to go.

The door opens and Zia looks at me from the doorway. After a moment, he unwinds a bracelet from his wrist and lays it on my chest as he sits on my bed beside me.

"I see it too," he says and holds out his hand, palm up. A blue flame appears above his hand. He lays his other hand over my eyes and murmurs a few words. I see a bright flash of light from between his fingers. When it disappears, he lifts his hand from my eyes. "That's better."

The angry air is gone. I take a deep breath and hold it in my lungs for a moment before I let it go. The air tastes sweet.

Zia picks up the bracelet and winds it several times around my wrist before he ties the ends together. "These stones will deflect some of the dark energy, but you need training to gain control."

When he releases my hand, I look at the bracelet. It feels strange on my wrist. Zia leans over me and his hair falls over his shoulder onto my chest. I touch it. It feels cold like the night sky.

"Will you talk to me?" he asks. He takes hold of my chin and turns my face up so that I look into his eyes. "Show me when you decided to stop talking."

I remember another night when I was younger and I heard my hostling and father arguing. I felt pain in my head. Their words and the air turned colours for the first time and I was scared. When Dura came to check on me, he lay on my bed next to me, sobbing. I saw angry red words stuck to his skin like the hooks of briars. I didn't want to hurt any har like that ever.

Zia releases my chin. "Words can hurt, but words can heal. Words can make laughter and friends. You're sensitive, Bear. Other hara don't see words the same way as you. It's a gift, even if it doesn't feel like it."

Zia moves his hair back over his shoulder. "Next time you feel like you can't breathe, visualize a hard ball of white light here." He taps my chest with a long dark fingernail. "And then breathe into it to make it grow large like a shield around you."

My hostling comes into my room. "What happened? Was he having a bad dream?"

Zia shakes his head. His hair moves around his shoulder and tickles my arms. "Your voices woke him."

Dura touches my face. "I'm sorry, Bear. No more arguing tonight, I promise. Go back to sleep. You need to rest. Tomorrow we're going on a journey."

I leaned against the wall outside of Bear's room and sighed. Aris approached me and I held up my hand to stop him from coming any closer. "I don't want to argue," I said.

"Neither do I," Aris said, "but I want you to see why this is wrong. We all make mistakes, but you can't treat the family like we don't exist. What would you do if Bear turns his back on you some day?"

I rubbed my forehead. "Aris, I've agreed that Bear and I will go. Beyond that, I can't say what will happen."

Zia left Bear's room and closed the door. "He's asleep."

"Thanks, Zia," I said. I wanted to hug him to thank him, but I knew Zia didn't like casual touches from anyhar except Aris. "You two can take my bed. I'll sleep on the couch or with Bear."

Aris wrapped his arm around Zia's shoulders. "We like to sleep under the stars."

"Do you need anything?" I asked.

"No," Zia said. He bumped Aris with his shoulder. "Apologize to Dura or he'll dwell on your argument all night."

"What about me?" Aris asked.

"You don't dwell on anything," Zia said. "Good night," Zia told me and left Aris and I alone.

Aris and I looked at each other. Something in his eyes reminded me of when I first saw him sitting in a sunny corner of the medical clinic, his facial expression a mixture of pain, suspicion, and loneliness. I remember how much I wanted him to be part of our family because it made me sad that he had nohar. It was a long time before he trusted us.

Suddenly, Aris lunged forward and embraced me so hard my ribs ached. "I only yell at you because I care," he said.

I laughed and patted his back. "I know."

When I wake in the morning, I hear soft voices coming from the kitchen. I see the bracelet that Zia tied on my wrist. The white stones glow from the inside. I like wearing a bracelet from my hura, even if it is scratchy. I dress and walk to the kitchen. I smell breakfast. I yawn and rub my eyes and lean against my hostling's legs. He taps the top of my head, and I look up and see that it is Zia. I step back and stare.

Aris scoops me up and puts me on Dura's lap at the table. "Don't feel bad, Bear. Zia doesn't cuddle with me either," he says.

"That's not true," Zia says.

Dura hands me a half a piece of toast off his plate. I nibble on the toast and watch crumbs fall onto Dura's arm. I brush the crumbs off him and feel his arm for the scars that my father's words left on him, because sometimes they open and seep sorrow. Today they are closed.

"Back to what I was saying, we can take my transport and arrive later today."

"Where's the fun in that?" Aris asks. "As Zen always said, the journey is as important as the destination."

"If there were transports back then, I'm sure Zen would've seen the advantages in expeditious travel."

Zia sits in the chair beside Aris. "I cuddled with you last night."

"The ceremony is in two days," Dura says. "We wouldn't make it by horse on time."

"Nothing our family plans starts on time," Aris said with a shrug.

I finish my toast and pick up the other half from Dura's plate. Dura moves me over to my own chair. I notice my hostling's light is brighter than yesterday. The gray is less visible.

"I'm not debating this. I've agreed to go, but we travel my way." Dura says.

Zia lays his hand over Aris's. "I'm holding your hand," he says.

Aris lifts Zia's hand and kisses the back of it. Their light grows stronger and more of it mixes together. "I was just teasing about cuddling," Aris says.

Zia pulls his hand away and crosses his arms over his chest. Their light stays the same even without the physical contact. I watch them closely. Adults do this. Their bodies and words say something different than what their light shows.

Aris tries to put his arm across Zia's shoulders, but Zia is stiff and doesn't yield. "Zia and I could go by horse and you can take Bear by your transport," Aris says. "I don't trust those things. What if we accidentally get sucked into a different dimension?"

Dura shakes his head. "They're thought-propelled, Aris. They have no connection to other dimensions. Besides, we're going together. This was your idea. You have to see it through to the end."

"It would be fun to go by horse. Remember when Terzah used to leave us in the mountains to find our way home?"

Dura stands up and takes his plate over to the counter. "That wasn't fun. That was abuse."

Aris laughs and nudges Zia. "Remember when David saw that rabbit?"

Zia's mouth twitches into a small smile.

"It looked scarier in the dark," Dura says. He moves behind my chair and strokes my hair. "Maybe when Bear is older, we can take him to the mountains and show him the places we used to go."

Aris gasps and clasps his hand to his chest. "Why, David, that sounds like you're trying to reconnect with us."

"It's *Dura* and I think you're saying my old name on purpose."

"Aris, let him be," Zia says. "Dura doesn't have to put up with your teasing like I do."

We arrived in New Hope by sunset. Although I recognized some of the main buildings, the town had changed and grown larger. It was hard to believe this place started as a human refugee camp with clusters of sod houses and lopsided structures made of stone and clay.

Aris directed me to Illan's house. I got out of the transport and looked up at the smooth brown curving exterior of Illan's house. I didn't recognize the material it was made of, but it had no straight edges, except for the tall wooden doors. I sensed Bear's distress and saw him beside the transport with his eyes closed and his hands pressed over his ears. Zia leaned over him and took his hands. He said something to Bear, and Bear took a deep breath. I felt him centre himself.

"I think I'm going to be sick," Aris said as he staggered up to me and collapsed over the front end of the transport. "I told you I don't like these transport things."

"You'll live," I told him. "Trust me, I'm a healer."

The doors to the house were flung open, and Illan strode out. For a moment I was shocked at how much he looked like Zen; I had forgotten. He had Terzah's dark hair and height, but Illan's eyes and facial features were Zen's. "Aris," Illan said as he walked past me. "I can't believe you got a transport. You'll scratch up the finish lying on it like that."

Aris stood up and gave Illan a hug. "It isn't mine. It's Dura's."

Illan saw me then. I couldn't tell if he was glad or annoyed.

I picked up Bear. "Illan," I said as I swallowed nervously.

"I can't believe you came," he said. I sensed a pulse of power from his mind directed toward the house.

"You did invite me," I said.

"Actually, it was Drake," he said.

A har with long red hair came out of the house. He nodded at Aris and Zia. Illan put his arm around him. "This is my chesnari, Drake. Drake, this is my wayward brother, David, and his harling, I presume."

"Bear," I said. "His name is Bear, and I go by Dura now."

Drake smiled at me. "You look like Michael."

"Drake, take Aris, Zia, and Bear inside. I'll show Dura where he can leave his transport," Illan said.

Drake nodded. "We were just sitting down to dinner," Drake said. "I hope you're hungry."

"Depends on who did the cooking," Aris said as he grabbed our bags out of the transport.

"You're safe," Drake said. "I cooked."

I put Bear down next to Zia. "Will you take Bear, Zia? You're good with him."

Zia nodded. "Come, Bear."

Bear grabbed hold of Zia's shirtsleeve and followed him inside with Aris and Drake. Illan got inside my transport. I took a deep cleansing breath and joined him.

"Pull around the side of the house," Illan said as he checked out the interior. "Your transport is prime. I have two, but not this nice."

"Thank you. A har traded it for a healing."

Illan instructed me where to park and we got out without another word. Illan didn't seem to be in a hurry to go back inside. He lit a cigarette and gave it to me before lighting another for himself.

"Illan, if you don't want me here, I can go," I said.

Illan waved his cigarette in the air. "No, stay. I'm just surprised you came. It's been so long, little brother."

It annoyed me when he called me his little brother. "I *am* older than you."

Illan shrugged. "The human years don't count."

I dropped my cigarette on the ground and stomped on it. "How dare you say that. I lived through more in my insignificant human years than you ever have."

Illan hugged me roughly. "Finally. I thought you were going to stay hidden behind polite words forever. I can't change our past, but I promise in the future I might say or do something that hurts you again because I'm an ass. When that happens, yell back at me. Don't run away again."

"I'll keep that in mind." I tried to pull away from Illan's embrace, but he held me in place. "I need to see if Bear is okay," I told him.

Illan released me. "He's fine. He's with family."

"Bear is different. He doesn't talk."

"You should take him to Bela," Illan said. "Bela knows everything about harlings. He's brilliant."

I crossed my arms over my chest. "I'm a healer and Bear's hostling. I know exactly what he needs."

Illan smiled. "There you go. See how easy that was."

As we enter the house, I see a tree. I stop and wonder why it is here. I let go of Zia's sleeve.

Drake gets down on one knee beside me. "Do you like my tree?" he asks as he peels off a small strip of curling white bark from the trunk and puts it around my thumb. I see a flash of a forest of white trees with yellow leaves.

"Do you think it's wise to leave Illan and Dura alone?" Aris asks as he sets our bags down by the staircase going upstairs.

"Let them sort it out on their own," Drake says and presses his hand against my back to move me away from Tree. "How about some stew, Bear?"

"Bear doesn't talk," Aris says.

"You don't talk?" Drake asks me.

I look to Zia and slip closer to him. "No," Zia says. "He doesn't talk, but he *is* hungry."

Drake takes us through a door into the kitchen. I run my hands over the rocks in the walls to see in any will speak to me, but they are sleeping. Aris and Zia sit at a long table, and Drake calls for me to sit. I can't be still yet. I see colours on the walls. Pinkish orange and gold like Drake's colours and deep orange red with bright yellow and gold edges like Illan's. I try to touch them.

"Be careful," Drake says. "Don't make it fall. It will hit your head."

I freeze, not sure what these words mean. Colours don't fall. The edge shifts and I realise the colours are on a big square.

Drake takes my shoulders in his hands and steers me to the table. "You can see more of my paintings later," he says.

After we start to eat, Dura and Illan join us. Over dinner, Dura and my huras speak of hara and places that I don't know. Dura is comfortable. When I finish eating, I sit on my hostling's lap and close my eyes. Their voices go on and on until I fall asleep.

As much as New Hope had changed, the Blackwater Clan had not. We met the rest of my family the next day outside of town. According to Illan, the town leaders had asked that they dismount from their horses before entering the town because the last time they rode in, Nahala and some of the others raced through the streets and shot out the street lights.

I held up Bear so he could watch them ride toward us. I heard my brother Michael shout my name when they got closer. He broke away from the others and rode straight at me. I put Bear down and stepped away from him, not sure what Michael was going to do. He leapt off his horse and on top of me. We rolled in the grass laughing.

"Stupid. So stupid," he said. "You can't hide from family forever. I could have told you that."

"I missed you too," I said.

"Was that a harling I saw you holding?" he asked.

I motioned toward Bear who was watching Michael's horse sniffing at the grass around us. "My harling, Bear," I said.

"Hello, little one," Michael said.

Since Bear didn't respond, I explained, "He isn't rude. He just doesn't talk."

"Oh," Michael said as he stood up and brushed himself off. "He'll get along with my high harling then. River talks enough for two harlings."

The others around us dismounted. Horses stomped and shook their heads. Hara greeted Illan and Drake. Jewel stood over me and extended his hand. I took it and stood up.

"I told them you would be here," Jewel said. "No har believed me."

I smiled at him. "They should know better by now."

Michael rolled his eyes. "Jewel doesn't need any compliments. His ego is big enough as it is."

I introduced Bear to Jewel and the others. I hugged Solace, Terzah's brothers – even Nahala. I met the new hara and laughed at old jokes as we walked into town together. It felt like I had come home.

I sit in the courtyard alone with Tree. I relax for the moment away from all the adults who want to pick me up and touch me. It is not like Tree at home because this Tree does not need me to climb high to tell me its secrets. I touch Tree's smooth bark and I know it is happy in the shelter of the house and with the sunlight in the open courtyard. It likes to hear Drake sing.

River sees me as he comes down the stairs and shakes his head. He is a little older than me with feathers in his brown curly hair. "Drake doesn't like anyhar touching his tree."

I take my hand off Tree's bark, although Tree didn't seem to mind being touched.

"You're new. You don't know the rules," River says. "Drake won't yell at you, but Illan will. When Aris tells you he is telling the truth, he's probably lying. And never ever climb on Zia or Jewel because they don't like it."

It seems like a lot of rules. I look up at Tree's leaves. Tree is not listening to what River says.

"You're younger than me, so you probably don't know everything yet," River says and moves rocks from around the bottom of Tree onto the pavement. "Your hostling and my high hostling were humans."

I've heard this from my hostling. I don't know the meaning of this word but it is darker and larger than the others he says.

"That means you're more human than me," River says as he lines up the stones on the floor in a spiral. "I think that's why you don't talk."

River's hostling, Blanco, leans over the balcony overlooking the courtyard. "River, what are you doing? We have to get the courtyard ready for the party tonight. Take Bear outside and find something else to do."

"Okay," River says. "Let's go, Bear."

We explore outside the house for a while. I look at Illan's transports, but River gets impatient and grabs my hand. He pulls me up and down streets and past somehar selling sweets and fry bread to a long building where harlings of different ages are playing.

"Look, Bear," River says and points at an odd harling with a head too big for its body and giant eyes. Its light is weak and thin even for a harling. It runs slow and clumsy. "A human."

Dura was like this once but I can't imagine my beautiful hostling as a deformed harling.

River releases my hand. "Let's play," he says and runs to the other harlings.

I watch him easily join the harlings chasing each other. I don't like harlings. They laugh and mock me. One harling at school back home pushes me to make me talk. They don't know how to Be. I stand still and listen for Wind to speak to me.

A har with long dark hair and tan skin walks toward me. He has a light made of many shades of blue. I wonder if he is my hura too since I seem to have so many. "You must be Bear," he says. "I'm Bela. I grew up with your hostling. Would you like to help me with some papers?"

I like his face and his fingernails are painted the same colour green as his shirt. I give him my hand and we walk together toward the building that the harlings are playing around. When I get to the door, I realise that it is a school. I stop.

Bela looks down at me. "It's okay. Your hostling will know where to find you."

I go inside with him and he gives me a stack of papers and lets me sit at a big desk while he leans over the papers beside me. The room is cluttered with interesting things like rocks and dried flowers and plants and books and twisted metal scraps.

Bela gives me a pen. "So far, every harling wrote the wrong answer for number three. Either they all cheated off each other or I messed up that lesson. Look, this one is wrong too. Can you put an X on the number three?"

I do as he says and look at him to make sure I did it right. He smiles and squeezes my shoulder. We go over a few more papers. I mark what he tells me. I turn to a new paper and see a different answer for number three. I pick it up and point at it.

Bela laughs. "Finally, a correct answer. Maybe I'm not such a bad teacher after all."

Bela's relaxed energy is soothing after being around my loud huras. I sense Bela's attention shift from me. "Bear, do you think if I ask your hostling to dinner he'll say yes?" he asks.

I look up and see my hostling in the open doorway watching us. "You look good, Bela."

"So do you," Bela says. He moves around the desk and hugs Dura. "I was hoping I would get a chance to see you alone."

"So you kidnapped my harling?"

Bela chuckles. "It worked, didn't it?"

Dura glances at me. "I'm surprised you got Bear in here. He doesn't like school."

"Some harlings respond to structure and some don't. Does your village offer alternatives to formal education?"

Dura shakes his head. "It's a small village."

Bela takes Dura's elbow. "Let's talk outside."

Bela led me past the door to a patch of bare earth beside a concrete wall. I kept my back to the school. I didn't like remembering what happened here when we were young. Bela brushed his hair from his face with both hands. His clothes were as neat as always.

"Illan spoke with you?" I asked.

"I saw him this morning," Bela said as he turned his face up toward the sun. He was close enough that I noticed his hair smelled like apples and cardamom.

"What did he say?" I asked.

Bela shrugged and looked at me. I felt desire tug in my chest. "Do you really want to talk about Illan?"

"There's nothing wrong with Bear," I told him.

"I know," he said and brushed his fingers across my forehead to move my hair over my face to one side. "He seems normal to me."

My knees felt weak. I leaned back against the wall. "You're the first har I haven't had to convince of that."

Bela laughed lightly. "'Normal' might be the wrong word. I think he's brilliant in some way you haven't figured out yet. Does he have an affinity for anything?"

I shrugged. "He likes rocks, trees, and the river. Nothing unusual."

"So nature, then. If I was his teacher, I would use that to keep his interest and work on a lesson plan to address what he needs and what you want for him."

"Sounds like you're trying to get me to enrol Bear in your school."

Bela smiled. "Is it working?" He motioned to the door with his head. "We should get back to Bear."

When we went back inside, Bear held up some papers. Bela leaned over the desk and shuffled through them. "Good work. I need to hire you as my assistant," he said.

Bear grinned. I was surprised by how responsive Bear was with Bela.

"We should let you get back to your students," I told Bela.

Bela looked up at me. "Will I see you at Illan and Drake's party tonight?"

"Perhaps," I said with a tilt of my head and a small smile. "Let's go, Bear."

Bear stood up and hugged Bela. I almost gasped. Bear never hugged anyhar besides me unprompted.

"Well, Bela, you work fast," I said. "You've made quite an impression on Bear."

"Hopefully, I can make an impression on his hostling later."

"I bet you say that to all the hostlings," I said.

Bela grinned. "And the fathers."

When we return to the house, it is decorated with pine and juniper and candles. Tree is wearing long strips of knotted red cloth, which makes Tree proud. I eat dinner in the kitchen with Dura and River and then take a bath. Dura has never let me go to a party before and I am anxious to see what adults do at parties.

Once hara from town arrive for the party, River and I keep close to the edges so the adults won't notice us, in the hope that we will be overlooked. My hostling and huras are dressed in fine clothes and move among the other hara with a grace that I have not seen before. Drake and Illan shine so much that it is hard for me to look at them. Bela arrives late. I sense Dura's excitement, but he remains on the other side of the courtyard.

Aris gives River a taste of his sheh and River giggles. River becomes more daring and tries to steal another har's drink, but his father notices and tells us that it is time for us to go to bed. As we walk up the stairs, I see Bela with a drink in his hand watching Dura. I wonder if they will spend the whole night watching each other.

River tells me that he is going to sleep in my bed with me. He falls asleep quickly, but I can't. When River starts talking in his sleep, I get out of bed and put on my clothes and sneak to the balcony overlooking the courtyard. I see Dura and Bela still glancing at each other.

I watch them for a while but I begin to feel a humming sound in my feet. I go back to the hallway and find an open bedroom door. Jewel is meditating. Bright lights in shifting colours radiate from him like a rainbow from the sun. A hand touches my shoulder.

"Leave Jewel to meditate in peace," Zia says and he closes the door.

He takes me back to my room and sits cross-legged on the floor at the foot of the bed in front of a tall mirror. I think for a moment that Zia is going to meditate too, but he holds his hand out to me and I sit on his lap. We look at each other in the mirror.

"You should reconsider your decision not to talk," Zia says. "It upsets your hostling and it keeps other hara from knowing you."

I don't want to hurt anyhar with words. It seems better not to talk.

"Silence can hurt too," he says.

We are still for a moment and then Zia asks, "Do you see your own aura, your light?"

I shake my head. I don't have an aura.

"When you come into your power after feybraiha, you'll shine like the moon." He holds his hands in front of me and in the mirror I see a glimmer of lavender and silver above them.

I look down at his hands, but they are empty. I look up at my reflection again and see the shimmer of colour in Zia's hands.

In the mirror I see Aris appear in the doorway behind us. "Zia, are you okay?" he asks.

Zia nods and says, "Just clearing my head."

"Are you coming back to the party?"

"In a little bit."

Aris sits on the floor beside Zia. I watch in the mirror as he moves Zia's hair over his shoulder and stokes his neck. Zia shudders and closes his eyes.

"I think...I think we should have a harling," Zia says and he opens his eyes slowly.

Aris shakes his head. "You're just saying that because we're with the family and you're holding a cute harling on your lap." He taps the top of my head with his index finger.

"But you want a harling," Zia says.

"I would love to host our harling, but I don't want you to do something because it's what *I* want. You became har because it was what I wanted, even though we didn't know if you'd survive, and your althaia was horrible. I promised you that I wouldn't force what I want on you again. I don't want us to have a harling if it isn't what *you* want."

Zia grabs the front of Aris's shirt with his fist. "That's a ridiculous analogy. I've never regretted becoming har because of how awful my althaia was and I *did* survive, in case you forgot."

Aris lays his hand over Zia's fist. "To me it sounds like you decided to do this in the moment. I know you, Zia. You don't make decisions without first casting runes and then consulting omens five or six times."

Zia narrows his eyes. "We could cast runes now."

Aris laughs and jumps up to his feet. He picks me up and puts me on the bed. He makes me lie down. "I hope you realise that if we have a harling, he could be like River."

River starts muttering in his sleep again.

"Then you'll finally have somehar who will appreciate your jokes," Zia said.

Aris pulls the blanket around me. "That was almost funny, Zia."

Zia lays his hand over my eyes and whispers the word "sleep." And I do.

I sighed and watched Bela across the room. He was talking with Illan but his body was turned toward mine. His hair was pulled back from his face and I couldn't stop staring at the hollow at the base of his throat. He saw me watching and smiled. His eyes held my gaze. Illan looked over his shoulder at me. I turned back to Michael.

I groaned. "I don't remember Bela being so beautiful."

Michael laughed and handed me a drink. "Bela was always beautiful. You never noticed because he only had eyes for Illan."

"I've known him my whole life. He's practically our brother."

"But he isn't our brother," Michael said and pointed at the glass in my hand. "Drink."

I swallowed my drink in one gulp. Sweet spicy syrup coated my tongue and the back of my throat. I made a face. "What was that?"

Michael grabbed me by the shoulders and spun me to face Bela. "Stop trying to figure everything out. Go get him," he said and gave me a shove.

I stumbled a bit before I regained my balance. Warmth and numbness from my drink crept through my muscles and down to my fingers and toes. I locked my eyes on Bela and crossed the rest of the way in what I hoped was a seductive manner.

Illan and Bela stopped talking. "Sorry to interrupt," I said as I brushed past Illan. "I need Bela for a moment."

Bela raised his eyebrows. Before he could say anything, I leaned forward, grabbed his short collar, and pressed my mouth over his. Bela chuckled and opened his mouth to mine. His hand settled on my shoulder. I closed my eyes and his breath-vision of a lightning-scarred oak tree in a pale green prairie at twilight unfolded around me. I could hear locusts chirring and feel the heavy heat of mid-summer.

I pulled back and took a deep breath. "Um, wow."

Bela grinned. "Was that all you wanted?"

"Maybe a little more."

"I think I can manage that," Bela said as he grabbed my hand and pulled me toward the door. I heard Michael cheer as we left.

"My place isn't far," Bela said as we got outside.

The cool night air cleared my head. I released Bela's hand. "Wait. I can't leave. If Bear wakes up…"

Bela shook his head. "You're right. I wasn't thinking." Bela embraced me and I was surprised at the heat of his body, like his skin held the warmth of the sun. "I know another place," he said.

Bela led me around to the side of the house to a small outbuilding. He pressed his hand to the door and I felt pressure in the air build and then pop as Bela deactivated the wards on the door. "It's Illan's workshop," he said. "It's close enough that you can go to Bear if he needs you."

"You must think I'm silly," I said. "The whole house is full of my family."

Bela opened the door and motioned for me to follow. "Of course not, they're strangers to Bear."

I felt relieved, but I should have known Bela would understand. He dealt with hostlings and harlings all the time. It was dark inside Illan's workshop but I saw dark metal shapes scattered over the floor. The air smelled crisp and acidic.

Bela took my hand again. "Careful. He's modifying a transport. There are parts all over the floor." He led me through the clutter to a shell of a transport with a hull that gleamed like an opal in the moonlight. The door squeaked as Bela opened it. "Ever taken aruna in a transport?" he asked.

"No," I said. "Won't Illan be angry if he finds out?"

Bela laughed. "Do you really care if Illan gets angry?"

Something in the tone of his voice reminded me that Bela and Illan had a long off and on relationship. Maybe I wasn't the only one with past grievances with Illan.

"Not at all," I said and pulled Bela into the transport with me.

In the morning Dura wakes me in a rush. "I overslept," he says. "The ceremony's started. We have to hurry."

I see that River is gone. I dress quickly and we run downstairs to the courtyard. Dura leads me through a crowd of standing hara toward Bela. I hear Jewel singing. Gold and silver words float up through the open courtyard. I watch the words in the sky. An eagle circles around them.

Dura picks me up. A flash of light reflects off a knife and blood runs down Illan's arm. I bury my face into Dura's neck and he whispers. "It's not bad, Bear. It's good."

I look up again and Jewel ties a silver cord around Illan and Drake's bleeding arms to bind them together. As he does, I see their lights merge and blend in the same way that Aris and Zia's lights do.

Soon everyhar is cheering and hara move forward to congratulate Illan and Drake. Bela leans over to Dura. "Let's go outside," he says.

Outside Bela lights a cigarette and he sucks on it before he hands it to Dura.

"I always thought that would be you up there with Illan one day," Dura says.

Bela shakes his head. "Drake is a good har. I don't wish them ill because it didn't work between Illan and me." Bela watches Dura breathe in smoke from the cigarette. "Are you really leaving tomorrow?"

Dura nods.

"Are you in a hurry to get back to Bear's father?"

Dura laughs. "Bear's father is long gone... for me anyway. He visits Bear when he can, but he never wanted a family. He said it was too much pressure."

"Why did you decide to have a harling with him?"

"Terzah had just died and I realized how much I missed being part of a family. He was the one I was with at the time. It wasn't a well thought out plan."

"Let's walk to the hill," Bela says and he takes Dura's hand. I run ahead of them because I am glad to be outside with Wind and

Earth. I get to the hill first, but I don't see them so I run back. They are sharing breath. I grab their hands and pull them forward.

Dura laughs. "Bear is impatient."

The hill isn't big, but at the top I see the whole town. I run from one side to the other and back to Dura and Bela.

"I lived here up here when I was young, Bear." Dura says as he looks over the town. "I'm surprised no har has built up here,"

I try to imagine my hostling as a deformed harling with a big head living on this hill with my huras but I can't.

Bela sits on the ground. "Terzah hasn't been gone that long."

Dura sits beside Bela and they lean their shoulders against each other. "I assumed he went back to the clan. There was nothing really keeping him here."

"He did, but he would come back from time to time."

I sit behind them and take off my shoes. I want to throw them over the side of the hill to watch them tumble to the bottom, but I leave them beside Dura instead. I stand up and feel Earth cool and firm under my feet. I hold out my arms and Wind wraps around me and tugs at my clothes.

"Did Terzah ever say anything to you about me?" Dura asks Bela.

Bela leans back on his elbows. "He was proud of you for striking out on your own. He changed. In the past few years, he grew more introspective."

Dura laughs. "I can't imagine a serene Terzah."

"I didn't say serene, but it took a little longer for his temper to show up. I think he needed time to reflect on who he was without Zen."

I feel something under my feet. Earth wants to show me something. I kneel down and start digging with my fingers.

"You and Terzah were close?" Dura asks.

"We were close. I don't want to make you sad, but Terzah told me he had a dream about you. He said he felt it was time to end the silence, but he wanted to go to River's naming day first because he knew it would take time to settle things with you."

I uncover something in the dirt with gold metal circles and dark blue stones. I pick it up and a shock travels up my arm. I see silver eyes in my mind. I shout for Dura and fall backwards.

Dura grabs my arms and pulls me up to my feet. I realise that my eyes are closed. When I open them, I see Dura and Bela above me. "Are you okay, Bear?" Dura asks.

I open my hand and show them what I found. The psychic energy that was on it when I first touched it is gone now.

"That's one of Terzah's earrings," Bela said.

"Bear, you said my name," Dura says and hugs me hard. "I like the sound of your voice." His green light tickles and I wiggle out of his arms. I see such happy colours in his light that I know I pleased him. Maybe Zia is right that words are good too.

Dura takes the earring from my hand and attaches it to the collar of my shirt. "This is a gift from your high hostling," he says to me.

Bela watches Dura's face and then touches his cheek. "I like you, Dura." His soft words stroke Dura's skin like feathers.

Dura smiles and says, "You made that clear to me last night."

"Is there any way I can convince you to come back?"

"I think we can work something out."

They share breath. I roll my eyes and I feel Wind tugging on my clothes. I run to the far side of the hill where it slopes into a flat field. I hold out my arms like eagles' wings and run as though I am flying. Laughter bubbles out of me and Wind whispers Be.

Epilogue

I gazed at the outside of my house. The setting sun cast long shadows under the eaves, which made me think the house looked sad. Bear was leaning against my legs examining a locust shell that he found.

"Are you going to miss our house, Bear?" I asked.

No response. Bear was speaking more each day but there were times when he was caught up in his inner world. I touched the top of his head and he looked up at me. I repeated my question and he shook his head.

Surprised, I asked, "Not even a little bit?"

He shook his head and pointed at Bela, who was trying to shove another bag into the backseat of my transport.

"I don't know what you're trying to say," I told him.

"Live with Bela," he said.

I stroked Bear's face and nodded. We had spent a few months travelling back and forth from each other's houses before we decided to live together. "Living with Bela is one of the advantages of moving to New Hope," I said.

Bela cleared his throat. Bear and I looked at him. "I'm not complaining," he said as he held out a lumpy bag, "but do you really need all these rocks?"

"Mine!" Bear shouted and threw himself against the bag.

"Sorry, Bear," Bela said. "I didn't know were yours."

Bear took the bag and sat on the ground. He reached inside and took a rock out. "Rock from water," he said as he placed it in front of him on the ground. He took out another rock and said, "Rock from next to water." After the next rock he said, "Rock from next to tree."

I gave Bela a look that I privately call the "Terzah stare" and crossed my arms over my chest. "You thought those rocks were mine? What kind of a har do you think I am?"

Bela shrugged. "A beautiful, eccentric har."

I smiled. "Good answer," I said.

I sat on the front end of the transport and absentmindedly stroked a rough scratch in the paint from when Bear rolled rocks over it. I'm sure Illan would have had a fit if he saw it. The transport looked full and there were still more boxes around Bela's feet. "It isn't all going to fit," I said.

"I'll make it fit," Bela said as he ran his hands through his hair and looked at the boxes around him. "Maybe Bear can ride on the roof?"

Bear gasped and turned to me with his mouth open and eyes wide. "Can I?"

"No!" I said.

Bear sighed and turned his attention back to his rocks. "Rock from under tree," he said as he held up another rock.

I stood up and went to Bela. I wound my arms around his waist and rested my head on his shoulder. "I'll come back for the rest of it tomorrow while you're teaching."

"I can do it," he said. "I want you and Bear moved in by tonight."

"Why tonight?" I asked.

"I want you and your stuff in one place, so you don't change your mind."

I gave Bela a shake. "No way. Besides, you might change your mind about us, too." I saw movement from the house next door. I sighed. "My nosy neighbour is watching us."

"Let's give him something to watch," Bela said and shared breath with me.

I felt a light pat on my thigh that I knew was Bear. I picked up Bear and held him in the centre of our embrace. Bear reached his hands above our heads and gathered air in his arms like as in a hug. He laughed and said, "Be."

Antiques

Wendy Darling

Antiques

I deal in antiques. Some hara say I'm an antique myself, but strictly speaking, that's not at all true. Sure, I've been in the business twenty years, but I'm only thirty years old, and for a har that's really just getting started. As it happens, I had a reminder of that very fact today, which is what's prompted me to share what I'm about to share – a day in the life of my shop and the hara I met there.

My shop, which I opened fifteen years ago, after I ran out of room in my apartment, is just off the main street in Galhea. It's on the ground floor of an old human dwelling – appropriately – while I myself live upstairs in a comfortable space with two cats and a collection of antiques I love so dearly I kept them for myself.

All sorts of hara come into my shop – locals, tourists, traders, and people like me who just can't help collecting the rarities on which I've built my life. Nearly all of what I sell is from human times and thus stuff that's not made anymore, whether because the resources aren't available or there's no longer a need. Plus a lot of human culture just died, rejected by the young males who were incepted and afterward decided to start over. But fortunately, a lot of it has lingered here on this earth and by now, two hundred years after the rise of Wraeththu, hara are beginning to become more interested in their cultural heritage. The younger hara, who are generally separated by generations from humans, grow more and more curious about their forebears and want to learn more – fortunately for me.

I'm a youngish pureborn myself of course, yet the fact I even use the term "pureborn" – dated at this point, when there are no more inceptions – is a sign there's something a little different about me. It's that difference that got me into antiques in the first place really. You see, unlike the hara I just mentioned, I'm not generations away from my human ancestors, but just two generations away. My highparents, on both my hostling and

202

father's sides, were human. "But how can that be?" hara wonder. It's called being born late. My parents had me when they were both over a hundred years old! Given that they're both scientists, I've always joked that they had me as an experiment to see if it was possible. How long do hara remain fertile? They always denied this, saying it happened spontaneously and they were nothing but happy about my coming along. I don't doubt the happy part, but I still think it was a bit of an experiment.

But now I've gone and gotten off track and even gotten nostalgic, thinking about my parents, who sadly are no longer with us. They faded out, as it's said, only about five years ago. Sometimes I think they are still around – watching me, skulking around the shop, walking beside me when I take long walks – and I suppose I'm not wrong, for it's said hara's souls are immortal and some stay around long after their bodies have gone.

Anyway, back to how I got into antiques. (I did start to explain that, didn't I?) First, I had parents whose parents had been human. Second, those highparents of mine, all incepted, had stayed more attached to their human past than most hara. Not that they stayed in touch with their relatives (all dead, I'm afraid), but they didn't reject human culture and history the way I mentioned earlier. They enjoyed old books, old furniture, and collected things like photos, maps and drawings showing the way things had been – *before*. My hostling actually grew up in a large old house elsewhere in Megalithica, out on the plains, before coming to Galhea – and taking a good deal of his family's human past with him.

And so the chain has continued. I grew up with old parents, in an old house, and surrounded by quite a lot of old things. Not to say I don't like some new things or am bitter about "hara today," like some old crotchety types, but there's something that resonates in me when I'm around these old things, and so I gravitate towards them. Having an antique shop, the stuff even gravitates towards me, as hara come into the shop looking to sell or to ask questions about pieces they've found. Which leads me to where I wanted to go, which was to tell the story of a day in my shop – and the hara who come into it.

As I said, my shop is on the ground floor of an old house, about three hundred years old, in fact. It was referred to as "turn of the century" at one time, but of course all this time later that reference doesn't exactly work. It's a solid wood house, with cedar siding, solid wood floors and doors, all of which have heavy brass knobs and handles that somehow never got stolen. (Or maybe somehar went and collected a set of them and installed them before I got here. In any case, they're there now!) The ceilings are high and there are two cozy fireplaces, one on each floor. Though the ground floor was converted as shop space decades ago, the kitchen is still at the back of the floor, which works, since it saves me having to go upstairs every time I want toast and tea. There's also a basement, where I keep some overstock, plus a backyard with a garden and shed, which is also, yes, filled with overstock. (Antique dealers never have too much stuff – they just have overstock.)

My place in the shop is at the front opposite the entrance. Hara ask me why I don't have the desk right at the door, and it's because I don't want to intimidate customers. Who wants the saleshar looming over them when they might not even know what they're looking for? (Not that I *loom*. I'm a little har. Perhaps it comes from having old parents?) So I have a broad desk, with a lamp and file cabinets and bookcases. I have a nice old chair, solid oak, with a seat shaped like my butt, which might not be comfortable for everyhar but is quite suitable for me. (Often, one or the other of my cats will try to claim the seat is made for their butts, but I quickly relieve them of that notion with a sweep of my hand.) There's an old patterned carpet below all this, belonging to my father's parents who got it from someone or other in the family's past. So I sit on human history every day in the shop.

So picture me, in the shop at the desk in the chair shaped like my butt on top of this old carpet, listening to music. Did I mention music? No, I didn't. Well, in addition to all the other stuff I got into as a harling, all the books and photos and maps and tools, I was especially interested in the music collection that had come down from my highparents. This was actual old human music, recorded, and listenable via various players. Now, most of this stuff has been tossed, because the fact is that most technology nowadays doesn't run on the type of fuel these gadgets need. However, my highparents were devoted to this collection and always kept their machines in shape, collected more when they found them, and also collected power sources. In the end they went with solar batteries, of which they amassed a mighty collection, many of which I still have myself. And this is how I can spend my days listening to music from two hundred years ago or more and also wow my customers, many of whom have only heard *of* old-style recorded music, not actually *heard* it.

I was at my desk this morning, listening to some zither music (zither is a type of old stringed instrument) on speakers when in walks a young har. Right away I guessed he must've just gone through feybraiha, because not only did he give off that vibe, but he was wearing all new clothes, presumably since he'd rapidly outgrown everything he owned. He was tall and lanky, with scraggly black hair and an air of uncertainty.

"Good morning," I said, making sure he was looking my way before I spoke. (I hate startling customers!) "First time in here?" (Of course I knew it was.)

"Hi," he said, approaching the desk. "Yes, never been in here before, but my parents have, which is why they sent me. Said you could help me with something."

"Perhaps," I said. "What do you need help with?" (Meantime I was thinking I would like to help him upstairs to my bed, because despite the scraggly hair, he was rather appealing. But I am what they used to call a gentleman.)

So the used-to-be harling digs into his coat pocket and pulls out something I recognize instantly. "My high-high-hostling gave it to me for my feybraiha," he explained (proving my judgment had been right) "and he said it was really valuable, a treasure, but I don't know what he meant." (I was still keeping what I knew to myself.) "I've poked and prodded and shaken it, but nothing happens I think because we don't have the electricity it needs."

I picked the object off the desk where he'd placed it and looked it over. Very good condition, despite the aforementioned poking and prodding and shaking. "Your high-high-hostling didn't tell you what this is? What kind of 'treasure' it is?"

The harling shrugged. "Nope. He actually said he would expect me to figure it out. He laughed when he said it, but he laughs a lot at his age, so I really can't guess what was so funny."

It was time to come out with it. "Well," I said, "I'll tell you what you have. Or actually, if you don't mind, I'll *show* you."

I got up and went back to the table where I kept all my audio equipment. Then I fished out the cable I knew I'd need, plugged it in, and pulled out a spare speaker set, along with another cord. Then hooking cable and cord to the object of the young har's inquiry, I stood back.

"Ready to see what it is?" I asked, finger hovering.

The har stepped back around the desk onto the rug. "Sure."

And so I pressed the big white button and sure enough, it lit up, along with a digital display. I press another button and music, really loud, metallic, human music, blared out of the speakers.

"This is—" I began, fumbling with the volume buttons, "what you call an iPod. Extremely popular. Plays digital music, all kinds. 'Digital' means computer files basically. Unlike a record or a tape, neither of which you've probably heard of. Those take up space."

I pressed another button, skipping to the next song, then pressing again, on to another. "This device stores music so it doesn't take up space. I'll have to check the model but I think this iPod might have hundreds, even thousands of songs on it. All still, as you can hear…" I punched to a quieter song, "in playable condition."

The har's eyes lit up. "Wow! Can I hold it?"

I handed it over. "Of course you can, it's yours."

He turned it over, peering at the digital display, pressing some buttons himself. "Wow. Just— wow. I can't wait to listen to all of this, see what's on it!"

I smiled. "Happier about the present now than you were when you got it, aren't you?" I kidded.

"Yeah," he agreed, "and my high-high-hostling is going to get a thank you note as soon as I get home. Wow!"

After a few more moments, he handed the device back to me and I unhooked the cord and cable. The music stopped – and the har's smile disappeared.

"Oh, no," he groaned. "Stupid me. How can I go listen to this when I don't have any way to do that? No power, no speakers, no cable."

I had anticipated this and while he had toyed with the buttons, had come up with a solution. "Tell you what," I said. "I have solar batteries enough that I sell them and surplus cable and speakers. Let me fix you up."

The har grinned and soon we were on our way to constructing a human music exploration kit. He left with a box of goodies and

I was left with more spinners than I'd spent on the things I'd sold him. And such is my business.

The next interesting customer who came in made me laugh. Well, not that I laughed at him, but I chuckled inside as I watched him. He was a trendy young thing – younger than me, but at least a decade older than my iPod-owning customer – and he was digging into the clothing section apparently filled with glee.

Clothing doesn't have the lifespan of some antiques, or at least most of the clothing from history doesn't. What I mostly had in the shop, however, was clothing from the last few decades of humanity's reign, when clothing was made durable. These mostly weren't cotton or linen or flax or wool clothes, but synthetic stuff, made from chemical concoctions human engineers invented at a time when it seemed like a good idea to make things that never broke down. So there were shirts, dresses, skirts, pants, hats, shoes, and all sorts of other things that looked like they were right off the rack, two hundred years on. And this young trendy thing was loving them!

After at least twenty minutes of pawing and oohing and aahing, the har came up to me as I looked through a box of newly-acquired books. "Do you mind if I try these on?" he asked. "They're so lovely but eek, need to be sure they fit."

I waved to a door along the back wall. "There's a bathroom back there with a big mirror. Just promise me you'll come out and show the stuff off, assuming it fits."

"Sure," he said, walking off jauntily with an armful of antique clothes, none of which were the same color or even vaguely went together.

Ten minutes ensued – during which various muffled exclamations were heard through the thick bathroom door – before the har re-emerged, decked out head to toe in polyester.

I stifled a laugh. (Don't laugh at customers.) The har had put together an assemblage a magpie would envy. To start there was a form-fitting leopard-print (leopard: extinct wild cat) dress with a plunging neckline and a mid-thigh hemline with a vertical slit in it. Then there was a bright pink coat (well, a small coat, a *coatish* thing) made out of some sort of fluffy synthetic that included a good quantity of silver thread. On top of this was a ridiculous black and white scarf sort of thing made out of pom-poms the size of grapefruit. And the pom-poms had cat faces on them. (When I saw this thing at a swap meet, I just had to have it!) There was more: a couple of beaded chokers, pink earrings (which at least matched the coatish thing), and a gold-sequined purse. Finally, there were white high-heeled sandals with knotted ties going up to the knee.

"What do you think?" he asked, giddy.

I was tempted to tell him I thought he looked like what two hundred years ago would have been called a "tramp" or a "trashy whore," but instead I told him he looked fabulous and wound up with a tidy pack of spinners. The har didn't even bother changing out of the outfit, just begged a bag off me, stuffed his old clothes in it, and fairly bounced out the door, whistling a tune from the zither music collection still playing on my stereo.

My next memorable customers can in an hour after my own lunch. A sweet couple with a very young harling.

"Is it all right if we set him down?" one of the parents asked me. (I don't know which because oddly they looked so much alike. I think I can guess what the harling will look like grown up!)

"Um, that depends where you set him down," I said. "The books are fine, the clothes are fine, but the tools and gadgets and breakable things – not so much."

The har headed off towards the books, harling in tow. Meanwhile the other har, his lookalike, approached me at my desk. "I was wondering if you could help me?" (An oft-repeated line in my shop.) When I simply waited for him to go on, he glanced back toward the harling, then back at me. "I came here looking for some type of antique child's toy, an old human toy. I thought it would be something unique."

"Ah," I said. "I think I can help you out."

I got up and moved to a section near the clothes (which, I noticed needed rearranging after the trendy type had dived through them) where I keep a couple tables and a large case filled with toys.

The har stood and stared. "I had no idea," he said. "My friend who recommended I come here said he thought you had *some* human toys, but this is amazing!"

Unlike the clothes, the toys I had were made with both synthetic and organic materials. There were wooden toys, which somehow had not been burned for firewood, but closely guarded, and there were plastic figurines and child-sized ceramic teacups. And there were many, many dolls.

These were what caught the har's attention. "Wow. Female dolls! And— well, they're all females," he said, clearly puzzled.

"Almost all humans' dolls were female," I explained. "These here are Barbies – extremely popular, and as you can see from their condition, pretty durable, thanks to the 'wonder' of synthetics. These here," I gestured, "are baby dolls, and those down there are children."

The har goggled. "Amazing. I've never seen humans."

"Me neither," I said, "though I want to emphasize, these are doll versions of humans. Women didn't actually look like these Barbies."

The har reached out to examine one. "May I?" I nodded and he gently picked up a woman in a very tight dress. Her plastic hair was blond and tousled, her feet were pointed (but barefoot, as the shoes had been lost), and her chest-to-waist ratio was highly unrealistic. This I'd learned from photos of actual women and from what I'd read about Barbies, and this is what I explained to the har as his other half went about the safer sections of the shop with the harling.

"I'll take it," he said, holding up the first doll he'd grabbed. "I know there are more to choose from, but this one just feels right." He leaned close to my ear. "Can I pay you here and then slip it in my bag? Make it a surprise?"

After a quick exchange of spinners (and a trip to my change box, which I disguised as me needing a sip of my cooling tea), we were all settled, and the har walked towards the door. "Come on, darlings, it's past time for lunch and unfortunately this dear shopkeeper doesn't quite have what I was looking for."

The other parent wore a comical look of confusion for a moment, wondering how his chesnari had spent so much time looking at nothing, but quickly bent to catch the harling's hand and lead him toward the door.

"Thanks for all you help," the secret buyer said, with a wink, and he and his family left to enjoy lunch. I wondered what the harling would think of the Barbie.

A mid-afternoon customer was a har I don't particularly like. He's a local and while I don't know much about him, I do know he tends to come into my shop with "antiques" that often turn out to be rubbish. They might be "old," but more often than not they're not even from human times or if they are, they're broken or damaged beyond the point of salvage. Or they're just so common I can't possibly buy them off him, which is what he wants. What he always wants: "Found this in a basement I was renovating. Give me a hundred spinners for it?"

This was in fact what he was in for today, although as it turns out, this time he had not brought me rubbish. What he had brought me was a box of two dozen shiny old CDs. (CDs, non-antique-dealer readers, are "compact discs," one of the old music formats I referred to earlier when talking about the iPod.) A few were still in their cases (called "jewel cases" in the day, for they were made of hard, clear plastic) and had their covers. I was delighted, although like any good dealer, I concealed this as much as I could. A good way to lose advantage in a buy is to make it obvious how much you really want something.

"Found these in an old basement. Give me fifty spinners?" (I told you this har was predictable.) He looked hopeful.

I dashed his hopes. "Look," I said, "I'm interested. This one here…" I fingered an album with a fanciful illustration of a floating head, "is one I would love to have. But," I explained, "half of these are scratched and unplayable, and several others don't have any identification. So between half the CDs being junk and a fourth of them being unknown entities, I don't really see fifty spinners worth of stuff."

The har sighed out his nose. "Well, OK, how much would you give me, then?"

"Fifteen," I said.

"Twenty," he bargained.

"Seventeen."

He nodded and a few minutes later, I had a box of CDs, probably worth more than a mere seventeen spinners, and the har went off, his pocket more full than when he'd come in, whistling one of the zither tunes. (I was slowly infecting the city, you see.) A good trade!

The last customer I want to talk about is my favorite and the one who inspired me to write this in the first place: a har by the same of Seth.

He came in just an hour before closing time, while I was fixing a cup of tea in the kitchen. I heard the ring of the metal bell on the door and quickly added cream to my mug.

"Hello," I called as I made my way out. I didn't want anyhar thinking the shop was empty.

As I turned around a high bookcase, I saw who'd come in: A towering har with blue-black hair, high cheekbones and of an age I could hardly credit. He was a har nearing the end of his life, with that stretched, almost-not-there look hara get when they approach transition to the next life. I'd seen my parents go through it. I was very surprised, but also quite pleased, to have such a har in my shop.

"Welcome," I said. "Feel free to browse as long as you like. I'll be over here at the desk."

He nodded but did not speak. This was not unexpected, as fading hara often become ghostlike and act different to hara who are more in this world.

The har went slowly through the store. He was much more appraising of the merchandise than most hara, except for the occasional shopper from Kyme, who came with an eye towards adding to the city's famous collection. He held the books reverently, fingered the old clothes, and I saw his fingers moving to the music (now a woman singing old folks songs, not zither) playing on the stereo. I kept one eye on the book I was supposedly reading and the other on him. I was so curious!

Eventually the har disappeared into a section I couldn't see from my desk. I read a while, with both eyes, then began to tally up sales from the day and tidy up for closing. I was thus engaged when suddenly there was a cry from the back: "Oh my GOD!"

I rushed over, fearing perhaps the har had met with some accident, or perhaps moved right on to the next world. But neither had happened. Instead he was standing in the old photo section, a color portrait in his hands, staring. And then he began to cry.

I was bewildered and didn't know what to do. The har kept on crying. He didn't seem to notice me. His fingers stroked the outline of the face in the picture.

I focused on the face. It was that of a woman, late human period, from what I could judge, and she looked serious but kind.

Her hair was blue black and she had high cheekbones. She looked like—

The har suddenly looked over to me, apparently sensing my thought. "She was my mother," he said.

Flabbergasted, all I could do was blurt out, "Really?" I steadied myself against a display case.

He nodded, eyes brimming with fresh tears. "I remember this from our living room." He turned it over and looked at the back. "Yes, here's my father's handwriting: Geraldine."

I pushed myself into speaking coherent sentences. "Excuse me, but you must be very—"

"Old," he said. "Yes. Obviously." He gestured at himself and then at the photo. "I'm an antique."

Seth, as he introduced himself, then explained how he had been a late child of humans near the end of purely human days, and had grown up in a world rapidly being taken over by Wraeththu. Eventually, though not until he was twenty-one human years, he became on of them. And then lived a long, long time.

"You must be my highparents' age," I said as he wrapped up his story. "They were humans, incepted, too."

Seth looked me up and down. "Your parents had you very late," he guessed.

I nodded. "Good guess."

Eventually Seth offered to pay me for the photo, which somehow had wound up in my shop and in Seth's hands – despite the fact he had just moved to town, coming to Galhea for his last months, staying with some high-high-high-harlings of his. But of course I couldn't possibly sell him the photo. I gave it to him, along with a few other things he admitted he liked as well. Who better to give antiques to than an actual antique? And not just an antiques dealer, like me.

And so I sit back in my armchair, where I've been writing all night, upstairs, with cats snoozing on the couch nearby. On my stereo I'm listening to one of the albums the basement-digger had sold me. It was the album I'd really wanted. You see, I'd recognized the man on the cover from albums handed down to me from my highparents. With his wild black hair, kohl-lined eyes and harish good looks, I'd known right away the floating head on the album cover could only be Robert Smith of The Cure. *Disintegration* is in the air. But history is not disintegrating, at least not as long as hara remember to care for it as the treasure it truly is.

Give us This Day

Fiona Lane

Give Us This Day

Apparently, the local nayati burning to the ground was not excitement enough for one day.

Meridian had about half a second to reflect on this thought before a small stone missed his left ear by three inches. And hit him accurately on the nose.

At this point, his lofty intention to remain a disinterested bystander to the events playing out on the other side of the street evaporated in a stream of invective. He flung open the small wooden gate in back of his house and stormed across the road to inform the gathered mob of his displeasure. The gate flapped and banged behind him, disturbing a small grey cat sitting on top of the fence, which fled in alarm.

Out in the street, a tight and disapproving huddle of hara was gathered. Among them Meridian recognised many of his neighbours and regular customers. Standing opposite them, with a confrontational air about them, was a group of individuals he had never seen before. The interlopers were accompanied by two very large dogs restrained by metal chains — restraint which Meridian had no doubt could be released in very short order should the situation merit it. It was obvious that this was a delicate situation, one which would require a har with diplomacy to defuse without it erupting into further violence. A har with tact and discretion.

Unfortunately for all concerned, Meridian was not that har.

"What in the name of Aruhani's arse is going on here?" He stabbed a belligerent finger at the assembled throng.

One of the group of strange hara, a tall individual with a single plume of hair arising from his otherwise shaved head favoured him with a condescending look.

"Calm yourself, citizen, there's nothing to get excited about. It's just a routine search."

"*Citizen?* And what exactly is a *routine search?* Searches are not routine round here, I can assure you. This is a respectable and thoroughly unexciting residential district of Kyme, not some primitive backwater in Jaddayoth. Who are you, and what do you think you're doing barging your way into our peaceful neighbourhood and throwing stones at innocent hara?"

A small murmur of approval arose from the local hara, which ceased almost immediately when one of the over-sized hounds raised its hackles and growled menacingly, revealing alarmingly large teeth.

"I think you'll find, *citizen*, that the stones were thrown by your peaceful neighbours."

A har Meridian recognised as the occupier of the dwelling directly across the street from him half-raised his hand and smiled weakly, mouthing the word *sorry* at him.

"That still doesn't explain who you are or why you are here, provoking innocent hara into becoming tiresome stone-throwing militants," Meridian challenged the strangers.

"We are searching for a fugitive, tiahaar," the leader informed him, the slight emphasis on the word *tiahaar* deftly converting the honorific to insult, a fact that Meridian noted and gave credit for. "A wrong-doer whose actions have caused distress and fear to innocent hara such as yourselves and your law-abiding neighbours."

"Is that so? And what do you intend to do with this miscreant once you catch him?"

"Rehabilitate him, tiahaar. What else?"

"What indeed. Tell me, why is the local Law Enforcement Guild not dealing with the hunt for this desperado, as one might expect?"

"Sadly, tiahaar, the Guild finds itself stretched very thin these days. What with the Troubles and everything. The Concilium in its wisdom has decided to delegate some of the Guild's duties to external agencies."

"And that would be you."

"Precisely."

"Mercenaries and thugs."

The har bristled visibly and Meridian internally adjusting his inner scoreboard in his own favour.

"I hardly think, *tiahaar*," the har pronounced slowly, "that the Concilium would employ hara in whom they did not have *the fullest confidence.*"

'Oh, do you? Well you obviously don't know that bunch of

incompetents and freeloaders that make up the Concilium as well as I do. It doesn't surprise me that they can't manage to maintain law and order in Kyme — I doubt if they could organise a mass rooning in a musenda."

A hand flew up to the mouth of one of the local hara at this shocking heresy, whilst a small outbreak of tutting swept around the rest.

Meridian took no notice. "Much as we appreciate your presence and the deep sense of security it brings to us all to know that you are vigilantly patrolling the streets in search of criminals and ne'er-do-wells," he said, "I regret to inform you that you are wasting your time. There are no fugitives here. None at all. Only this fine group of hara you see before you who rise early, work hard, and retire at a reasonable hour to have aruna in one of three officially sanctioned positions before sleeping the deep and untroubled sleep of the blameless and clueless.

"You are, of course, welcome to search my own humble abode," he continued, "and I will assist you in every way possible, looking down the back of the seat cushions, pulling up floorboards, knocking holes in walls and digging through my pungent collection of domestic waste. I don't get a lot of excitement, so it'll be an experience to cherish, I'm sure."

The plume-haired har gave Meridian a sour look. "That won't be necessary, tiahaar. We have satisfied ourselves that the fugitive has not taken refuge in *this* particular street. We do, after all, believe him to be a har of some intelligence."

"Well, the very best of luck in finding and apprehending him, then. Can't have common felons outwitting the chosen representatives of the Concilium, can we?"

The har favoured Meridian with one last milk-curdling glare and then nodded to his companions. With a quick tug on the dogs' leashes, the group set off down the street, swaggering slightly and taking up more space than was strictly necessary. Meridian watched them go, debating with himself the advisability of employing a favourite hand gesture to their retreating backs.

The har who had thrown the stone cleared his throat nervously.

"Well, that was very—"

"Oh shut up, Chestnut, no-har's interested in your half-baked theories."

Without waiting to hear the unfortunate Chestnut's reply, Meridian turned and stalked back across the road towards his own home, leaving the small band of hara to discuss the evening's events among themselves with much indignation and exaggeration.

It was evening, the last grey of dusk quietly dying over the rooftops, and the yellow lamplight within the small back room of the house was warm and inviting. Meridian carefully closed the wooden gate of his small back garden, making sure the latch was firmly in place. The gate barely reached his waist, and any har of even moderate physical fitness could easily have climbed or stepped over both it and the equally self-effacing fence without difficulty, but it provided, in Meridian's mind, a psychological barrier against the outside world; a metaphorical "Keep Out" sign. And for any hapless har who failed to recognise a metaphor when he saw one, the physical "Keep Out" sign nailed to the gate performed a similar function.

Meridian entered the house and closed the door behind him. Inside was a narrow hallway, which ran the length of the building from back to front. At the front, the shop was dark and silent, and the room to the left of the corridor was also unlit, but the room on the right, his small inner sanctum where he spent most of his non-working hours, was cosy and cheerful with a log fire burning brightly in the grate and his favourite chair drawn up close to it. The warmth from the fire was welcome after the chill of outdoors. Despite the yellow flowers, which were everywhere announcing the arrival of Bloomtide, winter had not yet fully departed and the evenings were still cold after the sun had gone.

Meridian was looking forward to settling down in his chair beside the crackling fire, picking up the book he had discarded earlier and enjoying a good few hours' reading before he started work.

His plans for the evening, however, were thwarted by the presence of a small grey cat sitting in his chair with paws neatly folded and tail curled around its body. Its fur was striped in a darker grey, all the way down to the tip of its tail, and it had large grey eyes with which it was regarding Meridian calmly.

Meridian recognised it as the creature he had startled earlier. It must have run in here and found the warmth inviting. He decided to withdraw the invitation.

"Shoo!" he barked, waving his arm at the cat. "Get out! Off you go! Scat!"

"I don't think so," said the cat reasonably.

Meridian was not often lost for words, but then, (as he would reassure himself later), he was not often confronted with a talking cat. After several seconds of staring at the cat, he uttered the most profound thing he could think of.

"...What?"

The cat flicked its ears in the direction of the street outside. "I said I don't think I'm going out there again. Didn't you hear?"

"Yes, I heard quite clearly. I'm not deaf."

The cat crossed one of its front paws over the other and twitched the tip of its tail slightly. "There are dogs out there, you know."

"I know, but..."

"With fangs." Grey eyes blinked, once. "*Big* fangs. I am not keen on fangs. Especially when they come attached to bad-tempered dogs."

"Who is? But that's hardly the point, is it?"

"What is the point, then?"

"The point is that you are in *my* chair, taking up the space reserved for *my* backside, absorbing the heat from *my* fire, and breathing *my* oxygen. And also you are talking. Cats do not talk."

The cat licked the back of one front paw and fastidiously tidied a small patch of fur behind its left ear which had become disarranged.

"The empirical evidence would suggest otherwise," it said.

Meridian scowled. "Do not get clever with me. I refuse to stand here in my own living room discussing scientific methodology with a cat! Cats are not creatures you have conversations with, cats are creatures you put a saucer of milk out for — unless you are me, because I don't put saucers of milk out for cats, because I don't like cats, and I particularly don't like *talking* cats, so you are doubly unwelcome here."

The cat sighed, an almost inaudible exhalation, which was followed by the precipitation of what appeared to be a handful of sparkling dust. Meridian coughed and blinked away the particles, and when he looked again the cat was gone and in its place was a small and undernourished har with short grey hair sitting in its place on his seat.

"Explanation," Meridian said, slowly and deliberately. "Now."

"What exactly would you like explained?" asked the har.

"The whole cat thing would be a good start."

The har smiled disarmingly. "It was a disguise."

"Is that so? Most hara find a false nose and wig suffices."

"Ah, but most hara are not being pursued by the Forces of Evil."

"And you are?"

"I am indeed! You saw them! The bad-tempered dogs!"

"With the big fangs."

"Yes, and with the big owners who are big on hunting down fugitives with their big sticks."

"So you're the fugitive."

"Does that come as a hugely enormous surprise to you at this stage in the proceedings?"

"No, it doesn't, thank you very much. Why are they after you?"

The har tucked a stray strand of hair behind his left ear in a gesture eerily reminiscent of that performed by the cat earlier. "That's a long story."

"Who'd have thought? Does it have anything to do with you turning into a cat?"

"No, it doesn't, surprisingly enough. And I didn't turn into a cat, don't be silly. Hara cannot turn into cats. That would defy all the known laws of physics. Hara are much bigger than cats, as you've probably noticed, and for a har to turn himself into a cat he would have to disassemble himself at the molecular level then reassemble himself into the shape of a cat *and* find somewhere to put all the spare molecules left over from being a har. Can't be done." The har shook his head firmly.

"Then how did you..."

"I just make hara *think* I'm a cat."

"And the laws of physics are okay with that?"

"They're perfectly fine with that. The laws of the Concilium, I'm not so sure about, but I've broken so many of them that I don't think one more will make much difference."

"Again, I find myself in the unsurprised segment of the population."

"Don't be so judgemental, it's not nice. Anyway, the making-hara-think-you're-a-cat thing is quite easy really. Most hara are weak and simple-minded creatures, it doesn't take much to fool them." The har made a wavy gesture with his hands in front of his own eyes by way of illustration.

"Thank you. Well, now that you've had your fun here, you can shove off and do your party trick somewhere else."

"No, I can't."

"Why not?"

"I'm on the run from the Forces of Evil, remember?"

"Then I suggest you get on with the running part of that."

"I thought you might offer me sanctuary." The har blinked hopefully.

"What gave you that impression?"

"The way you spoke to those hara with the dogs. You don't like them."

"I don't like *anyone*. That includes you, by the way. I am very fair and even-handed that way. Now is there any reason I shouldn't call our dog-loving friends back and have you arrested?"

The har thought for a moment. "The satisfaction that comes from defying authority?" he suggested. "I bet you're the sort of har who enjoys defying authority."

"You're quite wrong." Meridian said tartly. "I am no such thing. I'm a baker. I enjoy living a completely dull and uneventful life based around the making and selling of bread."

"You don't look like a baker."

"Really? And what does a baker generally look like?"

"I don't know. Covered in flour?"

"I'm not baking at the moment. Later on, I'll be baking the bread for tomorrow, and I will be sure to sprinkle myself with flour the better to conform to your expectations. In the meantime, if you look above my shop, you will see the sign 'Baker' and below that in smaller and more modest letters, my name, Meridian har Suhl. If that fails to convince you, ask around the neighbourhood and many of those brave hara you saw standing up to the Forces of Evil in their own inimitable way earlier will confirm it for you."

"Fine. I believe you." The har thought for a moment. "This...er... bread you bake?"

"Yes?"

"You wouldn't happen to have any of it going spare at the moment?"

"Why?"

"I'm hungry."

"In which case there are charitable institutions which will provide you with something to eat tomorrow. I am not a charity. I am a baker. You are a nuisance. Go away."

"Just a little bit." The har smiled winningly.

"No."

"Please?"

"No!"

Meridian did not understand how the apparently simple and satisfying process of throwing out into the street an unwanted har who could change himself into a cat had mysteriously ended with the har sitting on his rug in front of his fire eating his bread, but it had been one of those days all round. He resolved to do better tomorrow.

The cat-har, on the other hand, seemed to be having an altogether better experience of the day. He tore at the bread with enthusiasm, stuffing chunks of it into his mouth rapidly.

"This is really good!" he declared, between mouthfuls.

"No it isn't, it's stale." Meridian told him. "It's yesterday's bread. That makes it stale, and that is the reason why I shall shortly be baking tomorrow's bread. Bread needs to be fresh."

"When you haven't eaten for three days," the har said between mouthfuls, "even something as disgusting as day-old bread can be quite welcome." He stopped eating for a moment and inspected Meridian's face.

"I'm joking." he assured. "It's not disgusting. It's really good. You're a good baker. Don't look so sullen."

"I'm not sullen. That's my normal expression."

"How unfortunate."

"And you're dropping crumbs on my rug. Don't. It'll attract mice."

"You should get yourself a cat, then!" the har suggested. "It's always good to have a cat around the place." There was a brief suggestion of sparkling dust again, and the image of a small grey cat appeared, then disappeared.

"Stop that. And no, you can't stay here. As soon as you've finished that bread you're leaving."

"That's what you said before you gave me the bread."

"Well, I mean it this time. I don't harbour dangerous criminals."

The har was indignant. "I'm not dangerous! Do I look dangerous?"

Meridian scrutinised him carefully. He had to admit that he looked about as far from being dangerous as it was possible for a har to get. His natural slenderness had been enhanced by three days of not eating, and his flesh seemed very thinly distributed across his bones. His pale grey hair was fine and fluffy and it stood up as if attracted by static, forming a downy halo around his head. Meridian could imagine blowing on it and seeing it fly off like dandelion seeds. His face was pale and moon-like, and dominated by the large grey eyes which watched everything intently.

"I notice you didn't deny being a criminal," Meridian countered.

"Circumstances can make criminals of the best of us."

"Trite. Try again."

The har pulled a face. "Why should I? I don't have to justify myself to you. You're a bourgeois baker, enjoying your peaceful, bread-based lifestyle without a care in the world while everyhar else in Kyme walks around in fear and terror."

"I'm not bourgeois, I work for a living."

"So you say. And what about the Fear and Terror?"

"I'd call it apprehension, myself."

"Ah, so you *do* admit it!" The har raised one finger and wagged it in Meridian's face. Meridian pushed it away crossly.

"I'm aware of the situation," he said.

"Of course you are. Everyhar is. How can you not be?"

"Ask the Concilium. *They* seem blissfully oblivious."

The har took the poker from its stand on the fireplace and gave the fire a prod. Flames shot up, and a shower of sparks disappeared up the chimney.

"If the Gelaming were here, this sort thing wouldn't be happening," he announced.

Meridian laughed unpleasantly. "Oh, I think it would. The Gelaming were never quite as amazing as they liked to pretend."

"What about Tigron Pellaz?" The har gave Meridian a triumphant look, as if this statement constituted the final word on the matter.

"What about him?"

"Tigron Pellaz will save us," the har declared, with evident conviction. "He will protect Wraeththu-kind from the Forces of Evil and usher in a new era of Peace and Prosperity for all."

Meridian gave a dismissive snort.

"No, he most certainly will not, for reasons which I could spend all evening enumerating, the most pertinent of which being that he has been dead for the best part of two hundred years."

The har gave him a pitying look. "Haven't you heard of reincarnation?"

"Yes, I have, but that still doesn't support your theory, since received theological wisdom says that no-har will remember any of his previous lives."

"Not ordinary hara, maybe, but Tigron Pellaz is different!"

"How so?"

"He was the first Tigron! He was... *Tigron Pellaz!* He united the entire Wraeththu world and brought Peace and Prosperity, showed us all how to be better hara, and he travelled to other dimensions and spoke with the dehara — and he could talk to animals and walk on water and jump higher than the legendary palace of Phaonica!"

"Amazing. Could he turn himself into a cat as well?"

"Yes! He could do anything!"

"I think you've been listening to too much Gelaming propaganda, my friend."

"It's true!" the har insisted, "And he's not dead, he's just sleeping, on the island of... I forget what it's called... and he will return to Wraeththu-kind in their hour of need and save them. Everyhar knows this."

"Tell me," asked Meridian, not even attempting to disguise his sarcasm, "is there a magic sword in this tale anywhere? An aquatic sorceress perhaps?"

The har's eyes narrowed suspiciously. "There might be," he conceded.

"In which case I think there's been a little recycling involved in your Glorious Myth of Tigron Pellaz."

"It's not a myth. What do you mean?"

"Go read a book and find out."

"Where would I get a book?" the har demanded.

"There's a rooning great library in the centre of Kyme. You

could start there."

"Oh, that place! It's haunted. Nobody goes there."

"It's not haunted, it's just suffering from neglect. The Concilium of Kyme seems to be as good at looking after our civic amenities as they are at maintaining law and order."

"There are ghosts there," the har said, shuddering slightly.

"Perhaps there are, but they are not the sort of ghosts anyhar needs to be afraid of."

"What sort of ghosts are they, then?"

"The ghosts of hara who could teach us many things."

"I already know everything I need to know."

Meridian made a disgusted sound. "Of course you do, my empty-headed little friend. You and everyhar else in Kyme — the Concilium, their hired thugs, the incurious and bovine hara inhabiting this fine neighbourhood, the Great and the Good of Kyme who show up to buy their daily bread, and not forgetting the occasional non-dangerous criminal, just passing through. Everyhar knows all they need to know about everything. Everyhar can stick their heads in the sand like the good little ostriches they are and let the entire Wraeththu world sink back into the slime from which it arose, and nobody will do a damn thing to stop it because they don't know what's causing it and they don't *care*. All they care about is drinking that vile slop the proprietor of the Mystical Badger sells as ale — and getting rooned on a regular basis."

The har stared at him thoughtfully. "What's an ostrich?" he asked. "And what is wrong with getting rooned on a regular basis?"

Meridian buried his head in his hands. "Dehara's droppings! I don't know why I bother!"

"I was only asking," the har retorted, "from the point of view of somehar who *isn't* getting rooned on a regular basis. Also, if things are as bad as you say they are, then why not ask the Dehara for help?"

"There are no Dehara."

"But you just invoked them only a moment ago. Somewhat blasphemously, I might add."

"It was a figure of speech," Meridian spoke slowly, as if explaining to a particularly slow-witted harling. "Hara say things like that all the time, it doesn't mean they're invoking anything.

I'm not expecting the Aghama himself to materialise out of thin air and answer my prayers."

"The Aghama answers all prayers." The har's grey eyes were large and serious.

"He didn't answer mine," Meridian said stonily.

"What did you pray for?"

"None of your business."

"You're supposed to pray for enlightenment."

"I don't need enlightenment." Meridian declaimed. "And I don't need deities that offer enlightenment. If we're going to have deities, then let's at least have deities that give you something useful."

"Like what?"

"Money, for example."

"You prayed to the Aghama for *money?*"

"No, I didn't. But I'd have much more respect for him if he answered prayers of a more practical nature. Like, *Dearest Aghama, please may I have twenty spinners to spend on unnecessary luxuries. What? You've only got enlightenment? No thanks, I'll pass.*"

"We are all striving for enlightenment. The Magister said so. He said the Gelaming could lead us and guide us. He said they were the most enlightened of Wraeththu tribes. He said they were seekers of knowledge."

"The Gelaming were a bunch of shameless poseurs whose seeking was mostly directed towards attaining power and admiration — and, oh yes, the general submission of all other tribes of hara."

"How can you say such a thing?"

"I can say such a thing, my wide-eyed and outraged young friend, because no thunderbolt will fall from the heavens and strike me dead for my heresy. No great hand of the Aghama will descend to smite me and wag a reproving finger at my lack of respect. The Gelaming will not spring forth from the Otherlanes upon their splendid white horses to show me the error of my ways, and Tigron Pellaz will not paddle himself over from his supernatural island having woken from his eternal slumbers for the sole purpose of setting me straight."

The har was quiet for a moment as he processed this. "Are they all dead, then, the Gelaming?" he asked

"Yes."

"You don't know that for sure."

"What I do know is that the Gelaming do not travel the Otherlanes these days, and neither do any other hara with any sense."

"Why is that?"

"It's dangerous. Hara disappear."

"The Vice-Archon says that is a nothing but a malicious rumour and we shouldn't believe any of it."

"The Vice-Archon is a fool and a liar."

"And I suppose you know better than him?"

"Yes, I do."

"Then why aren't you Vice-Archon, then?"

"Listen to me, um— what is your name anyway?"

"Perricat. And please do not shorten it to Cat, I'm not a cliché."

"The thought never entered my mind for a second. Listen to me Perricat, just because a har holds a position of power does not make him infallible. In fact, it does not even imply basic competence in most cases. The Vice-Archon and his minions on the Concilium do not want hara to know the truth about the dangers, because then they would have to do something about it, and they don't know what to do."

"Tigron Pellaz would have known what to do."

"I'm sure he would, but that doesn't help us one bit. Tigron Pellaz is busy enjoying the glorious afterlife and we are stuck here in Kyme, for our sins. Now if you'll excuse me, I need to go and start preparing the bread for tomorrow. After that I shall be retiring to bed for a couple of hours, and then I will be up again at an un-deharly early hour to bake it. I expect to find you gone by then."

Meridian noticed that Perricat had stretched out along the rug which lay in front of the fire, luxuriating in its warmth and occasionally digging his fingers into the worn woollen pile of the rug. He did not look to be in any hurry to move.

"Do you make cakes as well?" Perricat asked.

"No. Just bread."

"But cakes are nice. Especially the kind with icing on top."

"Bread is useful. Hara need bread. Cakes are unnecessary luxuries."

"But still nice. I bet you could make really nice cakes if you wanted to."

"I don't want to. I told you, I only make bread."

Without waiting to hear Perricat's opinion on the merits of other baked goods, Meridian rose from his chair and left the room, leaving Perricat still stretched out in front of the fire grinning cheerfully to himself.

The next morning Meridian arose before dawn and fired up the great brick oven in the kitchen to begin the day's baking. He tied back his long dark hair and donned a meticulously clean white apron. While he had slept, the bread dough he had prepared the night before had risen miraculously and the shapes he had moulded in neat and regular sizes had grown wayward in the manner of an unruly adolescent.

Taking his sharpest knife, Meridian cut a narrow slash down the length of each loaf to ensure that they rose evenly on top. His customers did not like lopsided loaves, and neither did Meridian – he took great pains to make certain that each loaf was perfect both in form and function. The kitchen was unheated most nights to guarantee that the dough rose slowly. The muscles in his arms were hard from the lengthy kneading given to each batch of dough; the punishment he meted out to the flour to give it the strength it required. As with life, it was the hardship that tempered. *Through suffering we rise,* Meridian thought caustically, surveying the array of risen loaves and rolls before him.

Checking that the oven was now at the correct temperature, he began loading the tins onto the long-handled shovel and then transferring them quickly into the back of the kiln with one smooth movement before the precious heat was lost. When it was full, he closed the black-leaded metal door firmly. There was no way to see into the oven once the door was shut, no way of telling how the bread was baking, whether it was rising lopsidedly due to uneven heat distribution in the oven, whether it was baking too slowly because the oven was cool, or whether it was scorching on the top due to the oven being too hot, to emerge blackened and burnt and rejected by his discerning customers.

Meridian was unworried. He knew this oven more intimately than he knew any har. He knew how long it took to get to just the right temperature, and how long it would remain at that heat. He knew not to put anything in to bake right at the very back left corner because it was sure to burn

He also knew the bread, knew from the feel of it, the weight of it, the smell of it and the sound of it how it would bake, and more than that, he knew — from a thousand other identical nights-and-mornings of kneading and baking and kneading and baking — exactly how long it would take to bake to perfection. There were no indicators on the oven and no timepiece in the kitchen, but Meridian had no need of them.

There was a blackened kettle sitting next to the oven with steam rising vigorously from its spout. Meridian wrapped a cloth around its handle to lift it and poured some of the boiling water into a cup, then added a pinch of dried herbs. A sharp mentholated aroma joined the other kitchen scents. The room was hot from the fire of the oven and Meridian was hot from his exertions, so he took his cup and went out into the narrow corridor separating the kitchen from the living room. The living room door was still closed, as he had left it upon retiring to bed, and as it had been when he arose. He opened the door and entered the room.

It was empty.

The fire in the grate had gone out, but the ashes were still warm. The cushions on his chair were plumped up and there was no sign of breadcrumbs on the rug. It was as if the previous evening's encounter had never happened. Meridian shrugged and walked over to the window. He stood there, looking out at the garden and the street beyond.

Dawn was approaching. Often from this window Meridian had watched as night gave way to day and a bright backdrop appeared behind the dark silhouettes of the houses opposite. When the sun eventually cleared their rooftops its rays would land on the wall above the fireplace in his room. Meridian did not know if he found it amusing or tragic to consider those photons having travelled a hundred million miles only to end up in a small back room expending their tiny spark of energy on the incremental fading of the pigments in the flaking paint on his wall.

But today there was nothing to see because rain had set in overnight. Not a lashing downpour of the type that would cause a har to dodge from doorway to doorway with his coat pulled up around his ears were he to unwisely venture out into it. Not even good old standard rain with discrete raindrops of regulation size and shape all falling at a rate within acceptable parameters, but the sort of low, heavy drizzle which was really only mist with an over-inflated ego — but which nevertheless could soak a har to the skin in a short space of time regardless of the thickness of his clothing, and which could wrap the sky and world and everything in it in a deadening shroud of grey.

For long minutes, Meridian gazed out the window into the half-light beyond, his hands wrapped around the mug of hot liquid, but he neither saw nor felt anything. Inside his head he was replaying the image of the dream he had had last night; a dream which might not have been a dream. A dream of a warm body in his bed beside him; of skin against skin, mouth against mouth, heartbeat against heartbeat. Of hair as soft as a cat's fur, or thistledown, and of his own body, warm and wet and willing beneath the har's insistent thrusting, because it had been so long, so very, very long...

Meridian shook his head to rid himself of the dream. Outside it was still grey, nothing had changed. The sun could well have cleared the horizon by now, but it would be impossible to tell. Inside his head, a small voice wordlessly informed him that the bread was baked to perfection and should now be removed from the oven. He carefully set down his cup down, half-drunk, and returned to the kitchen.

For the rest of the day he was kept busy with a constant stream of customers coming to his shop to buy bread. The rows of perfect crusty loaves upon the shelves were soon whittled away, as were the rolls, plaits, twists and long thin batons, of which he always made a second batch just before lunchtime to ensure freshness, even though it meant keeping the oven fired and ready.

By late afternoon he was sold out, so he tidied away the baskets, pulled down the blinds on the display window and turned his thoughts towards preparing his evening meal. He flipped the faded sign on the front door round so that the side reading "Closed" faced outward, and he was just pulling the door closed when a small grey cat dashed in from the street and sprinted round behind the counter and through into the back rooms.

Meridian cursed imaginatively under his breath, closed the door and locked it firmly, then followed the cat through to the living room. To his complete absence of surprise, it was sitting on his chair, licking its paws, which were wet and muddy.

"Off!" he commanded.

A handful of shiny grit hit him in the eyes, and when he had blinked it away Perricat was sitting in the chair grinning at him and squeezing the rainwater out of his shoes.

"You're good at that," he said. "Takes most hara a lot longer to de-cat me."

"I already knew."

"Not the point."

Meridian ignored him. "I thought I told you to go away."

"I did! I went into the centre of Kyme, had a look around — you're right about the library, by the way — had a bit of a stroll around the marketplace, spoke to a few nice hara, got wet, and now I'm back. What's for dinner?"

"The invitation for you to depart my house did not include within it the expectation of your return. And I'm not feeding you again."

"But I'm hungry. I haven't eaten all day."

"Then go and buy yourself some food."

"I don't have any money."

"Well, find yourself some employment and earn some, then."

"Oh, right. So I'm supposed to spend days, if not weeks, searching for somehar to hire me to perform menial tasks, and then wait until this evil taskmaster grudgingly pays me a tiny pittance — if he ever does — and in the meantime I starve to death and there is nothing left of my once-lovely body but a pitiful heap of bones lying on the ground staring accusingly up at passers-by. You've really thought this through, haven't you?"

"Not half as thoroughly as you have, obviously. And bones can't stare."

"Mine would. They would stare at *you* in particular, as you walked by, and you would be overcome with guilt and remorse and say to yourself–, 'Why, oh why, did I let that tragic and beautiful young har starve to death. Woe is me!'"

"No, I wouldn't. Trust me, I really wouldn't."

"You're really rude. Has anyhar ever told you that?"

"Frequently. Now are you going to leave, or do I have to throw you out?"

Perricat looked at him appealingly. "I haven't got anywhere to go," he wheedled. "And it's raining."

Meridian was unmoved. "Go back to wherever it was you came from. Go back to your family, if you have one."

"I don't."

"Oh. So where did you spring from, then?"

"I didn't *spring*, I was hatched like any other har, in a town two days ride from Kyme, but I lost my parents at an early age, and I grew up in an orphan-home which burned down the year I reached my feybraiha."

"Excuse me while I get my handkerchief out."

"Then a kindly couple of hara took me in, and I lived with them for about a year until the sad day their house burned to the ground and I was homeless again."

"You appear to have the most appalling luck, if I may say so. So how did you end up in Kyme?"

"I moved to Kyme when I was offered a place at the Lectorium under Magister Squill."

"What were you studying?"

"Well, I wasn't so much *studying* anything as *being studied*. But I had to leave quite suddenly when the institute closed due to unfortunate circumstances."

"Which were?"

"It burned down."

"Really. Tell me, were you anywhere in the vicinity of the nayati yesterday?"

"Why do you ask?"

"No reason," Meridian sighed, recognising defeat when it poked him in the ribs and kicked him in the shins. "I suppose you can stay one more night. But you are definitely leaving in the morning. I will be cooking broth and dumplings for dinner. That is all. There is no choice."

"It sounds delicious, whatever it is."

"You can find some dry clothes in the bedroom upstairs, while your own are drying off." Meridian stood up. "You already know where it is," he couldn't resist adding.

Perricat grinned. "I can light the fire for you, while you're cooking dinner," he said, indicating the now-cold hearth. "I'm good at lighting fires."

"I don't doubt it. Is this some other supernatural ability you have, like turning into a cat?"

"No, I just light 'em with matches, same as everyhar else."

By the time Meridian had the large pot of broth simmering away on the stovetop, evening was drawing in. Soon the season would change, Bloomtide would give way to Feybraihatide and the delicate, early flowers would step aside to make way for the more vigorous growth pushing and thrusting from the earth and from the branches of long-dormant trees. And the sun would shine and bring warmth to the land. Or at least, that was the theory; Meridian had lived long enough to know that a certain capriciousness was the hallmark of whichever dehar was charged with bringing sunshine to Alba Sulh, and he organised his provisions of both firewood and solid, nourishing food accordingly.

The broth was thick with meat and vegetables. He dropped the small, walnut-shaped blobs of dough into the liquid where they landed with a satisfying plop. Then he put the lid on the pan and went to inform his guest that dinner was imminent.

In the living room, a fire now burned industriously in the grate, and the room was pleasantly warm, but of Perricat there was no sign. Meridian tutted under his breath, and went back out to the corridor, at the far end of which was the narrow staircase leading to the solitary bedroom upstairs under the eaves. At the top of the stairs it was practically dark, only a feeble gleam of light entering from a small skylight in the roof. The upper part of his dwelling was cramped, and full of odd angles and slants, as if it had been added as afterthought, which was indeed the case. There were two doors at the top of the stairs — one leading to a small cupboard where he kept his linen and sheets, and the other into the bedroom. Meridian's height was half-a-head more than either of the doors, a fact which had caused him inconvenience, not to mention bruising on many an occasion. He grasped the handle of the bedroom door, opened it, ducked instinctively, and entered.

The bedroom ceiling sloped down at a steep angle dictated by the pitched roof directly above. There was a window opposite the door, but due to this gradient of the ceiling it was small and almost at floor level. To Meridian's right was the bed, hard up against the gable wall. In the opposite half of the room there was a large dresser with a mirror where Meridian kept his clothes. In the dim light of the dying day, he could just see the figure of a har dressed in well-made clothes admiring himself in the mirror, turning occasionally to view himself at a more favourable angle.

Meridian froze. All the oxygen seemed to drain from the air, leaving him unable to breathe. He could hear his own heartbeat ringing in his ears, too loud and too intrusive. He blinked, and looked again.

"Juni," he gasped.

The har turned at the sound of his voice, surprised to see him standing there. "I found these," he explained, indicating the clothes he was wearing. "They were at the back, I..."

He never got to finish the sentence. In three angry strides, Meridian was upon him, seizing him roughly by the shoulder. "What do you think you're doing? Why are you wearing those clothes?!"

"I told you, I found..."

"Get them off! Get them off now!" He pulled at the expensive fabric more roughly than he had intended and the shoulder seam parted.

Perricat stared at Meridian in shock, as if had unexpectedly transformed into a snarling tiger before his eyes. Realising what he had done, Meridian released Perricat and took a step backwards. "Not those," he managed to say, his voice choked. "The other ones. In the top drawer." He indicated the dresser.

Perricat did not move, struggling with the unexpectedness of the situation.

Meridian seized the handle of the dresser drawer and pulled it open. He snatched some clothing from within and threw the garments at Perricat. The clothes fell to the floor. There was a long, silent pause, then Perricat slowly bent down to pick them up, then stood up again equally slowly, his eyes remaining fixed all the while on Meridian.

With an effort, Meridian regained his composure. "Dinner's ready," he said, in something approaching his normal voice. "Downstairs."

Without another word, he walked out of the bedroom, leaving Perricat still staring at him, clutching the bundle of clothes to his chest.

Dinner was eaten in silence, broken only once by Perricat announcing brightly that it was the best broth he had ever tasted, an observation which was met with silence. When they had finished eating, Meridian gathered up the dishes, took them through to the kitchen, rinsed them off and then began preparing the dough for the next day's bread.

He mixed up the first batch, then turned it out onto the tabletop and began kneading it, digging the heels of his hands into its soft folds, turning and stretching, pushing and pulling, turning again, a quarter turn. There was an almost hypnotic quality to the repetitive movements. Knead and turn. Turn and fold. He could empty his mind of all thoughts and focus only on the rhythm and the softness of the dough under his hands. Knead and turn. Turn and fold.

The sound of the kitchen door opening behind him broke his meditation, but his hands continued with their work. With his back to the door, he felt rather than heard Perricat approaching him, his soft, cat-like footsteps und on the stone floor. Perricat walked around to the other side of the table and watched him work the dough for a few moments.

"I'm sorry," he began. "I didn't mean to do anything I wasn't supposed to. The other clothes just fit better." He held up one arm, displaying the sleeve of one of Meridian's own garments which dangled loosely beyond his fingertips."

"It's alright," Meridian said, continuing to pummel the dough. "It wasn't your fault. I shouldn't have shouted."

"Who is Juni?"

"Juniper. My chesnari." The rhythm did not alter, but the dough slapped down on the table with a louder thwack on its next turn.

"And those are his clothes?"

"Were. He's dead."

"Oh. I'm sorry."

"You said that already. There's no need to be. You didn't kill him."

"Who did? I mean, what happened?"

Meridian gave the dough one last turn, then patted it into smooth hemisphere. No point in ruining a good batch of dough by over-working it. He wiped his hands on the front of his apron, leaving floury marks down it.

"Some years ago, Juni and I were working for the Concilium. We were investigating some strange events involving travel in the Otherlanes. Hara would enter the Otherlanes, but never appear at their destination. There were different theories amongst high-caste hara as to what had happened. Some said that the hara had merely misjudged their exit point and had ended up somewhere different, possibly even another realm altogether, and would reappear eventually when they found their way back. Some said that these hara had achieved *enlightenment* while in the Otherlanes and had moved on to another dimension of existence. Others – and I was among those – felt that something more sinister was happening. I was making numerous Otherlanes journeys, and something seemed... off. Not right."

"In what way?"

"I sensed the presence of somehar... *someone...* *something...* else in the Otherlanes space. I never saw anything, but it was like there was something standing just behind me that I could catch a glimpse of in my peripheral vision, but when I turned my head it vanished. And there was a sense of danger, of foreboding — some undefined threat that I could provide no rational justification for, yet which existed none the less. For me, anyway.

"The Concilium were unimpressed by my 'mystical scaremongering' as they charmingly put it, and told me in no uncertain terms to keep my theories to myself. They said they didn't want Kyme to look like some sort of benighted superstitious backwater to the Gelaming and other Enlightened tribes. So I said nothing. To anyhar. Not even Juni.

"And then one day he didn't come home. He was late for dinner, so I ate mine on my own and left his by the oven to keep warm. And it was still there the next day, and the bed was empty beside me, and his clothes were still in the dresser, and his hairbrush was still by the side of the bed. But he wasn't there.

"I waited three days, then I went to the Concilium. I told them that Juni had been travelling the Otherlanes the night he disappeared. I explained that he had not returned, and that this was most unlike him. After careful consideration of some seconds in duration, they suggested that perhaps Juni had found a more attractive har and had decided to end our relationship." Meridian brushed the floury surface of the bread dough with his hand to remove some imaginary imperfection.

"In response, I informed the Concilium that I was putting an end to my relationship with *them*. And I told them a few other things besides, which I suspect they were less pleased to hear.

And then I left. And became a baker."

"But didn't you try to find out what had happened to Juni?"

"Of course I did. I even forced myself to make one last trip through the Otherlanes, even though I knew that wouldn't help. I spoke to some of the terribly important Gelaming who were in Kyme, and they were just as dismissive as the Concilium, but they must have known, or suspected something, because soon afterwards they left — by ship — and never returned. No visitors have come to Kyme from Almagabra since.

"And the Concilium—" Meridian laughed bleakly, "—the Concilium still deny that anything is wrong. Still insist that one day the Cultural Ambassador for Creative Fretwork and Whittling will show up from Immanion and all will be well. But the hara of Kyme are not stupid – they know that something is wrong, that their world is shrinking and diminishing and that their friends and neighbours still occasionally vanish without trace, even though they have never been anywhere near the Otherlanes. Yes, that's the dirty little secret the Concilium don't want anyone to know. Even if you're good and pure and say your prayers by night, and too low-caste for Otherlanes travel, you can still disappear. Nohar is safe.

"Fortunately, Kyme is blessed with an impressive library. A har can learn a lot of things in the library. For example, I learned that this is not the first time that strange phenomena have afflicted the Otherlanes. And I learned that we are not the only inhabitants of this green and pleasant Earth of ours."

"What do you mean? Are there still humans about?"

"No, the humans are gone. But there were beings here before them and before us, Perricat. Not like us — not of blood and bone and flesh, but beings who need this realm, and all that it has to offer, and they don't like having to share it with Wraeththu-kind, apparently. But they are patient. They are old, they have been here a long time, and they can wait, picking us off, one by one, and when we are all gone, this world will be theirs again."

Perricat bristled. "I do not like the idea of being picked off!"

"Neither do I."

"And that's what happened to Juni? He got picked off?"

"Yes."

Perricat rolled a small piece of stray dough he had found on the tabletop beneath the palm of his hand. "Magister Squill said that it does not matter when a har leaves his earthly flesh — I think he meant when he dies — because he will be reincarnated or move on to another level of existence, so there is no need for emotional distress."

"The Magister is a fool."

"Yes. I told him that. Only not quite so politely. In fact, rather rudely. Okay, *very* rudely. Which was instrumental in him getting a bit emotional himself and refusing to have anything more to do with me. Which tends to happen to me quite a lot. Would you like some cake?"

"What?"

"Cake. I bought you one. In the market."

"I don't eat cake."

"You should. It's good for emotional distress. Or so I'm told. I could probably do with a slice myself. And maybe some of that stuff you drink that smells like mothballs."

"It's peppermint tea."

"Great. I'll have a cup too."

Meridian considered himself a quick learner, and the short time he had already spent in Perricat's company persuaded him that this was not an argument he was going to win. Very soon he found himself sitting in front of the fireplace with a steaming mug in his hand watching as Perricat cut a large slice from a lopsided cake covered in sticky green icing, which he placed carefully on a plate and handed to Meridian. Meridian nibbled it cautiously. "I could make better," he said.

"Of course you could! Why don't you?"

"Because I don't make cakes. I make bread." He set the slice of cake back down on the plate. "Where did you buy this?"

"From a har with a stall decorated with dried flowers. He had green hair."

Meridian looked disgusted. "I might have known! Bellis will never be a good baker. He buys the cheapest flour, and thinks putting lurid-coloured decorations on things will disguise the poor quality."

"Tastes okay to me," Perricat judged.

"That's because you are young and ignorant and have no experience of anything better."

"I expect you're right. When I'm really old and miserable like you I'll probably hate cake. I'd better make the most of it now."

Perricat took another bite of cake then licked the sticky traces of icing from his fingers, making exaggerated expressions of ecstasy as he did so, much to Meridian's annoyance. He washed it down with a gulp of tea, then wiped his hands on himself.

"Those are my clothes," Meridian pointed out

"I know."

"I just thought I'd point that out."

"Duly noted. So what are you going to do about these Old, Patient creatures in the Otherlanes?"

"Me?" Meridian's eyebrows raised a fraction. "Nothing at all. It's not my concern."

"Yes, it is."

"No, it isn't. I am a baker, not an Otherlanes Guardian and Saviour of the Wraeththu World"

"Is there any reason you can't be both?"

"I can think of many."

"But you can do things most hara can't," Perricat reasoned. "You can see them. Or feel them. And you can do that Otherlanes travel stuff." He thought for a second. "Do you have one of those magic horses? The big white ones?"

"No, I was able to travel the Otherlanes without the assistance of a *sedu.*"

Perricat's large eyes widened even further, giving him an almost comically startled appearance. "I thought only the Gelaming could do that. Are you Gelaming?"

Meridian sighed heavily. "I was, once. A long time ago. When I was young and idealistic."

"You still are!" Perricat insisted.

"What – young and idealistic?"

"No, Gelaming. You're still one of them. You can't just... *resign* from that sort of thing."

"I can, and I did."

"Why?"

"Because I got fed-up pretending to be something I wasn't," Meridian snapped, a sudden flash of anger in his voice, "Pretending to be powerful and lordly and composed and serene. Pretending to know what to do. Pretending to be *enlightened*. Because I'm not. I'm just stumbling around in the dark like everyhar else."

Perricat observed him with forensic detachment. "So you're

sulking because you realised you're not better than everyhar else?"

"No, I'm not. I'm sulking because everyhar else is even worse than me. And they don't deserve to be saved."

"What has that got to do with it? Lots of hara don't deserve lots of things, both good and bad — that's an entirely different thing to whether or not you are obliged to save them, and if I'd paid attention to the Magister — which I didn't because he was boring and I fell asleep during his lessons — then I'd be able to explain why, using long words, but since I'm an ignoramus you're just going to have to go and read it for yourself in a book. I expect there's one in your precious library. We are getting picked off! You said so yourself! And the entire Wraeththu world is sinking back into the slime from which it arose! Doesn't that bother you?"

"No. I don't care."

"Yes, you do! You *do* care, or you wouldn't shout at people in the street or insult the Gelaming and the Vice-Archon. You wouldn't grumble about the state of the library and the ignorance of young hara today and look down your nose at cake. And if you didn't care you wouldn't take such pains over the bread, you'd just make stuff like Bellis."

"I have no idea what you think that proves," Meridian said. "I make good bread because somehar has to."

"Somehar has to save the Wraeththu world as well."

"That somehar is not me."

"If not you, then who? Tigron Pellaz?"

Meridian did not answer. He looked down into his cup where a few flakes of leaves lay stranded at the bottom.

"I did try," he said. "I told the Concilium."

"You didn't try hard enough."

Meridian looked up at him angrily. "No! I didn't! I didn't try hard enough at all! I didn't tell Juni. I didn't warn him, I didn't tell him to stay away from the Otherlanes. If I had he might not have... He might still be..."

He failed to finish the sentence. An awkward silence filled the room, during which the ticking of the clock on the mantelpiece seemed louder than it had a right to be.

"He would just have laughed at me," Meridian said at last. "He wouldn't have believed me, any more than the Concilium did. He would have gone anyway. He always thought he was invincible, he... I had no proof of anything. Not then, not now. No-har would believe me."

"I believe you." Perricat announced, grey eyes blinking earnestly.

"That's because you are gullible and stupid."

"No, it isn't. I mean, yes, I *am* gullible and stupid, but that isn't why I believe you."

"Oh really."

"Yes, really." There was another slightly awkward silence, followed by a heavy sigh from Perricat. "You never asked me why the authorities were after me."

"Yes, I did. You said it was a long story. And then failed to relate it."

"Did I?"

"Yes. I mean no, you didn't. Stop confusing me. Why should I be interested in why they were after you?"

Perricat looked at him steadily. "I see Angels."

"Now you're just being ridiculous," Meridian chided. "And I take back what I said. You are gullible, stupid *and* delusional."

"No, I'm not. The Concilium of Kyme didn't think so. They thought it worth their while keeping me locked up in their Lectorium studying me like an experiment. They know. They really do. They just don't want anyone else knowing." He plucked at the loose fibres of the worn rug in frustration.

Meridian regarded him thoughtfully for several long seconds. "Go on," he said at last.

"There are – creatures, beings, whatever – like you said. They're here. They're all around. But you can't see them. I think they hide themselves – disguise themselves, in the same way that I do. Make hara think they're something else. Only not cats."

"And what *do* they disguise themselves as?"

"Anything at all. Or nothing. It doesn't matter; they just need to make themselves invisible."

"But you can see them?"

"Yes."

"And what do they look like?"

"I don't know."

"What do you mean, you don't know?"

"I mean, they look like... something I can't describe. Like air and light. Solid and liquid. Darkness and love. They look like

Angels." Perricat made a gesture of frustration with his hands.

Meridian considered this information. "If they have to hide," he said slowly, "it means they are afraid."

"Afraid of what?" Perricat asked.

"Of us. This is not their world or their dimension. In the Otherlanes they are powerful — perhaps that is their natural realm; we hara are the intruders there, we are vulnerable when we pass through, but perhaps here the situation is reversed. They would not hide if they did not have to. They would not be slowly picking us off one by one if there was an easier, quicker way."

"I know one thing they are afraid of," Perricat said. "Fire."

"It's good to know that the practical experiments were not in vain."

"The Concilium said I was to stop doing that. That it would only antagonise them. They said we should just keep our heads down and not cause any trouble and they would leave us alone."

Meridian gave an explosive snort, not unlike an angry llama. "Idiots," he declared. "The only way to deal with these creatures is from a position of strength. We must learn their weaknesses and demonstrate to them that we are not defenceless."

"And then we will destroy them all!"

"No, we will not. Even if that were possible, which I doubt, it is not an option. They have as much right to exist as we do. What they do not have is the right to destroy *us* for their own selfish ends."

"If it was up to me, I'd just destroy them all."

"I know. That is why it is a good thing that it's not up to you."

"I can help you, though. I can be your sidekick."

"My *what?*"

"Your accomplice." Perricat bounced excitedly on the rug. "Your second-in-command. Your loyal companion. You can't be expected to save the entire Wraeththu world all on your own, you said so yourself. You need... staff. I mean, not *lots* of staff, obviously, just the one. Preferably one who can see what we're looking for. That's what you need. A singular staff. What's the singular of staff? Stuff? No, that isn't right. An assistant? A partner. You need a partner. I can be your partner. For saving the world. And anything else you might need a partner for. Can't I?"

Meridian stared at him in disbelief, the rebuke already forming, but then he looked into Perricat's wide grey eyes and saw the mixture of hope and pleading within them. He looked at him as if seeing him properly for the first time, taking in the cloud of soft grey hair and the moon-pale skin, in stark contrast to the brown of his own hand, oddly now resting over Perricat's own. And much to his surprise, the word "No" which he had so carefully formulated within his mind, exited from his mouth somewhat differently. "Alright."

"Really?" Perricat's eyes opened even wider, if that were possible.

"Yes. But you must do as I tell you and perform your duties without complaint or question."

"I always do!"

"And your first duty is to wash up the mixing bowls in the kitchen."

"Why?"

"Because if you don't, there will be no bread for tomorrow."

"I thought you were going to be a Guardian of the Otherlanes and Saviour of the Wraeththu World, not a baker!"

Meridian gave him a serious look.

"Is there any reason," he said, "why I can't be both?"

***

"If you had no money, how were you able to buy that cake?"

"Well, a very strange thing happened while I was in the market place. I was standing looking at the cakes when a har came up behind me and asked me if I wanted one. I said yes, but that they cost 20 spinners each and unfortunately I was destitute. I told him my chesnari couldn't afford to keep me."

"I am *not* your chesnari. And how *dare* you imply that I cannot afford to keep you!"

"He said: 'There are no destitute hara, my dear!'" Perricat uttered these words in a more-than-passable imitation of one of Almagabra's ruling elite, stretching on tiptoe to gain imaginary inches, and looking haughtily down his nose.

"And then what did he do?"

"Then he gave me twenty spinners."

"Just like that?"

"Yes."

"Who was this har?"

"I don't know — I've never seen him before. He was very tall and had red hair. Perhaps I will dye my hair red. Do you think I would look good with red hair?"

"I think you would look like a rusty pot-scrubber."

"You really are the rudest har I have ever met!"

"You're still young. Give it time. You have so much to experience. I almost envy you. Now go and scrub the pots."

Destiny Of
choice and chance

Suzanne Gabriel

Destiny of Choice and Chance

Prologue

So far, my second day of school ever had been as marvellous as the first. I was in love. My teacher was the most amazing har in the world, and I wanted to be the best student in the world.

We were sitting in a semi-circle on the grass in the school yard, the warm summer sun shining down on us. Art class was to be outside that day; we were going to draw the large tree that stood in the school yard. I sat with my sketch pad on my lap and my crayons at my side. I was ready.

"I want you to draw the tree," the teacher said, his silky black hair moving around him as he walked amongst the students. "But before you do, I want you to really see the tree. Study it! Look at it hard! Notice the details that make this tree unlike every other tree. I want you to notice the variety of colours, and textures, that make up the bark covering the tree's trunk. Notice the different shades of the leaves, and patterns the sunlight makes…"

I studied the tree for a time, taking in all the details that our teacher had spoken of, and then I bent my head over my paper and I drew. I put my heart into my work.

"That's wrong!"

I looked up into the scornful face of one of my classmates peering down at my work. His greyish-silver hair stood up in messy spikes around his face, grey-green eyes stared down at mine.

"That's wrong," he repeated. "You're supposed to be drawing the tree. Like this." He shoved his sketch book towards me. "Not like that. Yours is a dumb drawing."

"His picture is not dumb!" Mony hollered, springing to his feet. Mony is one of my best friends.

"Your picture is dumb," Ovide sneered. Ovide is my other

best friend.

Ovide, Mony, and I all broke free of our pearls during the same summer three years ago. We live on the same lane in the same town; we've known each other all our lives and we are always together.

I sat in the middle and looked from my picture to that of the spiky-haired harling, and then at those of Ovide and Mony; mine was very different. All three of their drawings showed a dark trunk topped with green leaves. My tree had many different colours in the trunk, and the leaves were made of vibrant colours with other colours swirling around.

I was horrified. I had wanted to impress the teacher.

Ovide and Mony had started a loud and vigorous defence against the spiky-haired critic, which attracted the attention of the teacher.

"Tiahaara! Please! What is going on here?"

"He," announced the spiky-haired harling pointing at me, "is doing it wrong and they…" he continued pointing at Ovide and Mony, "are being stupid."

"Shay's not doing it wrong!" Ovide sniffed primly, his blue-black hair flopping across his pale forehead.

"You're the one being stupid!" bellowed Mony, his light brown eyes narrowed in anger.

"Let's all calm down. I am the art teacher so I'm the only one who can decide who is doing things right or wrong in this art class. OK?"

"But," insisted the spiky-haired harling, "you said 'draw a tree and pay attention to detail.' His picture is wrong. There aren't those colours in real trees."

"Von," the teacher admonished, "there are many ways to draw a tree. You three are to shake hands, apologise to each other, and go finish."

Ovide, Mony, and Von grudgingly shook hands and muttered apologies.

"Very good! Thank you," said the teacher. "Now scoot!"

Once my friends and Von had retreated a distance, the teacher turned his attention to me. I tried to cover up my drawing; I wanted to crawl under a rock to hide.

He crouched down beside me and took the sketch book from my hands. "Wow" he said gently "that's very interesting. Tell me

Suzanne Gabriel

about all those colours?"

"You said to look at the tree carefully and draw what we see." My voice was barely a whisper.

"Can you see all those colours around the tree?"

I nodded.

"Shaymar, do you see those kinds of colours in and around other things too?"

I nodded again.

He pointed at his boot. "Can you see my socks?"

I shook my head.

"But I bet you know what colour they are..."

"They're dark grey," I responded immediately. "With a hole in the toe."

Sometimes I just know things like that.

"Indeed they are," he laughed. "I think you had better come with me."

He took me by the hand, and led me away from the class. He called out to another teacher as we passed, asking him to watch the other harlings, and then we walked out of the schoolyard up the road towards the Nayati.

My teacher bobbed his head politely to the hienama and offered him my picture. He explained the project and my 'interesting' drawing, as the hienama nodded thoughtfully.

"Thank you Philander," the hienama said. "If you would be so kind as to find this young har's parents and return here, I would greatly appreciate it."

My teacher nodded and left.

The hienama and I stood looking at each other for a time in silence. I could feel him studying me; I could feel his presence in my head. He was a very intimidating har; tall with piercing dark eyes and long, coarse, flaxen hair woven into dreadlocks. But what both intrigued and frightened me the most was his right hand; he only had four fingers, no baby finger.

"Walk with me Shaymar Brialith har Hadassah," he said suddenly.

I hesitated.

"You're not in trouble," he said kindly. "I just want to talk with you about all the wonderful colours you put in your drawing. Come, let's go sit in the garden."

I followed him into the garden. It was an ornate walled garden

250

filled with flowers, herbs, and white pebble walkways.

"My name," he began, "is Fahrim. I'm originally from the Teraghast tribe, but I've been the hienama here for years. In fact, I remember your parents when they were harlings."

He motioned for me to sit next to him on the bench. I sat carefully on the end of it, as far away from him as possible, trying to sneak a peek his damaged hand.

"Your picture interests me. Do you see these colours around a lot of things? Are they just around trees? Tell me about them."

"They're around most things. I can see them when I concentrate."

"Do I have colours around me?"

I studied him for a moment. "There is some pink... and some purple... and a lot of blues."

I glanced at his hand again; in addition to the missing finger, his tanned arm was crisscrossed by many white scars.

"Would you like to know what happened to my hand?"

"Yes," I nodded sheepishly. I had not wanted him to notice me looking.

"A long time ago, before I was a hienama, I was a soldier. I was injured in a great battle."

I glanced up at him and frowned.

He studied me, a slow smile spreading across his face. "You don't believe me, do you?" his eyebrow rose.

I let the story bounce around in my head for a moment, and then I shook my head.

He chuckled. "You're right. Can you tell me what did happen?"

I stared at his hand and let images come and go in my head. "You were attacked by a wolf?"

"Bang on!" he said as he studied me. "This is fascinating. Are your parents teaching how to do things? Do they even know that you can do this?"

"We do meditations at home. My parents make me sit with them and be quiet. My father tells me I should focus on sending good thoughts to help people. They taught me how to keep my toes warm when my boots get full of snow in winter." I paused for a moment before adding proudly, "I can also start fires by thinking hard about the flames."

"Your parents taught you that already?" Fahrim sounded

surprised.

"No, I just watch Potz. He's my father, and he makes pottery in a kiln. I've watched him light the kiln, and the fire in the fireplace at home, too. I saw what he did and I did it, too."

"Goodness. Do us all a favour and don't do that on your own until you're a bit older." He shook his head in a bemused way. "How about telekinesis? Can you make things move just by thinking about it?"

I frowned. "No."

"'No' because you can't? Or 'no' because you've never tried? See that red ball over by the rose bush? It belongs to my dog. See if you can get it to roll around; concentrate on it and give it a shot."

I looked at the ball and concentrated on it, picturing it coming towards me. Nothing happened at first, but then the ball made a tiny jerky motion on the ground before it suddenly shot through the air towards Fahrim and me. We both ducked as the ball hit the wall behind us and bounced off, first smashing into a large urn, and then landing with a splash in the pond, startling the large koi swimming lazily in the sun.

"I'm sorry!" I exclaimed.

Fahrim was not angry; far from it, he looked surprised for a moment, and then howled with laughter. "Brilliant!" He managed to say.

Fahrim and I spent the next few hours sitting in the sun-drenched garden 'playing games'; we played guessing games, a game like I-Spy, and meditation follow-the-leader games.

After a time, my teacher returned with my parents. My hostling, Saana, is a landscape designer. He has violet-blue eyes, and fine strawberry-blonde hair, which he wears short and spiky. I think he is the most beautiful hostling in the world. My father is a potter, and everyone calls him Potz; I love him like crazy, and he's always making me laugh. That day, his unruly dark-brown hair was twisted into a messy chignon, and he had a streak of dried clay on his cheek. Both he and Saana looked very worried and a bit angry as they entered the garden.

Fahrim told my parents about the picture, and about what he'd discovered by playing some games with me; I had a gift. I had come into the world with skills that most hara have to learn.

"Tiahaara," Fahrim said, "your son is rare and exceptional; his skills are at a level usually not reached until later adulthood. I am unable to completely assess his abilities, as he is simply too young to understand what is being asked, but I believe as he matures his innate abilities will continue to evolve. We need to guide him, support him, and nurture him as he grows, so that he will have the resources to control his abilities and use them wisely. As parents you must continue to nurture him as you have been. Philander, the school needs to continue to teach him as you would any harling, and I will begin to teach him how to harness his gifts."

Destiny

It was hot. The late summer sun beat down on Ovide, Mony, and me as we lounged on the patio behind Ovide's parents' home.

Ovide's silky blue-black hair was swept up into a tidy roll, secured with shiny pink sticks. Somehow he'd made the pink match the bright tangerine shirt he wore; no matter what Ovide wore it always looked "right". He was currently sitting cross-legged on the ground, embroidering trim on one of his hand-sewn "creations".

Mony was sprawled on his stomach across a *chaise longue*, using the head rest to prop his feet. His sketch pad was on the ground, and he was busily sketching. Mony was always sketching; I often think that his art looks more real than the object he's drawn.

This was the lull between life phases; at ten, we were young adults, our basic education complete, preparing to move on to the next stages of life.

Despite the relaxed calmness surrounding me, I was feeling peevish and irritable. I shifted restlessly in the deck chair I'd draped myself over.

"What's bugging you Shay?" Mony drawled, without taking his eyes off his drawing.

"I should have just drawn a regular fucking tree," I muttered.

"Be reasonable, Shay! If it hadn't been the tree picture, they would have found you out another way." Mony flipped his fine white bangs out of his eyes.

"It's not fair!" I said for the millionth time. "It isn't you who has to go to some far away theological college to study shit you don't want to study. No, your future is something you get to decide; it wasn't decided for you based on a stupid drawing you made on your second day at school. I want to go to live in Belshore with you two."

Belshore was a large city not too far from our town.

"You don't know how lucky you are!" Mony countered. "I'm going to a *local* Belshore art school, Ovide is apprenticing with a *local* Belshore fashion house, and you, my love, are going to be at the Lyceum on an exotic, sun-soaked island a two hour ferry ride from Immanion."

The Lyceum was a renowned institution of higher education devoted to the cultivation and grooming of the most gifted and masterful hienamas. Consequently, everyone I knew was ecstatic that I had been invited to attend; everyone but me.

"Immanion!" Mony exclaimed again with emphasis. "As an aspiring artist, and an aspiring fashion designer, we can honestly say our hearts aren't bleeding for your 'misfortune'. I'd give anything to be going that close to Immanion; it's *'the'* place to be."

I sighed. "I don't want to go to the Lyceum. Everyone just assumed that since I'm a freak, I would be a hienama. "

"You're not a freak," Mony said evenly. "Everyone has always assumed I'd study art somewhere, because I'm good at drawing, and Ovide has always an eye for fashion, so it makes sense that he's going to study fashion. That's just the way things go."

"What else could you possibly want to do?" Ovide peered at me curiously.

"I don't know," I growled in frustration.

The prestigious Lyceum was on the island of Itamar, an exotic, sun-drenched vacation destination. It consisted of the main town, numerous beaches, luxurious small inns, and spas, all surrounding a singular mountain that rose dramatically out of the sea. The port town was bustling and energetic, filled with boutiques, restaurants, and beautiful hara.

I had arrived on Itamar a day early and had taken the opportunity to wander the town and explore some local lagoons and beaches.

There was only one main road on the island, since there were only two places to go; if you were at the shore, the only place to go was up the mountain, and if you are at the top, the only place to go is down to the sea. The road started there at the port, made a ring around the island passing by the small beach communities, and then spiralled up the mountain, passing through scattered hamlets that had grown wherever they could on the rocky plateaus. It twisted alongside the olive groves, citron orchards, and vineyards, until it finally ended at the Great Nayati built over a sacred spring, and the Lyceum that had grown and flourished there for over a century.

Self-talk and positive meditations had bolstered my spirits as I steadied my nerves and set out for the spot, near the Town Hall fountain, where the new crop of trainees were to congregate and be transported up to the Lyceum.

As I approached the fountain, I could see two luggage wagons, each already containing luggage; two horse-drawn covered-wagons, each with three rows of seats; and two separate groups of hara.

I approached the nearest of the two official-looking hara; he held a clipboard and exuded a sense of authority. He wore a long sleeveless tunic of saffron brocade that fell to his knees revealing the fine creamy linen shirt and leggings he wore beneath.

"Hi," I said cheerily. "I'm one of the new ones. I'm supposed to check in here, right?"

Grey eyes met mine, and then travelled up and down me. "Name?" he said coolly.

"Shaymar Brialith, from Woodnesse."

"He's mine!"

A tall tawny-skinned har with a heart-shaped face bustled over and grabbed my arm. He led me firmly, and quickly, away from the har in the yellow. When we were out of ear shot he turned to me and brushed his short, curly, brown hair out of his eyes, and straightened his slate-grey tunic.

"Why on earth did you present yourself to the Chrysanthos?"

"What?"

"Them! The Chrysanthos!" His tone was exasperated. "You are Argenteus; you should have presented yourself to me."

"Does it matter?" I began. "We're all going up to the same place."

"It does matter," he said snippily. "You are Argenteus – never forget that. Our orders are very scrupulous in maintaining our distinctness. Do not make that mistake again."

He grabbed my arm again and led me towards a group of hara standing next to one of the wagons.

I didn't like being chastised as if I was a harling; I hadn't done anything wrong. My upbeat mood threatened to retreat into a harling-esque sulk. So what if we belonged to different sects?

A tall, pretty har, with light blue eyes and neatly-bobbed red hair approached our group. "Lirell Rose," he announced with an officious air, as he made his luggage levitate into the nearest wagon. "I'm one of the hienamas at Grey Light."

I had never heard of him, or the place he was from, but he annoyed me already. I could sense the shifting reactions of other hara as they evaluated, and judged, sniffing the new arrival like wary old tomcats; all that was missing was the arched backs and the hissing.

Lirell shook hands with several of the hara, and nodded to the rest. When he came to me, he paused and raised his eyebrow.

"Has the Lyceum opened a crèche?" His laughter was light and musical. "Sacred colouring books? Nap times and story circles perhaps?"

He laughed again, and several hara glanced at me grinning.

I think I had already noticed that I was the youngest har there, but now it was hard not to. I had expected to be to be joining a group of hara my own age, but every har here was older, and, judging by the snippets of conversation I was overhearing, already hienamas.

"Oh, very clever!" I said as cuttingly as I could. "I am not a harling."

The attention turned away from me as the new Argenteus arrivals circled each other, making strained conversation. My heart sank at the thought of enduring a long wagon ride up the mountain with these twits.

"I'm going to hike up to the Lyceum," I announced to no one in particular. "Anyone want to come?"

"I'd go with you," a har with chocolate-coloured skin said, his black eyes peering out from under his dark brown bangs, "but I didn't bring the right kind of shoe." He shrugged apologetically as he extended his foot so I could see his well-manicured feet in delicate sandals that certainly would not survive a hike.

I nodded, and turned away without waiting for the grey-attired har from the Lyceum to say whatever he looked like he was about to say.

Down the street, just past a small bright yellow café called *The Sun Flower*, I remembered seeing a sign for 'The Trail to the Great Nayati.'

The farther I walked from the group, the lighter my spirits felt; I needed to think. Everyhar knew of the existence of the two main sects in the Immanion Nayati structure. Fahrim had given me a thick tome explaining the history, and philosophy, of the rift, but I hadn't read it; I'd skimmed it, barely. The Chrysanthos and Argenteus sects had emerged about a hundred years ago. The differences had initially been seen as useful adaptations to accommodate the multitude of tribal deharic traditions assimilated, and embraced, into the Immanion 'central' Nayati system. Different tribes, different deharic dogma, all simmering together, in a melting pot of rich ritual traditions, that made allowances for each sect's uniqueness, in exchange for coming under the umbrella of the Aghama, and by default, the control of Immanion. But over the generations, minor differences became big cracks, and eventually the Chrysanthos and Argenteus sects emerged. I did not care about the differences: I didn't care to debate ritually-appropriate verse, the sun versus the moon, ritual order, or the subtle nuances in the complex hierarchy between the main dehara, minor dehara, hienamas, and all other living things. Nor can I ever remember the proper words to incantations, and if called upon to create my own, they never rhyme.

I'd grown up knowing we were Argenteus, just as I imagine those in Chrysanthos regions grew up knowing what sect they were. It bothered me that the rift seemed much deeper than I'd chosen to believe; where we lived, we were fairly isolated, and Fahrim was far from militant. We heard of occasional clashes between sects, but I'd never paid attention to those stories; hot-heads and fanatics could cause trouble anywhere.

I tried to remember more details of the differences between the two sects, and how they had started, but I couldn't. I knew that the Chrysanthos sect identified with gold; they wore ever-deepening shades of yellow as they progressed through the hierarchical ranks, and decorated their Nayati with gold. We Argenteus had chosen silver; hienamas wore progressively darker, more elaborate greys, and we used silver to decorate our Nayatis. There were other differences, too; the Chrysanthos drew on the power of the sun, while the Argenteus drew on moon; the

Chrysanthos calendar was based on the sun, while we used the lunar calendar. Debates raged about whether ritual invoked the presence of the dehar, or the essence of their presence, and about whether life events, such as emerging from a pearl, feybraiha, and blood bonds, required real rituals, or whether they were merely life events to be imbued with a sense of ceremony. The Gelaming had been highly accepting, and adaptive, in absorbing cultural elements from many tribes, but this acceptance, and the hybridisation of different cultural and deharic practices led to many interpretations, and those different interpretations had eventually led to a parting of the ways. As I climbed along the trail, I tried to make sense of it all, but I couldn't remember all the details. I wish now I'd actually read the book.

Wait, I thought angrily. *No, I don't wish I'd read it.* I wanted nothing to do with this whole mess; it wasn't my problem. I hoped it was not going to be forced on me, but as both the Chrysanthos and Argenteus sects used the Lyceum, it probably would be.

I mulled this over as I trudged along the upwardly-winding trail through the hills, which was steep at times. The trail ran close to the edge of the cliffs, where one could see truly breath-taking views of the ocean and island, and then it would turn back inland through cultivated lemon orchards, olive groves, and vineyards; everywhere showed the signs of the same drought that affected my home.

As the trail snaked inland again, it led up a wooded hill and onto a flat bit of land that must have once been a field, but now lay fallow and overgrown; small saplings encroached around the edges and wildflowers and grass stood tall. The sun had dropped low in the sky, casting long shadows across the pathway that ambled more or less straight through the field passing a derelict old barn before disappearing into the wooded hill on the other side.

Perhaps Fahrim had warned me about the depth of the divisions and I had failed to listen, but now I really wished I could sit down at his kitchen table the way I used to and ask him a bunch of the questions that were swirling around in my head.

The cry stopped me in my tracks; it was harsh, primitive, and sent shivers along my spine. It's just a bird or an animal I told myself, but then I heard it again; the piercing bloodcurdling sound of a har screaming out in pain. My heart was racing as I bolted off the path and dropped down behind a bush. I raised a ward around me, shielding myself from detection. I could see no movement in the surrounding woods; whatever was happening must be happening in the barn.

I started to move towards the barn. Using wards to avoid being seen is something I was pretty confident using; I'd perfected the skill as a harling sneaking out of my bedroom, and satisfying harling curiosities about all manner of adult things.

When I peered through a space between the broken boards in the barn wall I could see three hara standing over the prone bloodied body of a fourth; a cold panic rose in my chest.

By appearances the three hara were among the affluent and well-to-do crowd; I had seen many of their type seated in the fashionable bistro patios in the port town and at the beach resorts that dotted Itamar's coastline. By contrast, the har lying on the dusty floor of the barn wore loose black drawstring trousers, a light linen shirt, and sturdy canvas shoes; practical garb favoured by the islanders who worked in olive groves, orchards, and vineyards.

The lankiest of the three bent over the prone har and punched him hard in the face three times; I recoiled as if I was the one who'd been hit. When the attacker stood upright, his knuckles were smeared with blood. I knew I had to do something, but I did not know what; I'd never encountered violence. I was terrified.

I did the first thing I could think of; I sent energy to rattle a pile of wooden planks that I could see lying on the far side of the barn.

The hara all started; the lanky har froze and I could feel him scanning the area. I had assumed these hara were just thugs, but this lanky har had considerable power. I focused on my shield as his gaze momentarily hovered on the spot where I stood.

"What? What is it?" One of the other two asked. "Is someone out there?"

"I sensed a presence for a moment," the lanky har stated, "but it's gone now."

"Do we kill this one?"

"We have the amulet; there is no need – let's get out of here."

Without another look at their victim, they headed down the path in the direction from which I had just come, quickly disappearing from view.

As soon as I considered it safe to do so, I dropped to my knees beside the injured har. "Are you OK? No, of course you're not, what a stupid thing to ask. We'd better get you out of here in case they come back."

He had shoulder-length dark brown hair and his skin was pale. I could not see what colour his eyes were as they were both almost swollen shut.

I dragged him to his feet; he leaned on me heavily, muttering something I could not understand.

I pulled his arm across my shoulder, and snaked my arm around his waist. Outside, the barn, we began making our way up the trail in the fading light.

The going was tough, as sometimes the injured har leaned on me so heavily that I was almost carrying him. As darkness descended fully, we made it to the outer courtyard of the Nayati complex.

"Help!" I cried.

We were immediately surrounded by hara; the injured har was carried away, and I was led inside. My experience during the next few moments was confusing and surreal, as hara wearing various shades of yellow and grey took it in turn to chastise, challenge, question, and accuse me. The grey-clad Argenteus were relieved I'd made it safely, but regarding my rescue of the injured har, as he was a Chrysanthos and I was Argenteus, they were adamant that I should not have gotten involved. The yellow-clad Chrysanthos were convinced that I knew more than I was telling about the attackers and demanded I return the amulet.

I was feeling confused and angry, when yet another har entered the austere windowless room in which I had been deposited shortly after my dramatic arrival at the Lyceum. He had short silky, bleach-blonde hair; he was not tall, but the way he carried himself made him seem taller. His black eyes stared at me, and I could feel his mind touching mine. I blocked the contact and glared at him; he was unperturbed.

"Shaymar Brialith from the Nayati at Woodnesse, I presume?" He adjusted the heavy silver grey brocade robe he wore; his voice was an octave or so higher than I had expected it to be. "I am Dalsea Ribenny, Provost of this Argenteus hermitage.

"I'm glad you turned up of your own accord. We were in the beginning stages of planning a search," he continued. "As long as you are unharmed, then no damage is done. As for the ramifications of your actions, we will have to attend to them…"

"Ramifications? I didn't do anything wrong. All I did was bring an injured har here for help."

"You are Argenteus. He is Chrysanthos," Dalsea said with a slight shrug. "But never mind, you weren't to know. I'll deal with this."

"I wasn't to know what?" I demanded. "The Chrysanthos was beaten and left for dead. I helped him; Argenteus should get bonus points for helping, shouldn't they? Unless," I said, narrowing my eyes, "unless we were the attackers. But we aren't, right?"

"No, of course not! Don't be silly," Dalsea said lightly.

I could sense enough evasion in his tone that I doubted him. *Damn*, I thought, *this is messed up.*

I tossed and turned most of the night. My brain replayed recent events endlessly and produced a series of brilliant things I wish I had had the wherewithal to say. The next day, I woke sulky and still tired. I pulled on my Lyceum uniform of cream-coloured drawstring pants, loose shirt, and light grey tabard, and went to join the other new acolytes.

"Just follow the schedules you received yesterday," said the cheerful har wearing a dark grey robe. "If you have any questions, just ask!"

"I don't have a schedule," I said.

"Of course you don't have a schedule," Lirell smirked. "You were too busy rescuing prominent Chrysanthos."

There were a few titters; I glared hard at Lirell.

"Be fair!" said the cheerful har. "He wore nothing that identified him as Chrysanthos, and being new, Shaymar would never have seen him before."

I was still glaring at Lirell. "I would have helped him even if I had known," I said defiantly.

"Why?" somehar asked.

"It was the right thing to do."

"Had the positions been reversed, Shaymar, he probably would have left you to die." The cheerful har smiled gently.

"If you believe that Argenteus are better, they must behave better, must they not?" I asked airily.

The har in the dark grey robe raised his eyebrow and studied me. "Perhaps," he said softly.

The first few weeks were horrid. I was miserable; our classes were not so much 'educational', as 'indoctrinational'. I felt isolated, although I admit I did not do anything to improve my situation; I flat-out refused to participate. I did no assignments, or readings, and I skipped most classes.

During the second week, they tested us to assess our ascension skills. My skills were so far above the others that I was singled out for special one-on-one "advanced" studies; rather than feeling privileged, I felt even more isolated.

One afternoon, as Sirius, the cheerful minder of the first year novices, was escorting me to a private session with one of the higher-ranked hienamas, we were almost bowled over by a tall Chrysanthian har in gold-trimmed robes. His aquamarine eyes flashed dangerously in our direction as he and his entourage swept past. He was gorgeous.

"What an asshole," Sirius muttered, more to himself than me.

"Who was that?" I asked.

Sirius looked amused. "You don't recognise him? That's Mithras, right-hand to the Provost of the Chrysanthos section of the Lyceum – you hauled his ass up the mountain when you arrived."

"Oh…" I said as I looked after them.

It took me nearly a whole month of skipping classes, not doing my work, and general insolence to end up in the Provost Dalsea's office.

He read out a lengthy litany of complaints and misdemeanours, and then looked up at me.

I shrugged. "Kick me out," I said simply. "I do not want to be here."

"That is not possible."

We argued back and forth until the Provost suddenly seemed to lose interest in the debate, and dismissed me.

In a fit of pique, I stomped out and slammed his office door hard, noting with grim satisfaction the crash of items falling from the wall. That earned me a penance; I was to report to the kitchen gardens and help the gardener with weeding.

Since I like gardening, I was looking forward to quietly communing with the earth. I was slightly annoyed to find that I was to be serving my penance with a first year "yellow-jacket"; he looked equally displeased.

He was of medium height with a stocky build. He raised his chin and squinted at me. "You're that freak who can do everything already," he stated. "What did the star of the Argenteus freak show do to get stuck with penance?"

"Skip class. Fail to do assignments. Fail to do assigned reading. Slam the door of the Provost's office so hard things fell off the wall and broke. You?"

"I punched one of your friends in the face," he said with a smug little smile.

My memory conjured a scene of hara crowded around Lirell, who was holding a handkerchief to his bloodied nose.

"Was he a tall redhead with a bob?"

The yellow jacket crossed his arms across his chest. "Yes."

I laughed out loud, which brought a look of surprise to my companions' face.

"He probably had it coming." I grinned.

The Chrysanthos' eyes narrowed. "That doesn't sound like something a little 'silver-fish' like you would say."

"I don't really think of myself as Argenteus," I said, "but I don't consider myself Chrysanthos, either. I don't even think I'm somewhere in the middle. I feel like I'm on the outside looking in. It all seems so petty, so silly, so…" I paused searching for the right word.

"Human?" my companion inquired with a wry smile.

"I guess," I said doubtfully. "Did they fight about their dehar… or… gods… or whatever they had? I remember learning about humans in school. I thought humans were pretty cool, in a weird sort of way."

"I research human culture; they fought about everything, but their spiritual differences were among their biggest conflicts."

"Weed everything," had been the gardener's only instructions. The yellow-jacket and I began working our way through the garden beds, and I pressed him for information about human conflicts. I saw many parallels between the human quarrels and what was happening now to us. The work was not too hard; the drought had not given the weeds much of a chance to grow.

"I don't mind weeding," I said, hoping to keep the conversation going. "For me, it's not really punishment. I had hoped that they'd kick me out; I guess I'll have to try harder."

"They won't kick you out. They will never kick you out. They can't."

I looked at him in surprise.

He shook his head. "They're scared of you. Didn't you know that? Rumour is that you can do it all; they just have to explain what to do, and you do it effortlessly. They say you must be an old soul and that you no idea what you are capable of, and that terrifies them – all of them."

The weeding had not taken too long; we still had about an hour in our penance left when we finished the last bed.

"Well that wasn't too bad," I said.

"What about in there?" My companion pointed.

Through a simple wrought-iron gate at the end of the kitchen garden, I could see that the adjacent garden had rather forlorn, overgrown flowerbeds.

I shrugged. "Sure! Why not? We still have an hour, might as well."

My companion put his hand on the gate.

"STOP!"

The word was clear and held command; my companion and I both froze. Towards us along the pathway that lead back to the kitchen strode a tall dark-haired har; Mithras, the har I had rescued.

"What do you think you are doing?" he demanded.

"We …" stammered my companion. "We were told to weed the gardens… and …"

Words failed him at this point, and he merely pointed to the garden through the gate.

"We were told to weed the garden, and we were going to get started in there." I said. "It's a mess."

Mithras ignored me. "No one enters this garden. It is strictly off limits."

"Yes, hienama! I'm sorry, hienama," my companion babbled.

"Why?" I asked.

I wasn't ignored this time; Mithras turned an icy aquamarine stare my way.

I kept my gaze steady. "I am not challenging the rule," I said evenly. "I only seek understanding. Why is nohar permitted through the gate? It is easier to follow a rule if one understands the rationale behind it. Otherwise it's just another dumbass rule." I smiled sweetly.

"The Lyceum," he said coldly, "has a guest; a very revered and honoured guest. His meditations are not to be disturbed. Is that clear?"

"Crystal clear, tiahaar," I said with a nod of my head. "He shall not be disturbed."

I meant that; I had no intention of intruding on some mouldy, old hienama hiding out in an overgrown and weedy garden.

Mithras turned to the yellow-jacket. "Return to your other duties immediately."

I would not have thought that a har with that stocky a build could have moved that quickly.

"And you," he turned his attention back to me, "put the gardening tools away and report to the gardener to see what else you are to do."

I bent down to pick up the basket full of pulled weeds. "By the way," I said as I straightened up, "you're welcome."

Mithras stiffened and his eyes narrowed. "For what?"

"Hauling your ass up the mountain, you know, saving your life and all," I said airily, then spun on my heels and headed off towards the compost pile.

"Get back here, Argent!"

There was a powerful command in his voice, but I resisted it. I was feeling quite smug until he appeared suddenly, out of nowhere, in the path directly in front of me. He glared at me.

"Whoa!" I said. "That was a sweet trick."

"One you could no doubt learn easily, should you decide to apply yourself." He paused. "I am indebted to you for having come to my aid. Thank you. But tell me, would you have done so had you known who I was? Or that my attackers were Argenti?"

"Yes."

His raised eyebrow told me he didn't believe me.

"It was the right thing to do," I said. "I don't care whether a har wears yellow or grey."

"Gold and silver," he corrected.

"Whatever." I shrugged as I turned and walked away.

Nothing much changed over the next few weeks, I was a lonely loner, angry about being trapped there, and overwhelmed by the negativity I felt pulsating between the Argenteus and Chrysanthos factions. The only thing I found remotely interesting was exploring my power; I enjoyed finding out what I was capable of. But on days when there was no ascension work, I roamed the hills outside the walls of the Lyceum.

While tramping through the hills, I had made a discovery; a tiny spring, right below the walls of the Lyceum. It was barely more than a trickle of water seeping out from a crack in the rock, but it provided enough water to make the moss and rock flowers in its little grotto lush and green. I went there often. I felt a deep sense of peace in that spot; a welcome antidote to the negative, oppressive atmosphere within the walls of the Lyceum.

I looked at the thin trickle of water and put my finger in it, feeling the cool water run over it.

"You are the same spring that bubbles under the Nayati, aren't you?" I said. "And just like me, you come here to get away from all that craziness going on up there. Right?" I chuckled softly. "Listen to me. I'm talking to a trickle of water. It's because I need to find a friend. I need someone real to talk to. I don't like who I'm turning into, but I don't really know how to change."

I got to my feet and started to make my way back up towards the Lyceum. I tried a new trail which, although a little bit steeper, got me directly up to the backside of the Lyceum wall. As I made my way along it towards the Lyceum gate, I came upon a bright blue door. I grinned. I remembered that door! I'd seen it in the far end of the kitchen garden. I turned the door handle and went in, feeling quite pleased that I had discovered a shortcut.

It took a few moments, and a few steps, down the path before it registered that this was not the kitchen garden; this garden was quite overgrown and had a vaguely forlorn look to it. A strange tickle went up my spine as I spotted the simple wrought iron gate from the wrong side, and through it, the kitchen garden.

Instantly, I spun on my heel, intent on making a dash back to the door and getting out of the forbidden garden as fast as possible. Instead, I came face to face with a tall, black-haired har in a dark blue robe standing silently in the path along which I had just come.

"Hello, old friend." His voice was soft and low.

"I am so sorry, tiahaar!" I blurted. "I saw that blue door and I thought it was the blue door into the kitchen garden – the one just on the other side of the gate. I didn't realise there were two blue doors. I am so sorry, tiahaar. I didn't mean to disturb you."

"I'm surprised it took you so long to find your way here," he said. "Come have tea!"

He led me along a path to a neat little cottage, with a large covered veranda, and a sunny patio. On the patio there were chairs, and a small table already set for tea.

He poured the tea and handed me a cup.

"Sit!" he waved his hand in the direction of a chair.

He poured a cup of tea for himself and settled back in his seat; taking a deep breath, he stared off into the distance, and I sensed he was no longer here with me. I sat silently, taking the time to examine him. I could tell that he was very old, and very powerful, and as he sat there he seemed to glow with a soft, radiant white light.

He sighed deeply, and refocused his attention on me. "Advanced age!" He shrugged. "Other places call me..." He smiled. "What were we talking about?"

"You called me 'old friend', and said you were surprised that I hadn't dropped in sooner."

"Ah, yes," he smiled, and settled back as if he was waiting for something further from me.

I cleared my throat. "I'm sorry tiahaar," I began tentatively. "I don't remember you. There were many hienamas that came to test me when I was younger, and I don't really remember you."

That was awkward, and I squirmed a little under his gaze.

"You don't look anything like I thought you would," he said suddenly. "Tell me your name."

"My name is Shaymar; Shaymar Brialith"

He stared at me motionless.

"Har Hadassah." He nodded.

"... From Woodnesse," I added awkwardly.

He nodded again.

"I'm sorry. I'm confused. I thought you said we were old friends."

Suzanne Gabriel

"Yes, we were… once." He took a sip of tea. "But you have no memories, eh?" He smiled wistfully. "Too bad, really."

"What memories? Who are you?"

"Call me 'Darq'; it is short for Darquiel."

"Darquiel? Like the Tigron Darquiel?" I exclaimed, immediately regretting it. I sounded lame.

He smiled at me, and nodded encouragingly; slowly my brain began to click the pieces into place.

"You!? You were *that* Darquiel; the Tigron Darquiel?" I shut my mouth when I realised it was still hanging open.

"Yes, I was. I suppose I still am, but I left that life a long time ago, long before your high-parents emerged from their pearls."

"Then when did we meet?" I asked.

"We haven't, at least not in this lifetime, or rather, not in *'your'* this lifetime. I'm ancient, even for a har." He sighed. "I have seen hara fade, and then return." He looked down at his tea cup. "And you have not only returned, but you've returned with your ascensions intact. You know," he said, wagging his finger at me, "that is *so* you!"

"So me? You knew me in my previous life? Who was I?"

He shook his head. "Oh no! No, no, no. I can't tell you that; either you will remember or you won't. It wouldn't be fair to who you are now. The 'you' now must develop as he is meant to. I shouldn't have even told you that there was a previous you. That was very naughty of me. But Shaymar," he said, "*someone* has to get your attention. "

"Get my attention?"

"Fate! Destiny!" he exclaimed. "You are here at the Lyceum for a reason. You don't like it? Tough! If you can't change your fate, change your attitude." He harrumphed, and sat back, glaring his reprimand at me. "Drink your tea."

Mortified, I did as I was told, as Darquiel's attention drifted away again.

"Do you remember?" he asked, in a soft dreamy voice. "Do you remember that little chiffchaff? The one with the damaged wing? It was a smart little thing. It stayed inside the tropical bird enclosure? It would come when you called it. Do you remember his name? I've forgotten."

"A chiffchaff?" I licked my lips nervously. "That's some kind of bird, right? No, I'm sorry, tiahaar, I don't."

He was silent, lost in another world, for a time.

"I must not keep you," he said suddenly, "or you will be missed. It was a pleasure to meet you Shaymar har Hadassah. Please come again."

I beat as hasty a retreat as I could, politely.

I did not sleep that night; too many thoughts swirled through my head. I had met a Tigron! He knew me, or rather who I had been in a previous life. Who? That question played through my mind on an endless loop. A Tigron would have known many hara. I was, or had been, somehar who had done ascension work, but who? The possibilities were endless.

I was mortified that my behaviour had been noticed by the Tigron; he had called me on my bad attitude. I fully admit that I had not been a pleasant har. I had become difficult and sullen. No wonder I had no friends! I wasn't very likeable; I didn't even like who I'd become. I felt very alone and very sorry for myself.

The next morning at breakfast, I sat subdued and quiet. I looked up to find Sirius watching me.

"You need to go to class," he said, as he did every morning.

"OK."

His eyebrow shot up in surprise.

I did go to class; all of them. I sat at the back of the class, ignoring the odd looks I got, and read quietly. I was by no means a model student. I refused to read the biased, prescribed texts. Instead, I read histories of the earliest days of Wraeththudom. I read about the rise of Immanion influence and about the development of the current Nayati traditions. I read background histories about the major tribes, and comparative histories of tribal ritual traditions.

Darquiel's chastisement had catalysed my change of attitude, although I was genuinely curious about the past, and wanted to understand this ridiculous yellow and grey theological split. As I devoured memoirs of Tigrons Darquiel, Pellaz, and Calanthe, as well as those of Thiede, and Loki, there was another motivator as well; I searched for anything that seemed familiar. Sadly nothing did, and no memoir mentioned a little injured chiffchaff.

One afternoon in the library, our instructor closed the memoir I had been reading, and insisted that I get a poetry book, so as not to "dry out my brain." Much, I'm sure, to his surprise, I dutifully returned to the stacks to find a poetry book.

I went in search of a book of poems by Chrysm Luel; I found his poems entertaining, slightly bawdy, but with an unexpectedly deep perspective. As I pulled my chosen tome off the shelf, my eyes fell on the book next to it: *Ornithological Compendium, Volume 4: The Birds of Immanion and Surrounds*. The librarian would have a fit if he saw that somehar had miss-shelved this. On a whim I pulled it off the shelf, too.

I returned to my spot, and flipped open the bird book; I had no idea what a chiffchaff looked like.

The book was very thorough. Each entry consisted of an extensive write up about the bird species, its habitat, habits, and all and sundry information about it. Each entry was also accompanied by a lovely colour painting of each different bird. I flipped through the pages slowly.

On one page, the Armenicus seagull stared regally off the page at me. A few pages later was the entry for the black-eared wheat-eater, a striking black and white bird, drawn with wings spread as if it were about to take flight. I spent several minutes admiring the painting of the blue-cheeked bee-eater, a pretty little intelligent-looking bird with mostly green feathers, blue cheeks, and a black eye stripe. Next was the cattle egret, a stocky, angry-looking white bird with large ungainly feet.

I turned the page, and there it was: the common chiffchaff, a tiny little bird with a dull green upper body, creamy belly, and slight tinges of yellow around its wings.

As I gazed down at the painting, I felt a cold shiver run up my back, my heart began to pound, and my palms started to sweat. I could see, in my mind, a large sun-drenched enclosure filled with tropical trees, flowers, and large noisy birds with vibrantly coloured plumage. Sitting on one of the cages' crossbars, directly in front of me, was a chiffchaff; he bobbed and chirped at me impatiently. I stretched out my hand, palm up, and the bird hopped onto it and pecked at the crumbs I held; it tickled. The tiny creature then hopped back onto the crossbar, and spread his wings. As he glided back into the enclosure, I could see that one of his wings was misshapen. I knew his name.

I slammed the book shut and stood up. My sudden movement caused everyone to look up.

"Shaymar? Is everything okay?" The instructor appeared concerned. "You look ill."

I opened my mouth to say something, but it was too dry to speak. My heart was racing and I felt dizzy. I swayed a little and griped the table for support. Now everyhar was looking at me with alarm.

"I have to go," I stammered, and bolted from the library.

I fairly flew down the halls and staircases until I found myself in the kitchen garden, at the gate to Darquiel's forbidden garden. Without a moment's hesitation, I pushed it open and ran along the path towards the little cottage.

When I got there, I found Darquiel sitting on his patio drinking tea, but he was not alone; Langsol, the Provost of the Chrysanthos part of the Lyceum, and Mithras sat with him. An unmistakeable look of fury crossed the Provost's face. Mithras jumped to his feet and tried to intercept me, but I dodged him, stopping only when I stood in front of Darquiel.

"What the hell are you doing here?" Langsol sounded furious. "Mithras, remove him!"

Darquiel halted Mithras with a hand gesture, and smiled up at me. "Well, little one?"

"Otis," I blurted out. "His name was Otis."

Darquiel's eyes sparkled. "Indeed!" He beamed.

Word must have spread quickly about my odd behaviour in the library, and of my appearance in the forbidden garden. I found that I was being stared at a lot: some hara stared openly, some more covertly, and some looked genuinely nervous as if they were afraid I'd have a bizarre fit in front of them. I ignored the stares, and immersed myself deeper in my readings.

Thirteen days after the chiffchaff incident, I returned to my room after lunch to find that someone had slipped a small purple envelope under my door. The note was written in a flowery, formal script and the words were equally flowery and formal. Langsol, Provost of the Chrysanthos, was inviting me, a first year Argenteus, to have tea with him. The note spoke of important matters that needed to be discussed, and he acknowledged the delicate nature of his invitation and the need for discretion to avoid unnecessary questions. He even suggested a circuitous route to his private garden.

I laughed out loud as I flopped onto my bed, tossing the invitation onto my dresser; I wanted a nap. But I could not sleep; my curiosity was piqued and it would not let me rest. What important matter could he want to discuss with me? Delicacy? Discretion?

"Oh heck," I said out loud. "Why not?"

I followed the Chrysanthos Provost's directions and felt like a naughty harling by the time I slipped into Langsol's private patio garden. The brief gleam of triumph I saw in his eyes was quickly hidden behind the façade of a polite and gracious host.

"I must confess," he said with a laugh, as he poured me a glass of lemonade and pushed it across the table, "that I have been watching your antics here at the Lyceum with relish. I enjoy watching Dalsea Ribenny contend with your shenanigans. Would I be correct in postulating that you are not entirely comfortable with the Argenti? Because be assured that the Chrysanthos would welcome you to the true path with open arms."

Ah! I thought. *He wants me to switch sides; this is the 'important matter' he needed to discuss with me.*

"Actually, I'm not comfortable with the whole sect concept," I said truthfully.

Langsol's eyes narrowed. "Have you no interest in the one pure path to truth? Argenteus beliefs are weak and misguided; you follow the wrong path."

"I believe there are many paths to truth," I said carefully. I did not feel ready to debate a hienama of his standing.

"Ah, yes," he sneered. "I have heard that saying before: 'There are many paths to the top of the mountain, but only one view.' Only the Chrysanthos path is the true one, the others will lead you astray; there are no views on dead-end paths."

"Hienama, even if we came up the same path together, and you faced north and I faced south we would still not be seeing the same view; we would be seeing different parts of a great panorama. It is only if we stood side-by-side that we would share the same view. I believe that the Truth is like the panoramic view, too vast for us to see from one vantage point; once we truly understand Truth we will see that there is no real difference between our paths. I believe that the diversity and differences between Chrysanthos, Argenteus, and the other minor sects that still exist in the outer tribal areas are like separate languages but we all discuss the same concepts and we all speak of the same truth."

I stopped. I hadn't really planned to say that and it was sort of an epiphany; I'd never really solidified those thoughts into words before. I also noted with some exasperation, that what I had just said sounded exactly like something a hienama would say; I have been amongst these hienama too long.

Langsol glared at me, his lips thin. "You're a fool."

I shrugged and an awkward silence settled; Langsol glowered as his fingers drummed fitfully on the table and I wondered how I should make my excuses and escape back to the Argenteus dorms.

"So be it," Langsol said bitterly, "we are at an impasse."

I nodded. "I'd probably better go."

"Before you leave I want you to tell me something." Langsol's voice was hard. "Are you The One?"

I stared at him blankly. "Which one?"

He rolled his eyes and made an exasperated *tsking* sound. "*The* One. The One spoken of in the prophecy."

"What prophecy?" my curiosity was once again roused and I felt an intense desire to know of the prophecy begin to gnaw at me.

His eyes narrowed. "You're lying. You must know of the prophecy; its origins are Argenteus."

I shook my head.

"Ribenny never mentioned it? None of your teachers? Not even Darquiel?" He sat back, as if assessing me. "That is interesting as well as telling. It would make sense they wouldn't speak of it to you, especially if they believe you to be 'the one'."

"What is this prophecy?" I asked. "Tell me. Please."

"It's not my job to educate an Argenteus harling in his own sect's divinely-inspired revelations," he said peevishly.

"Please!" I desperately needed him to tell me about this prophecy.

He contemplated me for a moment, as the corners of his mouth twitched. "Very well," he said finally, "but we will do this properly; in a deep meditation."

I followed him into his office which was ornate, stuffy, and overwhelmingly purple.

He indicated that I should sit opposite him on a matching pale purple meditation mat and cushion set. "Are you comfortable?" he inquired, in a manner which clearly conveyed that he didn't care either way.

"Whatever." I shrugged.

"How deep have you been?" he asked.

"I have no idea."

"Perhaps we shall just have to see what you can manage." He sounded patronising, as if he did not think I would be up to the task.

We settled in and began; I followed him as we sank deep down. He drew me deeper than I had ever been.

"What do you see?" he asked, his voice echoing slightly.

I let my visions settle.

"I see rock tunnels," I responded. "The ground is sort of sandy, and there is a dull orange-ish light, but I can't see where it's coming from. What are we trying to accomplish? Should I follow along one of the tunnels?"

"As you wish," was the only response.

I began to move carefully along the tunnel to my left. It went on a ways, but I could see darkness further up.

"The tunnel doesn't seem to go anywhere. The light ends farther up this way," I called back.

"Oh!" I exclaimed. "There are markings on the walls. It looks like some kind of ancient writing... almost like a... a..."

"A tomb?" Langsol's voice seemed a very far way off.

"Yeah, kind of like an ancient tomb," I said.

I spent a few minutes examining the markings; they were fascinating. When I looked up, I thought the darkness at the end of the tunnel seemed much closer. I related this to Langsol, and turned back the way I'd come in.

But Langsol did not answer, and there was no more tunnel entrance, there was only another wall of darkness. The darkness oozed towards me slowly; I backed up quickly.

"Langsol!" I hollered.

But there was no reply. Panic rose quickly and I backed up again. The darkness at the other end of the tunnel was also moving closer, too. I was being sandwiched in between; there was no escape.

"Langsol! Help!" I yelled.

There was no response. I knew in that instant that there was no prophecy; Langsol had lured me into a trap.

One wall of blackness ooze was almost upon me. I reached out to touch it; it was thick and sticky. When I pulled back, I could not get free. First my hand, then my arm, and then I was engulfed. The harder I struggled, the thicker and tighter around me the black ooze became; I could not breathe.

"When an attacker pushes you, use his momentum to pull him off balance; if he should pull you, use your momentum to push him."

The words of an old martial arts instructor floated through my head. I tried to calm myself; if the black ooze wanted me still, I would be still. I forced myself to relax, and let my body sag into the ooze. Nothing happened at first, but in the blackness I become aware of small glimmers of green. In an effort to avoid panicking, I focused on these, and gradually the glimmers fused, and grew, until I felt surrounded by a living halo of agmara, the life-giving energy of the universe. Slowly the ooze started to loosen; I began to sink through it.

I sank faster until suddenly, I tumbled free. Falling head over heels, I found myself floating free in the blackness of the heavens. I laughed. I knew where I was now; I knew how to get back.

I breathed a deep, cleansing breath as I floated back into my conscious body. My eyes fluttered open; I was back in the office. Langsol sat across from me, still in meditation.

I was surprisingly calm as I sat there staring at him, while he too returned to this world. His eyes flew open, and his nostrils flared. I could sense his fury, fury with tinged with fear. We stared at each other in silence.

"You tried to kill me." My voice was calm and quiet.

"Who are you?" he hissed. "What are you? Get out! You're a freak! An abomination! Get out!"

I stood up in a single graceful move, and strode calmly from the office. It was not until I had reached my room that I allowed myself to fall apart. I leaned against the closed door, and began to shake; Langsol had tried to kill me.

I could hear a commotion out in the hall; a lot of yelling, and then pounding on my door. I opened it a tiny crack, and was forced back as Mithras and two yellow-jackets pushed their way in.

"I've been ordered to take you to Darquiel."

Suzanne Gabriel

"Thank you, Mithras." Darquiel dismissed my escorts, waiting until he heard the clank of the gate before turning to me.

"Are you okay?" His voice was soft.

I could feel him inside my head; he was not relying on me to answer, he was checking for himself.

"No!" I was shaking again; I could feel a storm building up. "He tried to kill me."

"I know. But it is now in the past. You are OK."

"I hate it here," I whispered. "I hate it here!" I repeated this over and over until I was yelling. The dam had burst; I could no longer hold things inside. I paced around the patio, and vented everything that I'd kept bottled up. "I never wanted this! I never wanted to come here!"

I ranted about never having been given a choice about my life and how much I resented it. I ranted about how neither sect actually knew their own history, how things had been twisted, and how we were behaving as our ancestors, the humans, had.

"We're all spiritual creatures! We are all capable of so much more! The sects are keeping truth caged up in places like this. How does fighting about the levels of existence of the Dehara Demitto create the silence we need to find that place where our life force truly is?" I shouted.

I ranted about pettiness, hypocrisy, and how we had lost touch with the true path. I cursed and swore about every lie, half-truth, and every problem I saw. I raged about the damage the recent escalation in the conflicts beyond the Nayatis, and how we should be focused on positives rather than negatives.

And then the storm was gone.

I found myself standing still in the middle of the patio, breathing heavily, and feeling completely spent; I covered my face with my hands and burst into tears.

Darquiel had kept silent as I vented; he remained quiet now, too, but he gathered me in his arms, and held me as I sobbed.

Eventually that storm also passed, and I pulled away from Darquiel's now damp shoulder. "I'm sorry," I mumbled.

"Better out than in, and quite understandable, given that an attempt has just been made on your life."

"And I'm really sorry about all the bad language I used. It was uncalled for, especially in your presence."

"Judicial use of colourful language is best, of course," he

276

chuckled. "You were indeed enthusiastic in your usage. Now," Darquiel smiled, "let's go sit and have some tea."

I nodded. "Yes, tiahaar"

"I have a confession to make," Darquiel said as we settled into our seats. "I am by some degree to blame for this theological schism that you are currently presented with. We saw the beginning of it generations ago; my fathers did nothing, and I also did nothing. I saw the schism develop from slight differences to barely-veiled hostilities. The hegemony chose ... I chose... to ignore it. They say 'every dogma has its day', and I believed that the ideals that nourish and enrich us are eternal. I had hoped that these highly-skilled adults would eventually work it out. I wish now I had been more proactive. Perhaps this is why I have not yet faded."

He sighed.

"We tend to judge others by their behaviour, but we judge ourselves by our intentions. Don't make that mistake Shaymar. If you judge them," he waved his hand in the direction of the gate, "by what they say and do, make sure that what you say and do lives up to your intentions; cast your shadow with purpose."

He was silent for a long time staring into his cup of tea.

"I believe that you and I are alike in many ways. We were both born 'different', and considered 'freakish' by some. We were both propelled down a pathway not of our choosing, and now we have both had somehar try to kill us. That means I also think you are strong enough to deal with this situation.

"This afternoon's 'unpleasantness' will be dealt with; you need not fear, or worry. I will be dealing with this personally; despite my retired status I still wield considerable influence." He smiled wryly. "Langsol is a fool and his actions are inexcusable; he risked open warfare between the sects. News of this incident will travel fast. I have sent for Dalsea, as well as the heads of both the Argenteus and Chrysanthos Precincts in Immanion; we will have to move quickly to head off the backlash I expect is already threatening. Your role will be to do nothing and say nothing further in regards to this incident. Understand?"

I held his gaze for a moment before nodding and looking down. "Yes, tiahaar."

Darquiel and I chatted about dull ordinary things for some

time longer before he deemed me calm enough to send back to the world beyond his garden.

And the situation outside Darquiel's garden was dire; crops were failing, rivers were no more than trickles, wells were running dry, and even the trees had begun to look wilted. No relief had come despite the Argenteus' and Chrysanthos' Grissecons performed by highest of high hienama. In fact, the universe seemed to thumb its nose at their attempts by banishing even the puffy white clouds; the sun had beaten down out of unbroken blue skies for weeks.

Nerves were frayed. The whole world was unnerved, as the highest ranked from Immanion, Almagabra and beyond returned once more to the sacred spring, and as expected, the halls of the Lyceum, and the spaces of the Great Nayati were filled with discord, and with rhetoric.

As the atmosphere at the top of the sun-drenched island paradise became more tense and unsettled, everyhar began to be feeling the effects; I found it almost unbearable.

I had tried to duck out of the General Conclave that had been called, but Sirius had intercepted me.

"We are *all* required to go," he had said sternly. "Nohar *wants* to go, Shaymar, so if I have to, you have to, OK?" He sounded exasperated.

So there I sat, sandwiched between Sirius and Lirell, in the Great Nayati at the sacred spring of Itamar. With the notable exception of Langsol, the whole Lyceum was present, along with many respected hienamas from Immanion, and the lands beyond. The Great Nayati was filled with vests, tabards and robes of yellows and greys, deep golds, and dark greys, gold and silver threads, brocades, and trims.

As we sat silently, watching the high hienamas from both sects standing outside, on the terrace next to the sacred spring, performing competing opening rituals, I snuck a glance at Lirell. He had been increasingly subdued as letters from home arrived bearing dire news; the crops were failing, and his family suffered.

He was sitting quietly with his head bent, and his eyes closed; I knew what he was praying for. Instinctively, I reached out and put my hand on this arm. He looked up startled.

Everything will be okay. My mind touched his.

He nodded uncertainly. I really wished there was something I could do to help.

The hienamas entered the Nayati proper, and the great doors were closed, blocking out the glare of unrelenting sun. It felt instantly stifling, with the sun beating down on the great dome; I was sure we would eventually bake. I shifted restlessly.

Any hopes that we had been called together to look for solutions were dashed almost immediately as sect leaders rose to give fiery addresses that laid blame and made accusations. These, in turn, were met with passionate rebuttals and furious tirades.

I closed my eyes and shrank away from the turmoil; I felt sick. These hara were powerful, and their words were firing up the emotions of those gathered. Feelings of anger, resentment, and hatred all swirled together, rising with the sweltering heat in the high-domed chamber. These were not the words of leaders trying to reach compromise; this was vitriol fanning the fires and widening the gulf.

Why? I screamed silently to the universe. I did my best to push the dark, oppressive atmosphere away, but it pushed back, threatened to take hold of me. I extended my mind beyond the walls of the Nayati, desperate to reach the coolness of my secret spring, but I could not quite reach it. I put my mind out in search of Darquiel. I could sense him, but he did not respond; he seemed only to be monitoring.

I put my hands up to cover my ears.

Stop it! Stop it! I felt suffocated. I was being crushed by their anger, and torn apart by the widening chasm between the two doctrines.

"Enough!"

I hadn't realised I'd said that out loud, but I found myself standing, echoes reverberating around the great dome and hundreds of shocked faces looking my way.

"Enough!" I repeated.

Instead of feeling mortified, I felt a rush of confidence; I felt emboldened. I had their attention; I would cast my shadow with purpose. I began moving out of the row where I was seated, towards the centre aisle. Hara pulled back from me, as if they were afraid that touching me would burn.

"Do you hear yourselves? Does your rhetoric solve anything?" I asked quietly. "'Be careful with fire' is good advice. 'Be careful with words' is better advice. Watch your thoughts, they become words; watch your words, they become actions. If you preach hate, how can we ever find peace?"

Words began to flow out of me. Not my own words, but as I listened, I found myself in complete agreement with everything I heard myself say. I opened myself completely to the source, and let his words flow through me.

Nohar moved; all sat as if frozen. I walked towards the dais, addressing our highest leaders with my voice pitched so that my words reached all assembled there. I climbed the three steps of the dais, and turned to address the audience; my voice rose and fell, pitched perfectly to the tenor of the words.

And then I was done; silence hung in the Nayati and hundreds of pairs of eyes stared.

Now what? I thought. Suddenly the door through which I had come in seemed very far away. A quick calculation established that my closest escape route was through the great doors behind me that led out to the terrace.

I turned towards the high hienamas, who still sat frozen in their chairs on the dais. I pulled the grey tabard I wore over my head, and held it out to them; still no one moved. I let the tabard fall; it landed with a soft rustle on the white marble. I walked past them towards the exit.

The great doors swung open easily, and soundlessly. I stepped out onto the terrace expecting sunshine, but there was none. As far as the eye could see, the sky was a dark and stormy grey. As I tilted my face upwards; I felt a large raindrop hit my nose, and then another, and another; it was raining.

I raised my arms up towards the sky, letting out a joyful whoop. Within seconds, the heavens opened up and it poured; the rain falling so hard that it bounced as it hit the marble of the terrace. I was soaked and grinning as I sprinted off the terrace.

I ran without stopping to Darquiel's garden. I found him sitting quietly under the covered veranda of his cottage watching the rain.

"It's raining!" I cried happily.

"So I see." He smiled.

I dropped to my knees in front of him.

"Why did you make me do that?" I asked. "Why did you make me say those things?"

"I made you do nothing; the courage and conviction were all

yours. All I did was take your tirade from the other day, and polished your words; more oratorical, less... colloquial," he said with a smile. "Bravo, my friend, you finally found your bite. Perhaps now things will change for the better."

I shook my head. "I doubt it. After what just happened, they won't keep me here. I was coming here to say goodbye and ... thank you."

"Goodbye?" He smiled. "I wouldn't be so sure. I just threw you under the chariot of destiny."

His gaze shifted. A group of eight hara came towards us along the path through the now steady, gentle rain. Mithras and Sirius still wore their coloured surcoats, but the others did not. I stood to face them as they stepped under the veranda.

There was silence as I looked from face to face.

"The rain was a nice touch," Mithras said.

"I didn't do the rain," I said. "It just happened."

"Don't be so sure," Sirius said. "Months of work, rituals, prayers, and Grissecon by both sects go unanswered, and then you stand up and give everyone a verbal kick in the head and suddenly it's raining. As far as we're concerned – the universe has spoken."

"You're not even aware of what you did, are you?" A tall har with wide hazel eyes said, brushing his wet bangs off his face. "Your words held magic; they broke the spell."

I looked nervously at Darquiel. "They weren't my words."

Sirius spoke again. "The Nayati is in chaos. There is a pile of silver and gold garments on the steps. Everyhar is agitated and they want change."

"This is more than one har can be expected to do; he can't fix it alone." Darquiel's voice was calm.

"We will not follow you blindly, but you can count on our help," said Mithras.

"I don't know..." I began uncertainly.

"You broke it," Mithras smiled. It was the first time I'd seen him smile – he really was beautiful.

"You broke it," he repeated. "You fix it. Let's go."

The group turned back toward the Nayati; Mithras and I brought up the rear.

"Mithras! Shaymar!" Darquiel called

Mithras signalled the others to continue as he and I returned to stand in front of Darquiel.

"Later this evening," he said, "when the panic has abated, I want you two to find somewhere private and share aruna. Share aruna as often as you over the next few weeks; get it out of your systems. In due course, a deep love with grow between you, and you will come to trust each other more than you trust yourselves. But know this..." Darquiel surged to his feet, his black eyes flashed, and the air around us sizzled with power; for an instant I knew what he must have been like as Tigron. "Know this: no matter how right it feels, no matter how easy it seems - you are not meant for each other."

He closed the short distance between us and he placed his hand gently on Mithras' shoulder. "Mithras, my friend, the next time you are in the port of Sumosea, climb the hill, find the restaurant known as *The Overhang*, order the Chef's Special, and sit by the window."

Mithras nodded.

Darquiel took my face between his hands and leaned forward to touch his forehead to mine. "If you walk out the front door of Immanion's hegemony building, and walk straight across the piazza, you will see a street. Down that street is a tiny coffee shop; it's barely more than a hole in the wall. When you get the chance, go have a coffee."

Epilogue

Time is relative; seven years can seem like forever, or they can feel like they pass in the blink of an eye.

So it was for the seven years since my 'coup'; it felt like a long time, and yet the time has flown by. Sadly, although not unexpectedly, there has been no miraculous mending of the rifts between Argenteus and Chrysanthos, but there has been progress in many areas; the tense powder keg has been diffused.

I had initially locked myself away in Itamar, and pushed older, more seasoned, hara to the foreground while I immersed myself in ascension studies. I had travelled the world, visited other tribes, and gained perspectives beyond Immanion's influence.

This was my first official visit to Immanion. I was now comfortable in my own skin and aware just how much power I possessed.

I had made peace with not knowing who I had been in my former life, although this visit was stirring up some strange sensations; every so often, something quite mundane felt achingly familiar.

A door opened behind me, and a har entered. I kept staring out the window at the piazza in front of the hegemony building, and at the space between the buildings on the other side where a particular street began.

"Are you still here?" Mithras asked pointedly "Quit stalling."

"Shut up! I'm not stalling. I'm thinking."

Mithras crossed to where I stood by the window and leaned against the casing, crossing his arms in front of him.

"Destiny happens every day in so many little ways, most of the time we're not even aware it's happening. Every time we react to a situation, or make a choice, we affect our path. In Sumosea, I went to the *The Overhang* restaurant, I ordered the Chef's Special, and I sat by the window. I met two fabulous hara, and we had a fabulous evening; I hadn't laughed that much in ages. They invited me to visit them sometime. When I chose to take them up on that offer, my mind was completely blown by one of their younger brothers. Destiny is both choice and chance!"

I walk out the front door of Immanion's hegemony building, walked straight across the piazza, and down the street directly across. About a third of the way down the street I spotted an elegant black and gold sign; *The Java-lope.*

I took a deep breath and opened the door.

Ai-cara 1515

Martina Luise Pachali

Ai-cara 1515

Special thanks to my writer friend Elin Gregory for putting this into story shape from the jumbled ruins of an abandoned fanfic I felt rather at a loss about. She's as much the author of this as I am and can be found at www.elingregory.com

Present

The unrecognisable object Cael was knitting today was green.

He looked up at me while his hands continued their task. His hair was already straying from its improvised knot. "Where's Siwi?" he asked.

"At the harlingry. I've been giving Stella a run on the beach and just popped in to get what I need to fetch him – in fact, I must hurry to get him before the storm breaks."

Dismayed, I noticed the first fat raindrops appear on the large, arched window that looked upon the Aphaia Centre. "It's raining already – I'll have to run."

Cael nodded and looked back at his knitting, but I found I couldn't tear my eyes from him. Cael had never been so moving and alluring than at this precise moment, sitting cross-legged on the living room sofa, surrounded by pale grey and dark green clews of wool intermingled with a few of Siwi's toys. His sweater and socks were large, greyish brown, and shapeless, his hair was a mess, and his knees were bare and bony.

I walked around the low table and squatted in front of Cael, taking his cold fingers in my hands to try and disentangle them from the wool.

"What do you think you're doing, Gurdah?" he asked.

"I just realised that I'm alone in the house with a delicious young har, and that there's a thunderstorm outside. The worst of the rain will probably be over in an hour, and getting Siwi off that damn rocking horse in the harlingry will be just as hard then."

I grinned up at him, tugging at the knitting. He took it from

286

my inexpert fingers, pinned it up against the clew with the needles, and dropped it over my shoulder onto the table. He snaked his head down towards my face like a graceful bird and covered my lips with his. His energy poured into me, filling me with a calm awe. I closed my eyes, suffused by his brilliant clarity, and felt bereft when he broke contact.

"You're like dark furs before a fireplace – a luxurious heap that I want to burrow into," he murmured, his head snuggled close to mine, a swathe of his hair gently brushing the nape of my neck. "Do you realise we've never taken aruna in this room, leisurely and relaxed like civilised hara? It's always been over in the bedroom, and us always alert in case Siwi needed us, apart from the few times we went to the Grissecon temple."

Pushing aside his escaping hair, I looked up at him with mock sadness. "Do you think it's too late now?"

"I don't know. We can give it a try."

I dropped my head into his lap, tunnelling under the big sweater that smelled sweetly of Cael. In the close darkness, surrounded by the vibrant energy and the beloved scent of his groin, I felt I was contained and protected inside his gentle power like a fish in a warm, sunlit sea. Below my cheek, something withdrew. I followed it with my nose. Cael, sensing my movement, undid the top of his shorts to allow me access.

I refrained from teasing the pale, tightly closed petals of his ouana-lim as not to confuse him in his passage into soume and instead sought the sweet liquid of his soume-lam with my tongue. He gave a deep moan and opened his legs wide, tugging at my shoulders to pull me up. I heaved myself up on my elbows to face him, sharing breath again while he undid my clothes to free me and draw me inside.

After this we did undress, in front of the fireplace, having shoved Siwi's toys out of the way. I was soume for him, and he drowned himself in me, moaning, shouting, and heaving, as if he wanted to push his entire slight body into me. Outside, the thunderstorm raged; rain veiled the air and whipped against the windowpane, its fierceness driving us on.

As the rain subsided, so did we. When the power of the lightning subtly permeating the room withdrew, we looked up into the vestiges of the sunset reflected from the Aphaia Centre and returned to our surroundings. On one of the turrets, two hara were standing and looking at us; when they saw us stirring to reason, they departed.

Cael laughed softly, put his sharp elbows on my chest, his chin on his fists, and looked into my eyes.

"My sweet Gurdah," he said, possessive pride in his voice. "Whatever it was that gave you to me, gave me the most important gift of my whole life."

"Apart from the Nahir-Nuri who gave you Siwi, of course," I hastened to amend.

"Siwi is not a gift, not something extra, not something for me; he's there for himself, at the centre, unassailable." Cael scowled, his hands balled into fists. "But you always threaten to up and leave me as soon as that Nahir-Nuri shows his face round the corner, as if he had a right to take over our lives just because he dropped his seed in me without even asking first. I swear to you, on the power of our aruna, that I will not let you go without putting up every kind of resistance known to Wraeththu-kind and then some. I love you, Gurdah. I love you because you're you, and not because you're useful. Get that!"

He shouted into my face. I pulled his elbows apart and tugged him closer to share breath again; his was still fraught with his energetic resolve and roared into me like a firestorm – so different from his accustomed taste. But while we shared breath, his taste changed, and he dissolved in my arms, sobbing my name. His hair, damp from the exertions of aruna, clung to us both and entangled us.

I put my arms around him. "I do love you, Cael," I murmured into his hair. "It's just that I fear that our love and our free choice will be weak as autumn leaves before the advancing willpower of that mysterious har. We'll be swept away kicking and screaming, but just as helpless as Siwi when we lift him off that damn rocking horse in the harlingry. Speaking of which, we should really go and get him before the night shift comes in and puts him to bed over there."

Cael lifted his head, hair and tears streaming, nose red and sniffling – not a pretty sight, but one to melt my heart.

"I love you, Cael," I assured him again. "Whatever I can do to keep you, I will! However, I can't shake the fear that it won't be enough."

"Nohar can ever swear that the world won't come down and

crush us. One day, it inevitably will. We are not immortal. But short of that, I will not let you go!"

Wrapping his hair around his wrist and knotting it into a loose loop again, he stood up. His skinny frame still glowed from the power of our aruna. He stood and stretched, uncaring of any potential watchers from the windows of the Centre.

He turned around and started collecting his clothes, wiping his nose and eyes on some undergarment as he went.

Earlier That Year

If you believe the silly old song that "it never rains in southern Almagabra" – forget it! When I was leaving Phaonica after my audience with the Tigron, it was raining as hard as in the Gimrah plains. Well, not *my* audience, really; I had been there with a whole bunch of provincial dignitaries. It was one of those occasions scheduled years in advance where you'd do exactly as you were told in order to get noticed for a moment. Now, my mission was over; our house had been represented at court, and our gift of half a dozen fine Gimrah-raised yearlings had been well received.

Taking a bunch of skittish young horses, gifted but not able to travel the Otherlanes like *sedim*, had required our party to come by sea. My attendants had gone back the same way, anticipating a leisurely voyage. I claimed I was going to stay a few days longer, perhaps, and then go home with Stella, my mare – who was a *sedu* and who'd helped to keep the young ones disciplined – via the Otherlanes. In truth, I doubted whether I'd ever go back. Cyriel, my chesnari, had died two winters earlier in a fall from a horse, my sons didn't need me, and my daughter had gone to her training at Shilalama in Roselane. I was, in the middle of my life, at loose ends. As long as I answered my family's loving but perfunctory enquiries over the thought transference network, I was free to do whatever: get some higher caste training, spend an entire year in a Grissecon temple, or wander back into the southern deserts I'd come from.

The liberating loneliness was aggravated by the weather. Although I didn't know what to do with the eighty or so years of life still ahead of me (Aghama willing), I definitely knew what to do next: Get out of the rain.

I had been so eager to leave my former life for the unknown

Martina Luise Pachali

that I felt I couldn't stand another day and night at the guesthouse with my former compatriots. I hadn't even looked at what the weather was like. Only now, as I was passing the majestic walls of Lower Phaonica with its administrative buildings and power hubs, the rain was starting to get at me.

There was a cab pole flashing its signal, but of Immanion's famous Grissecon-powered public transport system there was no trace. Too many of them needed at once, I guessed, what with the downpour. Nohar in his right mind would want to walk a step outside if he could ride a cab, although the har – the hara – waiting at this pole definitely needed the cab more than most. At the sight of them, my heart melted with sympathy.

The har didn't even have a cloak; he stood there, just letting himself and his precious burden get soaked through. His hair was longish, darkened by rain. It stuck to his face and his clothes; it stuck to the bundle in his arms, of which only two small hands clawing into the wet hair were visible, all else concealed by a large, wet blanket and a small, wet woolly hat.

At the sound of Stella's hooves, the har lifted his head, regarding me with enormous, passive sea-green eyes, hopeless and resigned. The harling turned his head as well; he pointed at the horse and chirped, grinning at me with his four perfect little teeth. His eyes, I could see from my horse, were amber. His woolly hat was dripping into them, but he didn't mind – he was seeing the very first horse of his young life, I suspected, and he liked it.

I brought Stella to a halt.

"Can I take you anywhere?" I enquired of the har. The harling, at the sound of my voice, squirmed to reach out towards the huge and beautiful animal, smelling sweetly of hay – and almost succeeded in falling out of the har's arms. The har held the little one in front of him, pressing the delicate bundle gingerly and insecurely against his chest. I held on to my saddle horn and leaned down to catch the little one before he fell. I grabbed him by his clothes, hoisted him up onto the saddlebow and secured him with my cloak, just as I'd always ridden with my children when they were that small. This one was cute, and peered at me, his eyes learning to focus. By the Aghama, he must have been hatched that very morning!

The sea-green eyes of the grown har never showed any panic – after all, this was Immanion. Not everything was perfect here, perhaps, not by a long run, but nohar would harm a harling. Confusion, perhaps disbelief at my offered help, was all that I read in those eyes.

"Come on up and I'll take you out of this rain and home," I offered, bending down again, the harling snug and safe in my cloak between the saddle horn and my belly. The har bent down to retrieve the drenched blanket. Tucking it under his arm, he gripped my proffered hand, I pulled, he pulled – and nothing much happened. Seemed this har didn't know how to get on a horse.

"It always looked so easy when the nobility was doing it in the sunshine," he murmured, his voice low and a bit roughened. I took the harling into the crook of my arm – the little creature, warm now, was already fast asleep – and jumped off the horse in order to help the hostling up. He, however, wasn't ready yet – he was looking at my face under the hood.

Hara come in all hues, of course, but my skin is pitch-black with an almost bluish sheen. I come from a tribe right at the circumference of the Earth. My people had converted from human tribe to harish tribe as a whole back in the Aghama's time – all the young males being incepted at once, or so our tribal legends say. Human traditions and harish traditions had combined to form a close-knit backwater that I fled even before my Feybraiha – on account of not wanting the mighty tribal leader they'd chosen to perform for me on that occasion.

Despite the rain, I shrugged off my hood to let him look his fill before he joined me on Stella's back. At the movement, the harling woke. He looked up at my face and grinned, grabbing – like all the small harlings I have ever known – for the multitude of small, coloured beads I wear at the end of my braids. Back home in the Southern desert, that hairstyle is commonplace. Cyriel found it so exotic when he met me that I'd kept it ever since, and the harlings love the colour, the glitter and the whispering sound of the beads.

I grinned, letting them see the whiteness of my teeth. The wet har smiled back at me and the harling grabbed for my braids again, succeeded, and yanked – making me yelp. We laughed out loud, the little one joining us, although he couldn't yet have the slightest idea what was so funny about it, and the mood was broken.

"How do I get on this?" the hostling said, shyly, huskily. I smiled at him again and showed him which foot to put in the stirrup. He blushed a little – his skin was fair, but ruddy from the cool rain – and tried again. He pulled at the saddle horn, I pushed at his bottom, and up he went. He landed with a plonk; Stella turned her head to look at me, deep hurt in her dark eyes. I held out my hand and scratched her nose; the harling, totally absorbed, reached for the horse as well and I let him touch her, leaning forward so the little one could reach her. The harling's small fingers touched Stella's nose, and she very gingerly nibbled them. The harling was entranced.

The hostling, however, gave a little frightened groan, so I tenderly separated harling and horse and told the hostling to take his feet out of the stirrups so I could get on. He did, fist white-knuckled at the saddle horn, and I mounted behind him, putting the harling into his free arm and securing us all with my cloak, to make sure that neither of them got dropped accidentally. A minimal mental command to Stella, and we were off again, following the red brick wall of Phaonica's business end.

When we turned the next corner, I could see an enormous crystal cupola, shimmering with the magic power stored there. I thought of all the aruna needed to make that amount of power and wished that I had headed for the nearest Grissecon Temple and let myself go seriously wild for a time before doing anything else. I had not lacked since Cyriel's death, but I felt like luxuriating in my harishness for a bit. It seems my fate always to be landed with cute harlings instead of beautiful hara.

I couldn't tell if the sea-green-eyed har in my arms was beautiful. In any case, with a harling, he was probably spoken for, perhaps even bonded. His hair was unpleasantly cold and wet where it touched my throat. The little one slept, and Stella just ambled along.

"Where are we going?" I remembered to ask.

"Wherever it's convenient for you to drop us," the har answered. "Where are you headed?"

"Nowhere, really. I can take you anywhere you want."

"Anywhere? For that, you would need a *sedu*," he said. "Short of that, home would be enough."

"She is one, actually. A *sedu*." I had nonplussed him. "So, where do you want to go now?'"

"Still home."

"Where is that? Should we stop and turn around?"

"This is quite okay. Just follow this road until you reach the big shop with the red sign. I live in one of the courtyards behind it, a few streets back from the avenue. I'll tell you where exactly to go; it's a bit complicated."

"Must be great to live so close to the Aphaia Centre," I ventured, hoping he'd tell a bit more about himself.

"I don't go there much; not much time for that sort of stuff. I spend most time at work – that is, I used to," he added.

"What happened?"

He nodded at the sleeping harling. "He happened. I can't come back to work for six months now. They say having delivered a pearl has done things to my energy conduits that could be dangerous to all of us on the team."

A-ha. Power worker. That explained many things.

"The boss even bawled me out for not telling beforehand, as it could have been dangerous in an emergency – but I didn't know. He just didn't believe me. Said that only happened in old legends – hara delivering pearls without the slightest idea they were going to."

I couldn't believe it, either, but I kept my mouth shut. If anyhar could manage it, it would be a totally self-absorbed power worker with his head up in the sparkly clouds. You had to be a bit mad to do the job in the first place – all that knowledge and trained perception, and then do nothing but let other hara's magic flow through you all day, controlling the crystals, routing resources and requests. It was supposed to be glorious, but I wouldn't take such a job for anything in the world – I'm sure it's infinitely boring.

However, something impels me to be cheerful around harlings and their parents. "If you were that surprised, do you have everything you need for the little one, then? Can I help you to get something from the local harlingry? You'll need a lot of clothes. If you look away for minute, they're an inch taller already."

He giggled, actually noticing that this was a joke.

"Or do you have enough help?" I added, fishing.

Astonishingly – especially for a power geek – he laughed, getting my meaning at once. "No, I'm doing this all on my own.

No chesnari, nothing – I don't have the time for that sort of thing! Didn't, rather. The little one was conceived at the Grissecon Temple."

Inseminating a stranger during power-raising aruna at a Temple? Without him ever noticing? That sounded curiouser and curiouser. You had to be immensely powerful to accomplish that, Algoma, probably aiming for Nahir-Nuri already. And a har in caste training for Nahir-Nuri wouldn't go to a common Grissecon Temple where the energy wafting off anyhar at aruna is harvested off for everyday use – that is what the power workers work with, of course.

At home in rural Gimrah, we don't have such temples; every Grissecon ritual is used for its special purpose, mostly physical healing. But large places like Immanion or Oomadrah or Ferelithia, or the large cities of Megalithica and all over the world really, they are run on this. Couldn't exist without them.

Nahir-Nuri and their apprentices, though, would use their finely honed abilities for more carefully chosen purposes. To blast it off with a stranger right into the public power conduits would be a terrible waste of resources, like using a *sedu* to carry large sacks of potatoes to market. And if we hara had learned anything from the bad example of the humans, it is to preserve our resources – as Cyriel always used to say. But even so, if the Nahir-Nuri just needed his rocks off urgently and more roughly than planned, what in the world possessed him to impregnate his unknown partner with his powerful seed? Had he been insane, perhaps?

Much more believable to think the hostling was lying – even to himself, probably. And to suspend somehar with such a fracture in his self-knowledge for half a year, expecting him to get himself together again during that time, was only too natural. Without a doubt, the scene with his boss couldn't have been very pleasant. What a pity for the little one to be welcomed into the world in this way. Well, I'd try and pamper him a bit, if the har would let me. The Grissecon Temple could wait; first, these two could use my help. Anyhar can make aruna power, but how many have raised several harlings and a Kamagrian, as I had?

"Don't be frightened about doing this wrong," I told him. "Just follow your instincts, the way that you learned to follow your instincts during aruna. Just do what needs to be done. You love the little one, and if you do whatever your love for him tells you, you can't go far wrong."

I stroked his wrists to make him relax his grip. Shivering, he huddled back into my arms, brushing my face with a swathe of wet hair smelling strongly of sweat. I willed myself not to pull away. Instead, I leaned forward to give him the support of my warmth.

With a very small voice, he said, "I don't know that I love him – he's the most beautiful creature in the world, but I don't know him and have no idea what to do now. How can I say I love him – he frightens the living daylights out of me! I've never felt so helpless."

He started sobbing into the harling's woolly hat, making the little one nervous. I told Stella to get a move on while I held on to harling and hostling, trying to calm both of them with my mind. The little one reacted with surprising ease; the har was at first startled to find me in his mind and then relaxed into the emotional warmth I was projecting. He held on.

"You love him, no doubt about that," I said. "Nohar should have to do this alone. But I'm here for you and will see to it that you're all right, so don't panic, trust your feelings, and if in doubt, ask me."

"But you won't be here for long, will you?" he asked, with resigned hopelessness in his voice. "You must be busy with your life and the hara who share it."

Here I was, not even having looked at his face properly, my nose in his less-than-sweet-smelling hair, and I was almost promising to look after him and his son for as long as they'd need me. I doubted my own sanity for a second, but then the right words found me again.

"Cheering you up is all I have to do right now. My daughter always tells me this is what I do best."

I felt his astonishment at the mention of my daughter; curiosity got the better of him.

"Did you host her, or father her?" he asked in wonderment. All sorts of superstitions spring up around Kamagrians and their parents, all of which I found to be loosely rooted in fact – but still rooted there.

"I hosted her, and one of our sons before her. My chesnari hosted the other harlings, as pearl-bearing came considerably easier to him than to me. When I wanted to try it for the second time after all, the result was our daughter – and when we had her, we didn't make any more. She kept us all busy. They're all grown up now, Maryam is in Roselane, and I'm at loose ends."

Stella had turned left at the Aphaia Centre and now stood, awaiting further instruction. "Where do we go now? Don't tell me, just think of the way," I instructed. He was Pyralisit like me, even if he was a bit under the weather emotionally. I reached into his mind and made the connection to Stella, retreating from their communion.

"So this is how you ride them," the har said when the *sedu* went on her way without hesitation. She shook her mane as if in mirth, the coarse white hair flying into the harling's face. The little one, tickled, just giggled and put out his dimpled little hands for the horse's mane. Grabbing over the saddle horn, he sat up on his own and stuck his slightly reddened little button nose out into the fascinating – albeit dripping – world. The hostling held him by the waist and took a deep breath.

"Seems he knows already what he wants," he commented, heartened.

I had told Stella to be on the lookout for the common sign for a harlingry, and now she stopped right in front of the door to the shop. It was on a corner, in an unprepossessing building. The windows were framed in faded dark green, and the walls of the house were a yellowish taupe.

"One block further," the har protested, confused, as his description to Stella had been clear.

"We're exactly where we should be," I said, sliding off the horse and taking the little one down after me. I steadied him on my lower arm, and looked into the perfect little face again. His eyes were truly amber, with the tiniest violet flecks, and when he grinned at me with his six little white teeth, the most delightful impishness crept over his expression.

He reached up with both arms, giving me a diminutive hug. I smiled into his face from close by, and we both giggled softly together – after all, harlings need the occasional cuddle just as much as food, clothes and an education.

Stella reminded me, and I reached up to catch the hostling as he was trying to slide off the horse on his own. He came barely up to my armpits, large masses of wet and neglected hair still obscuring my view of his face as he pressed against me for a second.

"I have no idea who you are," he said, "but thank you for being such a good friend to us both."

He looked up into my face. His nose was somewhat too large for the rest of him, and the enormous sea-green eyes made you want to drown in them. I leaned all the way down to gently cover his lips with mine.

He tasted of crystal and wide open spaces in the cold, a taste the colour of his eyes. I felt the clarity of his purpose and the arrow-strength of his power. He was telling the truth – to himself and to the world. There was a memory there of amber eyes captivating him, and of ecstasy; of magic amber eyes that deepened into violet during aruna; of glowing eyes that turned his will to water while the fiery ouana-lim below gave and gave and gave in fierce and endless concentration that sent tsunamis of rapture through the tidal sea of his soume self. That had been the moment, but he hadn't known then. He knew now, and remembered through our shared breath.

"Excuse me," said a small voice somewhere in the vicinity of Stella's tail.

A small harling, perhaps two years old, stood there, not daring to push past us into the harlingry. Exasperation at grown-ups and their strange rituals blocking his way clearly showed.

"We are sorry," I said, letting him pass. He shot up the stairs and vanished inside with a clanging of the doorbell.

"Let's get this over with," I said to Cael – his name had come into my mind as we had shared breath. "I really want out of this cold, and to find a warm place to stay, where I won't have to leave before this rain stops."

I led the way up the stairs and into the harlingry, readying my purse. Cael, coming up behind me, must have seen my gesture. He gave me a little shove in the small of my back.

"You go right ahead, Gurdah, and find us the stuff we need for the first few days while I clear up the technical details with that har behind the counter."

So, he had his pride. My experience and advice he might need, but my money, definitely not – as a power worker, he would of course lack nothing.

I got myself a large basket and started loading pre-prepared food for freshly hatched harlings, but got called back by the attendant. "You need to sign this first, tiahaar," he called out, as if he feared I might disturb his merchandise and then leave without joining or paying.

"Don't worry, I'm just helping my friend here," I called back.

"But I need both your signatures here."

I put the basket down and walked back towards the countertop, leaned my elbows on the darkly-scuffed wood, and let the har admire the muscles in my arms, strengthened by years of handling horses and harlings. "Listen, fella, I'm just a friend. I don't have to sign anything here."

"I need two signatures on this," the attendant whined. "If you're helping your friend, you'll certainly want to get things from here later – just sign here, please. You friend's chesnari can always come and sign the form whenever it fits his schedule."

By the Aghama, this creature was dense! I could feel Cael tensing beside me, fearing to be forced to an explanation – again.

"Aren't you listening?" I tried to distract the attendant. "Or have you perhaps discovered some flaw in my friend's money?"

"Ummm, no," the har deferred.

"Good, then we don't have any problems here."

The harling extended his arms to me, wanting to be held and reassured my irritation had nothing to do with him. I picked him up and returned to my basket, letting the little one ride my hip and admire the all-new world from a secure vantage point.

I had piled the counter with things they needed and was choosing a musical toy with the little one – he wanted to hear the different melodies again and again and carefully singled out those he liked best – when Cael came and joined us.

He squatted down, put his arms around us both and leaned his head against my back. "That har sure loves to screw commas." He sighed. "Are we through yet? And don't take the duck one; if I have to hear that squeaky melody again I shall scream. Hated it even when I was a harling myself."

Perverse as all little ones – seems to be a law of nature nohar has a worse taste than your own harling – his son clung to the offending toy and dared his hostling to take it away.

"Bah!" he said, defiantly, brandishing the dread thing. Resolutely, Cael pulled it out of his hands and replaced it with a green frog that played different calming water songs. "Here, you can have this."

"Bah," the harling said, heartbroken, and grabbed at the duck.

"Let's take both and teach the duck some new songs later," I suggested to close the matter and move us on, but Cael kept me from getting up and stuck his beaky nose conspiratorially into my face.

"One important field on the form is still empty, and he won't let me take anything until it's filled. Name of harling, it says."

I took this as a question. One hour ago, I'd not yet met them, and here I was choosing a name for the little one. I closed my eyes, breathing in the sweet smell of the harling through his wet woolly hat, and thought of a beautiful legend I had heard of a lost little one left by the sweet water of a well, a lost harling bringing a plentiful bounty to the tribe that took him in. "Silivrio," I said.

The courtyard where Cael lived was spacious and lush with spring flowers, the fountain in the middle of the small, daisy-spattered lawn turned off on account of the season and the rain. Trees and bushes promised shade for the summer.

Always, when I come to a new place which I anticipate growing to know very well, I try to commit the first feeling I get to my memory. I want to remember how it felt when it was all fresh and new to me. The first time, the last time – those are the times that count, the times that we remember a place we know or love.

I knew this was one of those special moments.

Cael led the way to one flight of stairs that had cacti standing on the stairs and growing high beside the banisters. He looked up at them and gripped Silivrio tighter. "Those will have to go, huh?" he said, wistfully.

I asked Stella to stay where she was and carried some of the purchases up the stairs. "No," I said, putting them down in front of the locked door and returning to get more of the stuff. "You don't have to sacrifice all that is important to you in favour of your harling. Life is dangerous, and Silivrio will have the advantage of growing up with the knowledge that cacti sting."

Cael stood on the top landing with the little one in his arms, not quite sure what he was expected to do.

"Go and unlock the door so that we can get out of the rain," I said, and he complied, his translucently pale cheeks blushing a mottled red.

I brought up the folding bed. Taking the little one from Cael, I carried harling and bed inside while the hostling continued to unload the horse.

Inside, I found a spacious room, with large potted palms, marble floors and generous windows that afforded a spectacular view of the Aphaia Centre's architectural splendour. Low furniture invited you to sprawl luxuriously about the room. However, the room was a chaos of used cups and plates, half-read books and magazines, dirty clothes and blankets, and on top of this, somehar had apparently broken a glistening black vase, a wake of shards trailing all the way to one of the doors to the left.

After depositing Silivrio on a sofa that was free of broken pottery, I chose a spot near the window and cleared enough space for the folding bed. Its sides were made of sturdy but transparent mosquito netting, allowing the harling an almost unobstructed view of his surroundings while not giving him any means of egress – at least not until he was a bit older. I picked Silivrio up from the sofa and deposited him in his new bed. He sat there, staring after me as I went out to help Cael.

"I put him in a safe place so we can get this done," I assured Cael, who was carrying a bag of harling clothes up the stairs and was rather startled at my harling-less reappearance. It took two trips to carry two more bags, three boxes and a feeding chair as well as my own packs up the stairs.

"Where can I stable the horse?" I asked Cael.

"Around the next corner, there's a livery stable there for this whole block," Cael replied at once.

A livery stable per block? This was unexpected luxury; nothing but the best for the rising young power workers of Immanion, it seemed.

I made sure Stella was content and comfortable. There were some fine animals there, but the har in charge was obviously excited and happy at having a *sedu* to visit. "Don't spoil her too much," I laughed, leaving.

As I returned to the courtyard, I felt weariness all though my body. That very morning, I had stood before our young Tigron and bowed to his cool loveliness while he affected almost not to see me, despite my spectacular appearance. Since then, a whole new life – however temporary it might turn out to be – seemed to have accreted around me.

When I entered the flat, Cael was on the floor, open bags all around him. He had opened the doors of a tiny kitchen, a luscious marble-tiled bathroom, and a rather austere bedroom. Every corner was inhabited by a mess similar to that in the main room.

I bent down to help Cael. In the rising warmth, the har smelled rather rankly of sweat and blood and the indefinable juices of procreation. It was a natural smell – but not one that should be kept around too long.

I plucked Silivrio from his bed and took off his wet clothes. His hair was curly and reddish, the exact colour of his amber eyes – a beautiful effect. The translucent paleness of his skin he'd inherited from his hostling, but with those eyes and that hair, he'd be spectacular in a few years. This one was destined to break a few hearts in his life, I was sure of that.

Cael trailed after me to the bathroom with the bottle he'd filled with some juice. Silivrio marvelled at the ruby colour of the liquid but didn't yet associate nourishment with it. "What should we give him to eat?" Cael asked me, as I began to wash Silivrio in the tub. "All those packets are just plain confusing."

"Nothing," I answered. "When did he hatch? This morning?"

"Yes, just before sunrise."

"We'll have at least till tomorrow morning until he gets hungry, and when he does, he'll tell us – the wail of a hungry harling is like nothing else in the world. The juice will do for now, but let me dry him off first."

I discarded the first towel I found – it was stiff from something unnamed having dried on it. Cael found me a clean one from a cupboard. I let the water out, lifted the little one high and wrapped him in the towel.

"Go ahead and have your own bath," I said to Cael. While I dressed Silivrio, Cael ran hot water and dropped a handful of blue-green crystals into it. Unselfconscious, as any urban har would be who frequents the Grissecon temples, he discarded his wet clothes and slipped into the fragrant, steaming water. I tried to organise a corner of the bathroom for Silivrio's things, bringing in an occasional table and a small rattan bookshelf, and arranged everything that needed to be on hand.

When I turned around to ask if it was okay this way, Cael had relaxed into the bath, almost floating on the warm water. I decided to give him a bit of privacy and took myself, the harling and the bottle of juice to the main room, closing the bathroom door as we went.

I picked my way to the sofa, threw off everything and installed myself with Silivrio on my lap. We spent a very comfortable half-hour while he learned to drink from the bottle and hold it on his own. When I was sure little Silivrio had mastered the principle, I put him back into his bed and began tidying up around the room. I collected everything that had once contained food or drink and put it in the kitchen sink to soak. I collected all the clothes and towels and blankets in a heap and then went to look for a basket large enough for all the laundry.

The bedroom was a scene of rank desolation. It was very small and had been designed, at a time when Cael could spend time and attention on such things, to be austere and calming, but now, the floor was spattered with blood, food and coffee, and the bed had been transformed into a nest. The whole place stank to high heavens.

I opened all the windows, rain or no rain, found baskets and collected the most revolting items first to get it over with.

Carrying the last basket from the bedroom, I accidentally stepped on one of the black potsherds – which proved to be elastic under my foot. I put the basket beside the door with the others, trying in vain to ignore the evil stench that hung around them, and then turned back towards the mysterious leathery potsherds – that turned out not to be broken pottery after all, but the discarded shell of Silivrio's pearl.

This was something to be treated with respect and ceremony, not to be dropped on the floor and thrown out with the trash, and it pained me to imagine how alone Cael must have been with his pearl and then his harling that he hadn't even been able to collect the broken shell. Carefully, tenderly, I collected the thing in a stoneware bowl and, harling under one arm and bowl in the other hand, I went to the bathroom to ask Cael what he wanted to do with it. I sat down on the rim of the bathtub and cleared my throat.

Cael opened his eyes. They were deeply drowsy and very relaxed, the sea green darkening into turquoise in the steam. He grinned at us from under his prominent nose and said "Hi there," in a low and almost flirtatious voice. Silivrio tried to reach for his hostling, so I deposited the bowl on a corner of the tub and held on to the little one with both hands. Cael lifted a languid hand from the water and tickled the harling's nose; the little one giggled.

Then Cael noticed the bowl and sat up a little; the pale ouana-lim that had bobbed almost inanimate on the surface pulled under and sank into the opaque blue-green of the bath water. "Oh," he said.

"What do you want done with this?" I asked him outright. "I don't think I should just take it out with all the other things that are broken."

"By no means – that would be irreverent. As if this wasn't anything special. Let's just keep it in this bowl on the mantle until I can think about it." He took one piece from the bowl, turning it in his hand. "Strange to see it in there, all broken and lifeless, after I spent a week entirely focused on it. I'm sure it was the strangest week of my life; I didn't recognise myself any more. Frightening, really, how the instincts took over.

"When it began, I was sure I was going to die. It was the middle of the night, you know. I woke up from the pain and I sent out a Call for help to any healer – they must have heard me screaming inside their heads all the way to Phaonica. I'd never seen the one who came before and don't think I will again. When he told me I was dropping a pearl, I didn't believe him – I really didn't. But through the hours, when he stayed with me and encouraged me, it all became real. And when the thing was finally out, I just wanted to be left alone. He insisted on sending a formal notice to my boss, but I found I just couldn't be bothered.

"I didn't want to see anyhar. I just wanted to huddle in corners and brood over this glistening, swelling, ripening black thing. I know I should have called for help, and I'm sure my friends would have been glad to come, but I didn't really want them. I don't know what happened to me in that week. As if all my energy was flowing into that black thing and I had nothing to spare for anything else – not even to call for help and explain what I wanted done. I certainly had no thought or anger to spare for that har from the Grissecon Temple who caused it all. I hope you don't think I'm always that lazy and indolent, Gurdah."

"Lazy has nothing to do with it," I assured him. "Everyhar does it when he's had a pearl – I know, I've been there twice, and tidied up after my brooding chesnari a few more times. It's just that you shouldn't have to do this alone. What about your family – father, hostling, brothers?"

"No brothers, and my father lives in Ferelithia now. My hostling went east a few years ago to raise his caste and only sends a few short messages every month. Anyway, even if they'd been here, I wouldn't have wanted them. Sorry for the mess – that's all I can say."

I laughed aloud, putting him at ease. "You'll be sorry yourself before we're through cleaning it all. Speaking of which, can you move your pretty behind out of the tub so I can clean myself up a bit?"

I had a quick bath after this, not taking time to soak thoroughly, as I'd get hot soon enough from all that needed to be done. For one that had risen from brooding over a pearl only that morning, Cael bestirred himself quite energetically, although he frequently had to rest.

It was getting dark when I hung up the last of the washing. The rooms were clean now and looked the way they were meant to, apart from the scatter of harling things that was actually making the somewhat overly stylish place cosier. We had lit a fire and the rooms were warming. Cael was curled up on the sofa reading. Silivrio had fallen asleep on his hostling's chest. On the table beside the bottle with the juice, there was a large pot of hot tea, a half-filled mug and an empty one thoughtfully set out for me. I filled it, took a careful sip, and sat down on the other sofa with a sigh. I just sat there and idly watched the dusk over the Aphaia Centre, the flames in the fireplace, and sweet Cael almost asleep over his book.

They say that all hara are beautiful, though that sometimes seems more of an affirmation than a fact. Well, Cael really did need some affirming, what with his skinny limbs and large nose, but the overall effect was very moving. Now that his hair was dry, it was a honey-coloured mass that made me want to bury my face in it. He'd put on the most perfunctory of clothes, a tight black vest and trousers that hung low on his hips, slightly rounded to remind you what his body had so recently gone through. His bony ankles moved me to intense tenderness. He was seductive and lost at the same time, and I decided to do something about it.

I collected the soundly sleeping harling and put him into his bed, where he snuggled against the blanket that still smelled rather rankly of Cael, and slept on. It was then that I noticed something glinting below the bed, a little something that I must have missed when I had cleared the space at the beginning.

I picked it up; it was a crystal of the kind you use to store short messages or music. It wasn't marked. I offered it to Cael. "You wouldn't want to lose this," I said, expecting to get it tossed back and be told where to put it. Instead, Cael rolled it wonderingly in his hand.

"It's not one of mine; I don't use this kind." He held it out in his flat hand and let his breath pour over it. A mist rose from the crystal and formed a figure. A message from a high-caste har, very intricately done.

The figure wore the hooded cloak of a Nahir-Nuri. From the hood peered a longish face, pale, with intense amber eyes. "Hello Cael," he said, and grinned. "By now, the pearl should have hatched. I promise you, I did not plan to leave you in the lurch like this, but I have to go and deal with some unforeseen problems. I trust in your capability to get by. I'll be back when I can and do my share. Don't worry, Cael; all will be well. I know why I've chosen you. In the meantime, I am sure, you'll have capable help and shall lack nothing." He grinned again, outsmiling any shark, and vanished. On Cael's hand, the message crystal evaporated in pretty sparkles. Nahir-Nuri, indeed! I felt my bile rising.

Cael just lay there, staring unseeing into his hand. "Who does he think he is?" he asked, deeply troubled. "He expects me to hang around until he in his high-caste wisdom reappears and takes over my life again!" His voice rose and he rose with it from the sofa "Does he believe I'm even interested in his dubious attentions? Does he expect you to keep me warm and the little one fed until he comes to collect us like so much left luggage?" he shouted, standing in the middle of the room, enraged.

Silivrio shifted uneasily in his bed, so I went over to calm his hostling down. I took him in my arms and held him firmly, feeling the whole skinny har sinking into me, exhausted by his anger. He looked up, letting his luscious hair flow down his back, slow and sensual like honey. The glow in his sea-green eyes grew softer, sensual, enticing.

"That Nahir-Nuri can get lost, Gurdah," he declared. "I'd

much rather have you."

I gathered his lips with mine, tasting again the crystalline clarity of his soul. His anger dispersed through our shared breath, all the confusion drifting away like mist. I let my hands slip under his vest, feeling the pliable strength of his spine, the sweet sway of his hips as his soul heated for me. Now, I did bury my face in his hair, and it smelled sweet, a sensual variation of what had been harsh and ripe before.

We shared breath again. He was pulling at my shirt, wanting to get at me. I lifted him and carried him to the bedroom, leaving the door ajar. I let him slide out of my arms onto the bed and quickly discarded our clothes, lying down with him and welcoming him inside me, nourishing his bewildered soul with my soume submission.

Afterwards, he slept, curled inside my long and rangy limbs, trusting me to keep him warm and safe.

I would, I swore to myself, cradling his body in my arms.

Present

He turned around and started collecting his clothes, wiping his nose and eyes on some undergarment as he went.

I still lay on the fur in front of the fireplace, dazed by the suddenness of both his emotional outbreak and its end, strength sapped by the force of our aruna. Cael had the potential to go much further than me, perhaps already had.

I forced my reluctant limbs to push me upwards as there was a harling to be collected. Yet I couldn't let Cael carry on like this, even though he'd weathered his own outbreak rather well.

I collected my things and followed him to the bedroom, where I dropped everything into the laundry basket. Cael was stepping into simple and utilitarian clothes, his back to me, the closets thrown open behind him.

I went up to him and took him in my arms once more.

He turned around and smiled up at me. "You still haven't had enough?" he asked.

"Never, but I know we have to get a move on." I crushed him into my arms, just holding him, happy to have him here, now, no matter what the future might bring. He stood on his toes to share breath with me again, deepening our shared sense of belonging. In the closets behind him, my things had equal place beside his. This was home and he was mine; I could live with that and be content.

Cael went to fetch Siwi so I busied myself by making soup and tidying up a bit. I was making tea for myself and cocoa for Siwi and Cael when I heard the entrance door and Siwi's sweet chirping voice.

Cael was busy getting shoes and coat off the harling. Catching sight of my face, the little one came bumbling towards me, squeaking "Hat-tat-tat-tat!" as he went, which was his way of greeting anything pleasurable. I hoisted him up, high above my head for a second while he gurgled happily, then took him in my arms to hug him.

While Siwi and I greeted each other in this way, Cael came up to us to take off the harling's shoes and quickly nip my lips with his, before heading into the kitchen and towards our dinner.

While we ate, a second front of the thunderstorm made ready to assail the city. The rain began again; I was glad we were all safely inside. Perhaps we should bring the cacti in too so they wouldn't get flooded, I thought; we'd had to do it twice already since I'd come to live with them. Standing between the table and the sink, sluicing off the used plates prior to letting them sit until one of us felt like washing up, I was in the process of suggesting just that when the lights went off, the water stopped running, and all was very quiet. Then, some dim lights came on again, and a piercing mental Call shrilled from the direction of the bedroom. Cael flung himself towards it, bowling over his chair in his haste. I picked up Siwi from his high chair and followed.

Beyond the bedroom was Cael's office, where he kept his equipment – including a professional-grade thought transference unit. A skylight of coloured glass illuminated the room by day; now, it was lit by a screen that had come to life, despite the fact that the power was on emergency. I stood in the doorway, holding the harling, while Cael concentrated on the screen; then, it went dark, and Cael pushed past us, hurried towards the entrance and paused to put on some shoes and throw on a watertight cloak.

"What happened?" I asked.

He tore open the door and ran out; I followed him, Siwi still on my arm, despite the rain lashing at us. Cael hurried through the courtyard, not towards the gate but to stairs down to the basement.

"Dome blew in Lower Phaonica," he explained as we were hurrying along. "Seems the Thunder magic was a bit too much. Lots of power lost, many conduits blown to the utmost level, parts of the city not even getting emergency power, all the others on brownout."

"And this compels you to go to the basement?"

He guffawed, taking the last two stairs down in one leap. "My bike's down there. Need to go and help – they called in everyhar they could get for the emergency."

He reached our compartment and tore it open.

"Your work?"

"Yes, of course," he said, freeing his bike from some boxes that had accumulated in front of it. "They're reactivating everyhar able to crawl, and they've even called in the Tigron – it's that serious." He shouldered his bike and ran up the stairs again. "No idea when I'll be back – don't wait up for me," he called through the lashing rain as he pedalled away through the courtyard.

Siwi hadn't made a single sound since the power had gone; he just stared after his hostling. I carried him back to where our door was standing open, shedding dim yellow-brownish emergency light. I took off his wet clothes and wrapped him in a blanket, and sat him down on the threshold, telling him to stay there while I went out again to collect the cacti.

That, it seems, is my job in life. I take care of things and raise harlings and provide warmth and help to those who need it. Why do we drift through life like that, like branches in a flood that happen to fetch up against each other? This is where we happened to land, and where we stay now?

What makes us hara different, in that way, from our predecessor, humanity, whom we mostly know only through books?

Siwi gingerly picked up a cactus from the top step and carried it inside, held carefully away from himself, small spine braced against the weight. "Urr-gah!" he said, clearly meaning to say my name. "Look! Siwi big!"

He had dropped the blanket, and I was a bit worried about the combination of near-naked harling and cactus, and got ready to intervene, but he managed.

My name. The first thing that he'd clearly said had been my name. So yes, I had been brought here by the rain and my inclination to take pity on lost things, but I had found a place for myself. This wasn't temporary, something to leave behind easily when the rightful owner, that mysterious Nahir-Nuri, came back. This was mine now. Let him come.

Cael had his work back now, and I'd surely find something to do, with horses most likely, as that's what I'm good with. Teaching harlings to ride, for example. I'd see. The next time we were all at the harlingry, though, I'd make sure I'd finally co-sign that damn form. Cael's outburst had clearly shown me he wanted to keep me, no matter what.

We're all temporary, by our very natures. But I'm not any more temporary than anyhar else.

The Skies
Of Miyacala

Andy Bigwood

The Skies of Miyacala

A derelict factory, American continent
Year minus 10 ai cara, the human epoch

Kheops waited until the others were asleep before bundling what was left of the canned food into the pillowcase. As he slipped past the sleeping hara a glint of metal caught his eye. Thiede's carving knife, wedged between the bones of the dog they'd roasted for dinner. Yes, Kheops thought to himself, that arrogant bitch Thiede owes me a going-away present. Slipping the knife into his belt, the first har to steal from his own kind never noticed the steady penetrating gaze of the knife's owner as he slipped into the night and on into the pages of history.

The Nayati of Macupicua, The Mountains of Aahnd
Year 24 of the ai cara era

The tribe watched silently as the skies claimed another of their number. The new glider spiralled downward, its broken left wing fluttering like a flag. One by one the figures turned away, pulling up the fleece-lined hoods on their robes. The addition of condor feathers had not evoked any measurable improvement in performance. The loss of their brother was regrettable, but he had given his life in the highest cause. One day a brother would fly; it was a truth that they had each learned upon inception. It was foretold.

The Nayati of the Realm Gates, Alba Sulh
Year 538 of the ai cara era

Caline har Tuaththua ran his finger along the seam of his realm-suit, activating the majhahnic bonding that made the suit ether-tight. Four early aethernauts had been lost because they'd stepped into realms that were inimical to normal reality; he had no intention of being the fifth.

Suit check

Life support aura - active, personal reality stabiliser - invoked, deharic familiars - on standby, mission memory crystal – recording, suit lights – on, suit integrity – 100%, agmaric level – 6666.6 rels, replied the calm dreamlike voice of the suit's guardian dehar.

"Control. I'm ready for insertion when you are, Rolan."

"One moment on that, Caline. We have some Emissaries in the room."

"Which tribe this time?"

"The Opt. They're from..."

"...The Aanhd Mountains. The ones who invented those wing-construct gizmos?" asked Caline

"The same."

"Give them my respects and tell them that their devices have been very useful in our exploration of the world realms."

"Yeah, already did. Although this lot seem to have perfected 'enigmatic' as a default emotion."

Caline pulled a face. "Not more One-Realmists trying to disrupt the gate evocation ceremonies?"

"No," Rolan answered. "They seem comfortable enough that we're exploring beyond the world the Aghama gave us. It's something else. Probably one of them had a precognition about being here *'on this specific day'* or something."

"I wonder how many times predestination has been used as an excuse to crash a party?"

"Millions probably," Rolan replied. "It would be so much easier if you could tell which guests are *genuinely* predestined to be at an event. I'm pretty sure that last lot of Colurastes just turned up for the food and the aruna. Anyways, these Opt'hara are too serene for that sort of game. Ahh, there they go - Jorcel is ushering them into the room of respectful viewing to watch the gate guardians getting it on."

"Let's get this done, then. Twill and Life-Sung must be going frantic keeping themselves on the edge." Caline smirked at the thought of the two gatekeepers trying to keep their sweat-drenched arunic supernova in check.

"In three heartbeats, two, one."

May the Aghama watch over you, Caline.

Agmaric energy began to flow through the granite of the realm-gate, pulsing with the rhythm of the gatekeepers' aruna.

Caline opened his mind to the flow, feeling the passion, waiting for the ultimate moment before taking the step forward into the schism between realities.

For an instant he ceased to exist, his mind summoning up a host of dreams, nightmares, sensations and memories to fill the void. An untrained mind might go mad, which was why only those who had achieved a caste level of Pyralis or higher were allowed near a gate ceremony. Caline embraced the sensation like an old friend. It was his personal belief that a har could gain insights from the ordeal.

Time returned first as was its right. Quickly, Caline traced the symbol of Aruhani within his mind and observed the rate of decay as it faded. *Mission Note: Comparison of the temporal flow rate between reality Z1223L and Eartharuhani gives a ratio of approximately 1:1. Looks like we've found one in our universe this time.*

Realms often had time running at a differential rate. At first it had been considered a problem. Inevitably, a quick-thinking Kheopsid business-har figured out that you could craft your products more efficiently in a faster realm or take a long holiday in a slower one. There were of course four realms permanently off-limits. The Realm of Poor-Jaslin-in-Amber, where time ran at a billionth of the standard rate; The Realm of Tarbec's Bones, where time ran so fast you died instantly; Hourglass River where time was a liquid, and Rebound where time flowed backward ejecting you at the instant you entered it.

The personal reality stabiliser had been invented in response to Tarbec's death and a monastery in Suhl had been dedicated to finding a way to release poor Jaslin.

Space unfolded itself like a flower with three petals, stretching out toward infinity. Realms seemed naturally to have either three or eleven space-like dimensions. Both types could be habitable, although the Elevens were truly strange.

Mission Note: Looks like a standard type three, no scale compression of the straight run path, the sideways stepped direction, or the highness of the heavens. In old science notation X,Y and Z all =1:1

Light, colour and the sound of wind flooded Caline's senses, momentarily blinding him as the new reality grabbed at him like a hungry shark. The thought *Mine!* accompanied the surge of stimuli. Caline felt no particular concern at the stray thought. It was in the nature of universal-dehara that they believed everything within them was theirs.

His vision cleared and he found that he was standing on a cloud. The sky was a beautiful tropical blue, studded with small white clouds, similar to the one on which he was standing. For a moment Caline felt his guts clench in terror before his mind caught up to the fact that he wasn't falling.

Begin continuous record. I'm standing on a cloud, which is as weird as it sounds. It feels like very fine snow between my toes, my feet penetrate about two inches before the cloud-stuff becomes compacted. We might have some unusual physics on this one.

Moving cautiously, he eased closer to the edge of his cloud and peered over the edge.

No land mass in sight. This place looks like it's cloud and blue skies all the way down. I'll need a set of wing-constructs shipped through a lot sooner than we'd originally planned. Without them this exploration is going to be limited to the cloud I'm standing on.

Caline frowned; there was something he was missing, but he couldn't quite put a finger on it. Shrugging to himself, he set about setting up the rest of the standard tests. The time it took a feather to drop proved gravity was normal, which meant that it was the clouds that were odd. The weather globe indicated the air was identical to that of Eartharuhani and was at a pressure of 1000. Wind speed was ten knots set to increase to twenty-five knots by midnight. Thunder showers were predicted by dawn.

Thunder, wind. Caline's eyes widened as the missing thing fell into place. Quickly he glanced over his shoulder in the direction of the gate's distortion. As he'd suspected his cloud had behaved exactly like a regular cloud and had drifted clear. The gate was now in a good twenty feet away hovering in an empty sky.

It was one of those things; sometimes Murphii, the Dehar Dimitto of small things that go wrong, played his tricks. Sitting down, Caline removed one of the rune-covered crystals from his thigh pocket and used it to call upon the first of his three familiars.

Reality quivered and a small dehar manifested, sitting cross-legged on top of the rune stone.

If you are willing, please take a message to Rolan har Kheop.

Willing, willing message take, chirped the harling-like familiar.

Caline uncoupled the memory crystal from the realm-suit's

315

collar and pitched it in the direction of the gate. Taking flight the tiny dehar followed, easily catching the crystal in a bear hug and guiding it through to Eartharuhani.

Satisfied, Caline lay down to meditate, letting the ultimate blueness of the sky penetrate his soul. Gate Control would read his memory and quickly move the wings to the front of the delivery queue.

4256 heartbeats later the aura of the gate pulsed, spitting out a package wrapped in white silk with a gold trim. Like a theatrical majhahnic effect the package seemed to hesitate in mid-air and then dropped like a stone. Caline scrambled upright and watched it fall until it was nothing but a dot. ...a dot that unfolded into a pair of wings.

With gentle grace the dove white wing-construct spiralled upward, the sun glinting from the golden-tipped feathers. Homing in, the mecha-majhahnic device deployed a set of bronze landing legs and settled gently into the cloud-stuff.

Its job complete, the deharic familiar detached from the wings and flowed back into the pattern of runes on its crystal.

Caline quickly strapped the device to his back. The wing-construct housed an incredibly sophisticated majhahn; by evoking Miyacala, Prime Dehar of Elemental Air and Optera, Dehar of Winged Flight, the user could temporarily become a mecha-majhahnic bird. You controlled the feather, wax and bamboo-boned wings as if they were an extension of your own body. Needless to say, the discovery of a clean method of powered flight had earned the Opt a seat at the Tigron's table.

Miyacala, Dehar, Lord of Airs, Walker upon the North Star Road. With all respect, I don these wings and seek to enter the skies. I pledge to follow the winds where they may lead and give myself into your hand for my protection, Caline thought. Probing the interface, he visualised the feel of wind brushing through his feathers. Usually it took a few minutes to get one's mind attuned with a construct. This time it was different, sensation flooded into his mind like a torrent. His arms felt numb and clumsy as his soul surged into the wings.

Breathing deeply, Caline concentrated, pulling his essence back until both sets of limbs felt equally real.

Note for future investigation, looks like this realm has a higher than normal affinity for Miyacalan Majhahnics. We will need to run experiments *to see if one or more of the other prime dehara have a weaker influence here as a counterbalance. This reality is going to be a tricksey one.**

Caline shrugged, a gesture that now included a brief flap of wings. As he did so, something caught his eye. Holding his right wing out in front of him he took a closer look. Where the Opt'Haran wing-construct included a frame of bamboo and brass, his wing was now entirely etheric, the physical parts burned away, replaced with sinews of pure living agmara. The straps that had held the device in place were now stripes of white downy feathers running across his chest fading to nothing as if his skin was uncertain whether to be flesh or feather.

*Suit. What is the status of my personal reality?** he sent with controlled precision

*Personal reality compromised. Realm reality dominant,** replied Suit, his voice as happy and dreamlike as ever.

For the first time in years of exploration, Caline allowed himself a moment of real fear. The wings evidently had some sort of intrinsic affinity to the local reality. In essence they were more real here than he was. It was only slightly comforting that Suit didn't perceive the feathers as a problem.

A part of him wanted to flee immediately, slamming the gate shut behind and yet another part wondered what it would be like to go native, to be a part of something new and unknown. There was a freshness to the realm almost as if it were only a few minutes old itself. Was this feeling why his ancestors had so willingly shaken off their humanity?

*Get a grip,** he thought to himself. The emotions had come from the two extremes of his persona – neither represented his true feelings.

*Rolan, let's tag this reality as an amber travel zone for now. Miyacala's influence here is stronger than anything I've seen outside of a full-on primary nayati invocation. The wings fried my stabiliser so I'm a part of this reality now. Only the Aghama knows what that's going to mean. I'm still alive obviously, which is good. The catch is I'll have to use these malfing wings to glide back through the gate.** He sent this information to the message crystal, tossing it toward the gate with all the strength in his arm. *Oh, and be a dear and find out what those dehara-cursed, human-har, Opt'haran emissaries have to say about this!**

He flapped the wings a couple of times, getting used to the feel. The urge to take flight was almost overpowering, instinctive, like a fledgling taking its first steps. It would be easy to just let go and fly forever. It would also be selfish. His weakness of mind would be a mark of shame to his tribe.

Yes, thought Caline. *I'll fly, but only to the realm gate.*

Taking a run up, he leapt toward the gate spreading the wings to their fullest span. Almost immediately, an unexpected downdraft caught him, blowing him eastward and several hundreds of feet down. Adjusting his path, Caline landed on a smaller cloud and turned to glare up at the gate.

That could have gone better. The wind must be blowing stronger than I thought, he sent to his crystal, frowning at the reality distortion that marked the way home. A slight movement caught his eye; instinctively he refocused his sight so that he could sense the next higher etheric plane.

By the Aghama's breath! That's incredible! Rolan, I'm viewing the ether at the Pyral level. There's an agmaric wind in this realm. It follows the air currents, that or the wind follows the agmara. I'm seeing rainbows constantly merging and changing, swirling like... like nothing I've seen. This place is a natural wonder! Caline paused and then frowned. *It's also going to make things even more interesting, these 'etherwinds' are forming a vortex around our gate. I'm guessing that, because these wings are now more agmaric than physical, it's not the air of this realm I'm flying in, it's the ether.*

Caline stood for several minutes, hands on hips trying to understand the swirling mass of energy surrounding the gate. Having trained with Opt'haran wing-constructs, he had a good understanding of how difficult the journey now was. If he tried flying a normal mechanical wing into regular air turbulence it would rip apart. He had to assume that agmaric wings and etheric turbulence would be equivalent.

Finally it came to him; it wasn't impenetrable, there *was* a way. Taking flight again, Caline followed a strand of ultraviolet light that swirled upward far above the spiral skein of agmara braided around the gate. He quickly gave thanks to his tribe's patron dehar Daananan of the Mists, and Optera, and Miyacala himself. His hunch had been right; from above, the airs and energies were as calm as a meditation of Lunil. Folding his wings, he stooped like a peregrine falling upon a mouse.

Reality screamed. Caline screamed too.

The Nayati of the Realm Gates, Alba Sulh
Year 538 of the ai cara era

"...Quick get the next stabiliser majhahn tuned... increase the Miyacala invocation to maximum."

Caline groaned and tried to sit up, only to feel as if a vast weight were pushing down on him. "In the words of the first Tigron 'Ouch, that hurt'."

"Cal? Can you hear me?" said a voice.

It took Caline a moment to realise that it was Rolan. "I hear you. That transition was as rough as a sedu's backside."

"Cal. There's no easy way to say this. You are still part of that other realm. We've had to spin up all four primary nayatis just to get you this close to Eartharuhanian reality."

Caline opened his mouth to protest, but shut it with a snap, noting that the gate chamber was different. Additional majhahnic paraphernalia cluttered the area with totems, feathered charms and rune crystals. The assemblage had an improvised look, as if some-har had been making it up as they went.

"How long?"

"We had to slow time. Subjectively you've been unconscious for about 120,000 heartbeats. Out here it has been a day and a half. We've been working in shifts in order to keep the majhahns around you stable."

"I see," Caline said. He didn't need to glance at the wings to know that they hadn't reverted to their original form. "You had better get those Opt'hara in here. I'd like the opportunity to be rude and irrational in their presence."

"Don't get too human with them. In fairness, they've been more than helpful."

Caline nodded and propped himself up in a rough semblance of the meditation-upon-a-budding-rose position: legs crossed, arms outstretched to the sides. It seemed appropriate to hold his wings fully extended as if gliding on a thermal.

He sensed the Opt's presence without needing to open his eyes.

"We are here. Please feel free to express any rudeness, irrationality or other emotions that seem fitting," said a very young voice.

Caline opened an eye and glanced at the tall gangling har, who couldn't possibly have been an adult for more than a year. The anger that he'd been nurturing fled. It would have been like kicking a puppy. "I hear you've been helpful. Tiahaar...?"

"Forgive me. I'm Whitesnow Opt'har." The youth blushed and glanced away. "I. . . I invented the wings that fly."

"You?"

"Me. The correct majhahnics were obvious. As a harling I could never understand why my elders didn't see it that way." Whitesnow shrugged "In any event, it's the way of the Opt that I must face the consequences of my invention."

"Are you saying that you knew the majhahn was flawed? Why didn't the Opt'hara warn us?"

"When we follow the wind, the true path is often less than straight" replied Whitesnow reverently.

To Caline that sounded like a rote-learned catechism. "That wasn't an answer, tiahaar Whitesnow."

"Sorry," the Opt replied. "The answer is a bit complicated. Each tribe has its founding tale. Immanion has its Tigrons, the Varrs had Terzian and dread Ponclast's doom. The Opt'hara's human founders were a group of gliding enthusiasts, who fled to the ruins of the high mountains. Our tribe's secret name translates as 'those who have been promised the gift of flight'."

Whitesnow paused, clearly trying mentally to edit his tribe's oral history down to just the relevant bits.

"Most tribes count days using the ai cara calendar," he continued. "Our calendar counts backwards. The date of the tribe's creation was the year (minus) 538. Its caused endless confusion. Anyway... today is day zero of year zero. The day we are destined to learn to fly."

His shoulders slumped.

"In our hubris we assumed that it would be one of our high caste brothers who would be first to accomplish flight without the mechanical aids and that he would do so in our own territory, probably in Macupicua City itself."

"Strap on a pair, pop through the gate and there you go." replied Caline, feeling guilty for the sarcasm almost as soon as he'd said it.

"Oh, I intend to," Whitesnow said, "and my entire tribe will probably also do exactly that at the first opportunity... but first we still owe you a duty of care."

"You have a way to help me, then? You can return me to normal?"

"In theory. It's complex. Obviously we hadn't expected to encounter such an incredible bias toward Miyacala. That part of the majhahn is several orders of magnitude more efficient than expected. Your friends have been trying to force a rebalancing of the deharic influences. It's something of a brute force approach. It won't work."

Caline could tell that the young har was really excited about the maghanic intricacy. He was the sort of personality that humans would have praised as a genius and secretly hated for being so clever.

"Of course, the majhahnic aspects are only an amplification of my original work," Whitesnow said. "The evocations and wards that I created are still in there quite happily doing what they do... just better. For instance, the intention of a quick release on the harness still exists even though the physical harness doesn't."

"So if I punch myself where the release should be the majhahn will... will just fall off?" asked Caline, surprised by the simplicity of the solution

"Sort of... for about a heartbeat..." Whitesnow said, giving a crooked smile, "then the self-healing charm kicks in and re-establishes the majhahn. It's simply a matter of making sure that in that instant I am a better host than you are."

Caline's eyes narrowed. Whitesnow was too young to hide the subtle unease that permeated his aura and posture. "What aren't you telling me tiahaar Whitesnow?"

"Firstly we're going to have to do this in the other realm," Whitesnow replied, holding up a finger. "The majhahn that the gatekeepers are using would cause a defraction effect, similar to the one that nearly killed your great grandfather on Lunalunil."

"Secondly..." Whitesnow held up a second finger. "Well... we're already writing an entire new chapter of Majhahnic lore. I've told you what I think I can make happen. What actually happens is something for the dehara to reveal."

Silence followed; Caline had expected more. "So basically, forgive the pun, you intend to wing it."

The young Opt snorted a stifled laugh. "Ok. Yes, it's going to be an improvisation. But no more so than anything the first Wraeththu did. The curse the Lion of Oomar laid on the towers of She'Ka'Gee for instance. The scholars of Kyme are almost certain he changed his intention at least twice during that evocation."

"They also say he'd just drunk eighteen bottles of dehar-proof alcohol and had had a row with his lover about a kitten," replied Caline. "Not that it makes a difference."

Something metallic tinkled against the stone floor. The charm of Agave that Caline had worn tightly bound around his wrist had fallen free.

"Tiahaar Caline. That bracelet just fell *through* your wrist."

"Looks like I'm almost out of borrowed time. I'm in your hands tiahaar Whitesnow Opt'hara."

Realm Z1223L

To Caline the emergence into the other realm seemed like the easiest thing he'd ever done. It felt as if he'd been stretched as tight as a bowstring without noticing and was now released. He lay full length on a cloud soaking up the sun, whilst he waited for the Opt to stop screaming. As had happened on his first visit, the gate's presence was causing the multi-coloured agmaric winds to eddy and swirl with increasing force.

The sounds of distress finally lessened and Caline cast an eye in the young har's direction. "You forgot number three on your list," he said. "The one about never having used a realm gate before."

"I know...," Whitesnow said, sheepishly. "Fortunately I'll never ever need to do that again. Ever." He snapped his necklace-like reality stabiliser and threw it as far as he could.

Both hara watched as the stabiliser fizzled and sank through the cloud like a knife through butter.

"You'd better be quick, tiahaar Whitesnow," said Caline. "This place wants me to stay; I can feel it in my bones." He'd noted that the breeze was stiffening and blowing back his long hair almost horizontally.

"OK. Here's how it's going to go," explained Whitesnow. "Air is Miyacala's element, but he is also the Dehar of inceptions and new beginnings. So we're going to hold an old-style inception ceremony, like they used to use to convert humans." He took an engraved wooden box from his backpack and gently opened the lid to reveal what appeared to be an excessively sharpened carving knife. "According to legend, this was the vakei that Kheops the First stole from the round-table of Thiede the Red and used to incept the first generation of his tribe. It's a tool Miyacala knows well."

"Isn't that supposed to be in a museum?" asked Caline

"The Tigrons have shown a personal interest in your problem," replied Whitesnow. "They insisted that every aid be given." He held the powerful vakei by the blade in both hands, offering the handle to Caline. "For our purposes, you must take the role of harhune."

Caline reverently pulled the blade from between Whitesnow's palms leaving a pair of cuts that welled up with teardrops of fresh red blood. Swiftly he cut his own palms and returned the still bloody vakei to its case. Speed was essential; the wounds would already be healing closed.

"In the names of the Aghama I share my blood with this har," Caline chanted, "in sacred memory of the ceremonies that created our ancestors. Miyacala, Lord of Inceptions and New Beginnings, this blood symbolises the willingness of Whitesnow Opt'har to enter the crucible of your care." Caline stepped close and clasped Whitesnow's hands, bloody palm against bloody palm. The cuts in his hands stung, but the brief pain was surpassed by a sensation of flowing energies.

"I, Whitesnow Opt'har, accept the Aghama's transforming blood into my veins and call upon Optera, dehar of winged flight to fulfil his prophecy and guide my journey into Miyacala's realm," answered the young Opt, leaning upward to share breath with Caline.

The agmaric winds, which had been briefly quiescent whilst they'd been calling upon the dehara, began to blow with a sudden vastly-increased strength. Unprepared, Caline staggered backward, the agmaric wind catching in his wings, blowing both hara off the cloud and into the empty blue sky.

They fell, connected only by their blood-slicked hands. Instinctively, Caline spread his wings wide, trying to guide them toward the safety of another cloud, only for a second gust to send them tumbling. As he cartwheeled end over end, he glimpsed a shoe fly past followed by the sleeve of a realm-suit. Whitesnow's grasp loosened suddenly and Caline was alone. A moment later he felt his ass skidding through the cloudstuff and folded his wings protectively about himself.

"Wahoooo!" cried a voice above him

Looking up Caline saw a vision that at once filled him with despair and a burgeoning joy. Whitesnow hovered overhead slowly descending on wings that glowed intensely white. The inception had worked only too well, the wing-majhahn passing with his blood.

As Whitesnow glided closer, Caline noticed that the Opt'har had lost almost all his clothing to the agmaric winds. As if to underline the point the remaining shoe and the har's utility belt fell *through* him, their reality now too different from his own to adhere to him.

Glancing down Caline noticed that his own realm-suit now formed a pile about his feet like the discarded skin of snake or a chrysalis. Unsurprisingly, he found that his fears had fallen away with the trappings of his old life.

With two powerful beats of his wings he joined Whitesnow in mid air.

No regrets? sent Whitesnow with emotions of sympathy.

None, Caline replied. *And I trust you recall the traditional final act of an inception ritual?*

Oh? OH! That! sent Whitesnow, his wings blushing pink at the feathertips. *Yes. Yes that's probably appropriate, just to be certain. I wouldn't want to turn back because we didn't. Did you know some species of hawk go about it in mid-flight?*

It's a valid topic to research certainly replied Caline.

The Higher Realms

In a reality that boasted forty-eight spacetime-like dimensions the dehar Miyacala looked down from his throne. If he were perceived in only three of those dimensions he would look like a white-haired Wraeththu, his sightless milky eyes covered in a white blindfold that obscured nothing from his all-seeing gaze. A smile played briefly across his lips. It seemed that another of The Aghama's little ploys had born fruit.

A new life was being created and one of the dormant realms would soon flower with the quickening that only sentient beings could bring.

Beyond a Veil
Of stars

Storm Constantine

Beyond a Veil of Stars

In those days, there was a village called Long Marn near to the edge of the wilderness where no-one went by choice. Those who lived there were defiant remnants of human civilisation, scratching an existence from the wild earth and the angry river that rushed past the edge of their fields. The world belonged to Wraeththu, and had done for a long time. It was said that Wraeththu had brought back to the world an ancient knowledge, that they were neither men nor women but something of both; either a new form for human life or a reversion to a very old one. The people of Long Marn were aware that Wraeththu were able to breed among themselves, but had originally derived from human stock. Occasionally, but with increasing rarity, they might still seek to call the youths of human settlements to join them.

In Long Marn were young men who had not heeded the call and older men to whom the call had never come. There were women and children too, although not many. In the past, young men had sometimes heard whispers in the night that whistled out from the wilderness. In the morning, one of them might have disappeared, and tracks, like those of big cats, had marked the dirt around the skirts of the village walls. But, despite this, the community had survived.

They lived uneasily near to shrouded Caracanti, a city of the Wraeththu: believed in, but never truly seen. Sometimes, on a clear day, a ghost that might be the city could be glimpsed rising tall and splendid far away, winking like quartz in the pale sun, but on another day it could not be perceived at all. The people believed that sorcerous fogs eclipsed it from view. There were tales of how, long ago, in the vibrating night air, distant voices had sometimes been heard, raised in strange ululations. The sensual scent of incense had crept in tendrils down the narrow village streets.

There were stories too of how, when the city had been built, Wraeththu had come out of the wilderness to the village and told

327

the people where they might walk, and where they might not; where they might plant their crops and graze their herds. There were boundaries that must be respected, and if this was done, the people would not suffer harm.

The Wraeththu had spoken softly of conservation and co-operation, but they had been – and were – remote like gods. They had never offered assistance. The people of Long Marn feared them, because they were not human, because they had stolen the world.

The leader of Long Marn was a man named Jacob, who had a wife, Mara, and two sons: Ahtau and Attjan. One of the reasons Jacob led the community was because he and Mara had had children; it was a rare thing nowadays and regarded as a gift from the Land Mother. People so blessed were above all others, and there were, in all, only eight young people in the village of Long Marn and two of them were 'not whole' in the mind. There were other small communities huddled around the plains and forests, but Long Marn was the largest; it boasted youngsters. Most of the other small settlements were inhabited only by the elderly and frail and had been dying for a generation. Yet other settlements were now no more than the abode of ghosts, where lonely winds blew memories before them down the empty streets.

But not so Long Marn the Prosperous.

The sons of Jacob and Mara were long-limbed and hardy youths, and faithful to their people. Wraeththu would never steal them away. Each night, they burned certain herbs before their doors to repel the Whisperers in the Dark, those particular spirits believed to work with Those From Beyond the Wilderness. The boys had been raised strictly, and Jacob believed he had shaped their inner morals to repel all subtle forms of attack or seduction. Mara had taught them special words, which she said made a person immune to the magic of Those Beyond. If Caracanti had ever sought to woo these boys, it had long since given up trying.

Then Ahtau fell ill. The villagers had never encountered a sickness like it. The boy simply fell in his tracks as he walked in the long fields by the river. Very soon, all colour left his flesh and the temperature of his body fell to an unnatural cold. The people carried him to his home, wary of his iciness: it was a chill that spoke of death, but still Ahtau breathed. Ahtau and Attjan were not just boys to the people of Long Marn; they were sacred symbols. For ill to befall one of them was a dire omen indeed.

For thirteen days, Ahtau wasted before his family's eyes. It seemed impossible he could still live. His flesh seemed to fall from his bones; his ribs were a visible cage, and his closed eyes had sunk into pits above the blades of his cheekbones. He could not eat, and the only fluid Mara could force inside him was what she was able to dribble into his dry mouth with a sponge. Anything more than that made him choke and splutter.

She sought to revive the boy with herbs and poultices, and when this made no difference, she called for a healer man who lived in a cave in the forested hills across the river. He laid his hands on Ahtau's gaunt frame and sought to restore him through faith. When this also failed, Mara called for a woman known to be wise, who lived among the trees of Grey Crow Woods. She burned acrid resins in Ahtau's bedroom and invoked his totemic animal spirit. This did not help either. Nobody could tell Jacob or Mara what ailed their son. But some had their suspicions.

One evening, a new healer came to the village, a travelling woman who lived among the skirts of the wilderness, and who was always moving. She had heard of the trouble, she said, and had come to offer her services. She wrapped Ahtau in damp cloths, imbued with eye-stinging resins, placed hot stones upon his chest, and burned bitter herbs in a dish. Then she knelt upon the floor beside his bed and fell silent for some time. Jacob, Mara and Attjan stood by the bedroom door, watching anxiously. Presently, the healer sighed and placed one of the damp cloths over her burning herbs to extinguish them. She removed the stones from Ahtau's chest.

"What have you learned?" Jacob asked.

The woman would not look at him. She shrugged. "It is no ordinary sickness, but this you already know. I am tempted to say it is not a sickness at all, but something else."

"An enchantment," said Mara.

"Evil from beyond us," Jacob murmured softly. He closed his eyes.

Mara and Attjan watched helplessly as Jacob walked out of the house and went to stand in the dying sunlight. Quietly, they followed him, and saw that the other villagers, seemingly attracted by his distress, had all come out of their dwellings and in from the fields, to stand around him. All were silent. Then Jacob uttered a terrible, hoarse cry and banged his bunched hands against his eyes. The villagers flinched at the unexpected outburst: Jacob was normally a calm and measured man.

To Attjan, his father's cry was the most hideous sound he'd ever heard; it was the quintessence of despair and grief.

At sixteen, Attjan was Ahtau's junior by nearly two years. Like his brother, he was a striking youth; tall, with long black hair, which he wore tied back at the nape of his neck. For some days, he'd been unable to face visiting his brother, despite the urging of his mother, who felt that Attjan's voice might somehow soothe Ahtau's troubled soul. But the emaciated creature who rasped and trembled beneath the blankets hardly even looked like Ahtau anymore, and Attjan found the sight both repellent and frightening. He wanted to remember his brother as the vibrant and humorous person he'd once been.

They had been inseparable. Together, as young children, they had trembled beneath their blankets in the dark of moonless nights while eerie sounds had whispered in to them from outside. Then they had whispered of terrible monsters with blades for hands and fire for eyes, and when the wind sang its wild song on the night, Ahtau would always say in a low, sombre voice, "They walk tonight." And Attjan's skin would freeze momentarily with a delicious horror, to be savoured because he believed their parents' house was so safe. Then he and Ahtau would laugh together, fearing nothing in the warm darkness of their beds.

As time went on, the childish games had ceased, but sometimes, when the wind was a hollow voice above the fields, they would talk of Those From Beyond. It was almost impossible to resist, even though it went against the laws of their people. The Wraeththu had not been seen for three generations by any of the people of Long Marn. What proof did they really have that they still existed? And yet here Ahtau lay, a husk amid his damp blankets, barely able to draw breath, the flesh visibly melting from his bones.

How could this happen now? Attjan wondered. He knew from his father's veiled words that Jacob believed the Wraeththu had exhaled a toxic breath from Caracanti to ensorcel Ahtau. But did Attjan believe this himself? He knew it was forbidden even to think of the Wraeththu and perhaps he and Ahtau had provoked this situation by doing so. They had felt so secure and strong, sneering at the folklore that spoke of how a simple thought of Those From Beyond gave them power over you.

The healer came out of Jacob's dwelling and Attjan was moved to speak to her. His voice sounded absurdly loud. "Is there nothing you can do?"

The woman looked at him in silence, tying a cord around her ritual cloths.

This unsatisfactory reaction brought Attjan's helpless anger to the surface and he spoke without thinking. "It *is* Wraeththu work, then! Why not admit it? When do we cut his throat before they come for him?"

He was unaware of a swift movement behind him, and only realised his father was there when he'd been swung around. For a second, he looked into his father's eyes – his savage, despairing gaze – then Jacob's open hand smacked him hard across the jaw. Attjan was knocked backwards against the wall of the house, where he slumped dazed.

After a few moments, he picked himself up and ran away to the edge of the wilderness, his eyes streaming silent tears. Here, at the very place where the verdant green of the West Pasture gave way to the rocky stubble of the wilderness rim, Attjan flopped onto his stomach on the bristly ground. His jaw throbbed with pain and his vision was occluded by boiling spots of light. He thought he could see eternal Caracanti shining in the distance, but it was only a cloud, towering in the sky.

The evening meal in Jacob's dwelling was consumed in uneasy silence. Four of the other village elders were present; two couples, Bethy and Orin Wheathook and Sharn and Mirkis Rakehollow. It was clear that they expected an announcement of some kind from their leader. Attjan had come creeping home at sundown, and now sat in a corner of the room, being ignored by his father. His mother had given him a plate of food, which he picked at without appetite, his jaw still painful. Jacob sat at the table, eating slowly and carefully, a thoughtful expression on his face. When he had finished, he drank deeply from a cup of ale set beside his plate. Six pairs of eyes glittered at him fearfully.

Jacob drew in his breath. "There is no hope for Ahtau," he

said.

At once, the tension in the room was broken. Mara uttered a choked, sobbing sound, her fingers pressed to her lips. The four elders mumbled in response, without words. In such a situation, words were difficult.

Jacob raised his hand for silence. "I have decided that *something from the wilderness* is responsible for my son's condition," he said. "However, I might be wrong."

Silence fell. It appeared that no-one felt capable of agreeing or disagreeing with his conclusions, although Attjan knew Jacob had merely voiced aloud what others had been whispering behind his back.

"Even if I am wrong," Jacob continued, "it seems to me there is only one way to save Ahtau's life. We do not have the knowledge ourselves, but *others* do."

Mara uttered a shocked sound. She was the first who dared to speak. "What are you suggesting?

Jacob stared above the heads of all present. "Tonight, I will go to the wilderness and beg *them* for aid."

There was a further moment's silence and then – pandemonium. Everyone spoke at once – except for Bethy Wheathook, who remained silent, her arms crossed across her chest. Mara was clearly horrified. Attjan's mouth hung open in mute shock. Jacob seemed to lean away from the onslaught of words, then smashed his fists against the table-top for silence. "I know you think I should go to Ahtau now and end his misery with a knife. I cannot!"

"But Jacob, are you really suggesting we surrender your first-born to... to *them*?" Mirkis Rakehollow enquired, in the most reasonable voice he could muster. "It is unthinkable."

"Our community has survived," his wife Sharn added, "as many have not. This act would be seen as submission by our people, Jake. You cannot do it. It will crush their spirit."

Jacob shook his head. "No! We will still survive. Do you not understand? I love my boy more than life itself, and I would rather he lived with *them*, than died, than suffered."

Mara put a hand upon his arm. "I love Ahtau too, but I can't bear to think what might happen to him with them. Death would be preferable. You don't know what you're saying. It is grief. It is..."

Orin Wheathook interrupted her. "Jake, the boy might suffer more with them than he does now. You, as much as any of us, know the stories of grotesque mutations and slavery. Is that really a better fate than death? You are clutching at nothing!"

Mirkis nodded vigorously. "Our way has always been death rather than submission," he said. "*They* have stolen our future generations. *They* have slaughtered most of those who escaped humanity's fate. They are *not* our friends, nor our helpers. And we once made a pact between us they would have no more of us. Jake, see sense. Don't be lost in the marsh of emotions. You mustn't give Ahtau to them. You must save him from that fate in the only way we know how. Of course we understand you might not be able act yourself, but one of us would perform this sacrifice, with honour and humility."

Jacob stared Mirkis in the eye for long uncomfortable seconds. It was clear he was considering what he'd heard. He did not look like a person lost in the marsh of emotions. Eventually, he dropped his gaze, sighed and stood up. His eyes were fixed upon the back wall of the room. "This involves our son, and it is our decision." He glanced at Mara. "Will you hear me out?"

She nodded.

Jacob sighed heavily. "*They* are all the things you said. I don't deny that. But what has befallen Ahtau is not their way. In the past, when they took people, it was simply a siren call that lured our sons from their homes. There was never sickness, never... *this*. Those Beyond the Wilderness either steal or kill quickly, and it has been many years since they have done either of those things. We are nothing to them now, no more than wild sheep grazing on the fields alongside their homes. We are no threat and no attraction. I don't believe that what has befallen Ahtau is their doing. But if any living creature has the power to heal our boy, it is them."

Mara uttered a sad moan and pressed one hand across her eyes.

Jacob laid a hand upon her shoulder. He spoke softly now. "I promise you all that no ill shall come to any of you, or our people. If sacrifice is to be made, I shall make it, not you."

The silence was broken only by the hunger of the flames burning in the home hearth. Then Orin shook his head. "Jake, you are insane. We should bind you with cords to prevent this thing."

"Perhaps he *is* insane," agreed Orin's wife Bethy softly, "but I think that we've been lucky and that sometimes sacrifices *have* to be made. Perhaps, in this instance, the sacrifice is something other than the death of a beloved son."

She addressed Jacob. "I have trusted you for many years, and if your heart speaks to you now, I know it speaks in truth."

She fixed each of her companions with her deep brown stare. "Change is the nature of the world and we resist it at our peril. Although comfort and safety lie in what is known, sometimes situations arise that require the courage to walk into the unknown. I think we have little to lose, for as Jake has rightly said, we are nothing to *them*, tolerated simply because we are not even a nuisance. But perhaps we have something to gain."

She turned her stare upon Jacob. "There is another dreadful thing we must consider. What if others among us should also become afflicted like Ahtau has? Is it not better to seek aid or advice before that happens? We do not know what caused this ailment, but something did. It might be that Those From Beyond would thank us for informing them of what has happened and could prevent further tragedy. We have no way of knowing, not truly, but in my opinion – Jake must follow his heart."

Jacob held Bethy's steady stare, while the other elders considered this for a while. Of all of them, Bethy was the quiet oracle who did not speak much, but when she did it was usually with wisdom. After a minute or so, they grudgingly nodded their heads.

Mirkis sighed and addressed Jacob. "Bethy has voiced a truth. I still think what you propose is madness, Jake, but if you are determined, I will not stand against you."

"Nor I," said Sharn.

"I trust Bethy's feelings," Orin said, although he did not look too happy about it.

Mara curled a hand around her husband's clenched fists. "They might kill you," she said miserably.

Jacob shook his head and looked down at her. "They never kill us," he said. "Not now. I shall simply go the Western Crossroads and speak aloud, as was the way in the days of our ancestors when the ancient contracts were devised. I shall ask for their aid. They might comply, they might not. They might take Ahtau, they might not. It is a risk we shall have to take. In my heart I feel the worst outcome is that they will ignore me."

While Mara served coffee to her guests, Jacob rose from the table and went out to the porch. It was his custom to smoke his pipe out here in the evenings. Attjan was moved to follow him. "Father," he said. His voice was low but carried easily on the still night air.

Jacob turned. He held out an arm and drew his son towards him as if in apology for what had happened earlier. They stood for a while in silence. Their house faced the village green, where seasonal festivities were held. In its centre was the well that was the heart of their community. It was named Deepest Life. Attjan knew that his great-great-grandfather had sunk that well and that it was a symbol of his people's will to survive. Sometimes at night, it gave off an almost imperceptible blue glow, and it was said that spirits dwelled within it and made the water sweet.

"I'm puzzled," Attjan said. "All my life I've been told that Those Beyond are to be shunned at all costs. Now you say you must go to them. Wouldn't their aid, if they were prepared to give it, be an abomination in the eyes of Mother Land?"

Jacob squeezed his son's shoulder. "Listen to me," he said. "When your great-great-grandfather was very young, people made the world like this. Thoughtlessness, greed and cruelty made the Wraeththu happen." He paused. It was not often that word was spoken aloud. "Humanity flayed their Mother, tore Her skin, infected Her body with disease. No one cared, and something came seeping from the Mother's wounds. A great many somethings, like rats from the cellars of a great burnt out house. Perhaps She made them on purpose, to punish us, to remind us for eternity of all we'd done to Her. Who are we to call Those from Beyond evil or wrong?"

"Does She hate us that much?" Attjan asked, appalled.

"She is our Mother," Jacob replied. "I believe She is mostly sad for us."

"Let me come with you tonight," Attjan said hurriedly. "I can throw a spear. I'll protect you."

Jacob laughed softly and patted Attjan's shoulder. "Throw a spear, eh? Those From Beyond throw spears with their eyes, spears of fire. You must remember that once they coveted the sons of humans. They might not have taken anyone for many years, but that's only because there are few to take nowadays. I can't risk losing you as well, so I won't take you anywhere near them. If Ahtau is taken from us, you must and *will* be the next leader of our people."

Attjan went cold inside. "It sounds as if you don't think they *will* be able to help Ahtau. If so, why bother going to them?"

Jacob rubbed his eyes wearily with one hand. "Even if Ahtau survives, in a way we *will* lose him. I'm sure that if he is cured, Caracanti will have him, if only because the cure itself will reveal too much of them. I didn't speak of this at the table back there, but let me trust you with these words, Attjan. The Wraeththu will ask a price, and that will be Ahtau himself. I have a strong feeling that will be so, but, strange as it might sound, not through ill will, but to protect their secrets."

"Then why...?"

Jacob put a hand over Attjan's mouth. "Hush now. Humanity's day is done, my son. We will never rise to reclaim all that was once ours, and perhaps that is the right way. We will continue here, as we always have, and it is not a bad life, but through Those from Beyond, Ahtau might still have a life too, whatever happens to him."

Attjan stared silently; his father's hand was still over his mouth.

Jacob seemed to remember he'd put it there, and took it away, patted Attjan's shoulder again. "My thoughts are strange to you. They are strange to me too, yet something speaks to me...it feels deep and ancient. I cannot let him die."

Hours later, after the twilight hour, Attjan watched his father walk away from Long Marn, until his figure became a silhouette in the dusk, then not there at all.

In the morning, Jacob came back to the village. His face was set into a weirdly blank expression, but his steps were sure. People saw him come, saw him walk down the main street to the green and the well; many had been watching for him all night. Perhaps watching also for something worse. They came out of their houses and, following Jacob, congregated on the green outside his dwelling, clearly anxious to hear what had transpired in the cold wilderness night. Before entering his house, Jacob paused with his back to them. The people saw his shoulders slump, then rise. He turned to them and said, "They will come." And then he went inside.

The Wraeththu took two days to comply with Jacob's request. On this day, not long after noon, Attjan was squatting on the porch to his home. The day was hot but brooding. Although the sky was clear, it was haunted by the impression of thunder clouds. Long Marn was mostly empty, since the people were at work in the fields. Jacob would not speak of what he'd seen and heard when he'd met with Those From Beyond, and perhaps had been forbidden to. He was anxious, haunted; he renewed all the wards about the house every day. And every day Attjan wondered whether whatever price they must pay would be worth it.

Musing glumly on this matter, Attjan saw two girls run past the house: Merri Wheathook and Janna Fairfly. He became alert at once. The girls' white dresses blew out behind them, along with their hair – auburn and blonde. They kept looking behind themselves, holding on to each other's hands. Jacob wasn't sure whether they were laughing or crying. He stood up.

Tension filled the humid air, which shimmered at ground level and glowed almost blue. A few old people came out of their dwellings, gazed up the street in the direction the girls had come from. Something was coming. The people could feel it. They were drawn in from the fields, perhaps against their will. As they gathered in the centre of Long Marn, three proud, high-stepping horses came towards them from the wilderness road.

Attjan did not want to stare but could not stop himself. His skin prickled, as if he was cold, and his heart beat quickly. The leading horse, a beautiful white creature with a dark nose and black eyes, bore a figure swathed in black cloth. All that could be seen of this individual was his eyes and his booted feet. His two companions were not so disguised. They were tawny-skinned and their hair was white like the coat of the leading horse. They wore silvery grey cloaks that were draped over their horses' hind quarters. Their eyes seemed to flash in the hot air like amethysts and they were armed. They looked superficially like humans, but there was an ambience about them that suggested otherwise: it might be a smell too subtle to detect with the physical senses. They looked like faery folk, creatures of legend from a distant romantic past that had never existed. They looked like beings from a dream.

Jacob emerged from his house just as the riders were dismounting from their horses. The Wraeththu had come to a halt by Deepest Life, and now the horses stood patiently, shaking their fine heads. Jacob went to the well. Attjan could not hear his father's words, but could read the movements of his body, which seemed at once both accommodating and anxious. The air smelled electric. The figure clothed in black appeared to be paying close attention to what Jacob was saying. He was a leader, certainly; he had an air of command. But why did he hide himself? What did he hide?

Now, the group approached Jacob's home, villagers moving slowly behind them, keeping their distance. Those From Beyond might be seen as the enemy, but their presence conjured curiosity as much as fear. No one had actually seen one of these creatures for generations. Two worlds had overlapped, and somehow it seemed too ordinary, as if it happened every day.

Attjan braced himself against the door of the house. He could flee if he wanted to, but instead he moved carefully to the side, to hide behind the chair where Jacob liked to sit in the evenings. They were passing by him now, so close, and he couldn't smell anything, couldn't hear anything different. What comprised their difference went beyond superficial senses. Two of them had approached the house; another remained with the horses upon the green. The Wraeththu swathed in black mounted the three steps to Jacob and Mara's house. He paused at the threshold, and then directed one glance at Attjan crouching behind the old chair. His eyes were dark, his expression remote, but they were eyes like any seen in a human face and perhaps more terrible for it. He did not pause long.

After the Wraeththu had gone inside, Attjan covered his face with his hands. He was filled with a dread compulsion to see the face beneath those human yet not human eyes. He wanted to see what lay beneath the cloth. To kill it. No. No. That was the call of Caracanti. Suddenly afraid of the dark in his mind, he opened his eyes.

The Wraeththu who had remained outside stood before him, staring down. His mouth was smiling, but his eyes were hard, or perhaps it was the other way around. "There is no need to fear," he said in a low voice.

Attjan could not respond. It was forbidden, wasn't it? Around him, his neighbours had turned to watch. For a moment he was the condensed essence of his community. "I fear for my brother," Attjan managed to say. "He is very sick."

The Wraeththu nodded. "I would like a drink from your well" he said. "I feel the water is very good. May I?"

Attjan still wasn't sure if he was doing the right thing by communicating with this creature, and he could feel keenly the eyes of his neighbours still upon him. But since childhood he had been reared to offer hospitality to those in need, and to share the bounty of his family's hearth. Without speaking, he got to his feet and went to Deepest Life, where he drew up clear, cold water. This he poured into a clay cup that was attached to the well with a chain and offered to the Wraeththu, who drank freely. His flawlessness was marred only by a white scare on his long neck, where it showed very prominently against his tawny skin as he threw back his head to drink. Had blood once come from that wound? Was it red as human blood, or like light or fire?

The Wraeththu handed the cup back to Attjan. "Thank you for your kindness." He inclined his head and strolled back to the horses.

Attjan felt quite empty. After a few minutes he walked back to the family home. Here, he went to his room, which was next to Ahtau's. There were many cracks in the wood-panelled walls. Attjan knelt down, his face against the wall, and turned his eyes to spying.

Ahtau's room was filled with an unfamiliar smoke; its scent could have come from another world. Jacob and Mara were not in the room; the Wraeththu had been left alone with Ahtau. The leader began to remove the concealing cloth from his face and body, but moved out of Attjan's line of sight before all was revealed to him.

The leader spoke. "They think we did this," he told the other. "They think us capable of killing flesh like this. And so we were... once." Attjan saw a shadowy dark hand touch his brother's brow. "Fortunately, we are not too late. Asneis, come here to me."

The other paused. "Tiahaar, forgive me... should you be

doing this? Send healers... somehar else. It should not be you."

"Why not me?" the leader replied. "I remember we all come from humble beginnings, even if you do not. It was no coincidence it was me who heard when the plea for aid came. I am interested to see where the omen of that leads."

"As you wish, tiahaar Tashmit." The guard bowed his head and came forward. "I meant no disrespect. Only that generally dedicated healers would be called for such tasks."

The leader had a smile in his voice. "I know that. Sometimes we *have* to intervene, Asneis, and quickly. I know many hara believe the humans should be left unmolested, but to be *humane* sometimes you cannot turn your back."

"You will incept this boy?"

"No. He is in no condition for it. I am puzzled as to what's caused this."

The one called Asneis pursed his lips. "As you said, we were once very capable of killing. Things happened around here, a long time ago, and the taint of it still haunts the land in places. Such taints lie in wait and are triggered when the unwary walk over them."

"It has waited a long time, then. How selective. What intelligence drives such a taint?"

The other shrugged. "I only offer an explanation."

"Well, we shall see. First we should dispel this blight."

"As you wish."

There was a soft crackle, and then more smoke came into the room. The one named Tashmit began to chant in a soft hissing voice. It seemed the smoke danced to the tune of his words, which were of no language that Attjan knew. Those musical yet alien sounds attached to him like an invisible chain. They wound around him, spiralling like a helix, holding him in their grip. He heard voices, his brother's among them. Ahtau was shouting for aid, as if he was lost. Another voice; "Follow the sound, Ahtau. It is the light in your darkness."

Attjan came to his senses suddenly and found himself sitting against the wall of Deepest Life. For a moment he was disorientated. Surely he had gone inside the house and spied through a hole in the wall? He couldn't remember coming back outside. The entire population of the village appeared to be waiting on the green. Jacob came outside first, followed by the two Wraeththu. For a moment, the Wraeththu leader leaned against the wall of the house. It seemed that whatever he had done had drained him.

Attjan could not remember how, but suddenly he was in front of the creature and a strange voice spoke from his body. "What sort of monster are you? What lies beneath the cloth?" He was aware of his father's hands on his arms and a worried, frantic voice without words in his ear. But he was free. Free, and his rebellious hand tore the cloth from the Wraeththu's face. He gripped the creature's shoulders, feeling its warmth for a moment, before he *saw* what he held.

Within a week, the whole incident was practically forgotten. The people of Long Marn appeared to push it from their minds and got on with the business of living. But subtly, they avoided Attjan and his dark, haunted eyes. They dropped their gaze when they came up the revived Ahtau walking among them. It was a wonder to Jacob, to them all, that Ahtau was still with them, but maybe Jacob was the only one who was not sorry.

Ahtau had tasted Wraeththu sorcery. Attjan and his family had heard the whispers: one day, *they* would come again, and Ahtau would walk the streets no more. Was it not better he went now, this living ghost among them? He *had* changed. No one could say how, and perhaps even, in some strange way, they *wanted* the change to be there and therefore made it be, but Ahtau was not quite one of them anymore.

Attjan knew his brother was different, but this did not drive him away. They became closer, avoiding everyone else. Ahtau did not speak of what had happened, and Attjan did not press him. If a time came when Ahtau needed to speak, he would have an ear there waiting for him. Attjan shared the communal feeling that one day his brother would be gone, lost forever to ephemeral Caracanti, the city of mists and dreams. The ache within he felt about that could not be quelled by this newfound, silent closeness.

Neither did Attjan speak of what he had seen when he'd ripped the cloth from the Wraeththu leader's face. But surely others must have seen it too?

One evening, Ahtau and Attjan went out to hunt. Long Marn had no pressing need for meat or furs, since their domestic animals provided well enough, but it was Ahtau's suggestion. Attjan sensed his brother wished to escape the village for a while and was happy to provide company. They went up into the forested foothills of The Lean Guardians, where bears or mountain cats might lurk. But the night was silent, strangely so. Ahtau made them pause on a rocky platform that looked out over the diminishing forest to the east, form whence they'd come. "Build a fire," he told his brother.

Attjan, unquestioning, set about finding branches. A dead thornwrake jutted out from the rock; its white-crusted limbs would do well enough. They cracked like bullets firing as Attjan broke them from the trunk. The night was too quiet, the air humid and heavy on the skin.

Ahtau looked round and made a sound of irritation. Behind him a noiseless trident of lightning broke from the sky and speared the forest. Attjan saw a flare of flame. "A storm comes," he said. "We should find shelter."

"More comes than that," Ahtau said.

Attjan looked up at his brother and for the first time wondered whether in fact the person who stood in front of him was Ahtau at all.

"What comes?" he asked, but he could feel the air stirring around his body; a wind that came from the ground, from the wilderness. But they were far from the wilderness road here; Caracanti lay a long way to the West. This was mountain territory, the home of ancestral spirits and other less clement presences.

"Can't you feel it approaching?" Ahtau murmured. He glanced beyond Attjan, at the stony path that rose up behind them.

Perhaps it was only Ahtau's uncanny words and tone that made the shivery feeling slither up Attjan's spine. They were not alone. "Is it Wraeththu?" Attjan asked, daring to speak the word aloud. "Are they coming for you again?"

"They never came for me. What are you talking about?" Ahtau snapped. "I knew where it lived when it touched me. I knew it rolled down the mountain to lie in the ground."

"What was it?" Attjan asked breathlessly.

Ahtau shook his head, frowning. "Hatred," he answered, "like a hole in the ground that leads out of this world into somewhere dark and cold and utterly without life. Tashmit brought me back. It scarred him, I think. I smelled his blood."

Attjan shuddered at the sound of the Wraeththu's name. "I saw him," he said abruptly. "I tore the cloth from his face. His skin was scaled like a snake."

Ahtau stared at his brother. "They are not like us," he said. "Don't imagine that they should be."

"What is coming?" Attjan asked. "This hatred you spoke of?"

Ahtau peered over the lip of rock. "You can see," he murmured. "Look."

Attjan went to stand beside him, glanced down. There was an eerie light to the land, which made it easy to see the rocks, the trees, the glint of water between ancient trunks. But there was also a ring of darkness about the hill, darkness that was simply a hungry *absence* of life and light. "It's all around us," Attjan said, "We must leave, do something..."

Ahtau did not seem to be afraid, which in itself added to Attjan's fear. Again, he felt it was not his brother standing beside him. "It is like graves opening," said Ahtau, "the past spilling out." He raised his arms, holding them out to the side, his head thrown back. It seemed almost like a gesture of welcome.

"Ahtau, what must we *do*?" Attjan cried. "We can't stay here. Should we try to run through it?"

Ahtau expelled a snort, but did not lower his arms. "You've seen what happens if we try that."

"Then...?"

"I'm sorry, Yan," Ahtau said, "perhaps it was wrong of me to bring you, but I didn't want to be alone."

"What?" Attjan shrieked. "What?"

The darkness was covering the hillside like a sleeve, creeping ever closer. Attjan had no doubt that once it touched them, they'd be lost.

"I had to pull it out of the earth," Ahtau said. "I'm sorry." Now he threw back his head and closed his eyes. His jaw dropped open and from it came a sound that should not derive from a human body.

Attjan dropped to his knees on the rock, shut his eyes, pressed his hands over his ears. This was madness, a dream. Surely, it could not be real. The echo of Ahtau's cry rang around the mountains like a bell; weirdly beautiful now it was not attached to his body.

"This has to be done," Ahtau said in a chillingly calm voice, "otherwise it will kill everyone, not just our community but everyone else who is left."

"You mean... we let it kill us so others might live?" Attjan asked.

"No," Ahtau said. He turned to his brother, a ghost of a smile across his lips. "I was simply the lure." He raised his head to the sky once more and Attjan could see the planes of his face illuminated by a silky starlight that did not derive from stars, at least not those in the sky above them.

Attjan looked up also and saw a strange whirling shape above him comprised of light, of stars, of mist, perhaps even water. He'd never seen anything like it and lacked the words to describe it even to himself. This bizarre maelstrom grew larger as he gazed at it, until it burst asunder and something, or a pack of somethings, spewed out of it in a burst of blinding radiance. Attjan smelled ozone, and bizarrely the scent of hyacinth. He crouched down and covered his head with his arms, as what seemed to be immense shapes comprised entirely of stars leapt over him, down into the encroaching shadow.

Ahtau pulled roughly at his brother's arms. "Don't hide your face," he snapped. "Look!"

Attjan did so.

The darkness was like the sea, throwing up black waves, with droplets of black flying off them. Amid this whirled the shapes of white horses, but they were glowing with icy fire, constellations within their semi-transparent bodies. Only one of these creatures bore a rider, a near-naked form with skin like that of a serpent. He wore a veil of shimmering cloth around his hips, nothing more. His black hair was filled with sparks of light and he sang to the creatures he'd brought with him; a high, eerie mantra that made Attjan's skin prickle over his entire body. The star-horses appeared to be devouring the black sea; snapping at it, *eating* it.

"I don't know what I'm seeing," Attjan murmured, clinging to his brother's legs. "What are we seeing?"

"I had to call it out, only me," Ahtau replied. "Then Tashmit can destroy it." Now, he lowered his arms and hunkered down beside his brother, took Attjan's body in his arms.

"You'll leave with him now, won't you?" Attjan murmured, still aware of the ringing cries of the star horses around them, a strange almost mechanical thumping sound, the high clear voice of the Wraeththu who rode the brightest star.

Ahtau laughed. "What makes you think that? I'll be the leader of our people one day. My place is here. Even if I wanted to leave, I couldn't."

"But..."

Ahtau hushed Attjan's words with his hand. "Be silent," he said. "It is over."

Tashmit and his eerie host stood now at the base of the hill. Around them the night was clear. Attjan could see in the trees nearby the fire of animal eyes, creatures drawn to see. They had no fear of the Wraeththu nor of the strange beasts he had brought with him. Now the horses looked more real – perhaps had always been that way – although their startling coats glowed in the starlight so that it seemed the light came from inside them.

Tashmit turned his horse and waved to Attjan and Ahtau, then he was riding towards them up the precarious trail.

"Thank you, Ahtau," Tashmit called. "That was well done. Not that I had any doubt." Once he reached them, he jumped lightly from his horse's back.

"My brother fears you will steal me away," Ahtau said, his grin so wide Attjan found it insulting.

The Wraeththu laughed. "Well, I understand this fear." He looked Attjan in the eye. "The time has come for change," he said. "But first I must explain something. Come, let's sit."

The three of them arranged themselves around the fire Attjan had made, which he now fed with more wood. Ahtau produced an earthenware jar of his mother's berry wine, which he passed to Tashmit. Inclining his head in thanks, Tashmit uncorked it and took a swig. "Now that is a taste of early autumn," he said. "Very fine."

"Last year's batch," Ahtau said.

Tashmit handed the jar to Attjan. "You know, of course, there has never been commerce between our people and yours," he said.

Attjan nodded. "You used to steal and kill." As soon as he'd said those words, he wished he hadn't.

"That was a long, long time ago," Tashmit said. "Those times live in the memory of your people more than they should."

"Perhaps because we were the ones who lost most by it," Attjan couldn't help saying.

Tashmit nodded thoughtfully. "Not all hara – Wraeththu – wanted to destroy humanity entirely. We knew their time was done, and that was not our doing, but what was meant to be. The next step. Evolution of the world. But my race was birthed in blood and screams as much as any human child. The transition was not... easy." He fixed Attjan with a stare. "You might want to take a swig of that wine before I continue."

Attjan grimaced and did so. The autumn fire of it warmed his flesh.

"Some of us became guardians," Tashmit said. "All that you see around you, to the invisible perimeters of your territory, is the world we gave to you, that we created for you. This place... it was never upon the Earth. That's not where we are."

Attjan stared at Tashmit in silence, then said inadequately, "What?"

"It is... another realm, another world, if you like. We created this copy of Earth for you, untouched, untainted, but perhaps we were not careful enough. We took from Earth some lingering parasites perhaps, parasites of consciousness. That is what Ahtau unwittingly ran into. It was an evil that had lain dormant for many generations."

Attjan shook his head. "But this is real, this is home..."

"Of course it is," Tashmit said gently. "The only thing you didn't know about it was that it was not quite *where* you thought it to be." He reached out and briefly touched Attjan's arm. "We were never your enemies here, Attjan, although we believed it was in your people's best interest to believe us so. We wanted you to continue as you were, and if we'd share the new world with you, that would not have been possible."

Attjan blinked. "Like animals in a farmyard or in the zoos humans once had," he said.

Tashmit nodded once. "Yes, it might be seen like that. Preserved, a rare species. This is the nature reserve in which you live safely." He paused. "Your people have been here a lot longer than you think."

Tashmit's words were shocking, and yet Attjan was aware

that in some ways he felt relief, as if a burden had been lifted. It was as if he'd suddenly been given proof of the existence of benevolent gods; they'd been cared for all along. He shook his head, laughed shakily, then glanced at his brother. "How long have you known this? Since you were sick?"

Ahtau nodded. "Tashmit told me everything then."

"It was because I could not conceal it, given how I had to pull him back," Tashmit said. "There's another thing I'd like you know. I've been involved in the maintenance of your community for around fifty years, and almost since the beginning I've had doubts about the way things have been run. Luckily, it was me who heard your father's call when Ahtau fell ill. It might have gone differently if certain other of my colleagues had received it." Tashmit grimaced. "But that is not your concern. I heard it, and here I am."

"Are you not ruler of your people?" Attjan asked.

Tashmit laughed. "By the dehara, no! I am ruler of my own small office, I suppose." He shook his head, still smiling. "Anyway, I have since spoken at length with those who *do* govern our city, and have persuaded them that your people should no longer be kept in ignorance. It might be that now we can help you repopulate. The danger always was that if our species should mingle, share our means of travel between worlds, your young would leave home and seek to become Wraeththu. Sometimes it is not just the whims of nature that can destroy a community but the lure of what is beyond it. That is why we instilled within you the belief that we were... evil... that inception to Wraeththu was a terrible thing."

"Why would any child born of our people not want it?" Ahtau asked. "Humans are frail vessels as you've show me so plainly. You can't force people to remain that way if there is an alternative, an evolution, as you call it."

"I know," Tashmit said. "That is the dilemma."

"I will stay," Ahtau said. "I've already told you this, but I can't speak for everyone, nor those who might be born to us."

"We can only let events unfold," Tashmit said. "It might be the preservation of your species is at an end, being a conceit on our part, or a misguided delusion."

"We will go back to our people," Ahtau said. "We shall come down the mountain with the knowledge, as was the way in so many old stories."

Tashmit smiled. "There is a sweet mythic quality to it, I agree," he said. "But first, you might remember from other old tales how those who met angels on the mountainside were often given glimpses of the cities of angels, sights they could not adequately describe with the words available to them. Would you like to see my city?"

"Yes!" Attjan said at once, although part of him was aghast he so readily accepted as truth all that this inhuman creature had said to him.

Ahtau laughed. "I might've known. My brother has always been headstrong and rash."

"Would you like to see it, Ahtau?" Tashmit asked.

Ahtau paused for a few seconds, then shook his head. "No. I'm to stay here. I would love to see it, but... no."

Tashmit nodded. "There will be a time, have no fear." He stood up. "Come Attjan, choose a *sedu* and climb onto his back."

"A... *sedu*? The horses?"

"Yes, but not quite horses as you know them. Come." Tashmit remounted and turned his beast with a light touch of his hand upon its neck.

Attjan felt as if his feet weren't truly on the ground. Perhaps he would soon wake from this strange fever dream. But then the dark eyes of a *sedu* were upon him and he swore he heard a whisper inside his head saying: *Come ride the stars with me...*

He went to the creature, plunged the fingers of his left hand into its thick mane and vaulted onto its back. At once a ripple of energy coursed through him; he felt... *connected*. There was no other word.

Hold tight... whispered the voice in his head. *Hold tight and I will not let you fall.*

The air around them was swirling, fracturing, creating patterns that could be felt rather than seen. The scent of hyacinth and ozone was building up again.

Attjan saw his brother's face: serene, contemplative. He raised his hand in farewell, and a wave of love passed between them. Ahtau had paid the ultimate sacrifice for being healed, but it was the opposite of what his people thought. Staying with them was the sacrifice.

And then the stars began to sing and far galaxies were

pulsing against Attjan's inner eye. Reality opened to him, to countless new realities, and he was on his way to a city of fiery rivers and radiant thrones, to the unimaginable dream of all dreams.

History Lesson

Maria J. Leel

History Lesson

"Welcome. Welcome, my children, to this truly momentous day. Come forward and see, you who have been granted this final privilege. You stand in this chamber, a bubble of pure thought, safe and protected from the world outside. Come and see that world - after all, it's what you're here for. Do not be afraid. Look out and what do you see? A world that is dry, barren and lifeless. All life, save us, is gone from here and has been for millions of years. The sun, once golden, fresh and young, is now swollen, red and jaded and fills most of the sky with his sickly glow. We stand, of course, upon the Earth; a significant world in all our histories but one coming naturally to the end of her days. The animals, beasts and creatures are long extinct; the swamps, heaths, forests and fields all perished; the rivers, oceans and seas boiled away long, long ago and the atmosphere finally escaped to space.

"But still it is possible to see the Earth's face. We stand here on the site of an ancient city. The oldest there ever was, known by many names through the millennia; the City of Flowers; Athens; Immanion; Hemepterchron; Zanthilia and all her other incarnations. Throughout history a mighty city has always stood here. You can see where the sea would have been and the myriad of islands beyond. You can see the seven hills the city was built around, as so many of the ancient cities were, and in the distance the spines of the encompassing mountain ranges. You have, I know, visited this place many times in your studies and in your dream quests. Bring that knowledge here now, now that you are here for real. Paint the skies blue again and allow the clouds to gather; fill the ocean beds once more with sparkling and iridescent waters; reclothe the hills and the mountains with pine forests and olive groves; let the flowers bloom in the fields and the city spires gleam in the sunlight.

"I don't wonder that you gasp, for it truly is a wondrous world. Now, hold this image in your minds and we shall consider further. Not only are we here to pay tribute to this extraordinary world, we are here to remember one particular species she gave life to. That species is our common ancestor. They were known as *Wraeththu*.

"Know that, in her attempt to understand the nature of being, our great mother, the Universe, projects out parts of herself, creating separateness, and she encourages those individual parts to interact together. These projections are, naturally, life-forms. The desert rats, mountain lions, jungle fowl, sea-bound eels, arctic wolves and forest ants... these are all part of her great plan. Even you and I, through the relationships we have with each other and with all things, are part of that mission *to know*. Through these relationships the Universe gets to know herself better.

"In her youth the Universe made the error of giving her neonate life-forms longevity, millennia to accomplish their task, and progress was slow. As her children believed they had all the time in creation, there was no urgency. And so the Universe thought again and to her new creations she gave shorter lives. Progress and the acquisition of knowledge accelerated rapidly and the Universe was pleased. Her creations, conscious of their ephemeral natures, worked hard, striving for understanding, for sapience.

"But then in one corner of the cosmos there arose a species more destructive than any ever known – then or now... although in the beginning this was not apparent. For millions of years this species appeared benign, living by the universal laws – that they belonged to the world and did not seek dominion over it or any of their fellow creatures. The Universe was pleased with the progress they made. But then things changed. After some three million years, a new culture came into being, new ideas formed – and these creatures began to see themselves as masters; the world belonged to them and they were made to rule it. The Universe was discomforted; this was not what she had intended. But still she gave her wayward children a chance and hoped they would reconsider. They did not. In just ten or twelve short millennia these creatures had brought their world, their home, to her knees. These creatures were known as Mankind and the world they had devastated was the Earth, the very world we stand upon now.

"When the Universe looked again she was horrified by what she saw; her beautiful daughter lay bleeding and dying. In their thirst for progress Mankind had allowed their numbers to grown unchecked and now they spread as a plague across the surface of the Earth. In their greed they had poisoned her oceans, destroyed her forests, despoiled her mountains and driven countless numbers of their fellow species to extinction. In their blind folly, Mankind had confused progress with profligacy. 'Progress is an advance towards an objective.'[1] Mankind had no idea of their objective and instead squandered their resources, consumed their capital and lay waste to the world that supported them.

"Not every member of that species agreed with the culture of consumerism. Many spoke out eloquently against it but, oh my children, by and large their voices went unheard. Search the libraries and you will find them; Malthus, Jensen, Farnish, Orr and Lovelock to name but a few. I'll quote you one now. A philosopher by the name of Quinn. "In a billion years, whatever is around then, whoever is around then, says, 'Man? Oh yes, Man! What a wonderful creature he was! It was within his grasp to destroy the entire world and to trample all our futures into the dust – but he saw the light before it was too late and pulled back. He pulled back and gave the rest of us a chance. He showed us all how it had to be done if the world was to go on being a garden forever. Man was the role model for us all!'"[2] Well, my children, sadly Quinn did not get his wish. The beings that came after Mankind thought quite differently about him and his name was reviled.

"And the Universe looked upon the destruction wrought by the hand of Mankind and she learned something new: *rage*. It boiled black within her and spewed forth in terrible vengeance. If, she reasoned, if this foolish species, even with all its sense and sapience, could not control its own numbers then she would do it for them. She first removed from them their ability to procreate and then she sent a mighty pestilence to decimate their numbers. Like her mother, the Earth too sought to rid herself of the troublesome parasite that plagued her. She shook the ground beneath them, scorched them with lava flows, washed them away with huge tidal waves and drowned them with torrential rains. And then, my children, the Earth discovered something quite unusual... and she bid the Universe to stay her hand. From the ashes something new had been born; there arose a mutation.

Mankind had created their own nemesis. A new species: *Wraeththu*.

"Now, in her quest for understanding, the Universe experimented numerous times with many methods of reproduction in her children: sexual and asexual, sporulation, hermaphrodites and half sexes... She continues to do so even now. I see such variants among you here today and even tri-sexes. There is nothing better or worse about these variations – merely difference. And difference is food and drink to the Universe; the greater the differences the greater the capacity for exploration and interaction. The Universe does not set one above another. She is blind to creed, colour, race or gender – to her they are all equal.

"And so my children, when Wraeththu emerged from the ashes of Mankind a curious thing happened – quite unique at the time in fact. Mankind had been a half-sex race of two genders, male and female. When the first known mutation occurred it did so amongst the males. A new being was born – a har. An interesting blend of both male and female but later discovered to be able to procreate; so, a fertile hermaphrodite. Sometime later, from the females, there also appeared a mutation – a parage. She had, in fact, manifested first but had kept herself well hidden. Like her brother she was also hermaphrodite but this time infertile. And this, my children, this is what was interesting. Both hara and parazha possessed an acute connection to the spiritual, but in parazha, who had forfeited the gift of procreation, the connection was vastly enhanced.

"The Universe paused. These new species interested her, as they had her daughter, the Earth, and she halted her desolation of Mankind. Perhaps, she considered, perhaps she had been unkind, too unyielding in rigidly restricting this species with its potential perspicacity to so short a life span – possibly this was why they had grown so desperate, so acquisitive. And then again it might well be that Mankind had reached the end of their evolutionary capacity. Certainly with their increasing intelligence they had reached a natural limit; giving birth to live young as they did, their cranial capacity had little chance of expansion due to the restrictions of the pelvic girdle in the females. Hara on the other hand, with their system of expelling the partially developed harling in a pearl, which allowed the newborn to continue their development outside the parental body, were subject to no such limitations... their developing intelligence was, potentially, boundless. The Universe was gratified and in her benevolence she granted these, her latest progeny, a lifespan at least double that of Mankind. And so, our forefathers, Wraeththu, came into being. And what a trail they blazed!

"My children, in just their very first generation, that transition generation from human to hara, they discovered the secrets of otherlane travel. And, piqued by the actions of this young species, the ancient race who dwelt between the realms, the Sedim, took an active interest in them. Hitherto this had been unheard of – the Sedim keeping themselves much to themselves. And so hara and parazha were able to travel easily and quickly from place to place merely by an act of will. This made the dependence on fossil fuels, that which man had enslaved himself to, obsolete and the Earth breathed freely again.

"At first their use of otherlane travel was restricted to the boundaries of the Earth herself but then, accidently, the wider possibilities were glimpsed. Doubtless in your studies you will have encountered tales of the great librarian, Lileem? Ah, I see that you have. She, a second generation parage, in union with a har, travelled to a distant world of knowledge, but their passage through the Otherlanes was wild, uncontrolled, chaotic, and replicating it was deemed unwise. In later generations, ways were found to recover the lost continents of Earth, Atlantis and Lemuria, and on these sacred lands the vibrational energies of physical beings were raised high enough to traverse the universal conduits with ease... the mind travelled and the body followed.

"The Otherlanes gave our forefathers the ability to travel to other worlds and other realms, far distant from the Earth, in the blink of an eye, but still our ancestors wished to travel through space itself. Mankind had desired this also and had built monstrous, heavy, brutal machines of metal that required vast amounts of fuel to get them space borne. Wraeththu chose not to follow that example. One particular phyle, adept dreamers by the name of the Frodinne, learned how to manipulate matter at considerable distance. It was their research that led to the creation of the impenetrable chambers, like the one we stand in now;

bubbles of pure thought made solid that allow us to manifest here physically and protects us from any hostile conditions outside. And so it was with the craft they built for space exploration. With their minds, the Frodinne took the cosmic dust and, far, far above the Earth, in the vacuum of space, they fashioned it into beautiful ships of light; their cabins carved like turtle shells surrounded by gossamer wings radiating out some several miles. These solar sails caught the sun's radiation and propelled the vessels at high speed through the solar system; thus our ancestors were able to view their world from above and visit their neighbouring planets. These light ships never made landfall, remaining always in the velvet blackness between worlds, and they were reached by otherlane travel. You can view a replica of one such craft at the Stellar Museum on Goth. And so you see, my children, our forefathers earned the mastery of creativity and pushed the boundaries of possibility to the absolute limit.

"The Universe watched all this and was well pleased. She granted Harishkind a wondrous gift; a great honour. She invited them to travel to young worlds where life was in its infancy. There, she bid them seed the primordial oceans with their own genetic message so that all new life in these new worlds would be in harish image. A process our clerics and scientists now refer to as the Panspermia Project. In his time Mankind had aspired to similar glory but, as they approached this blessing in a spirit of conquest, they failed. Our ancestors went forth in a spirit of creativity and so were fruitful... And we, standing here, are the result. There was much to admire in this young species, Wraeththu, and we are here today to offer our gratitude.

"But I am being remiss! So far I have said little of Wraeththu's sister race, the Kamagrian. And we are just as indebted to them. You remember that they came from the female aspect of Mankind? And that they were infertile? As such their numbers were always low. What human females could be were incepted by the mingling of blood and, rarely, very rarely, a Kamagrian child was born to hara. But these wonderful beings were highly gifted in the realms of the spiritual and their assistance to Harishkind was beyond measure. They paved the way for numerous spiritual technologies, explored the ethers in depth and realised the full potential of the Otherlanes. In a few short generations Kamagrian chose to transcend the physical and become beings of light. After all, without the capacity for procreation, being flesh merely held them back. They became the spirit guides for Harishkind and were instrumental in the Panspermia Project. Without their efforts we, none of us, would exist.

"There is one more accomplishment I have to tell you of. By just their second generation a young har, a unique individual by the name of Darquiel, was able to commune directly with the spirit of the Earth herself. She appeared to Darquiel as a barefoot woman clad only in leaves and feathers. The Earth had learned her lesson with Mankind and in future intended that all the sentient life she gave rise to should directly hear her voice. That is why each of us on our own home worlds can commune directly with the spirit of our planet. The precedent was set here on Earth – much to think on then, my children.

"And so, at last, we come to our final task. We, the descendents of this beautiful world pay homage to her and the life she created. To our forefathers - Wraeththu, whose genetic code we still carry - to Kamagrian, our continuing guides in matters of the spirit - and finally to Mankind who showed us how easily we might stray from the path and how life should not be lived. We honour them all.

We will take a last look at the time worn and ravaged face of the Earth, now barren and devoid of life, and bid her adieu for none of our kind shall visit here again. Soon, very soon, the mountains will melt and the lands become liquid. No recognisable feature shall remain. The spirit of the Earth has spoken and has asked to end her days in peace and so we shall not trouble her again. In a few million years the sun will swell and the Earth shall be engulfed, returning to whence she came. Our task, my children, is to keep her memory alive and to pass that memory on to our descendents. We, the ambassadors of the children of Gaia, we must remember always – *the joy of the sweet green Earth.*"

[1] Quote from *Chocky* by John Wyndham
[2] Quote from *Ishmael* by Daniel Quinn

Afterword

We Might Be Doomed, But That Aside...

Wendy Darling

I suppose I've always been a little terrified of the future, in particular the future of this world. While other kids would get excited about flying cars, self-cleaning houses, robots, cures for every disease, no more inequality, world peace, a large part of me was always thinking, "No, it won't be like that."

This world, I thought, isn't just going to go on the way it (supposedly) has been, getting "better and better" — it's bound to crash and burn, unless there's radical change. These thoughts of mine were born out of 1970s environmental consciousness and 1980s nuclear holocaust fears, but they have continued ever since, solidifying with every year and every new threat, from genetic engineering to climate change to drone warfare. The world as we know it is not long for this world.

I'm a news junkie and a science geek, so of course I have followed with interest the growing body of evidence, dating back decades, that climate change is a real and serious threat, that the world's ecosystem is on the brink, that species are disappearing by the dozens every day. Like millions of others, I watched Al Gore's presentation in *An Inconvenient Truth* and was yelling, "We can't ignore this!" Yet it wasn't until some recent reading that I got some serious, heavy-duty scientific backing for this growing feeling of panic and doom.

The first book I read was Alan Weisman's *The World Without Us*. This book received a huge amount of press and was the inspiration for a couple of television shows (for example the History Channel's *Life After People*), but it wasn't until the hype had died down, and a close friend had told me I *had* to read it, that I sat down and took it in.

For those who haven't heard of it, the book describes what would happen to this planet if people just one day disappeared. (There's no explanation, like a plague, mass alien abduction, the Rapture, war, etc. People are just *gone*.) It begins on Day One, then goes to Day Two, then the first week, then the next months, then years, decades, centuries.

What happens to earth in our absence? What happens to buildings? Household pets? Highways? Nuclear power plants? Garbage dumps? The book covers it all, from how long it takes paper to turn to dust to how and when the Hoover Dam will burst. Skyscrapers will turn into vertical jungles, city streets into streambeds. It's fascinating — and all backed by scientists, engineers and others who know how things work and how they would survive (or more often would *not* survive) without people.

Some of the book's predictions present hope: The world can in some measure heal itself. Nature abhors a vacuum. Survival of the fittest and evolution can handle changes to the environment. Concrete crumbles and grass grows through. Ticky tack suburban McMansions will fall and become home to all the pesky wild critters and crabgrass that humans tried so hard to beat back. Nature is strong and will survive long after we are gone.

On the other hand, some of Weisman's speculations are scary, like what will happen to nuclear power plants, nuclear and chemical waste dumps, the industrialised world's groundwater (beneath factories, dumps and other sites that will decay and drain), and the plastic in the world's oceans. (Did you know that plastic, say a soda bottle, never goes away, just gets smaller and smaller and smaller, until it's so small it can be ingested by the tiniest creatures and even become *part* of those creatures, so that you have animals on the most basic level who are *made* of old human garbage?)

And it gets even weirder, when you consider the fact that one day other animal species may one day evolve to the point they start looking at stuff like nuclear waste facilities and, not understanding the warnings, decide to pop open some containers, which won't stop being bad for millions of years, which sounds comforting to us humans but is plenty long enough for that evolution to take place. All the badness humanity has left behind will kick those future species' asses.

So. Comforting book number one.

Now on to the second, which was even more sobering: *The End of Nature* by Bill McKibben. I actually had this book on my reading list for years but kept putting off reading it because I was scared of what it would tell me. Cowardly, but when I finally did read it, I realised my fears pretty much mirror the fears of a lot of people today.

There are many who know something is wrong with the world, yet choose to ignore it. Nature (capital N) will be able to fix itself, no matter how badly humanity has screwed things up, right? So climate change, rising sea levels, invasive species, dwindling habits and all those other problems will be as nothing against the force of Nature, which since time immemorial has been a force bigger than us, bigger than anything.

But does Nature even exist anymore? In his book, McKibben argues that in fact, the thing we call Nature is something that no longer exists. In the past, Nature referred to all those things that happen in the world that have nothing to do with Man (capital M) and can't be controlled — at least not totally. So for Nature, think of the seasons, certain types of trees growing where they have always grown, turtles laying eggs on the same beach as always, birds migrating along set routes at certain times of years, night being a time of darkness, water being made of water. (Already you can see we've blown it with the ocean.)

Now think about how many of those elements of Nature have been corrupted or are so far gone that it probably is too late to save them. Climate change — which at the time McKibben was writing, in the 1990s, was a proven theory but without *as much* proof as we have — is something that is affecting (*present tense*) the world globally. Populations living on islands in the Pacific are going to lose their land; they have started moving already. The weather is becoming more and more unpredictable, storms more violent, seasons unseasonable. Every year has an average temperature higher than the year before it. People everywhere, from farmers to winter coat makers, know the weather and seasons are broken.

Now, look at a few of those other "immutable" aspects of Nature. Trees, for example. You might think of a certain type of pine tree, which has been living in a certain section of New England for centuries, millions of years even. It has managed to adapt to some climate changes, ones that have occurred over a long period of time, but when faced with a jump in temperature and season changes in a period of say twenty or thirty years, it cannot adapt. It doesn't get the water and light it needs — and it dies. Imagine thousands of forests around the world dying because they can't cope with a world that's five, ten or fifteen degrees warmer.

A similar situation threatens thousands of animal species, especially egg-laying ones, who need a very specific temperature to breed. Turtles, for example, often bury their eggs in beach sand, which is a certain number of degrees cooler than the exposed sand. For some species the depth of the holes (and thus the temperature) even determines the sex of the eggs; deeper and cold might be all female, higher might be male. Now imagine if the turtles keep on what they've been doing, expecting if they put an egg in so deep, their babies will hatch. But they don't, because they get roasted or they do but they're all male and what the species really really wanted was all female. Species die out. This is true for birds and fish and frogs and many other species: they have adapted to a very specific environment and drastic changes — taking place over decades rather than over centuries or millennia — are too much for them.

I could go on with further examples, but McKibben's point is that many fundamental aspects of what we think of as Nature are threatened to the point they will cease to be. We humans can protect some species and launch projects to fix the environment, but in a very real way, that again reinforces the fact that Nature is ended. It can't fix itself after Man has maimed it. Climate change is not natural — not Nature — but man-made. Deforestation, pollution, habitat destruction, and most of all the rest are not things that just "happened." Likewise the only way to end those things is for Man to end them. So Nature really isn't in control, Man is. We may think otherwise, but it's no longer the case.

Right now, however, I will leave off on *The End of Nature* —

which of course I highly recommend, along with McKibben's astounding *The Age of Missing Information* — and move back to the theme of this story collection, which is our imagined future.

Not surprisingly for someone who's been convinced of coming doom, I've always loved dystopian fiction, in books and movies and any form really — everything from *1984* to *Venus Plus X* to *Blade Runner* to of course the world of Wraeththu. I'm a life-long *Star Trek* fan, but that future vision seems infinitely less likely than the dystopian scenarios. (Also way too sterile and boring and inhuman, in my opinion.) So I've gobbled up tales of futures where things aren't very nice or where there's been some kind of apocalypse or a whole new species has taken over. In fiction you can imagine all sorts of scenarios, from how the world "ends," to how it gets fixed again.

The vision in Wraeththu is actually quite hopeful. Yes, the world does go horribly wrong (as it's doing right now) but just in time (spoiler alert for the later Wraeththu books!) beings who sort of oversee the world intervene and make Wraeththu happen. Man dies off at an alarming rate, so the world is minus billions of bodies it didn't need or want anymore. The Earth flushes itself with earthquakes and storms.

Wraeththu rise up and have to deal with a lot of unpleasantness, but they also have the ability to enact healing and to have less of an impact on the world than Man had. They are more connected to the Earth, more conscious of its singularity, and also less apt to force Nature to do things it doesn't want to do. True, it might be unrealistic to expect Wraeththu to have figured out what to do about all that plastic in the ocean or nuclear waste sites, but it is a fantasy series so perhaps we can imagine the possibilities.

And speaking of possibilities, I hope you have enjoyed the possibilities presented in this collection. Authors have come up with a wide variety of future visions, from the familiar to the strange. In one story, Wraeththu have to contend with some epic bureaucracy. In another they're not even on Earth anymore. A familiar fictional location is the setting for one of Storm's. I wrote a story set in what was once Germany. Wherever and whenever they're living, Wraeththu present an appealing vision of the future in so far that there are living things left on this planet.

Wendy Darling
September 18, 2012
Atlanta, Georgia, USA

About the contributors

Storm Constantine

Storm is the creator of the Wraeththu Mythos, the first trilogy of which was published in the 1980s. However, the influences and inspirations for the Wraeththu world go much further back than that, and continue into the future as she plans more stories for it. Storm is the founder of Immanion Press, created initially to publish her out-of-print back catalogue, but which evolved into the thriving venture it is today. She has written over thirty books, including full length novels, novellas, short story collections and non-fiction titles. Her interests include magic and spirituality, Reiki, movies, music and MMOs. Among her many occupations, most of which are unpaid, she runs a Reiki school, the Lady of the Flame Iseum, which is a magical group affiliated to the Fellowship of Isis, and a guild called Equilibrium on the EU servers of World of Warcraft. She lives in the Midlands of the UK.

Wendy Darling

Based in Atlanta, Georgia, USA, Wendy Darling is co-author of *Breeding Discontent*, published by Immanion Press in 2003 as the first *Wraeththu Mythos* novel. She has been involved in Wraeththu in many different capacities, including editor of the revised *Wraeththu Chronicles*, webmaster of the *Inception* and *Forever Wraeththu* fan web sites, and staff at several Wraeththu conventions. She also co-edited the first Wraeththu Mythos story collection, *Paragenesis*. Her full-time job is as a web projects manager at Emory University, but she engages in many side projects and hobbies, including photography

and writing. She has also forged relationships with Wraeththu fans around the world and has been fortunate to meet several authors whose work is included in this collection. At home she is ruled by two cats, cats she did not have in her life until she met and visited with Storm, who as usual had a strong influence on her. Wendy enjoys international travel and tries to visit Storm and her husband Jim as often as she can. Connect with Wendy online at about.me/wdarling.

Martina Bellovičová

Martina was born in Brno, Czech Republic, where she successfully finished English and German studies at the Masaryk University and received her Master's degree. Subsequently, she spent a year in Austria, Finland and Luxembourg, working as a translator for the European Commission. She is currently studying creative writing and publicity in Prague, while working as a freelance translator. Her first published short story, "A Piece

of Meat" appeared in the fantasy collection "Rytiny" Martina also enjoys creating comics and in 2011 won a contest in the "KomixFEST Revue", which published her surreal comic "The Waiting Room". Prior to focusing on writing, she devoted many years of her life to theatre and music, and is currently the keyboardist in the dark electro band "LateXJesus". She considers herself a lifestyle Goth and spins CDs at alternative parties under the pseudonym DJ Zlyhad. She is also the owner and main editor of the gothic subculture webzine www.cavern.cz and occasionally writes book reviews for the steampunk webzine http://www.steamzine.cz/

Andy Bigwood

Andy Bigwood is a Wiltshire-based bridge engineer, cartographer, artist and author. Two time winner of the British Science Fiction

Association's - Best Artist for his covers *for disLOCATIONS* and *Subterfuge* (Newcon Press).

Through Immanion Press Andy has published an anthology of Art and fiction entitled *The Sixty: Arts of Andy Bigwood,* and has a short story 'Specimen 16' in the Wraeththu Mythos anthology *Paragenesis.*

Andy has also contributed cover art and a short story 'An American Were-hypnotist in Bristol' for the ebook *The Colinthology* (Wizards Tower Press) profits from which go to the Above and Beyond Charity in memory of Author Colin Harvey.

Brad Carpenter

Brad's career in the television industry began 15 years ago with Rob Tapert and Sam Raimi, working on their shows "Hercules: Legendary Journeys" and "Xena: Warrior Princess." A move to New York brought Brad five seasons of HBO's, "Sex and the City," followed by 67 episodes of Bravo's "Queer Eye for the Straight Guy." After having worked the first Emmy-award-winning season of NBC's "30 Rock," Brad went on to produce three seasons HBO's "Bored To Death," and is now beginning his fifth season of Showtime's "Nurse Jackie."

Brad currently has a few new projects in development, with a special eye towards developing a SciFi/Fantasy TV series called "Raythu," based on the fantastical "Wraeththu Chronicles" book series by Storm Constantine.

Victoria Copus

Victoria was born in the middle of nowhere at the dawn of the Age of Aquarius and grew up on a small farm where she sang show tunes with her siblings while hanging off farm equipment to drag in the dirt while her father planted soy beans. After many years trying to decide what she should do after high school, it was a book that made her decide to go to college. It was another book on Alexander the Great that led to degrees in Interdisciplinary Anthropology and Classical Civilization. Victoria authored the Wraeththu Mythos novel *Terzah's Sons* in 2005 and is grateful for the opportunity to revisit some of those characters again. She is currently employed by a large corporation where her main duty is the dying art of letter writing. Her interests include hiking, reading, writing, dead languages, archaeology, Native American religions, bubble baths, and preparing for the zombie apocalypse. She lives with two perfectly sensible cats, one ghost fish, and the world's most destructive kitten.

Jason Fullwood

Jason describes himself as a city boy born and raised in.... the West Midlands. He studied Illustration, Animation and Art and Design at university, as well as taking a couple of teaching qualifications. He employs what he sees as a traditional style, which covers painting, drawing and sculpting but also creates digital imagery and graphic design, finding that a mixed media approach is the best.

He has had experience of a variety of projects over the years ranging from the basics of photography to photo manipulation, graphic novel covers, album covers, character design, conceptual artwork, book covers, editorials, and logo design.

Jason feels he's still working on establishing himself for quite some time, and can list numerous exhibitions and favourable work, but still thinks he has a long way to go feeling accomplishing his goal. He had many inspirations and people that fuel his ambitions.

Suzanne Gabriel

Born to nomadic Canadian parents, Suzanne grew up in Canada, the UK, and USA. She is a wife and mother. She completed a Master of

Science degree in Food Science and Nutrition and spent time working in the food industry and currently works in a university as a budget officer. Suzanne is fascinated by antiquities museums, old cookbooks, old etiquette books, and documentaries about old things.

Even when there isn't any music, Suzanne is likely to be dancing and she will go out of her way to hug a tree. She adores animals, travel, historical re-enactment, science, hiking, yoga, and way too many other hobbies.

Although Suzanne would love to be thought of as quirky and unorthodox, she's incredibly normal, and probably a bit boring.

Fiona Lane

Fiona born and brought up near Glasgow during the Time Of The Flared Trouser and Unfeasibly High Platform Shoes. By the time we all came to our senses, she had relocated to Aberdeen, and spent several years waiting for a number six bus, in a horrible collision involving the nature of time and the Aberdeen weather. During the eighties, while she was waiting for the Internet to be invented, she acquired a husband and a couple of replacement units, and they all now live in a field full of sheep in Aberdeenshire, along with the odd cat or two and Fiona's posse of obsolete computers, many of which she has single-handedly restored to a completely non-functioning condition. She once kept chickens, but they were messy and she couldn't use them to buy vintage shoes from Ebay. The eggs were good though. She likes gin and hats, and dislikes the oppression of the proletariat. Her hobbies include cooking, gardening, and staring into the abyss.

Maria J. Leel

In a wide-ranging career Maria has been many things from urban ecologist to first aid trainer to reflexologist and most recently an assistant in a medical library. Originally from the flat lands surrounding Peterborough, she moved in 2006, with her husband, to Shropshire and continues to find the excess topography challenging. Between them they manage a half-acre veggie garden with the

assistance of two cats and a varying number of hens. Maria spent a year travelling the world volunteering on various environmental projects. She looked after bilbies in Australia, bees in New Zealand and condors in California. She also lived for a while on a kibbutz in Israel and, as a result, she has an abiding interest in alternative lifestyles and communal living. Maria lists her hobbies as dancing, playing guitar, rowing, making jewellery, sitting on the back of a tandem and applying for new jobs. She has been writing plays and stories from the age of ten and has contributed to several Wraeththu Mythos projects including her first novel *Song of the Sulh*.

Martina Luise Pachali

Martina Luise Pachali was born in Germany in 1967 and has been inventing and telling stories all her life. She has studied Japanese and Medieval Latin in Munich, Germany, where she lives with the obligatory two cats. Wrangling databases for a living and reviewing books for additional pocket money, her interests as a writer mostly lie with collaborative storytelling, net literature, and the grassroots entertainment movement fuelled by the Internet and the possibilities of cloud computing and user generated content.

Daniela Ritter

Daniela was born in the little German town of Salzgitter on a Leap Year February 29th Rather a loner until she discovered the Internet, Daniele then became involved in writing and fan-fiction. She still uses her old nickname DodyLuNatic. Daniela plays the violin and claims she is unbeatable at karaoke! She is involved in pen & paper roleplaying sessions with her Shadowrun group and online in World of Warcraft. Daniela took her first steps on the spiritual path as a Reiki practitioner, and has since found a home in Dehara Magic, about which she is passionate. Supported by a loving husband, she now lives in Hamburg, where they are building their private paradise. Maybe they'll add some children in a while.

Ruby

Ruby is the official artist for the Wraeththu Mythos, who creates all the covers for the Immanion Press editions. She started drawing from her imagination long before she could or indeed would talk. Still heavily influenced by the fairy tales and myths absorbed from her childhood, Ruby has grown into a multimedia illustrator interested in exploring the darkly sensual, symbolic and surreal undercurrents of life. Ruby's illustrations blend perfectly the mythological, the classical and the future fantastic and are also evocative of Beardsley and Mucha. She is now a much sought-after cover artist and interior illustrator for books across many genres, and is the creator of the ongoing Wraeththu Tarot project.

Ever increasingly working on commissions for private clients and their collections, Ruby is up for designing anything as long as it fits in with her bohemian aesthetic and animal-loving ethos (her dream is to run a combined cat sanctuary and art gallery by the sea). On any one day she might be fleshing out a tattoo design and then the next sketching concept art for a theatre set or perhaps sourcing unusual props for a photo-shoot. Ruby's future plan is basically continuing to avoid the average 9 'til 5 as much as possible, for as long as possible and without starving.

E. S. Wynn

E.S. Wynn is the author of over thirty books, the chief editor of Thunderune Publishing (and the associated magazines: *Daily Love*, *Weirdyear*, *Yesteryear Fiction*, *Farther Stars Than These*, *Linguistic Erosion*, and *Smashed Cat Magazine*.) He manages dozens of websites, has written hundreds of articles and short stories for a number of publications, has taught classes in literature, creative writing, marketing, math, spirituality and guided meditation, voiced fifteen albums as a voice actor and even spent time working as a model for stock photography. He has a bachelor's degree in English, has been trained in Reiki and other forms of energy healing and is a proud Freemason.

Storm Constantine's Wraeththu Mythos

Also published by Immanion Press

By Storm Constantine
The Wraeththu Chronicles
The Enchantments of Flesh and Spirit
The Bewitchments of Love and Hate
The Fulfilments of Fate and Desire

The Wraeththu Histories
The Wraiths of Will and Pleasure
The Shades of Time and Memory
The Ghosts of Blood and Innocence

Wraeththu
(omnibus edition of the Wraeththu Chronicles)

The Hienama
Student of Kyme

Other Mythos Novels and Anthologies

Paragenesis, edited by Storm Constantine and Wendy Darling
Breeding Discontent by Wendy Darling and Bridgette Parker
Terzah's Sons by Victoria Copus
Song of the Sulh by Maria J. Leel

Visit http://www.immanion-press.com for details of these and other
Immanion Press publications